Lifetime

of a

Chance

Wayne Brown

Llumina Press

Requests for permission to make copies of any part of this work should be mailed to Permissions Department, Llumina Press, PO BOX 772246, CORAL SPRINGS, FL 33077-2246

ISBN: 1-59526-253-9

Printed in the United States of America by Llumina Press.

Library of Congress Cataloging-in-Publication Data

Brown, Wayne, 1970-
  Lifetime of a Chance / Wayne Brown.
        p. cm.
ISBN 1-59526-253-9 (pbk. : alk. paper) 1. Men--Fiction.
2. Self-realization--Fiction. I. Title.
PS3602.R725L54 2004
813'.6--dc22
                                              2004012772

Lifetime

of a

Chance

Dedication

This book is dedicated to General Jackson Johnson.
Long ago, he made me promise to follow through on my dream of writing a book.
I hope that wherever he is, he sees that I did.

Bill,
We greatly appreciate your hospitality. The Beachtower is always a pleasure. Thanks

6/30/06

Prologue

M y name is Oliver Edward Chance.
"A real American name," my father would always say.
I was born in an apartment in New York City, three stories above the street corner where my father ran his produce stand. We were poor, but we always had good food to eat, and I always had new clothes to wear to school every year. I was the only child of Alice and Sam Chance. Actually, the names they left Italy with were Alicia and Salvatore Ragoni. Pop changed their names to Chance after the man who gave him his first job in America said that hiring him was taking a big chance. That was 1939, and Pop was seventeen.

I was born April 12, 1945. Wednesday. Mama died Friday morning before daybreak. The doctor said that complications of a difficult delivery had left her too weak to make it. Pop did his best to raise me by himself until I was sixteen. That year Sam Chance died in my arms on the sidewalk in front of his stand with two bullets in his chest. The punk that shot him got away with the entire fourteen dollars from the cash box that night.

After that day, I was sent to live with the only relatives that I had left in America, Mama's sister Liz and her husband Nico Barbioni. Nico worked the midnight-to-eight shift in the guardhouse at the Livingston Freight warehouse. He never tried to deny that he enjoyed his job. Where else could he sit in a big comfortable chair, chain-smoke hand-rolled cigarettes, and listen to big band tunes on the radio that sat over in the corner for eight hours a night and get paid for it? He spent most of his off time drinking at Charlie's Tavern down the street, or passed out on the bed at home. Aunt Liz cried all the time and complained to me that she wished they had never left Italy. She hated America for what she said it had done to Nico. When Nico was conscious, whether drunk or, rarely, sober, he and I would fight. To him I was just a freeloader. He constantly ranted about how much I was costing him, and how much I owed him for taking me in. The two years that I lived with them were the worst of my life. Every night I cursed the bastard that killed my father.

April 12, 1963, the day I turned eighteen, I decided that I had had enough of Nico's abuse. I was finally old enough to get the money Pop had left me. Two thousand dollars that he had squirreled away over the years for me to use to go to college. I had a dream of living in Florida where the orange trees grew. I used to tell Pop that when I grew up, I was going to live in a big mansion in Florida and grow oranges for him to sell at his stand. He would laugh and say, "One day, Eddie, one day." Then he would hug me and rub the top of my head. At eighteen I still had my dream, and I had two thousand dollars in my pocket to start my new life. Pop had wanted me to go to college, but I wanted to be out among the trees.

Saturday morning, I got up early and packed what few belongings that I cared to take into the tattered duffle bag that I had bought from the second-hand store on Calhoun Street. I took three suits of clothes, including the one I was wearing, and two photographs. One was the last picture of Pop and me taken before he was killed, and the other was of Mama and Pop taken a few days after they first arrived in America. I had their wedding bands on a chain around my neck, where they had been since the day they buried Pop. I looked around the room, but I saw nothing else that I valued enough to take. I wrote a letter explaining to Aunt Liz why I was leaving. I didn't mention where I was going, but said I would keep in touch. It was a quarter to seven when I finished the note. I planned to leave it on the kitchen table when I left. She would be asleep, and Nico wouldn't be home from work yet. Leaving would be easier that way.

My departure did not go as smoothly as I had planned. Nico was sitting at the kitchen table when I came out of my room. He looked at me over the top of the morning paper, a newly-lit cigarette hanging from the corner of his mouth, as usual. He noticed the bag on my shoulder and took the cigarette out of his mouth, dropping ashes onto the floor.

"Where the hell you going?" he asked, his English weighted heavily by his Italian accent. I didn't answer him. I ignored his question as I wondered what he was doing home so early. He spoke again, "I say where you going?" This time he raised his voice.

"Out," I replied.

"Don't get smart with me, boy. I'll knock your damn head off!" he yelled back at me.

I ignored him again. I set the letter on the table against an empty beer can. I said nothing to him. I had no intention of telling him anything. I was going to leave my letter and walk away just like I had planned, but he wouldn't let it rest. He stood up, swaying slightly from the beer he already drank that morning. "You better tell me before I take a belt to you." He fumbled with the buckle of his belt, almost losing his balance several times. He finally gave up the idea and reached for the letter I had left. To make matters worse, all his yelling brought Aunt Liz from her room. She took her place beside Nico and repeated his question. "Where you going, Eddie?"

"Out," I said again. I wasn't trying to be smart with her, but I felt that it was better if I left without telling her I wasn't coming back. I turned to walk to the door. By this time Nico had managed to rip open the envelope and read my goodbye. Liz immediately started to cry. Everything I had hoped to avoid was now coming in spades. "Shut up, woman!" Nico yelled at her. "Boy, what you mean trying to skip out on us after all we've done for you? You owe us for feeding you and putting a roof over your head for two years. We didn't ask to take care of someone else's stinking kid."

"I didn't ask you to, either, and you know it. I'm finally giving you what you've said you've wanted since I got here. I would have left the day they brought me here if I could have gotten my hands on the money to leave. Now I've got it, and I'll never be a burden to you again!" I was now yelling back at him. I lowered my voice and said goodbye to Aunt Liz. I guess that was enough time for what I had said to Nico to settle into his clouded mind.

"Money? What money?"

"My money," I said. "The money Pop left for me when he died. It's mine, and I'm going to use it to get out of your life forever."

Aunt Liz ran over and grabbed my arm, "Don't leave, Eddie. It'll be better. I promise. It'll be better if you stay." She was sobbing uncontrollably.

"I'm sorry, Aunt Liz, but I can't take it anymore. I'm tired of all the drunken abuse that I've had to put up with here. I can't stand to live with Nico anymore." She collapsed on the sofa and sobbed into her hands.

"You're not leaving here with any money," Nico yelled to me. "You owe us for everything we've given you. You owe us everything you got." He reached out and grabbed my arm. I pushed him back. He lost his balance and fell over the arm of the sofa landing on the floor next to where she sat.

"I don't owe you anything. Any debt I had to you, I paid back on one of the hundreds of times I had to leave school to drag your drunken butt home from the bar so the police wouldn't haul you in. Not to mention the countless times I covered for you at work when you were too drunk to stand up. I would say my debt to you has been paid in full. Now I'm leaving, and if you try to stop me, I'll knock you down again." I didn't give him a chance to reply. I stepped through the door and slammed it behind me. I could hear Liz yelling for me to come back. I didn't slow down. I was free at last.

I had money in my pocket and I was headed south to find my fortune where the orange trees grew. I walked down the stairs to the street. I paused and looked up at the window of the apartment. I would not miss it. I thought for only a minute that I was leaving everything I knew; my home, my friends; and my past behind me. A solitary tear rolled down my face as I walked down the street toward my future.

For the next month and a half, I wandered from town to town on my trek to Florida. I had never been outside the city before, so I decided to take my time and see a little of the country that my father was so proud to have the opportunity to live in. Most days I just walked. From sunup to sundown, I would walk, but sometimes I would stop in a town that interested me. Sometimes I would end up staying in places longer than I should have. Once I spent four days sitting on the front porch of a general store in Oxford, Pennsylvania playing chess with a ninety-three-year-old man. I was determined to stay until I won a game. After four days, I gave up.

Fifty-two days and eight states later, I found myself sitting on a bale of hay outside a feed-and-seed store on the east side of Macon, Georgia. It was Monday, June 3, 1963. I had caught a ride with a trucker in Sandersville, and had spent a half hour helping him and a boy, who looked to be fourteen or fifteen, unload bags of animal food from the back of his truck. I was tired and hot and was drinking my third cup of ice water in the shade of the store's red and white awning. I took a sip from my paper cup and leaned back against the window to rest my head a minute.

Chapter One

A man dressed in dusty overalls and a battered straw hat emerged from the store and sat down in one of the wooden rocking chairs that occupied the storefront. He drank the last of the water from the cup in his hand and tossed the empty cup into the trashcan that sat against the corner post of the awning. He pulled a pipe and a pouch of tobacco from the middle pocket of his overalls and turned to me and asked, "Do you mind if I smoke?" I shook my head in reply. He began to pack the pipe with tobacco and added, "It sure is hot out here today, ain't it?" I agreed and took another sip from my water cup. He continued, "It's hot enough to melt the lard off a hog's hind end." I didn't quite know what he meant, but I couldn't help but laugh. He smiled and lit his pipe. "Smitty back there tells me that he picked you up hitch-hikin' up in Sandersville. Said you were headed to Florida or somewhere," he said as he puffed.

"Yes, sir," I confirmed.

"Where you from? Up north I would imagine from the sound of your voice. New York would be my guess."

I looked surprised that he had guessed so well, then asked, "How did you know that?"

"Son, I spent three months in an army hospital bed in England next to a fellow from New York City. He talked just like you. That was 1918, during the Great War. His name was Robert Bishop. Two days after he was released from the hospital, he was run over. Ain't that somethin'? Get wounded on the battlefield, beat it, then get killed walkin' across the damn street! Anyway, that was too many years ago to worry about now. Let's get back to the here-and-now." He leaned over toward me and extended his hand, then said, "My name's Zachary Brewster. Nice to meet you."

I took his hand and replied, "I'm Eddie Chance, Mr. Brewster."

He leaned back in his chair and laughed, "Mr. Brewster, please. I'm Zachary. You really headed to Florida? You look awfully young to be traipsin' off so far from home. Might I be so bold as to ask why?"

I smiled and said, "It's a long and complicated story, but I guess you might say that I'm off to find my fortune. I want to grow oranges in the Florida sunshine."

He laughed. "Well, anybody that has gumption enough to walk from New York to Florida seems like the kind to make it big at whatever he wants to do. I wish you the best of luck," he said. He pulled a watch out of his pocket, flipped open the lid, and asked, "You plannin' to hang around here all day, or are you gonna make a few miles today?"

"I was planning to make at least the next town, before I stopped for the night. Why do you ask?"

"Well, I'll be headin' south as soon as they get that horse feed loaded on my truck. I'm goin' about sixty or seventy miles, and I just figured that if you cared to ride along with me, it'd be that much less you'd have to walk. It'd give you a chance to rest your feet and give me somebody to talk to. The road between here and home gets mighty lonely, but you could probably tell me more about that, I'd bet."

I laughed and said, "You are right about that. I think I'll take you up on that ride."

"Good. Good. Let me go check on how much longer we'll be here." We both stood, and I followed him through the store to the loading dock where the kid I had helped was loading bags into his pick-up truck. Zachary walked to the edge of the dock and called out to the boy, "Jeff, you 'bout to get it done, son?"

Jeff dropped the bag he was carrying into its spot in the truck, and then replied, "That's the last of 'em, Zachary. I'll get the ticket for you to sign." He hopped onto the dock and disappeared into the building. He returned with a pen and a receipt book that Zachary signed and took the top copy. "I'll see y'all next month," he said before turning to me and adding, "You ready to ride, Eddie?"

"Ready when you are," I replied as we jumped down from the dock and climbed into Zachary's truck. "Where exactly are we going?" I asked after we had pulled out of the store lot onto the highway.

"Wixton," was his reply, "I'm foreman of a plantation just north of there. I'm goin' that far. I figure it's about ten or so miles on into town from the front gate. That be all right with you?"

"Fine. That would be better than walking the whole way."

"That's 'bout what I was thinkin'."

On the drive down from Macon, we passed through several towns. For every one, Zachary had something to say about it. Anything from historical events, something that happened to him, or something that happened to a relative of his that lived there. I listened and nodded and commented when he called for me to, but I can't tell you today what he was saying or what town he was talking about. I didn't pay much attention to their names. After so long on the road the names of towns had begun to run together. I'd remember a town but couldn't remember what state it had been in. Finally, I gave up noticing, unless something made it stick in my mind. Like Oxford. There were others here and there that I'll always remember, but, for the most part, they were just places that I had walked through. In between towns, he asked me about myself and what I was doing so far from home. I told him my story and about my dream of Florida. He wished me luck and told me about things that he had dreamed of doing. Some he had done, and some he had given up on. Many, he said, he chalked up to the recklessness of youth or stupidity, whatever you wanted to call it. He told me about things that he had done after the war. He told me stories about hauling bootleg whiskey from Wixton to the underground nightclubs during Prohibition. He said that he once had a drink with Al Capone in a speak-easy somewhere in downtown Atlanta. He talked about being shot at by "revenuers". He said that was what got him out of the moonshine business. "The sting of buckshot and shattered glass can teach a man a great deal about right and wrong," he said sternly. "The scars of that feelin' run deeper than just those you can see." He pushed the sleeve of his shirt up his arm to show me the dozens of tiny scars that speckled his arm. "My back and the back of my head look pretty much the same. I just thank the Lord that I didn't die that night. I figure that was his way of lettin' me know that I was in the wrong business. After that, I settled down and took up farmin', and I've been doin' that ever since."

His stories of his exploits made the trip more enjoyable. I was thinking that I would miss him when the ride was over, but I knew that all I could do was take his stories and his kindness and add them to my list of the many other memorable people I had met along the way.

The last few miles of the trip, we sat in silence. Zachary lit his pipe again, and I leaned my head against the window frame and let the wind from the open window blow against my face. I thought about the miles that I had traveled and about the people I had met and left behind. I wondered if my passing through their lives had left the same impression on them as theirs had on me. Somewhere in my memory, I curled up and went to sleep. The next thing I remember was Zachary shaking me awake and saying, "End of the line, Eddie." I opened my eyes. We were stopped in a driveway. I noticed a big house sitting way back off the road. The plantation where he worked, I supposed. I sat up and grabbed my bag from the floor of the truck. He added, "I'm sorry to drop you off this far from town, but there are a hundred things I've got to get done before sundown."

"Don't worry about it. I appreciate the ride this far. Thanks for your hospitality and your stories. I really enjoyed the ride."

He smiled and said, "You're welcome. It has been a pleasure to meet you, Eddie." He shook my hand. I stepped out of the truck and shut the door behind me. He pointed out his window and said, "Just follow that road, and you'll run smack into the middle of town."

"Thanks," I replied and turned to walk away.

"Eddie," he called after me, "good luck in Florida. I hope you make all your dreams come true. Write and let me know how you're doin'. Zachary Brewster. Wixton, Georgia's all the address you need." He waved goodbye.

"I'll do that," I called back. He drove through the gate toward the big house, and I turned and walked toward town.

There wasn't much to see along the road to town. Miles of fields and pastures lined either side of the road. Here and there a house broke the open space. Traffic on the road was sparse, too. The cars and trucks that did pass me were few and far between, and none of them stopped to offer me a ride. I can't say that I blame them too much for that. You can never be too careful of a stranger by the side of the road. Most people who walk from town to town with their belongings on their backs have a reason, and nearly all of them are running from one thing or another. Good or bad, it's hard to tell the difference when you drive by someone on the highway.

It was about eight o'clock when I walked into Wixton. I was tired and hungry, so I headed to the first diner that I saw, a tired little place called Max's Diner, to get something to eat before I went to find a place to spend the night. I stepped through a battered screen door that had once served to keep out the flies, but now screenless, it hung sadly to remind the regulars of the toll of passing years. The stained, hardwood floor creaked beneath me as I stepped inside. The diner was scattered with an assortment of characters from dust-covered farmers to suit-and-tied businessmen. They sat in small groups around the room drinking coffee and telling the latest news. Of course all talk ceased when I stepped through the door. I had seen the same scene a hundred times before. They were all giving me the "who are you and what the hell are you doing here" look. I had learned to ignore it. I nodded to those that I passed on my way to the counter. No one spoke. When I had taken my seat, all talk resumed, but it was much quieter now. The conversations were now all about me. The waitress set a glass of water on the counter in front of me and hurried off to refill the numerous empty coffee cups around the room. When she returned, she pulled a pencil and a pad out of her apron pocket and asked, "What'll you have tonight, sugar?"

"Can I see a menu?" I asked.

Her expression went serious for a minute like she was deep in thought, then she said, "We ain't got a menu. Until now nobody's asked for one." I thought to myself, what kind of place doesn't have a menu? I asked, "Do you have hamburgers?"

"Well, yes and no. We have hamburgers, but we're out of buns. We can just put it on a plate or we can put it on light bread."

Having no notion as to what "light bread" was, I said, "Just put it on a plate. French fries?" I kind of half told and half asked.

"Sure thing, honey." She scribbled it all down on her pad. "And to drink?" she asked.

"Just water."

She reached under the counter and pulled out a pitcher if ice water which she set on the counter in front of me. She disappeared through the kitchen door, returning in about fifteen minutes with my breadless hamburger. I had to laugh at the thought as she set it on the counter in front of me and asked, "You want ketchup with them fries?" I nodded, and she fished this out from under the counter. "Let me know if you need anything." She grabbed the coffee pot to make another sweep. I sat silently and ate. The hamburger was good, even without the bread.

As I ate, I wondered if any of these people had anything better to do than sit in the town cafe and drink coffee. In a small town, I guessed that the later in the day, the less there was to do.

"You want a cup of coffee?" the waitress asked as I was finishing up the last of my fries.

"No thank you. I'll just have the check now please." She laid the ticket down and put my plate in a pan behind the counter. I thumbed through my wallet and pulled out two dollar bills. She tried to hand one of them back to me, but I said, "Keep the change." That gesture was sure to turn a few heads in the room.

"Thank you!" she exclaimed.

"Can you tell me where I might find a room for the night?" I asked.

"The Wixton Inn's right down the street. Go out, turn left, and you'll see the sign out front."

I thanked her for the information, picked my pack up from where I had dropped it, and headed for the door. As before, all chatter stopped, and everyone watched me to the door. I pushed open the sagging door and stepped into the light of the slowly dimming sun. I headed down the street to the aging motel that sat on the corner opposite the courthouse square. I had noticed that nearly every small town I had walked through had a courthouse square. In the center of town, the old brick courthouse stood judiciously, always capped by a shining clock dome that always seemed to be running a step behind the watch on my arm. Actually, it seemed that everything was running slower than normal. Maybe I just wasn't used to life in a small town.

The trip introduced me to a lot of things that had not been common in my neighborhood. Some of them were bad, but, for the most part, my journey had been a good one. I could not believe the friendliness of most of the people I had met since I had left home. Anyone who took the time to meet me and listen to my story and my dream were quick to offer their help and moral support. Some even invited me into their homes for a hot meal and a good night's rest. They were as friendly as they could be to a wandering stranger. However, no matter how friendly I tried to be, I couldn't hide the fact that I "...ain't from around here..." That alone was reason enough for some people to dislike me. I learned quickly that I was a Yankee, and that Southern pride was alive and well in 1963 America. On top of being a Yankee, my Italian heritage was more than evident in my features. To some, I was a foreigner, though I had lived my entire eighteen years in America and could not even speak Italian. My father never spoke it around the house. He always said that Italians speak Italian, and he was an American. He was extremely proud of where he came from and always taught me to respect my heritage, but he was also proud to live in America. Anyway, more than a few people that I had met didn't care for a foreign-looking stranger in their town. More than once on my journey south I had been carried through towns and counties by the local law enforcement. Although it made me extremely angry, I let it go and kept walking. I didn't feel like it was my place to right a social wrong. I didn't quite know what to think of this town yet. I had been around long enough for the locals to notify the appropriate authority to escort me out of town. I thought, "Maybe I can stay here a while and rest before I hit he road again." I wasn't very far from Florida now, but I needed some rest from a lot of foot travel. I felt like a refugee in need of sanctuary, and before me stood my haven in the form of the Wixton Inn.

I stood on the sagging porch looking up at a sign that hung over the bright red double door. The sign gave me a relief of sorts. It read, **YOU'RE NO STRANGER HERE! WELCOME TO WIXTON, GEORGIA.** I sighed, hoping it was true, and walked inside. The inside was not consistent with the outside. The smell of the fresh paint filled the air, and I could tell that the beautiful front desk and the hardwood floor on which I walked had recently been refinished. I walked over to the desk and rang the bell.

From a side door, a man dressed in overalls and a red and blue checkered shirt entered behind the counter. He was a small man, not much more than five feet tall. His graying hair was combed down and slicked back, and his gray-touched temples continued down into an almost white beard that hung almost to the middle of his chest. He pulled out a pair of wire-frame glasses, the half lens kind that you wear on the end of your nose, and placed them on his face. He asked, "Good day, sir. May I help you?"

"Yes, sir," I replied, "I hope so. I would like to get a room for the night with an option to stay longer."

The old man looked at me for a moment, then reached behind him for a room key. He opened an antique-looking ledger, handed me a pen and said, "Sign here. Your room is two-twelve. Up the stairs, at the end of the hall on the right."

I took the pen, signed the book, and reached for my wallet to pay. He stopped me, saying, "You'll pay when you leave." I thanked him and took the key from where he had laid it on the desk. He turned to walk away, then paused and asked, "You ain't from around here, are you?"

"No, sir," I answered and walked up the stairs, laughing to myself. I wonder how he knew. I paused for a moment at the top of the stairs to look out over the lobby. It was a beautiful place, totally out of place next to what I had seen of the rest of the town. It almost seemed that I had stepped through that red door into another world. I stood for a minute or two, then headed to my room. I was long overdue for a hot shower and a good night's sleep. I was tired.

My room was the last one in the hall. Beyond it were the stairs to the third floor. All the doors along the hallway were each painted a different color. Mine was the same bright red as the front door. I slid the key into the lock, which squeaked as I turned it. The door gave a stubborn resistance before it creaked open. The room behind it was nice, although not as nice as the lobby had been. The centerpiece was a huge, ornate bed that sat against the wall between the room's two windows. The bedspread and curtains were the same dark green color, and rugs of varying colors lay scattered here and there on the hardwood floor. Against the wall opposite the bed sat a matching dresser and a worn, dull-orange wingback chair that was entirely out of place. I sat down on the bed that gave in to my weight with an inviting softness. I pulled off my dusty clothes and headed to the bathroom for a hot shower.

After spending what seemed like an eternity standing beneath the hot water, I climbed into that big bed to get some long-awaited rest. The night before I had slept in a chair in the lobby of a booked-up motel outside of Augusta, Georgia. The night before that, I slept under a bridge somewhere in South Carolina. I settled under the covers, thanked God for the bed and seeing me through another day, then closed my eyes to sleep.

I was just about asleep when someone knocked heavily on the door. I pulled on my pants and shirt and went to the door. "Who is it?" I called angrily.

"This is Sheriff Besmer, Mr. Chance, I just wanted to ask you a few questions?"

"What about?"

"Just some information."

I figured it was best to answer his questions so he would go away and let me sleep. I opened the door to a huge man, well over six feet tall, in a spotless uniform, and a wide brimmed cowboy hat. Behind him stood a smaller man, the deputy.

I stepped back to allow the two of them to enter the room. The big man took off his hat and looked me over and looked around the room. The deputy never took his eyes off me. He had a look in his eyes that I had seen a hundred times before. He didn't trust me just because of the way I looked. His beady eyes watched my every move, while his hand rested on the butt of his pistol. I shot him a disapproving look, then turned to the sheriff.

"Besmer, was it?" I asked.

"That's right." He motioned to the smaller man. "This is Deputy Watson."

I nodded to the deputy, but he just glared at me.

"Joshua downstairs said your name is Chance. Is that right?" Besmer asked. His tone showing his doubt of my name.

"Yes, sir," I replied, not trying to hide my irritation. "Have I done something wrong, Sheriff?"

"No. We just thought it best to stop by and introduce ourselves."

"Do you personally greet everyone who stops here in town, or have I earned some special treatment?"

"Listen son, I'm not here to harass you. Some of the people down at the diner thought it seemed awfully suspicious for a young drifter to be passin' out money like there's no tomorrow. You just passin' through?"

"Yes."

"Where to?"

I had had enough of him. "Look, Sheriff Besmer, I don't want any trouble with you or your town. I just want to spend a few days here to rest from a long time on the road. When I've rested I'll move on. Okay?"

He cocked his head and replied, "Son, I don't want any trouble with you either. I just wanted to check out the stranger with all the money."

"Are you accusing me of something?" I was now extremely angry. I glanced over at the deputy, who had unsnapped the strap from his holster and was grasping the butt of his pistol. I turned to him before I thought about it and said, "Are you planning on shooting me? I never realized that tipping was a capital crime."

That angered him, and he stepped toward me, pulling the gun from its holster, but the sheriff stepped in. "Billy, calm down. Put that damn gun away and wait for me in the hall." Billy let the pistol drop back into place. The anger in his eyes burned into me, but I gave it back to him. He backed out of the room, never taking his eye off me. I turned back to the sheriff. He looked disgusted, and I guessed that he was more upset with Billy than he was with me. He shook his head. I took it as his apology for the actions of his deputy.

I spoke first, "Just so you'll know, my father left me the money when he died. Most of it anyway. Some came from odd jobs that I have had since I left home. When you grow up the son of a vegetable vendor, you learn pretty early how to unload boxes from a truck. I've done that now and then along the way down, just to keep myself from feeling useless. I didn't steal it, and I'll spend it anyway I want. I am sorry that I make your townspeople nervous, but I don't plan on being here long. When I've rested, I'll hit the road, and you people can get back to doing whatever it is that you people do. But right now I want some sleep. So if you don't have any more questions, I'd like to get back in bed."

"Stay and get your rest, but I'll be keepin' my eye on you. Stay out of trouble, and I'll leave you alone, agreed?"

"Agreed. What about Wyatt Earp out there? Am I going to have to spend my time here dodging bullets?"

The disgust showed on his face again, and he said, "Don't worry about Billy. I'll take care of him." He turned to the door to leave, then asked over his shoulder, "How old are you, anyway?"

"Eighteen."

"What's a kid your age doin' so far from home?" he asked with a fatherly concern in his voice.

"Chasing a dream," I said. "Chasing a dream."

He smiled slightly and closed the door behind him. I locked it and got back in bed. I looked at my watch. Ten forty-eight. I went to sleep.

Chapter Two

The next morning I was shaken from sleep by the sound of hammering outside my window. It was seven-fifteen. I moaned and fussed and buried my head under my pillow, but I couldn't go back to sleep with the noise, so I decided to go to the diner for some breakfast. I stumbled to the bathroom to splash some cold water on my face to wake myself up. It didn't help. I went back and dug through my pack for my last suit of clean clothes. I'd have to wash soon. I dressed and pulled on the boots I had bought at an Army-Navy store in Durham, North Carolina after the shoes I was wearing fell apart from walking for three days in the rain. I combed my hair, then headed out the door to breakfast. I locked the door behind me and slipped the key in my shirt pocket. The door across the hall was open, and a small, gray-haired lady was making the bed. I assumed she was the desk clerk's wife. She didn't notice me as I passed her door.

Once again, I stopped at the head of the stairs to look out at the lobby. This morning a young woman, about thirty or so, sat in one of the high-backed, leather chairs rocking a baby and watching over another little one who sat on the floor at her feet playing with a battered fire truck. A man stood at the desk. A blond-haired little girl clung tightly to his leg as he paid the clerk, my friend from last night.

I descended the stairs. The clerk and the man looked at me. The little girl peeked at me from behind her father's leg. I smiled at her. She quickly hid her face again.

"Mornin', Mr. Chance," the old man behind the desk said cheerfully.

"Good morning, sir," I replied, then added, "You can call me Eddie."

"Okay, Eddie, you call me Joshua." He pointed to the lady from upstairs as she came down. "This is my wife, May." I smiled at her. She returned it. The man with the little girl just nodded and continued to tend to his business with Joshua.

"Is the diner open?" I asked.

"Every mornin' at five."

"Thank you," I said and left through the red door.

The diner was nearly empty. All the farmers would be in the fields by now, and the suit-and-ties would be dropping by soon enough. I took the same stool at the counter. The same waitress that had served me the night before was behind the counter again. She smiled big when she saw me and grabbed the pot of coffee and a cup and hurried over to where I sat.

"Good mornin', sugar, how you doin'?" she said, pouring the coffee.

"I'm fine, ma'am."

"Please call me Janie, hon," she said, pulling a dish of sugar and a pitcher of milk out from under the counter.

"My name's Eddie. Eddie Chance," I said, spooning sugar into the coffee cup.

She stuck out a hand and said, "Nice to meet you, Eddie Chance. What'll you have this mornin', Eddie?"

"Scrambled eggs and sausage."

She called the order through the little window to the kitchen, then went off to tend to other customers who were slowly beginning to accumulate around the room. I sat at the counter drinking my coffee and looking around the room. Janie came back to retrieve my food when the cook announced its presence in the window. She set it down in front of me and hurried off again. I sat at the counter and quietly ate my breakfast.

Most people in town were at least cordial to me once the initial skepticism wore off, but Janie had been especially nice to me. She was an attractive woman, or at least she had been before years at the diner had taken their toll on her. She looked to be in her forties, but tired beyond her years. The crow's feet were visible at the corners of her eyes, and she hadn't gone out of her way to hide the gray streaks that wandered here and there across her light brown hair. A gold wedding band hung on a chain around her neck. A widow, I supposed. She had taken a liking to me the first time I came in the diner. I didn't know why, but I was glad. She seemed like the kind of person who would bring home any stray animal that wandered up, so maybe she could see the stray animal in me. I really didn't care about the reason, but I appreciated it. A friend was something I could use in a strange town.

I had eaten my breakfast and was finishing the last of my third cup of Janie's coffee when she came out of the kitchen over to where I was sitting. She said, "You know, Eddie, I don't why, but I feel like I can trust you."

"Yes, ma'am," I replied, puzzled.

"Would you mind doin' me a favor?" she asked.

"I've nothing else to do."

"I'd sure appreciate it. A friend of mine is stuck at home takin' care of his great-grandma. She needs her medicine, but he's got no way to come to town to get it, and I can't leave here to take it to him. I was wonderin' if you would take it. Do you have a car?"

"No."

"You can take mine. Normally I don't offer my car keys to strangers, but, like I said before, I've got a feelin' that I can trust you."

"I appreciate that," I replied. I really did appreciate her confidence in me. I was glad to see someone who still had faith enough not to prejudge me because of the way I looked or the way I talked.

She smiled and handed me the keys and a sheet of paper with directions on it. She pointed to her car in the alley beside the diner and directed me to the drugstore down the street. "I'll call Doc Brown to let him know you're comin'. He'll let you sign for the medicine."

I took everything and headed out down the street to the pharmacy that was three doors down Main Street. The fading red and yellow sign over the door proclaimed, **Brown's Drugs**. I went inside. A middle-aged man stood behind the counter shaking a large bottle. He looked down at me and asked, "May I help you?"

"I'm Eddie. Janie from the diner called to tell you I was coming?" I answered nervously.

"Oh, yes. I'm just finishin' up Mrs. Johnson's medicine." He dropped the bottle he was holding into a paper bag and stepped down to the counter where the cash register sat. He pulled a big book from underneath the counter, wrote Janie's name, an account number, and then pushed it toward me to sign. I signed and took the bag from him. "Thank you," I said.

"Thank you," he replied extending his hand. "I'm Simon Brown."

I shook his hand and replied, "Eddie Chance."

After that, I headed back up the street to the car. As I slid in behind the wheel, I couldn't help but laugh. Here I was delivering medicine to a woman I did not know, driving a car that belonged to a lady I had just met yesterday in a town I had wandered into just a few minutes before. Somehow, though, I felt like I was just doing a favor for an old friend.

Janie's directions led me west on the highway about five miles, then another two miles down a winding dirt road that was barely wider than the big Buick I was driving. The weather-beaten old house was the first that I came to. It sat close to the road under the shade of three large trees. A tireless Chevy sat on blocks next to the front porch. I caught sight of a dog peeking out from under it. The dog barked once when I stepped from the car but made no move to come out from its resting place. I knocked on the door. It was opened by a young black guy about my age. He looked past me at Janie's car. He said, "Janie send you?"

"Yes. I'm Eddie," I said, sticking out my hand.

He shook it saying, "I'm T. Come on in." He took the bottle from me, and I followed him inside. He closed the door behind me and motioned for me to sit down on the couch that sat in the middle of the small room where we were standing. I did, and he headed off to another room to give Mrs. Johnson her medicine, I guessed. A few minutes later, he stuck his head in the door and asked, "Eddie, you want a Coke or somethin'?"

"A Coke would be fine."

He returned with two bottles of Coke, handing me one as he sat down on the opposite end of the couch. "Thanks for bringin' Grandma's medicine. Mama forgot to pick it up last night after work. Grandma Grace can't go long without it." He changed the subject. "I don't think we've ever met. You a relative of Janie's from out of town?"

I laughed, "Actually, I just met Janie last night at the diner. I'm just passing through Wixton, and I was eating breakfast this morning when Janie asked me to bring the medicine out to you."

He looked a little surprised, then said, "Well, Eddie, you must have made some impression on her. Janie's not one to give the keys to that big Buick to just anybody. There's people here in town that she's known for years that she wouldn't hand over her car to. You should feel privileged." I smiled. That did make me feel pretty good.

He continued, "You said you were just passin' through town. Where you headed?"

"Florida," I replied. I told him about the trip down and how I had ended up in Wixton. He really liked my stories of the road. He had never been outside of Georgia and was very interested in all the places I had been and seen. He was especially curious about New York and asked a million questions about what it was like growing up there.

We had talked for nearly two hours when I realized that Janie was probably wondering where I was with her car. T decided he'd better call and let her know that I hadn't skipped town. She said it was all right for me to stay as long as I wanted.

"She's a really nice lady," I said when he relayed the news to me.

"Yeah, Janie's an angel. She's like a part of the family. She grew up with my father. They worked together pickin' cotton on the Baxley place. They were like brother and sister. They were inseparable, which ain't all that common for a white girl and a colored boy in rural Georgia in the 1930's. When Daddy died, she was there to help us out. She helped take care of Grandma Grace durin' the day so Mama could work, then went to work at the diner at night."

"How old were you when he died?" I asked.

"Ten," he answered. "I don't think I could have made it if Janie hadn't been here to help. There's nothin' like losin' a parent when you're a kid."

"I know what you mean," I replied. "My father died when I was sixteen. He was shot by a punk kid for fourteen dollars." A lump rose in my throat. "I never knew my mother. She died when I was born."

"I'm sorry, Eddie." The pain in his eyes was comforting to me. He was one person who could understand how I felt.

Just then, a bell rang in the other room. He stood and said, "That's Grandma. I better go see what she wants."

I sat on the couch and thought about the day my father died. The tears had stopped long ago, but the heartache never would.

T came back a few minutes later shaking his head and smiling. He sat down and said, "She wanted to make sure I fed the horses before Mr. Baxley came home." He laughed. I was trying to find the humor. He laughed for a moment then explained, "Her mind wanders. She spends most of her wakin' hours in the past. She has no idea what year this is or where she is. She's Daddy's grandmother, and she's a hundred and twelve years old. She was thirteen years old when the Baxley's freed her and her brother Solomon. She thinks I'm Solomon and that we're still slaves to Old Man Baxley, who's been dead for eighty years. Uncle Solomon's been dead nearly forty, but she doesn't remember that, at least not today."

"A hundred and twelve," I said. "That's amazing!"

"Yeah. She's outlived all her children and nearly all the grandchildren. Those that are left don't want anything to do with the 'crazy old woman'. She's lived with us as long as I can remember, and, as far as I'm concerned, they're the ones who're missin' out." He smiled.

"What made you decide to leave home for Florida?"

"Well, I really haven't had a home since Pop died, so I didn't have a hard time walking away from anything." I told him about how it had been with Liz and Nico, about the money, and about my dreams.

"It must have been scary travelin' alone through all the strange places so far from home."

"Alone doesn't really bother me. I've felt alone since Pop died anyway. What's scary is walking through towns where the people would just as soon spit on you as ask your name. Some people have been genuinely nice, but there have been some that were nice as long as I kept walking. More than anything else, I'm just tired, and that's why I'm still in Wixton. My body's exhausted, and I need to take a day or two and rest before I hit the road again. I have the blessing of the local sheriff. As long as he's happy, I'm going to stay put."

"Besmer's okay. You won't have any trouble with him as long as you stay straight. He's not the one you need to worry about. It's that deputy of his, Billy Watson. That fool's a loose cannon waitin' for an excuse to go off."

I nodded my agreement, then added, "I had the pleasure of meeting Deputy Watson along with the Sheriff last night." I went on to tell him about the altercation with Watson.

"You better be careful around Billy," T said sternly, with an implied authority. I assumed there had been problems with the deputy in the past.

"How did an idiot like that get a job as a deputy sheriff?" I asked.

"He's Besmer's nephew. Besmer don't care too much for him, but hired him because of his sister. The sheriff spends half his time keepin' Billy out of trouble. One of these days, that temper of Billy's is gonna get him killed. The best way to handle him is to stay away from him." I had already made that decision.

"I have been dying to ask you since you introduced yourself," I changed the subject. "I have to know where you got a name like T. Is it short for something?"

He laughed. "Theodore Roosevelt Johnson," he said proudly, "but I been called T all my life. My brother couldn't say Theodore, so he shortened it to T, and it stuck."

"You have an older brother?"

His expression saddened as he said, "I had a brother. He was eight years older than me."

"What happened to him?"

"He was killed when I was twelve, " he said sadly. A distance appeared in his eyes as he remembered the time. I did not press him for an explanation.

"I'm sorry," I said. "I didn't mean to bring up a bad memory."

"No, man, it's ok. There hasn't been a day go by that I haven't thought about it," he replied, still offering no explanation.

We sat silently for a while, not knowing how to break the solemnness of our mood. We both drained the remaining Coke from our bottles.

Finally, T asked, "What you got planned for the night?"

"Nothing. Why?"

"You play pool?"

"Yes."

"There's a pool hall out east of town where I hang out sometime. You wanna ride out there when Mama gets home? I'll introduce you to some of my friends, and we can shoot a few games."

"Sounds good to me. I don't have anything else to do."

"Great."

We spent the rest of the afternoon swapping more stories and playing cards to kill the time until his mother got home. We talked about everything from girls to politics. Neither of us knew very much about either one, but we talked about them anyway. The hours passed quickly.

Chapter Three

About six o'clock, a car pulled into the yard. T looked out the window and said, "Mama's home." He opened the door to let her in. I stood up from where I was sitting to meet her.

My presence surprised her. She turned to T for an explanation. T stepped over beside me and said, "Mama, this is Eddie Chance. Janie got him to bring Grandma Grace's medicine out for her this mornin'." Her expression relaxed at the mention of Janie's name. T continued, "He's been keepin' me company all day."

She smiled and stuck out her hand. I shook it, and she said, "Nice to meet you, Eddie. You ain't from around here are you? You a relative of Janie's?"

"No, ma'am," I replied.

T spoke up, "Mama, Eddie just got into town yesterday, and I wanted to show him around a little tonight, if you don't mind."

"Go ahead. Just don't be out too late, you hear?" she said.

"Yes ma'am," he replied and kissed her cheek. He turned to me and asked, "You ready?" I nodded my head, and we headed out the door.

"First thing we need to do is take Janie's car back to her," he said once we were outside. "I'll follow you in our car."

Back at the diner, I parked the car where I had found it and went in to give Janie the keys. T waited outside at the curb. Janie waved at him though the window. I told her about our plans and headed back out to the car. I climbed in beside T and said, "Drive on, my friend." He laughed and pulled onto the street. He circled the courthouse and headed east.

The east side of town, I noticed, was mostly black. Once we passed the stores and parking lots, the sides of the road were lined with yards full of black children playing baseball or something like that. They all waved as we drove by. T turned left off the main road and drove down past some old warehouses. He pulled into an alley between two of them and stopped behind a blue pickup that was parked beside one of the buildings. He climbed out of the car and motioned for me to follow. I fell in step behind him and followed him down the alley to a stairway leading below ground under the warehouse. The door at the bottom of the stairs was open, and I could hear music coming from inside.

"This is the pool hall?" I asked warily.

T laughed, "Yeah."

"Under a warehouse?"

"Yeah. Place used to be a bar, a speakeasy, back during Prohibition. Rich white folks came down here to drink illegal whiskey and see the show. When Prohibition ended, they didn't have to hide anymore, so the place closed down. Back in the forties, Willie Shaker rented the place and turned it into a pool hall."

The door at the bottom of the steps opened into a long corridor that smelled of urine and cigarette smoke. The narrow space was thick with smoke, and the humidity I had come to realize was what passed for air in the south. A man sat on a chair just inside the door. He didn't speak when we entered. He just hummed along with the tune he was picking on his battered guitar. T pulled two quarters from his pocket and dropped them into the old man's guitar case as we passed, then continued down the corridor. I could see the light from another door at the other end. I followed T down the hall and through the door.

The room was crowded. Groups of varying sizes gathered around the dozen-or-so pool tables that sat in the middle of the room. More people sat at the tables that lined the walls of the room. To the right of the door was the bar. An old man in an apron stood behind it handing out drinks. No one noticed us when we walked in, but I noticed that, from everyone I could see from the door, I was the only white man in the room.

T motioned toward the bar and asked, "You want a Coke or something?" I shook my head so he kept going into the room. As we worked our way through the tables, the players looked up from their games. Most spoke to T and shot surprised glances and nods at me. I nodded back and continued behind T.

He stopped at a table where a tall, lanky guy was hunched over the table to make a shot. Two guys stood off to the side, waiting. We drew up silently while the third took his shot. The cue ball cracked against the other balls, and two stripes followed one another into the corner pocket.

"Good shot," T said, then added, "for a change." He laughed.

The shooter stood up from the table. He was at least a head taller than my five-ten. He gave T a menacing stare, then his mouth widened into a big smile. He said, "You think you can do better, you give it a try." He looked over at me but didn't speak.

T broke the awkwardness of the moment by stepping up and introducing me. "Eddie, this is Clancy, Bobby, and Peabody." Each of them nodded when his name was called. Turning back to me, he said, "This is Eddie Chance." I stuck out my hand. Clancy, the tall one, was the first to take it. The others followed suit.

T turned back to Clancy, "Where's Jawbone?"

"Work," he answered. "He'll be down when he gets off."

Peabody tapped Clancy on the shoulder with his cue and said, "I thought we had a game goin' here. We can have the family reunion later. It's your shot." He pointed to the table.

Clancy looked at the table, then shot one of the two remaining stripes in the same pocket as before. He sank the final ball and called his pocket for the eight. The ball fell quickly, and the game was over. Clancy looked at me. "You play?" he asked.

"Now and then," I replied.

"You wanna shoot?" he asked. I nodded, and he handed me a cue. "You break."

Peabody lifted the rack from the balls, and I lined up my shot. The balls scattered across the table. Three fell. "Solids," T announced, checking the pockets. I found my next shot. Seven ball, side pocket. The luck of the break had not left me another good shot, so I took the safe and hid the cue ball in a jumble of balls.

Clancy looked at the table, then at me, and said, "You shoot pretty damn good for a white boy, Cue ball."

"Cue ball?" I asked.

"Yeah," he laughed, "seemed to fit you. That's what we call all the other whites in the room." Everybody laughed. I laughed, too. The name did seem to fit.

He lined his shot the best he could, but the ball bounced from the rail miles from the pocket.

I sank the four ball in the side pocket and watched helplessly as the cue ball followed it in. Peabody smiled and said, "Tough break, Cue ball."

I had my back to the door, waiting for Clancy to make his shot. T nodded toward the door and said, "Here comes your buddy."

I looked over my shoulder to see what he was talking about. Billy Watson and two other men stood in the doorway. The deputy looked much like he did the night before, except that his ill-fitting uniform looked as if he had slept in it. The two larger men were not in uniform, but each had a badge hanging on his pocket. I guessed they were there solely because Watson was afraid to come into the pool hall alone. He probably grabbed two of his biggest redneck buddies and made them deputies for the night. They paused in the doorway and looked around the room. Most everyone in the room ignored them, even though, like mine, their white faces stuck out like sore thumbs.

I elbowed T, protesting, "He's no buddy of mine."

Clancy looked up from the table and shook his head. "What the hell does that crazy white boy want?" he thought out loud.

Watson's companions stood on either side of the door while he made his way through the tables. He scanned the faces of the players as he passed. He was apparently looking for someone. Unsatisfied with his search, he made his way back to us. He looked over at me with a hint of contempt in the smirk on his face. I nodded, but did not speak.

Peabody was the first to speak. He propped against our table and asked, "Why Deputy Watson, for what do we have the honor of your official presence?" Watson was visibly annoyed by the sarcasm in Peabody's voice. Mission accomplished.

"Don't get smart with me, nigger," the deputy barked back.

Peabody stood up from the table saying, "Watch yourself now, Deputy. I'd be a little more careful of my language if I were you."

Watson looked over his shoulder to see if his backup was still there. Relieved to see them flanking the door, he turned back to Peabody. "You ain't me, nigger, so shut up. I'll say what I want to say." Peabody let it slide. Watson continued, "You seen Joe Mack Smith tonight?"

Peabody thought for a minute, then answered in a mock slave accent, "Naw Suh." He turned to the room and asked, "Any y'all seen Joe Mack Smith?"

"No!" was the mass answer.

Peabody looked back to Watson, "No Joe Mack Smith 'round here, Deputy. Why you lookin' for him, anyway?"

"That's none of your damn business," the deputy growled, "and I know you know where he is, and you're gonna regret lyin' to me!"

Peabody shrugged, "Maybe. Maybe not."

Watson was fuming, but, rather than take on Peabody, he turned toward me. "Well, well, well, what do we have here? The Yankee boy come down to play with the niggers. What's wrong, boy, you too stupid to tell what color you are?"

I ignored his comment, and that made him even more angry. He screamed at me, "I was talkin' to you, Yankee boy. What the hell you doin' here, boy, and don't give me the shit about dreams. Besmer may be dumb enough to believe your lies, but I ain't. You runnin' from somethin' ain't you, boy?"

"Yeah, I'm running from a half-wit deputy sheriff, but I'll be damned if they don't have one here, too!" I answered.

"Don't get smart with me. I'll beat your Yankee ass." He poked his finger into my chest.

I pushed him back and said, "Don't touch me again, deputy. If I've done something wrong, arrest me. If not, back off."

He grabbed the front of my shirt and pushed me back against the table behind me. He got right up in my face. The liquor on his breath was nauseating. "Let me tell you somethin', Yankee boy. What you did wrong was show your ugly, nigger-lovin' face in my town. I'm the law around here, and I'll do whatever the hell I want to. You need to take your sorry ass and head back the way you came. We don't want your kind down here, and if you stay around much longer, you might just find yourself in a peck of trouble!"

"Is that a threat?"

"I'm just sayin' that we have ways of takin' care of troublemakers around here. Ain't that right, boy?" The last comment was to T. Watson looked back at me and continued, "Why don't you ask your friend Johnson what happened to his brother?"

I could tell that what Watson had said had cut deep into T. Although anger flooded his face, it was the sadness in his eyes that touched me. Peabody put his hand on T's shoulder to calm him down. While Watson was gloating over T's reaction, I wrapped my hand around a cue stick on the table behind me. I was about to swing it at Watson's head when I felt a large hand on my arm. My first thought was that the deputy's cohorts had joined the fight, but they were still watching apathetically from their post by the door.

"Let's not do somethin' you might regret later," someone said from behind me. From my position against the table, I could not see the source of the thunderous voice. I released the stick, and he relaxed his grip on my arm.

"You got business here, Watson?" the voice asked. The arrogance drained from the deputy's face and was replaced by what I would say was genuine fear. I still could not see who was speaking, but I was glad he had shown up. "How 'bout letting go of him."

Watson let go of my shirt, and I turned to face the speaker. He was a huge man, at least a foot taller than Clancy. His huge chest and arms strained against the confines of his shirt, and his shaved head added to his menacing appearance.

He repeated his first question, "You got business here, Watson, or you just here to harass us?"

The deputy's tone was considerably different when he answered. His voice trembled when he spoke, "I don't want no trouble with you. I'm just havin' a little talk with Mr. Chance."

"I don't know if you noticed, but you and this Mr. Chance look a little out of place in here. There has got to be a better place for two white boys to have a talk, so tell me what you're doin' here."

"I'm lookin' for Joe Mack Smith."

"Why?"

"Business," Watson answered nervously.

"Don't play that shit with me, Watson? What you want him for?"

The last hint of defiance drained from the deputy's face. "Old Man Ditwhiler wants him for some groceries and stuff he stole," he answered, more responsive to the big man's question.

"How much?"

"What?"

"How much did he take?"

"Three or four dollars' worth."

The big man pulled a five dollar bill from his pocket and threw it down on the bed of the table. "You take that to Ditwhiler. Tell him that him and Joe Mack's square, and you leave the boy alone. You mess with him again, and I come lookin' for you." The deputy scooped the money up from the table. The big man added, "Ditwhiler best get that money, you hear."

Watson turned back to me and said, "You better watch your back, Chance. Your time's comin'."

"Watson," the big man spoke again, "your business is finished here. You better take your scrawny white ass somewhere where it's wanted before you make somebody mad." Watson sneered at me, then carried his wounded pride out the door.

The big man turned to Peabody and asked, "Who let this white boy in here?" I knew he was talking about me, and for a moment I began to worry. He turned back to me and stuck out his hand, "You're Chance, I presume?"

"Eddie," I replied, shaking his enormous hand.

"Cue ball," Clancy corrected me. "Call him Cue ball."

"Well, Cue ball, you can call me Jawbone?" He nodded toward the door. "That son-of-a-bitch's gonna get his ass tied in a knot one of these days."

Somebody in the front of the room called out, "I'd pay good money to see that!"

"Me, too!" someone else agreed.

Everybody laughed.

Bobby said, "We might have seen it for free if Jaw here hadn't come up. Cue ball looked like he was gonna put that stick up side the jackass's head. Why'd you stop him, Jaw?"

"Figured that would be a waste of a perfectly good cue stick." Jawbone laughed, then added, "Seriously, y'all know some of the white folk in town don't like us havin' this place. Let the white deputy get the shit beat out of him down here, and they wouldn't rest until they closed us down. Ain't nobody gonna give a damn that a white boy done the beatin'." He laughed again and said to me, "Still, I would have loved to see you crack his skull with that stick."

Jawbone walked away. I turned back to T. I could see that he was still angry about what Watson had said. I handed my cue to Peabody and said, "I don't feel much like finishing this game. Maybe later." He nodded. I put my hand on T's shoulder and said, "I'm ready for a Coke now. You want one?"

"Whatever," he replied.

I bought two Cokes from the old man behind the bar, and T and I found an empty table. We sat silently for a while, sipping slowly from the cold bottles in our hands.

"You want to talk about it?" I finally asked.

"What? " he replied, skirting the issue.

"What he said. I could tell it bit into you. What did he mean about your brother? What did happen to him?"

"He was murdered." The anger welled in his eyes again. "Tortured and lynched."

"Watson have something to do with it?" I wondered.

"No, but he didn't shed no tears, I bet."

I wasn't going to ask for details, but T continued with an explanation. "The summer he turned twenty, Ray became involved with a white girl, Leslie Bloodworth, over in Smithville. I'm not sure how they first met, but for months they would meet secretly to be with each other.

"One night, her father caught them together, goin' at it in the hayloft of his barn. He was furious. He hit Ray in the back with a shovel. Broke his ribs and knocked the breath out of him. When Ray was down, Bloodworth kicked him until he was nearly dead. When Ray couldn't fight back any more, Bloodworth turned on Leslie, who had been tryin' to pull him away from Ray. He was beatin' her and yellin' at her for bein' with a   'good-for-nothin' nigger'. Though Ray could barely breath, he used what strength he had left to jump the old man. Caught the old bastard off guard. Bloodworth lost his footin' and fell out of the loft onto the blades of the disc harrow.

"Leslie climbed down from the loft and ran to the house to call the sheriff. He arrested Ray for killin' the old man and even tried to charge him with rapin' Leslie. But Leslie stood up for him in court. She told the jury what happened. They were disgusted by her admission to havin' sex with a black man, but they found Ray not guilty. They took a lot of heat over that verdict. Nobody 'round here could believe that twelve white folks let a nigger get away with murderin' a white man, and the idea that the nigger was screwin' the dead man's daughter didn't make things any better."

He paused a moment to collect his thoughts and take a drink from the Coke bottle in his hand before continuing. "Though Ray was a free man, his life was a mess. The whites didn't trust him, 'cause they still saw him as a murderer, and the blacks didn't want him 'cause he had been with a white girl. Leslie's life was worse. Her family turned against her. She had shamed the family and had killed her father. They threw her out of the house and told her to never come back. She had no place to go, so she came to us.

"Ray decided that the best thing for them to do was get as far away from Wixton as they could. He talked to our uncle in Chicago. He was gonna get Ray a job. Ray bought two tickets on the bus to Chicago. He was gonna take Leslie and try to make a new start."

T's face grew sad again. I could tell that the memories pained him. Tears formed in the corners of his eyes. He looked away to wipe his eyes, embarrassed by the emotion, saying, "I'm sorry."

I put my hand on his shoulder to comfort him. I said, "You don't have to tell me anymore. I can see that it hurts you to remember."

He wiped the last of the tears away and replied, "No, I'm okay." He took another drink before continuing. "The night before they were to leave, we had a bad storm, and the animals were restless. Ray went out to the barn to settle them down but never came back. At first we didn't worry because it was rainin' pretty hard and lightnin'. We figured that he was waitin' out the storm, but when the rain stopped, he still didn't come in. I went to the barn to look for him.

"The barn door was standin' wide open when I got there. Through the open door, I could see blood puddled on the dirt floor of the barn. I didn't go in. I just screamed and ran back to the house. An image of Ray lyin' on the floor bleeding to death filled my mind. Mama and Leslie met me on the way back. Through my hysteria, I tried to tell her what I saw, but I all I could do was sob and wheeze for air.

"Leslie ran to the barn. She collapsed in the door and began to cry. By that time, Mama had caught up with her. I stopped at the door, but this time I could see what was inside. It wasn't Ray's blood that I had seen. Someone had killed all the animals, cut their throats. I threw up."

I sat silently, listening to the horrible details of his story. The thought of what he saw made me nauseous. I took a long drink from the bottle of now-warm Coke in my hand. My mind filled with the image of my father's blood pooling on the sidewalk, surrounding the spot where I sat holding his dying body. A lump rose in my throat. I took another drink.

He continued, "Mama called Ray over and over, but he didn't answer. She searched the barn for him. He was gone. She found footprints in the dirt. More than one set. Mama and me helped Leslie back to the house, and Mama called the sheriff, who took his time comin'."

"Besmer?" I asked.

"No, " he replied, "Clarence Wood was the sheriff in fifty-seven. Besmer was just a deputy then. He took Wood's place in fifty-nine. Anyway, Sheriff Wood wrote Ray off as just another crazy nigger. He tried to say that Ray had killed the livestock and just ran off." The anger showed through the sadness in T's eyes. He went on, "Two days later Besmer came knockin' at the door. Somebody had found Ray's body north of town, beaten and hanged."

"Did they find the ones who did it?" I asked.

The anger showed in his eyes again. "Find 'em! Hell! Everybody knew who did it. Leslie's brother, Mickey, and his uncle, Bloodworth's younger brother, Leonard. He's a cop down in Albany. Hell, they even bragged about it."

"If everybody knew, how come they weren't arrested?" I questioned.

"No proof."

"But if they bragged about it?"

"Hearsay."

"But..."

"As far as the sheriff was concerned, the case was closed. Somebody had just done what the court should have. He said one more dead nigger was one less he had to worry 'bout. Carl Besmer wanted to do somethin', but Wood overruled him. Sent him off to some bullshit trainin' school to keep him from stirrin' up trouble."

"How come Besmer didn't go over his head, go to the state? Or something?"

"Clarence Wood was a powerful man. He had friends in all the right places. High and low places. Besmer knew if he crossed the man, he'd end up in deep shit, or worse."

"What about when he became sheriff? How come he didn't go after them then?" My opinion of the sheriff was dropping by the minute.

"No need to by then," T explained. "The two of them were both dead by then. You know what they say, 'What goes around, comes around'. Well, they got theirs." A smile played briefly across his pained face. He continued, "Mickey was killed the followin' spring. Gored by a bull. Took him three days to die. Bled to death on the inside." He paused to empty the bottle in his hand.

"The other one?" I asked. "The uncle."

"Two days before Christmas, in fifty-eight, he was shot."

"Trying to arrest someone?"

"No," he laughed, "got caught in the bed with another man's, another cop's, wife. Fellow shot him six times. He's at Folsom now."

"Folsom?"

"Prison," he clarified.

"What happened to Leslie?" I asked.

"She left town. The last time we heard from her she had married a soldier in California and was trying to start a family. That was two years ago." He finished his story with a shrug.

I was at a loss for words, not really knowing how to react to what I had heard. Even with all the heartache that I had felt in my life, I couldn't fathom all the pain and tragedy that T had endured. He was a lot stronger than I could claim to be.

Jawbone helped us through the uncomfortable silence that followed our conversation. He made his way around the room and back to where we were. He grabbed a chair from the next table and pulled it up next to us. Clancy and Peabody did the same. Bobby mumbled something about an early day tomorrow, then headed out the door.

Jawbone yelled for a round of drinks for us all, then turned to me and said, "Cue ball, what's the story with you and Billy Watson. It ain't natural for Billy to be harassin' a white boy when there's colored folk around. He must hate you pretty bad."

I shrugged. I told him about the night before, and the incident at the hotel room. He and the others echoed T's opinions that Watson was a loose cannon. When T told Jawbone that I was from New York, he laughed out loud and said that the only thing Billy might hate more than blacks was Yankees. He told me that I shouldn't worry too much about Watson because, even though he talked a good game, he generally didn't act on his threats unless he was sure he could win. Peabody laughed and said he spent most of his time picking on women, children, and old people. In spite of all the jokes, I knew that I had an enemy that I didn't need. He was the first bona fide bigot that I had ever met. In his eyes, I had three strikes against me: I was a Yankee, I was Italian, and my friends were black. I was not afraid of Billy Watson. He was just an idiot who couldn't see past his prejudice, but I was afraid of Deputy Billy Watson, because he was a bigot with a gun and a badge. Although justice didn't mean a damn thing to him, he was still a lawman, and trouble with the law was something I did not need. For some reason, I seemed to have gained the respect of Sheriff Besmer. T had reassured me that Besmer would be on my side as long as I stayed on the good side of the law. I knew that, with Billy Watson out to get me, I needed the support of the one man who had some control over him.

"What's the story on the two men Billy brought with him?" I asked. "Are they deputies?"

Peabody laughed, "Only when Billy's too scared to go somewhere alone. Like I said before, Billy don't jump nothin' he ain't positive he can whip. Takes along the big boys to handle the rest."

Jawbone cut in, "The bigger one's Dick Brinson. He's dumb as a post, and he's tough, but he won't mess with you unless you mess with him. Best way to handle him is just leave him be. Now the other one's a different story. Name's Sims. Dan Sims. He's a bad ass. He'll fight at the drop of a hat. Spent some time in prison a few years back for killin' a man in a bar fight. He made a pass at Dan's wife, and Dan beat him to death. Just stay the hell away from him, and you'll be ok."

Around midnight, we decided to call it a night. The guys took off for home, each of them complaining about work the next day. T dropped me off at the inn.

I walked quietly across the deserted lobby and up the stairs to my room. I was surprised and happy to find that all my clothes had been washed and left folded on the dresser next to a plate of chocolate chip cookies. I stuffed one of the cookies into my mouth as I undressed for bed and thought to myself that I would have to remember to thank May in the morning.

I lay in the bed and thought about everything that had happened that day. Total strangers had taken the time to get to know me and accept me into their group. With the exception of Billy Watson, everyone had gone out of their way to make me feel welcome. I did feel welcome, and I knew that I had made some new friends.

In the distance, I heard thunder rumble. I thanked God for the clean, dry bed and the roof over my head, then I rolled over and drifted into sleep.

Chapter Four

The dreams returned that night. I knew they would eventually. The dreams started the night Pop was killed. At first, it was every night. I would wake up screaming from the horror of what I had seen in my sleep. Liz would try to console me, but she was barely in control of herself. Her constant crying was no help to me. As time passed, the dreams came less often. Sometimes days or even weeks would pass before the horrible images filled my thoughts. They were each different, with each one more frightening than the last.

This dream I dreamed my second night in Wixton was no exception:

First, there is nothing. No light. No sound. Nothing. I am aware that I exist in this place where there is nothing else. I scream, but, still, there is no sound. I search the space around me. Nothing. Nothing above or below me. No walls, no floor, nothing. Just me and the darkness.

My nose fills with the smell of bacon frying. The smell is powerful, almost nauseating. The darkness disappears. I see my father standing at the stove with a frying pan in his hand. He glances at me and smiles. He says, "Breakfast is almost ready. You'd better hurry or you'll be late for school." I stumble to the bathroom to splash water on my face and to comb through my hair. The morning is like every other morning. When I come out of the bathroom, he is gone. The frying pan sits on the stove, and the smell of burning bacon fills the air around me.

Darkness again. I hear the gunshots. Two explosions break the silence. The sounds of the city surround me. There is laughing. Loud, almost deafening. The light bursts into my eyes. I am blinded only for a second, then I see hundreds of people around me pointing and laughing. I realize I am naked. My body is covered with blood. My father's blood, but he is gone. I scream, but I can't hear it. The sound is swallowed by the laughter. Everyone laughing. All of them pointing at me. No one offers help. No consolation for my loss. Someone in the crowd throws a rock at me. Then another. Another. Everyone is throwing rocks. I run down the street. They chase me. Still throwing things at me. I am running as hard as I can. The pavement beats mercilessly at my bare feet. My legs ache for rest, but I must run to live.

Suddenly, it is dark again. Not the void of before, but nighttime. I am still running, but the city street is gone. Now it's a dirt road. The buildings that had loomed above me have been replaced by open fields. Wide open space for as far as I can see. Rain beats down on my naked body. I am alone, no longer chased by the laughing people, but still I run.

In the distance, I can see a light. Just a speck on the horizon. I know that I must go to that light. Though my legs burn from exhaustion, I cannot stop running. Miles and miles I run down the muddy road. The light grows bigger in the distance until I can see that it is a fire. Burning in spite of the downpour. I am drawn to it. Then the fire is gone. I realize that I am running through a cemetery. Acres and acres of tombstones surround me. The weakness of my body overtakes me, and I fall face-first into the mud.

Music surrounds me. Dozens of voices singing "Amazing Grace" as a piano plays. I lift my head from the mud and look into the open door of the church before me. An open casket stands at the altar. I crawl from the ground up the steps of the church. My aching muscles tremble as I limp past the pews filled with people I do not recognize. No one seems to notice me. They continue to sing. I stop before the casket and look down at my own body, naked and muddy. I stand there looking at myself in the casket. Then the image changes. Now I am lying in the casket looking up into my own startled face. The face I see slowly changes into the face of a woman. She cries, mourning my death. Who is she? One by one the unfamiliar faces of the congregation pass over me. Each one talking about me as if they know me. I can do nothing but lie motionless in the box and watch them. The piano continues to play in the background. Finally, the faces no longer appear over me. The music stops. The room around me grows quiet as the people leave me behind. The lights of the sanctuary are turned off. Only the light directly above me remains. One solitary bulb that shines so brightly that it is all I can see.

I am alone for hours. Unable to move. Unable to do anything but stare at that light. Then a shadow passes over me. Something comes between me and my light. The figure of a man appears over me. In the brightness of the light, I can see nothing but his outline. He pulls the lid down toward me. He is closing me in the casket. For a moment before it closes, the lid shields my eyes from the light, and I can see the face of the man who is shutting me away. The face of Billy Watson. I hear him laughing as the lid clicks into place.

Then there is nothing. No light. No sound. Nothing. I scream, but there is no sound.

There was a loud, crashing boom. I screamed again and sat upright in bed. I looked around my room. The dream was over. Thunder crashed outside as rain pounded against the window. The sheets and I both were drenching wet with sweat. Tears rolled uncontrollably down my face. I held my pillow to my chest and rocked. I knew there would be no more sleep that night. I looked at my watch. Two-thirty.

A knock came at the door. "Eddie, are you all right?" Joshua's voice asked through the door. Before I could answer, the door opened. Joshua rushed in wearing his nightshirt. He asked again if I were okay. "We heard you screamin'," he added.

"Just a bad dream," I answered, embarrassed. "I'm sorry that I bothered you."

May came in as I was answering him. She looked at me with motherly eyes and said, "Look at you. You're white as a ghost." She sat down on the bed and put her hand against my forehead. "And soakin' wet. Joshua, get him a towel. Well, you ain't got a fever," she assured me, taking her hand down from my head. "But these bedclothes will have to be changed before you can go back to sleep." She left the room to get fresh sheets for the bed.

Joshua came back in with a wet washcloth and a towel. I wiped my face, then toweled the sweat off my body. I pulled on my jeans and tried to help him strip the bed. "You just go sit down, son," he said. "You don't look like you got the energy to stand up. That must have been some dream you were havin'." I nodded. "You wanna talk about it?" I shook my head. I didn't think I was up to reliving it right away.

May came back with the sheets, and the two of them remade my bed. I apologized again for waking them and thanked them for coming to see about me. I also thanked May for the laundry and the cookies. When they had finished with the bed, she came over and sat on the arm of the chair and put her hand on my shoulder. She said, "It's been a long time since I've had someone who needed motherin' around here. Makes me feel good to be needed like that again." She leaned over and kissed my forehead, then got up to leave. Joshua asked, "You gonna be ok, or do you need some company for a while?"

I shook my head. "I'll be okay now. I think. You go back to bed." Before they walked out I said, "May, it's nice to have someone to mother me, too." She smiled and closed the door behind her.

I climbed back in bed. The fresh sheets felt good against my skin. I was sleepy, but the images from the dream would not let me rest. Every time I closed my eyes, they would start over again. I picked up the Bible from the nightstand and opened it to Luke. Somewhere in the gospel, I found the peace-of-mind I needed to go back to sleep. I closed my eyes and fell asleep with the Bible open across my chest.

Chapter Five

When I opened my eyes again, my room was dark, except for the hint of light that crept in around the edges of the dark green curtains. Rain drops beat steadily against the windows, a pleasant departure from the merciless banging of the previous morning. The rain had temporarily suspended the construction next door. My watch told me that it was nearly ten. I was thankful for the extra sleep. I pushed back the covers and uncovered the Bible that had fallen into the bed sometime during the night. I leaned back against the headboard and looked at the book in my hand. I bowed my head and thanked the Lord for all the things He had brought into my life. Through the kindness of strangers, He was letting me know that, no matter how bleak things got at times, He was still there for me, and that, even in the worst of times, He was still in charge. I pulled the covers back up and continued to read what I had started the night before. After a while, I placed the Bible back on the nightstand and went to take a much-needed shower.

After I had dressed, I pulled open the curtains. The rain fell hard against the glass. In the distant sky, I caught the flash of lightning. A good day to stay indoors, I thought to myself as I made the bed, but I was starving, so I would have to at least make a trip to the diner for some breakfast. I pulled the door shut and again dropped the key into my shirt pocket.

Joshua and May were sitting in the lobby when I came down the stairs. May was sitting at one end of the sofa knitting what appeared to me to be a sweater for a child. Joshua sat reading the newspaper in one of two big leather chairs that sat at either end of the sofa. His slippered feet rested on the end of the coffee table in front of him. He looked up from his paper when I reached the bottom of the stairs.

"Mornin'," he said. "I reckon you slept better the rest of the night."

I nodded, "Yes sir."

"Here now. Come sit a spell with us. We sure wouldn't mind the company," he invited.

"I'd like that, but I'm starving. I was just on my way over to the diner for some breakfast."

May looked up from her knitting. "Nonsense! You sit down here, and I'll fix you somethin' to eat. You ain't about to go out in this rain to eat at some old diner."

I tried to protest, but she was already on her way to the kitchen. Joshua laughed and told me that arguing was useless. I conceded and sat down in the chair opposite him.

"I'm sorry I bothered you last night, but I do appreciate your concern for me, though. It was nice having someone there when I woke up."

"Son, you needn't worry 'bout that now. We were glad that we could be there for you. The way you screamed out like you did, you must have seen somethin' awful bad." I nodded. Joshua nodded, too. He continued, "Ben used to scream in the night like that when he first got back from Korea. Sometimes two or three times in a night, we'd have to change his bedclothes 'cause he'd sweat so in his sleep. It was years before he told us what he saw in his dreams that scared him so.

"Ben," Joshua explained, "is our youngest son. He and his wife Sarah live over in Columbus." He pointed over my shoulder and continued, "Columbus is about seventy, eighty miles northwest of here. In case you didn't know that." I shook my head. He went on, "Ben works for the newspaper over there." Joshua picked up the paper he had been reading and proudly showed me his son's by-line. "Been there about five years. Sarah's an elementary school teacher and expectin' number two by Christmas." He beamed proudly at the thought.

"You said that Ben is the youngest. How many kids are there?" I asked.

"Three in all," he replied. "May probably has breakfast 'bout done by now, Eddie. Let's go inside, and I'll show you pictures of the whole brood."

I followed him behind the check-in desk and through the door he had come out of the night I arrived. It led to the living room of their apartment. The aroma of breakfast floated through the air. Joshua pointed me to a small sofa, then went off to check with May about breakfast. He was back in a moment with an armload of photographs. He set them down on the table in front of me and said, "Food's not quite ready. I've got time to show off the family."

He picked up the first of the pictures. He pointed to the woman and said, "This is Margaret Ann. She's the oldest." He moved to the man in the photo. "Arthur here is a state senator. And these are Ruth, Bobbi Lynn, and Priscilla," he said, pointing to each of the girls in the picture. "Ruth, I figure, is about your age. She's in her freshman year at the university." He put the picture down and began to rummage through the stack of others on the table as he talked. "Marshall, our other son, is an attorney in Birmingham. He and Rose have one daughter, Samantha. Where is that picture? Here it is." He handed me the picture and added, "This one's a little old. Sam's nearly ten." The man in the picture could have been Joshua thirty years younger.

May stuck her head in from the kitchen to announce that my breakfast was ready. Joshua said, "We'll be there in just a minute. I'm showin' him pictures of the kids."

"Let the boy eat, Joshua. He can look at those pictures some other time," she scolded.

"Just one more," he pleaded. I looked down at the photo he stuck into my hand. "That's Ben," he identified, "and his family in Panama City. It was little Lisa's first trip to the beach."

"That's enough now," May scolded again. "Eddie's food's gettin' cold. Eddie, you'll have to just walk away if you want to eat. He'll keep you lookin' at those pictures all day if you let him."

After breakfast we returned to the lobby. May went back to her knitting as we continued to talk about their kids and grandkids. Joshua went on and on about the new baby. He was hoping for a boy. He said with five granddaughters, a grandson was long overdue. Someone to carry on the Wilson name.

Eventually, the conversation turned to me. Both of them wanted to know what I was doing on my own so far from home. I told them the story. I had told it so many times that the words flowed without much thought. I could see the sadness in their eyes when I talked about growing up with no mother, and May cried when I talked about the day they buried my father. They listened compassionately as I talked about my life and my dreams. Each offered words of encouragement when they felt like I needed them.

Joshua asked, "You headin' out tomorrow if this rain lets up?"

"Probably," I answered. "I have miles to go before I sleep."

"What?" he asked.

"Nothing. Just something I read once," I replied. I thought about what I had said for a moment. I did have miles to go. Although I was so close to Florida, I was getting so tired of traveling. Tired of sleeping in a different place every night. Maybe staying for a little while could replace some of the stability that I had lost from my life. I added, "I may stay a while longer if Billy Watson will leave me alone."

Joshua grimaced when I mentioned Watson's name. He said, "Has Billy Watson been harassin' you?" I told him about my run-ins with Watson. He shook his head knowingly.

"That boy's nothin' but a menace. He ain't got no business bein' a deputy." He continued, "Did I hear you mention somethin' about T Johnson? How did you meet him?" I told him about the errand I had run for Janie. He shook his head and said, "It sure was a sad thing that happened to his brother." I nodded my head. "How did you hear about that?"

"T told me about it after Billy brought it up when he was arguing with me."

Joshua's face flushed with anger. "Billy Watson is a sorry, sick son-of-a-bitch! Excuse my language, but he's just mean for the hell of it. He does things just to see how bad he can hurt somebody."

"Has he always been like that?"

"Pretty much," he answered. "I caught him out back in my hen house one time stuffin' lit firecrackers underneath my settin' hens. He's just plain mean. He gets some kind of joy out of inflictin' pain." Joshua paused for minute, then continued. "He came by it honest, I guess. His father was a mean one, too. He spent his life in and out of prison. Billy probably would have ended up in prison if his mother wasn't Carl Besmer's sister. When Carl became sheriff, Louise, she's Billy's mother, thought it'd be a good idea for Billy to work with him. You know, to give the boy a role model. She thought spendin' time with Carl would make somethin' of the boy. Carl's done the best he could, but givin' the boy a little authority just made him that much more of a menace. Now he struts around like he's somebody, wavin' that badge in everybody's face. One of these days, he's gonna cross the wrong person and, badge or no badge, he's gonna get knocked off his high horse." I agreed.

When the grandfather clock in the corner of the lobby chimed at eleven-thirty, May put her knitting into her sewing bag and said, "I guess it's time for me to make dinner." She turned to me and asked, "Would you like to join us?"

I patted my stomach and replied, "I'm still stuffed from breakfast. I couldn't eat a bite right now."

"Suit yourself," she laughed, then went off to the kitchen to cook.

Joshua threw his feet up on the coffee table in front of him and went back to the paper he had been reading. I walked over to the front window to look out at the storm. Though the sun had begun to peek out from behind the clouds, the sky was still dark, and the rain fell in sheets. I shook my head at the dreary day, but I had to smile to myself and thank God for the roof over my head. Since leaving home, I had spent more than my share of days in the rain. Some days I was lucky enough to find a bridge or an abandoned building where I could wait out a storm, but there had been too many days when I had no choice but to keep walking. Sometimes through rain so hard I could not see two feet in front of me.

As I stood and watched the rain dance in the puddles in the street, Joshua walked up behind me, put his hand on my shoulder, and said, "Today's not a very good day for walkin', is it?"

I laughed and said, "I was just thinking the same thing."

"Come sit back down, son. You don't have anywhere you have to walk today. That road'll still be there when you get ready to leave. Let the rain have it for a few days."

Let the rain have it. I thought. Let the rain have it. I just nodded at what Joshua had said, then followed him away from the window.

By the time May called Joshua to dinner, the rain had stopped. After declining another invitation to eat, I decided to have a look around the town. The two of them went into their apartment to eat, and I headed out the front door to see what there was to see.

Sweat beaded on my forehead as soon as I walked out the front door. I had hoped the rain would cool things off, but the extra moisture just made the air thick and sticky. The clouds, still heavy with the promise of more rain, provided a pardon of sorts from the otherwise relentless summer sun. I shrugged off the heat and walked down the steps onto the rain-soaked sidewalk. My first order of business was to find the post office to send my weekly card to Aunt Liz to let her know how I was. From where I was standing on the northwest corner of the town square, I did not see a post office. From all the towns that I had wandered through, I guessed I would find it somewhere around the square, or at least not far off from the center of town. Wixton was like hundreds of other small towns I had seen. All the main roads converged at the square like the spokes of a wheel, with life revolving around the courthouse at the hub. The area was the heart of city commerce, with all the businesses and offices surrounding the big brick building in the middle. The building itself would be home to the local powers-that-be, and, judging from the two patrol cars parked at the curb, the courthouse was also the headquarters of the local law enforcement. I guessed the post office couldn't be too far away from the seat of government, but, after circling the block, I was no closer to finding it.

On my second trip around, a building up one of the side streets caught my eye. I was sure the polished granite building was the post office, but it turned out to be the town library. I decided to ask directions, so I stepped around the huge fan that sat in the open door—a feeble attempt to relieve the heat of the Georgia afternoon. The interior of the building smelled of old books and cinnamon. In one corner, a girl, who looked to be thirteen or fourteen, sat in a rocking chair reading a book to a group of children who sat cross-legged at her feet. I saw no one else around.

The sound of my footsteps broke the quiet and brought the girl's eyes up from the book. "Mornin'," she said, smiling.

I was about to speak, but a voice from the head of the room interrupted. "Amber Lynn, you done readin' that book yet?"

"No, ma'am."

"Then I 'spect you best get to it," the heavy-set lady behind the counter said firmly.

"Yes, ma'am," the girl complied. She threw one last smile my way and went back to reading.

"May I help you, sir?" the lady then said to me.

I told the lady what I wanted while she looked at me over the top of the horn-rims she was wearing. She nodded as I spoke, then pointed over my shoulder to the street.

"Post office's in the courthouse down the street."

I laughed to myself. I should have known. That courthouse really was the center of everything in Wixton. I was almost surprised that the library wasn't there, too. I thanked the lady for her help, then headed back toward the center of town. More people were beginning to mill around after the rainstorm. Most everyone in town was hospitable to me. Most of those that I met along the street nodded and smiled or spoke as we passed one another. I even got a few friendly waves from passing cars when I crossed the street to the courthouse square.

I climbed the steps into the open front door. The sheriff's office was the first door that I came to. Its door also stood propped open by one of the large fans like the library. I glanced inside as I passed. An older lady sat leaning against the receptionist counter, fanning herself with a hand-held fan and puffing on a cigarette. Over her shoulder was the door to Sheriff Besmer's private office. To the right of the door, Besmer's big white hat hung on the top of the coat rack. Much to my relief, there was no sign of Watson.

I continued deeper into the building, looking for some sign of the post office. Finally, I had to stop and ask for help from an old man sitting on a bench outside the probate judge's office. He pointed to a door half hidden under the stairs to the second floor. This door, too, was propped open by another of the big fans. Again, I stepped around the fan and headed down the stairs. The stairs led to a poorly lit hallway lined with doors. Most of the doors were labeled "STORAGE" on frosted glass windows and appeared to be locked, but the last stood open. A handwritten sign taped to the wall beside it identified this room as the post office. A smaller version of the town fan sat in the door.

What I found beyond the door was exactly what I expected from a converted storage closet. It was, literally, not much bigger than a closet. The already tiny room was cut in half by a makeshift counter that was nothing more than a plank across some crates. Behind the counter, a young woman stood sorting mail into a series of baskets that sat against the back wall. She looked up at me when I walked in. She was about my age and very pretty. Her sandy brown hair was pulled back, tied behind her head in a ponytail. A few loose strands hung down across her face. She smiled brightly and pushed the hair away from her eyes. She dropped the stack of letters she was holding and came over to the counter where I was now standing. She pushed the hair away from her eyes again and said, "Well, you must be Eddie Chance."

I smiled, flattered by the recognition. "My reputation precedes me?" I asked.

She brushed the hair away from her eyes again and laughed. "Yeah," she replied, "I've heard a lot about you."

"Really?" I said. "All good, I hope."

"Well," she said coyly, "actually..."

"Let me guess. Billy Watson?"

She nodded. "You sure have Billy riled up."

"I do my best."

"Keep up the good work."

"I take it our Deputy Watson is not one of your favorite people."

"Hardly," she answered, again pushing the hair from her eyes.

"I'm glad to know I'm not the only one."

"You're definitely not the only one."

"Well, why are we wasting so much time talking about Billy Watson?" I said, eager to change the subject. "Since you know my name, I think it's only fair that I know yours."

She smiled, "I guess that's fair." She stuck out her hand and said, "Jenny. Jenny Besmer."

I shook her hand. "Besmer?"

"Yeah, I'm the sheriff's daughter," she answered, again brushing the rebellious hair away from her brown eyes.

I cocked an eyebrow, "Well, I must be the man your father warned you about."

She laughed. "Actually Daddy said you seemed like a pretty nice guy. It was Billy that warned me about you."

"I can only imagine what Billy told you about me, but I didn't realize that I had made such of an impression on the sheriff."

"Well, you did," she replied. "Daddy's not real big on praise, but he said he admired your courage."

"Really?" I replied. I was flattered and surprised, because our conversation had played more like accusation rather than admiration..

I leaned against the counter while she recounted what her father had said about me. Listening to her, I found myself watching how the expressions showed in her eyes as she talked, and laughed to myself every time she brushed the hair away. Sometime during our conversation, she caught on to my stare and winked. I felt myself blush. Embarrassed that I had been caught, I diverted my eyes. I just hoped that I had not made her uncomfortable. I was relieved when she broke into a huge grin, but I really didn't know what to say. She knew that she had embarrassed me, so she didn't say anything either. She just went on with her story.

We continued to talk for quite a while, and I tried unsuccessfully to not stare at her eyes. We talked about my trip, of course, and about her being the sheriff's daughter, and we talked more about how much of a jackass Billy Watson was.

I finally got around to asking for the postcard that I had come in for in the first place. I was just finishing it up and about to hand it to Jenny when someone yelled down the stairs.

"Jenny, you all right down there?" The voice was unmistakably Billy Watson's.

Jenny didn't answer him. She just rolled her eyes and asked me, "Did anybody see you come down here?"

I nodded, "Some old guy on a bench up there showed me where the post office was."

"That'd be Zeb Martin. He's the town snitch. That's why he hangs around the courthouse all the time. He probably ran and told Billy that you were here."

She had just finished her sentence when Billy stuck his head in the door. "Jenny, you all right?" he repeated. He glared at me while he waited for her to answer.

"Yeah," she answered, decidedly irritated. "What you want?"

He didn't answer her. Instead, he turned to me, his hand resting on the butt of his pistol. "What the hell you doin' down here?" he demanded.

I cocked an eyebrow and said, "Well, let's see. This is the post office. This is a postcard. You're a smart fellow. You figure it out."

He growled, "I told you about that smart mouth of yours!"

Before he could say anything else, Jenny piped up, "Billy, did you want somethin'? Eddie and I were havin' a private conversation before you butted in."

"Zeb said he saw him come down here a while ago," he said, pointing at me, "but hadn't seen him come back up. I thought I might need to check on you."

"Thank you, but I'm a big girl. You and Zeb need to mind your own damn business."

"But..."

"But nothin'," Jenny interrupted him. "Why don't you go back upstairs and let us be."

I took that opportunity to reach in my pocket for the money to pay for the postcard. "I really needed to get going anyway."

"You sure?" she asked. "Don't leave on his account."

"I'm not," I lied. I really wanted to get away from him before my temper got the best of me. I handed her the change, then added, "See you around?"

"I hope so," she replied.

I sneered at Billy as I walked by him. I walked through the door behind Billy, leaving him and Jenny inside. From the hallway, I could hear their conversation, or, rather, her lecture. Jenny was really letting Billy have it. He could not get a word in edgewise, and even when he did manage to complete a sentence, she would tear it apart. I had worried for a moment that I shouldn't leave her alone with that lunatic, but she seemed like someone who could take care of herself, and I was pretty sure that, as foolish as Billy seemed to be, he wasn't stupid enough to do anything to the sheriff's daughter. Although I could not help but laugh at the tongue lashing he was taking, I was angered by the small-minded attitude that had led to it. His ignorance was what drove him. Everything I had seen him do since I came to town was the product of his false sense of superiority. He disgusted me, but there wasn't anything I could do about him. No way I could undo a lifetime of stupidity in a couple a days. I just shook my head and climbed the stairs.

The old man was still sitting in the same spot when I came out of the basement. I nodded as I passed and said, "Afternoon, Zeb." He was noticeably stunned that I had called him by name. I continued, "If Billy asks, I'll be in my room." His face flushed with embarrassment. I just grinned and walked away.

I stopped at the water fountain to get a drink before I walked out into the hot sun again. I was drinking when Sheriff Besmer came out of his office and walked toward me.

"Mr. Chance," he said, sticking his hand out.

"Sheriff," I replied, shaking his hand. "Eddie, please."

"Eddie. Yes, of course. Of course. Carl," he offered his own first name. "I hoped I'd run into you today. You headed anywhere in particular?"

"No," I answered warily. "Why?"

"I was just about to make my afternoon rounds, and I thought you might like to tag along."

"Are trying to run me out of town, Sheriff?"

"Carl, please. No. No. Nothin' like that. I just have somethin' I want to talk to you about."

"What about?"

He looked over my shoulder at Zeb, who was obviously trying hard not to be obvious that he was listening to our conversation. "It'd be better if we talked in the car."

I nodded that I understood, then agreed to go with him. Before we walked away, I turned back to Zeb and said, "You get all that, Zeb? Change of plans. I'll be with the sheriff." His face turned beet red.

Besmer snickered and said, "I just need to stop by my office, then we'll head out." I nodded and followed him down the hall. Walking a couple of steps behind him, I saw confidence in the way he walked, and I realized just how big a man Carl Besmer was. His height had impressed me that first night in my room, but I was too aggravated to really pay much attention to much else. Although he wasn't as big as Jawbone, he had quite an intimidating presence. I could see where his size would be an advantage in his line of work.

I followed him down to the office. He stepped back into the inner office, leaving me outside with his receptionist, an older lady, sixtyish, who introduced herself as Lenora. Her face was drawn and yellowed, and she had a hoarseness in her voice that testified to a lifetime of cigarette smoking. She was at least polite, but showed no interest in carrying on a conversation with me. I shrugged it off and stood silently for the brief time that I had to wait. I took the opportunity to look around the room. Like the post office downstairs, the outer office's most prominent feature was the reception counter. This one, however, was built to stand up to the abuse I was sure it had endured over the years. Behind the counter, centered on the back wall, was the entrance to Sheriff Besmer's private office. He had pushed the door shut when he walked in, so I could not see what was inside. The area between contained an assortment of cabinets and shelves, as well as a pair of mismatched desks. One desk sat directly in front on the inner office door. From the lipstick-stained cigarette butts overflowing from the ashtray, I took this desk to belong to Lenora. For now, though, she had chosen a spot on a stool at the counter where she was thumbing through a catalogue of some sort and ignoring me. The second desk stood against the wall in the corner. Watson's name was engraved on a plaque that hung above it. On the wall to the left of the sheriffs door hung an aerial photo of the town. To the right was a huge map of the county. Elsewhere in the room, the walls were covered with various plaques and photographs. One in particular caught my eye. The fading, black-and-white image and the battered wooden frame that held it were, in themselves, unremarkable, but the two men in the photo drew my attention. Although he was decidedly younger than the man I had met, one of the men was Carl Besmer. Standing almost at attention in his crisp, clean uniform, he towered over the older man beside him.

That man was obviously the ranking man in the photo. He was almost dwarfed by Besmer's imposing stature, but he had an air of authority about him that I could see even in the aging picture. From the uniform he was wearing, I took him to be Clarence Wood. I could tell that a year had been written in the corner, and I strained to make out the faded numbers.

"Nineteen forty-six." Besmer's voice suddenly behind me gave me a start. He laughed at my reaction. "Sorry about that. I didn't mean to scare you."

"It's okay," I replied, embarrassed. "What did you say?"

"The picture. Nineteen forty-six. That's the year I became a deputy. I was just home from the war. Sheriff Wood, that's him in the picture there, thought I'd be good for the county. War hero and all. War hero, my ass. I was just a scared kid, glad to be home, who didn't have sense enough to tell the man no. But that's all water under the bridge, I guess, and that bridge was burned too damn long ago to do anything about it now." He seemed more than just disenchanted with the job, although he never came right out and said it. I just nodded to acknowledge that I was listening. "Well, " he continued, "enough reminiscin'. You ready to go?" I nodded. "Lenora, I'll be on rounds."

He lead me back out into the corridor. Billy was down the hall talking to Zeb, who was more than likely relaying my message and recounting what he could of my conversation with the sheriff. Besmer called out to him. Billy eyed me with contempt as he walked over to where we were. I just smiled. Besmer filled him in on his plans but offered no explanation of my presence. He knew as well as I did that Zeb had already taken care of that. We turned and headed toward the door.

"Chance," Billy called.

"What?"

"Later."

"Billy," Besmer broke in, "don't you have somethin' you can be doin'?"

"Yes, sir."

"Well, get to it."

"Yes, sir." He turned and skulked away, momentarily defeated.

"Let's get goin'," Besmer said, motioning me out the door.

The afternoon sky had grown dark again, and it had begun to rain. We dashed to the patrol car parked at the curb. I quickly slid into the passenger seat out of the rain as Besmer squeezed his huge frame behind the wheel. He started the engine and pulled out into the street. He drove around the courthouse once and took one of the side streets away from the center of town. We drove around many of the streets T and I had been on the night before. He made a circuit through the neighborhood and the blocks of warehouses, then went south toward what I found out was the cotton gin.

For the first few minutes, we rode in silence. Neither of us breached the subject of why he had asked me along. Besmer finally spoke. It was just small talk at first. Comments about the weather, the town, the inn, but nothing of any real consequence. We were on our second pass through town before he got around to what he really wanted to say.

"I hear you had a run in with Billy last night at Shaker's pool hall," he started.

"Watson tell you about it?"

"No, Billy knows better," Besmer replied. "Sam Ross told me."

"Sam Ross?" I asked, not recognizing the name.

"Jawbone," he clarified. "He called me last night at home. Said Billy was in your face runnin' his mouth pretty good. He also said that he came in just in time to keep you from crackin' a cue stick across Billy's head. I just wanted to hear your side of the story, before I say anything to Billy about it."

I recounted the events of last night at the pool hall. I told him about Watson's two buddies. I ran through his initial exchange with Peabody. Besmer listened with a frown on his face. He was noticeably angry by the time I had described our confrontation. I told him everything that went on between us. I did my best to relay everything Watson said and did and my reaction to it. I made sure to mention his comment about T's brother and the threat that accompanied it. I then confirmed everything that Jawbone had already told him.

Besmer shook his head. "Billy has a tendency to go overboard sometimes, so I want you to do somethin' for me." He paused a moment to gauge my reaction.

"I'm listening."

"As long as you're in town, I want you to stay away from him."

"I'd be glad to, but I'm not the one who's following him around town. Everywhere I go, he shows up."

"I know. I know. But try, ok, and I'll do what I can to keep him off your back. Agreed?"

"Agreed, " I replied, but I knew that, short of locking him up, there was nothing the sheriff could do to make Watson back off. Billy Watson didn't strike me as the kind to do what he was told, so I knew that I would need to watch out for him and his buddies.

Sheriff Besmer made one final pass along his circuit around town before heading back toward the square. The rain was still falling steadily, so I asked him to drop me off at the inn.

"You got plans for tonight?" he asked as he pulled up to the curb to let me out.

"No," I replied.

"How would you like to have supper tonight at my house?" he continued.

"That would be nice," I accepted.

"Great," he replied. "How 'bout I pick you up here, say, around six-thirty?"

"Sounds good."

I jumped out of the car and dashed up the steps for the cover of the front porch. Besmer threw up a wave as he drove away. He circled the square, then parked his patrol car next to Watson's at the courthouse curb.

I wiped my feet and went inside.

Joshua was behind the counter checking in a young couple. Newlyweds, it turned out. He was a soldier, a corporal from Fort Benning, with nothing but a three-day-pass for the honeymoon. She was young, barely out of school. Standing behind her new husband, she looked scared to death.

I walked by them to the stairs. She looked up at me as I passed. I smiled. She nervously returned the smile but quickly diverted her eyes, seemingly embarrassed that I had caught her looking. She was pretty. Long, chestnut hair, held back at the temples by a pair of pearl and lace barrettes, flowed down over the shoulders of her white, cotton dress. Her wedding gown, I guessed. There was an innocence that showed in her soft, brown eyes, but it was disguised by the surplus of makeup she had, no doubt, applied to look beautiful for her new husband. His look was all military. Tall and lean, he was decked out in his dress greens. With his cap tucked under his arm to reveal his shaved head, he was confident, almost cocky. He had the look of every good soldier. Primed and ready for action, combat or otherwise. I wondered how much of his confidence came with the uniform. Was he the worldly soldier about to dissolve the innocence of his young bride, or was he, too, a nervous kid about to take his second giant leap toward adulthood? I smiled once more at the bride, whom I caught looking again, then I made my way up the stairs and down the hall to my room.

The room was stuffy from being shut up all day. I pulled back the curtains and opened the windows to let in some air. My shirt was wet and sticky, so I pulled it off and hung it on the bedpost near the window. I stepped into the bathroom to wash my face. I heard the new arrivals passing my room and climbing the stairs to the third floor. Shortly after the sound of them on the stairs died down, someone knocked on the door.

"Eddie," Joshua called out, knocking again.

"Come in," I said, standing up to greet him at the door.

"You sure have been a popular fella this afternoon," he said.

"Really?" I asked.

"Well, the sheriff came by looking for you."

"I met up with him at the courthouse," I replied. "He invited me to dinner tonight."

"Then Billy Watson," Joshua continued, "asked if you were still in town."

"What did he want?" I asked.

"Didn't say."

I shook my head. "Nothing, apparently. I saw him at the courthouse, too, and he had nothing important to say. Just the same high-and-mighty routine."

Joshua shook his head, then said, "And T. Johnson called a half a dozen times. Sounded anxious to talk to you."

"Did he say what he wanted?"

"No."

"I guess I need to call him," I replied. "Can I use the phone?"

He nodded his head and motioned me out the door. I grabbed my shirt from the bedpost and followed him into the hall. I pulled my door shut behind us and glanced up the stairs. "Newlyweds?" I asked, pointing up to the third floor.

"Yeah," he replied, "soldier over from Benning."

"Looked scared to death, didn't she?" I snickered.

He laughed, "Yeah, she did, but you didn't get a good look at him. He was so nervous he could barely sign the book." He laughed again. "Oh, what I wouldn't give to be that young again." We both laughed. He looked sideways at me and added, "What you laughin' at? You are that young." I smiled and arched my eyebrows. He shook his head and slapped me on the back. We went down the stairs to the lobby. The smells of food cooking drifted in through the open apartment door. May was getting a head start on supper.

Joshua pointed to the back of the lobby and said, "There's a phone on the desk around the corner. You can call from there."

I thanked him and walked back toward the phone. He went around the end of the desk and disappeared into his apartment. I sat down at the desk and picked up the phone to call T. It was then that I realized that I did not know his phone number. I went to the desk and called for Joshua.

"What's wrong?" he asked, coming out the door.

"Did T leave his phone number?" I asked, feeling foolish. "I just realized I don't know it."

He said, laughing, "You city folk, I swear. I'll get him for you." He walked over and picked up the receiver. "Ramona, Joshua Wilson. Fine. Fine. You? Good to hear. Really, broke her hip? I'll be. Oh, she's fine. Mean as ever. Yeah, yeah, stayin' here. Nice boy. Well, I don't know that, Ramona. Listen, can you get Sadie Johnson's place for me? I know she's at work. I want her boy." He put his hand over the mouthpiece and said, "That Ramona loves to gossip." He laughed and handed the phone to me. "It's ringin'."

"Thanks."

"Anytime," he said, heading back around the end of the desk.

The phone rang a few times before T picked up. "Hello," he answered.

"T? Eddie," I identified myself. "Joshua said you called."

"Yeah, man. Where you been? I was beginnin' to think you had already skipped town on me."

"Not in this weather," I assured him. "I took a ride around town with Carl Besmer."

"Well, I was just callin' to see if you wanted to get together tonight," he said. "Clancy and Pea are going out to Baxter's Pond. Gonna build a fire. Do a little fishin'. You wanna come?"

"I'd love to, but I'm eatin' with the sheriff tonight."

"If you'd rather hang out with the sheriff than me, that's fine," he said with mock aggravation.

"Hey now, I can't help it if I'm so popular," I defended myself. "Besides, the sheriff is not the one I'm looking forward to seeing."

"You must have heard about the sheriff's daughter."

"I met her at the post office this afternoon. You know her?" I asked.

"You kiddin'? Every man in Wixton knows Jenny Besmer."

"You mean…"

"Oh, no," he quickly corrected. "I just meant that someone who looks that good gets noticed. She's somethin' else." I caught a hint of something a little more than admiration in his voice, but I didn't ask.

"You're not kidding about that," I replied.

"Anyway," he continued, "when you goin'?"

"Six-thirty," I replied.

"How 'bout after?" he asked. "Pea said they planned on pullin' a late one."

"Sounds good. Dinner and small talk shouldn't take more than a couple, three hours. Do you know where the sheriff lives?"

"Yeah," he answered.

"Good. Can you pick me up there around nine thirty?" I asked.

"Yeah, I can do that," he replied. "You figure to be done by then?"

"Should be."

"Okay," he agreed. "I need to go now, though. Grandma's ringin' her bell for me. I'll see you later." He hung up.

I placed the receiver on the cradle and checked my watch. Three twenty-five. I moved from the desk to the sofa. I sat back and closed my eyes. I had almost forgotten what it was like to have this much time to kill. I resigned myself to enjoy it, to just relax a while before heading upstairs to take a shower. I kicked back on the sofa and thumbed through the newspaper that Joshua had been reading. Eventually, the laziness of the afternoon must have overtaken me, because I dozed off.

Chapter Six

Joshua was shaking me awake on the couch. He laughed when I protested his prodding and swatted at him. Finally, when I was awake enough to realize what was happening, I laughed, too. I sat up and wiped my eyes, still groggy from my nap. I knew that I couldn't have been asleep more than a minute or two. Joshua laughed again at my reaction when he told me that I had been out more than two hours. It was nearly six o'clock. Joshua understood when I quickly excused myself and headed up the stairs to my room.

For the short time that I had been outside, the heat of the Georgia afternoon had left me sweaty and uncomfortable. I peeled off my now-sticky clothes and jumped in the tub. I was pressed for time, so I showered quickly, pausing only momentarily to soak in the cool spray of the water. I toweled off and set to the task of finding something decent to wear. Although my clothes weren't rags, they were showing the stains and scars of weeks on the road. Finally, I chose a pair of tan chinos that I bought a couple of weeks out of New York. Now threadbare, they were still my most presentable and, in fact, the only pair of non-jeans that I owned. I tucked in my black button-down and sat down on the bed to pull the weathered combat boots on over the green surplus socks that I had bought at the same Army-Navy store. I ran my comb through my shaggy hair. I stood in front of the dresser mirror and shook my head at how haggard I looked. Oh well, I did the best I could.

Downstairs, the sheriff had already arrived. May had brought out a pitcher of iced tea, and she and Joshua sat with the sheriff in the lobby. Carl and Joshua were involved in a very animated discussion, while May sat back on the sofa sipping her tea and looking quite amused at their antics. Carl stood up when he saw me on the stairs. He stuck out his hand as I approached him. Joshua snickered at my apology for being late. I shot him a sideways grin as I accepted Carl's handshake. The sheriff shook Joshua's hand and thanked May for the tea, then we excused ourselves. Joshua walked us to the door. He made a final remark concerning their previous conversation, at which Carl laughed, then closed the door behind us. We walked down the steps to the patrol car that sat waiting at the curb.

We shared only small talk on the drive out. More talk about the rain and the heat. The sheriff lived outside of town, just off the highway that lead out to T's place, on a small farm.

The biggest part of the farm, he told me, was pasture that he leased out to the dairy farm that bordered on his land. Not much farming going on anymore. There was the family garden and a few hogs that belonged to his oldest son, who lived on the backside of the property with his new wife.

Carl drove down the long, dirt drive, past the handful of cows grazing in the corner of the fenced pasture that separated the house and yard from the highway. The Besmer house itself was a modest two-story frame house, cream yellow with white trim, which sat almost hidden beneath the shade of several enormous oak trees scattered around the yard. We parked under one of the huge trees next to the family Nomad.

Carl lead me around to the back of the house. The kitchen door was open behind a locked screen door. Carl knocked. A woman, who I assumed was Mrs. Besmer, came over to unhook the screen. She looked over his shoulder at me and said, "Carl Besmer, you know better than to bring a guest in through the kitchen when I'm cookin'. Poor boy's gonna be scared to eat." She turned to me and said, "Please excuse the mess." She wiped her hand on her apron and stuck it out for me to shake as we came through the door. "Nice to meet you, Mr. Chance. "

"Nice to meet you, too," I replied, shaking her hand. "Please call me Eddie."

She smiled and said, "Okay, Eddie it is then. I'm Joanne." She was a tiny woman, not much over five feet. So small next to Carl. Looking at her, it was obvious where Jenny got her good looks. Though Jenny was much taller, thanks to her father, she was almost the spitting image of her mother. Joanne was just an older version of her daughter. She had the same face, the same eyes, and the same expressions. She even had the same sandy brown hair, which she had pulled up onto the top her head. She was a beautiful woman, like her daughter.

"When do we eat?" Carl spoke up. "I'm hungry." He picked at a plate of fried chicken that sat on the counter.

"Stop that." She popped him on the back of the hand. "It's not quite ready. Why don't you and Mr. Chance...Eddie go in there and have a seat. I'll call y'all when it's ready."

"Okay! Okay! Come on, Eddie. I guess we're not welcome in the kitchen." He reached for the chicken plate again.

Again, she popped his hand. "And that's why," she laughed. "You're gonna have to wait just like the rest of us."

Just off the kitchen was the dining room, so, while Joanne playfully scolded Carl, I looked inside. She had gone to a lot of trouble preparing for the meal. I was flattered by her effort. After Carl reluctantly accepted his reprimand, he nodded me toward the door. I followed him out of the kitchen into a short hallway. The walls of the hall served as a gallery of the Besmer family through the years. Most of the photos were of the kids. There were three all together. Two boys with Jenny in the middle. I guessed I would meet the other two tonight. I hoped Jenny would be there. Carl led me down the hallway to the foyer.

To the right of our entrance the stairs led to the second floor. The door to the outside was directly in front of us. It stood partly open. Carl shook his head and pushed the door closed, mumbling something about killing a kid. He looked back at me and laughed. "Our youngest," he explained, "won't shut a door to save his life." To the left of the outer door an archway opened into the family's living room. As in the hallway, the walls of the foyer, and what I could see of the living room, were covered with pictures. Sun from a huge bay window lit the whole area. I took a step toward the door, but Carl pointed me toward a closed door at the foot of the stairs.

This door opened into a room lined with bookshelves. This room, too, had the huge bay window, but it was covered by a thick brown curtain. Light here was provided by a few strategically placed lamps. Two walls were lined with shelves of books, and the fourth was split by a large stone fireplace. With no need for a fire, a large arrangement of dried flowers sat in the center of the hearth. Carl directed me to one of the two leather wing chairs that flanked the fireplace. He walked toward the small bar that sat in the corner. I paused for a moment to look at a rifle that hung above the mantle, then took my seat.

"You want something to drink?" he asked, as he poured himself a scotch and water. I declined. "Anything at all? Lemonade? Coke?" I declined again. "Suit yourself," he conceded.

While he poured his drink, I paused to look at the rifle that hung above the mantle. "Springfield '61," he identified it.

"What?" I asked, having been caught off guard.

"The rifle," he explained. "It's a Springfield '61. Civil War issue. It belonged to my great-grandfather."

"He was a Confederate soldier?" I asked.

"Actually," Carl laughed, "as much as I hate to admit it, Grandpa Sam was a Yankee." "Really?" I laughed.

"Yeah. Samuel Leonard. Born and raised in Ohio. The son of a state senator." "How did you end up in Georgia?"

He continued, "Sam came south to Tennessee after the war lookin' to make his fortune. He didn't. He did meet and marry, much to her father's dismay, Miss Catherine Wilson, then proceeded to father eight children." He stopped for a moment to refill his drink. He, again, offered me one, which I, again, declined. He shrugged and continued with his family history. "Their first born, Mary, met a young businessman from Birmingham by the name of William Besmer. He married young Mary and carried her back to Alabama." He paused, emptying out his glass. He considered having another, then sat the empty glass aside. He continued, "Where was I?"

"Alabama," I answered.

"Oh yeah. Alabama," he recalled. "William brought young Mary back to Alabama to start a family. On her twenty-second birthday, she gave birth to a son, the third of four. George Leonard Besmer, my father." Carl stopped. "I must be borin' you to death," he laughed. "You probably weren't expectin' the family history when you asked."

I laughed. Although he was taking the long way around to answer my question, his story fascinated me. "No, go ahead," I assured him.

"If you insist," he replied. "This is the good part, anyway. George was somewhat of a scoundrel in his younger days. Went places he shouldn't have with people he shouldn't have. You know the kind. Well, the summer he turned seventeen, he was drinkin' in some bar and made the wrong man mad. The guy stuck a Bowie knife through Daddy's kneecap. Buried it up to the hilt. Daddy said he just pulled it out, poured a glass of whiskey over the wound, and tied a bandana around it. Of course, it got infected, and after two or three days of limpin' around on it, he collapsed from fever. Medicine bein' what it was in those days, the doctor decided the only way to save him was to amputate. The doctor's office was built onto the side of his house, so he did the operation there, then put Daddy up in a spare bedroom to keep an eye on him for the first few days to make sure everything was healin' like it ought to.

"Now, Doc Mason's daughter, Wynnona, who was sixteen, was quite taken with the handsome young patient who slept in the room down the hall. She found every excuse to stop by his room. He soon grew very fond of her, too. One evenin' after Doc Mason and his wife had been out visitin' friends, the good doctor stopped in to check on George, before settlin' in for the night. He found a very naked Wynnona sittin' straddle an equally naked George, and, let's just say, she wasn't takin' his temperature.

"Needless to say, her father was outraged to find his sweet, innocent little girl engaged in such an unladylike activity. He hit the roof. First he yelled at her, then he threatened to kill him, and, all the while, they just kept doin' what they were doin'. That made Mason even madder. He dragged Wynnona, kickin' and screamin', off the bed and down the hall past the rest of the family who had by now gathered in the hall. She was locked in her room, and Granddaddy Besmer was called to remove George from the house.

"Although Wynnona professed her love for George, her father forbade her from ever seein' him again. Of course, small towns bein' what they are, word got around about the incident, and by the time Wynnona was visibly pregnant, the Masons could no longer deny it. Embarrassed by his very pregnant and unmarried daughter, Mason gave in to his daughter, and she and George were married. About six months later, my eldest brother Leonard was born."

The phone rang in the other room. Carl hesitated momentarily, then was about to continue when someone knocked on the door. Joanne stuck her head in the door and said, "Carl, sorry to interrupt, but that was Norma Jean on the phone. They've had some kinda breakdown at the gin, so J.R.'s gonna have to work late tonight. He won't be able to come to supper."

He muttered something under his breath, then asked out loud, "Is she still comin'?" "Yeah, but she needs a ride. I just sent Jenny down to Purvis' store, so one of us will have to go get her, unless you want me to send Jason."

"No, I'll go. I'll go," he agreed. Carl got up to leave. I also stood.

"I'll finish when I get back." With that, he disappeared out the door. I heard the front door open and close soon after.

I stood there for a moment, not knowing what I should do. I looked to Joanne for direction. Taking my cue, she pushed the door open wide. She looked around the room, shaking her head. "He keeps it dark as a tomb in here," she said. She looked back to me and asked, "You like sittin' in the dark?" I shrugged. "Well, then, come on over here where there's more light." I walked out by her and led the way to the living room across the foyer. She followed me into the room. "I want to get you out here where I can get a good look at you. I want to see if you're as good-lookin' as Jenny says you are." I felt myself blush.

"Mama!" Jenny's horrified voice called out. She stepped into the doorway where I could see her. Her face was as red as mine felt. In her arm was the bag from Purvis' store, I assumed. I moved to take the bag from her, but Joanne beat me to it. She waved me toward the sofa. "Sit down, Eddie," she said. "You're a guest." She took the bag from Jenny, and the two of them stepped back into hall out of view. I couldn't see them, but I could tell they were having a very animated conversation. Jenny, more than likely, scolding her mother for embarrassing her. I sat down on the sofa and waited for one of them to reenter, hoping it would be Jenny.

After a moment, it was Jenny, her face still flushed with embarrassment, who came around the corner to join me. She sat down at the other end of the sofa. "I'm sorry about that," she apologized.

"Don't be," I replied. "I'm flattered. Anyway, I thought the same about you."

She smiled and said, "Good lookin' and smart, too."

"You or me?" I asked.

"Both," she answered. We laughed. "I didn't expect to see you again so soon," she continued. "I'm glad, though. I was enjoyin' our conversation this afternoon, before Billy stuck his nose in it. I'm sorry about that, too."

"It's not your fault," I assured her. "You sure were giving it to him when I left. I was almost afraid to leave you alone with him. He seems to have quite a temper."

She laughed, "I appreciate your concern, but you needn't worry about that. I can handle him. Besides, bad temper or not, he knows Daddy'll beat the shit out of him if he lays a hand on me. Even he's not that big a fool."

"I guess not," I replied.

After a few moments, I heard Carl's voice from the kitchen. He came down the hall stopping in the living room doorway. "Y'all ready to eat?" he asked. We both nodded. "Good. Good. It's 'bout ready," he added, then headed up the stairs behind him. He had just topped the stairs when Joanne called us to the table.

Jenny stood, took my hand, and led me down the hall to the dining room. The table was set from end-to-end with dishes of food. There was certainly more food than I was accustomed to seeing at one meal. I eyed the generous spread hungrily.

Before showing me to my seat at one corner of the large dining room table, Joanne introduced me to Norma Jean, the wife of their oldest son J.R.; like the other women in the family, she was very pretty. J.R. obviously had his father's eye for beauty. Joanne excitedly explained that Norma Jean was pregnant with the first grandchild. I shook her hand, then took my seat. Joanne excused herself into the kitchen to bring out the last of the food to the table. Jenny followed her mother, leaving me alone in the dining room with Norma Jean. She was visibly nervous to be there with me. I wrote it off as shyness and tried to make small talk to ease the tension. She opened up when I asked about the baby. She was obviously as excited as Joanne about having a child.

Carl returned from upstairs. He had shed his uniform for something more comfortable. He stopped for a moment to kiss Norma Jean on the cheek. Following close behind him was the youngest, Jason. Although he was tall like his father, he, too, looked more like his mother. He didn't say much, even when Carl introduced us. He sat directly across from me, and Carl took his place between us at the head of the table. Soon after Carl and Jason arrived, Joanne returned with the platter of chicken I had seen earlier. Jenny came behind her with a pitcher of iced tea. She poured each of us a glass, then sat in the chair next to me. Joanne made one last trip to the kitchen, returning with a basket of biscuits. She placed them on the table, then took her seat opposite Carl at the other end of the table.

Before we began eating, Carl asked the blessing. He prayed, "Dear Lord, we come to You now to thank You for all that You have given us. Thank You so much for the food You have placed before us, and thank You for the opportunity to bring the family together. Be with J.R. while he can't be with us. And Lord, thank You for the fellowship You have allowed us with our new friend, Eddie. I ask that You be his guide and protector in his travels. In Christ Jesus' name I pray. A-men."

I was touched by his including me in his prayer. Silently, I thanked God for the friendship and kindness they had shown me.

Carl began passing the serving dishes around the table. He was the first to speak as I filled my plate with a variety of food that he passed my way. He asked, "Eddie, have you been introduced to Norma Jean and Jenny?" I nodded. He continued, "I took it for granted that you knew everyone."

"Yeah," Jenny piped up, "we met this afternoon at the courthouse."

"Really?" Carl questioned.

"Eddie came down to the post office," she explained. "We were havin' a pretty good conversation before Billy butted in."

"Billy?" Carl repeated.

"Yeah, he barged in like a jackass..."

"Jenny!" Joanne interrupted.

"Sorry, Mama," Jenny apologized. "Anyway, he came bargin' in accusin' Eddie of who knows what. I told him to mind his own damn business! Uh! Sorry, Mama." Joanne gave her a stern look.

Carl shook his head and said, "I'm gonna have to have a long talk with that boy.""He needs more than a long talk, " Jenny suggested. "He needs his ass beat."

"Jennifer Renee Besmer!" Joanne scolded. "Such language. Am I gonna have to wash your mouth out with soap, young lady?"

"Sorry, Mama," Jenny apologized again.

"Is that what you're teachin' her down at that courthouse?" Joanne asked Carl.

He shrugged. "Watch your language," he said to Jenny.

"Yes, sir," she answered. I got the impression that his reprimand was intended more to pacify her mother than to discipline Jenny. From the look on Joanne's face, she knew it, too.

Carl quickly changed the subject. He asked Norma Jean about the breakdown at the gin. She relayed what J.R. had told her. Something about an early bloom and needing to get ready for an early ginning season. Although I sat and listened like the rest, what she said was totally lost on me. I was only vaguely aware of what a cotton gin was, so the inner mechanics of the thing were quite over my head. Carl must have noticed my blank expression, because, after Norma Jean finished, he apologized for leaving me out of the conversation. He explained that J.R. was the foreman of the maintenance crew at the gin, and that the breakdown was the reason he had to miss supper. I noticed the edge of contempt in his voice as he talked about the gin. He was obviously not happy with his son's involvement with it.

Joanne interrupted. "Eddie, how long do you plan to stay in town? Carl tells me you want to go to Florida and grow fruit or somethin'."

"Yes, ma'am, " I replied. "If the rain holds off, I'll be leaving in the morning."

"Why so soon?" Jenny asked sadly.

"I don't want to let roots grow under my feet. I'm too close to the end of my road to give up now," I answered.

"What're you plannin' to do when you get there?" Carl asked.

"Get a job in an orange grove, I guess," I replied.

"Pickin' fruit?" he asked.

"If I have to," I said. "I have to start somewhere. Start at the bottom, learn the business, and work my way up." I really didn't care where I started. I just wanted to be involved in the business.

"You seem very passionate about it," Norma Jean observed.

"I am," I confirmed. "I owe it to my father."

"Your father?" she asked.

I told them my story. They all listened quietly as I spoke. Except for a question or two, no one spoke. Like all the others who had heard my story, they were overwhelmed by sadness of it all and surprised by the matter-of-fact way that I told it.

In the beginning, telling the story had been very painful, but since leaving New York, anyone who talked with me for more than five minutes inevitably asked why I left home. Regardless of how simple an answer I tried to give them, by the time I had answered all their questions, I had told the whole story. The more I told it, the easier it became. All the emotions were still there, but they no longer choked me up like they had at first.

When I finished, there was an uncomfortable silence hanging over the table. No one knew exactly what to say. I could see the tears welling in Jenny's eyes. She placed her hand on top of mine.

Joanne finally spoke. Her eyes, too, were brimming with tears. "I'm sorry about your father," she offered.

"Thank you," I replied. I felt the need to break the mood, so I reminded Carl that he still owed me the answer about his family. I said, "Well, that's enough about me. Now you know how I got to Georgia, but you never finished telling me how you got here."

He smiled. "I didn't, did I?"

Joanne interrupted, "Before you get too involved in one of your long-winded stories, is everyone finished?" We all nodded. She continued, "How 'bout y'all take the story- tellin' in yonder while Jenny and I clear the table."

"Mama!" Jenny protested.

"You heard me."

"Yes, ma'am." Jenny frowned.

Carl, Jason, and I stood to leave the table. Norma Jean opted to help the other women with the dishes. In spite of Joanne's protests, she picked up a handful of dishes and headed for the kitchen. Jenny and Joanne did the same, and I followed Carl and Jason down the hall to the other room.

"Where was I?" Carl asked when we had settled into our places in the living room.

"Leonard was born," I replied.

"Oh yeah. Well, that first grandchild really softened Mason up. He finally forgave Daddy for stealin' his daughter and accepted him into the family. By the time I came along, the bad blood between them had been all but forgotten."

Carl enjoyed talking about his family. I had noticed that while he told the story of his parents' "courtship." It was obvious that it was a story he enjoyed telling, and, now, he smiled incessantly. Only when he spoke about his brother, Howard, did the smile disappear from his face. Howard had been killed at Pearl Harbor. Though he was eight years older, Howard had been Carl's closest ally growing up, and his death had left a hole in Carl's life.

There were six children in all; four boys and two girls. Of the six, only his sister Louise, Billy's mother, was younger than Carl. Four of the six still lived in or around Wixton with their own families. Leonard, the oldest, was already grown when the family moved to Wixton. He was already married and had a good job in the steel mill, so he stayed behind in Birmingham. He and his wife still lived there. Beatrice, the oldest girl, had married a doctor and moved over to Americus. She had been widowed last year. William, young Watson's namesake, was born between Leonard and Beatrice. He was a Wixton city councilman. Of course, Louise still lived in Wixton with her husband and Billy.

Halfway through Carl's story, the women came in from the kitchen. Jenny plopped down on the sofa between Jason and me. At Joanne's insistence, Norma Jean took the recliner next to Carl. Joanne sat in a ladder-back chair that she had carried in from the dining room. Carl feigned annoyance as he paused while they all settled in. When all were in place, he went on with the story.

By the time he finished his family tree, I knew all about his brothers and sisters, their children, and their children's children, if there were any. With all the talk of family, I felt a pang of jealously. I could only imagine being part of such a large and apparently close-knit unit. My only family was one drunk uncle who hated me, and a terminally depressed aunt who seemed to hate everything else. Needless to say, I was envious.

After he was done, I reminded Carl that he still hadn't answered my original question. We all laughed, and he assured me that he was getting to that. Joanne commented that he could not tell a short story.

Carl playfully shushed her and said, "Daddy came here to build that damn cotton gin, and he dragged the whole lot of us along with him." He frowned. He went on to tell me how his father had gotten involved with the cotton gin and why he had uprooted his family from Birmingham. By the edge in Carl's voice, I could tell that the subject was a sore spot in Carl's life. As he talked, I learned that he blamed the gin for the death of his father, and was afraid that it was taking the same toll on J.R. He was not at all happy with his son's involvement with the business.

I could see by Norma Jean's reaction to what Carl was saying that she, too, shared the same opinion. Although she didn't say anything, I could tell something was weighing on her mind. The look in her eyes was distant and cold, and I got the impression that she felt she had spent too many nights like tonight. Too many nights at home alone while J.R. worked overtime at the gin. Regardless of the support from his family, she had to resent all the long hours, and, with the baby on the way, she was bound to hate the situation even more as time wore on. For now, she sat silently stewing, while Carl expressed everything for her.

As Carl talked, I glanced at Joanne. Although she undoubtedly harbored similar feelings, she had reached the limit of her tolerance for the subject tonight. The expression on her face implored me to move the conversation away from the cotton gin. The sadness in her eyes made me regret that I had pressed Carl to answer the question, so I was happy to oblige the subject change.

I knew from what Carl had told me about the picture on the wall of his office that he had fought in the war, and I was anxious to hear more. I asked him about his time in the army. Carl's expression softened to a smile. I already knew from my short time with Carl that he loved to tell a story, and I had apparently hit on a subject that he especially enjoyed. In fact, I had come to the conclusion that he enjoyed every subject except for the cotton gin and Billy Watson. However, the rest of the family was not overly enthused to sit through any of Carl's war stories, undoubtedly having heard them countless times before. Joanne just smiled and silently thanked me, but Jenny and Jason groaned beside me. Jason was the first to defect. He bolted for the stairs, throwing out some excuse about some work he had to do up in his room. We all laughed.

Carl started with the story of his enlistment against his parents' wishes. He told me about boot camp and about the boys in his barracks. He told me a dozen stories about confrontations he had had with his over-the-top drill instructor. It seemed that every story he told reminded him of another.

Joanne was the next to beg off. She excused herself and went out to the kitchen. Norma Jean followed her. Jenny stayed put for a while longer, but the stories eventually got to her, too. Finally, she excused herself and headed for the stairs. My eyes unconsciously followed her out of the room. When she disappeared from sight, I turned back to Carl, who had stopped talking and was looking at me coldly. I felt myself flush with embarrassment. Not knowing quite what to say, I just sat nervously.

After a few moments of very uncomfortable silence, Carl smiled, releasing the tension. He asked, "Eddie, have you ever been to a museum?"

"Yes, sir," I answered, not sure where he was going with it.

"Yeah, I like museums," he continued. "Room after room filled with beautiful and exciting things that are okay to look at but not touch."

"Yes, sir," I replied.

He took up his story where he had left off. He showed no sign that he harbored any ill feelings toward me. He had made his point, assuming I had understood his subtle warning, and left it at that. I had gotten his message loud and clear. I was welcome in his home, I was welcome at his table, but I was not welcome to his daughter. I could respect that. I put it to the back of my mind, sat back, and enjoyed the stories.

Carl was near the end of the story of how a stray bullet had earned him the first of three purple hearts and a hell of a scar on his left arm when Joanne walked in from the kitchen. She asked Carl, "You expectin' more company tonight?"

"No," he replied. "Why?"

"Somebody's comin' up the driveway."

"It ain't J.R.?"

"No, sir," Jenny answered from the stairs. "Somebody in a Chevy pick-up."

Carl got up and crossed over to the window behind me. By now, the pick-up had pulled up beside Carl's patrol car. The front porch light lit up the driver, so I could see that it was T. I glanced down at my watch. Nine-thirty already.

Carl announced to the rest of them, "It's T. Johnson."

"T. Johnson?" Joanne questioned.

"Sadie Johnson's youngest boy," Carl explained. He turned to me and said, "You expectin' company?"

"I'm supposed to go fishing with him tonight. I told him to pick me up here."

"Fishin'?" he repeated.

"Yes, sir."

"Can I go?" Jenny asked.

"No, ma'am," Joanne answered.

"But Mama," she protested. "Why not?"

"Because I said no."

"Daddy?" Jenny looked to Carl for support.

"You heard your mama."

Jenny grunted in defeat.

Carl walked out to open the front door. I followed him out the front door to meet T on the porch. Carl shook T's hand and invited him inside. He started to beg off, but reconsidered, so the three of us walked back inside. Carl introduced T to Joanne and Norma Jean. Joanne asked about his mother. Jenny greeted him cheerfully with a quick hug. I made a mental note to ask him about that later. Carl motioned for us to take a seat.

"Eddie tells me y'all are goin' fishin' tonight?"

"Yes, sir," T replied.

"Where at?"

"Baxter's Pond."

Carl sat for a moment, nodding to himself, then asked, "Who else's goin'?"

"Clancy and Peabody Dupree."

"Jawbone?"

"He's gotta work," T replied. "They had a breakdown at the gin."

"Yeah, how the hell could I forget about that?" Carl said with disgust. He added, "Old man Baxter at home tonight?"

"Far as I know," T replied. "Why?"

"Nothin'," he replied lamely. "I was out that way this afternoon. Willard Jenkins' boys, Seth and... oh hell, Jenny, what's the other one's name?"

"Warren," she answered.

"Yeah, Warren," he acknowledged. "Anyway, I saw 'em out at Baxter's place earlier this afternoon. Shootin' bottles at the clay pit out back of the pond. I just figured they'd be less apt to start somethin' with y'all if Baxter was home."

"You right about that," T agreed. "Mr. Baxter ain't one to put up with any kind of fool-ishness. Besides, we've been out there more than a couple hours now and ain't seen either of 'em."

"Good. Good. Maybe they've gone home for the night," Carl said doubtfully.

"Causin' trouble somewhere else, mor'n likely," T added.

"Probably," Carl agreed. He turned back to me and asked, "Fishin', huh?"

"Yes, sir."

"You fish much?"

"First time," I replied. He laughed.

"Maybe you should take him snipe huntin' while y'all out there." Carl grinned broadly.

"Maybe so," T agreed. They both laughed. T looked down at his watch and said, "We probably should be headin' back out there. If I'm gone too much longer, Clancy'll start worryin' about his truck."

Carl stood to walk us to the door. "Y'all try not to get into too much trouble tonight. I don't want anybody callin' me and runnin' me out of bed."

"We'll try," T replied, then we both said goodnight to the rest of them.

Carl followed us out on to the porch. He took T by the arm before we walked down the steps. "Y'all be careful," he warned. "Them Jenkins boys ain't the brightest boys in the world, 'specially if they've been drinkin'. Lord knows what they might do if they find y'all out there."

"We'll be all right," T assured him.

"Maybe so," Carl replied. "Maybe so." He then turned and went back into the house.

Chapter Seven

T and I climbed into the pick-up he had driven up in. I recognized the truck as one I had seen in the alley outside the pool hall. T backed it up and aimed it down the long driveway. He took a right onto the highway and headed back in the direction of town. A couple of miles up the road he turned left onto another road which we followed for a few more miles, then pulled into the yard of a house.

The house was a small, one-story structure that looked to be more porch than house. The huge porch wrapped around all of the house that I could see. Only after we came to a stop did I notice the old man sitting in a rocking chair facing the road. He pulled himself up from the chair and walked over to the railing nearest us. His bushy white hair and mustache reminded me of Mark Twain. He was slightly hunched at the shoulders, but he had a quickness in his step that you would have expected from a much younger man. He threw up his hand when he reached the rail.

T opened his door and stuck his head out above the cab of the truck. He called to the old man, "It's just me, Mr. Baxter."

Baxter pulled the big cigar he was smoking out of his mouth and answered in a strong but raspy voice. "Hell, I can see that it's you, boy. Who's that white boy you have with you there? He a relative of yours?" He threw his head back and laughed heartily.

"This is Eddie Chance," T explained. "He's a friend of mine from out-of-town."

"Chance, you say?" Baxter questioned. "You kin to the Chances that live over in Richmond Hill?"

"No, sir," I answered.

"Where you from, then?"

"New York."

"New York!" he repeated. "Helluva long way from home, ain't you, boy?"

"Yes, sir."

He turned his attention back to T and said, "Y'all try not to raise too much of a ruckus out there tonight, all right?" He looked back to me, still speaking to T. "Don't be takin' too many crazy chances!" He laughed again, louder than before. With that, he turned and went back to his rocking chair. He threw up his hand again before he sat down. We returned his wave before driving away.

"He's an odd duck, ain't he?" T commented when we were out of hearing range.

"To say the least," I answered. We both laughed.

T drove around behind the house toward a garage that sat at the back of the yard. The garage was backed up to a rail fence that divided the yard from a stand of pine trees. We cut across the yard between the two buildings. On the opposite side of the garage, the dirt drive led through a break in the fence. We drove through a gap in the trees and emerged at the edge of a field of high grass. The driveway reduced to a pair of tire ruts that disappeared into the expanse of grass.

"The pond's on the backside of the field," T assured me as the cab-high grass closed in around us. He added, "It's more a backwater off a creek. Baxter put in a dam down the creek a ways. Backed the water into the pasture here. Made for a fine fish pond." I just nodded.

On the other side of the field, Clancy and Peabody were sitting on a log at the edge of the water. The light from the fire they had burning played off the side of an old barn that sagged to the right of them. We parked in front of the barn at the edge of the circle of firelight. An old car sat half under the shelter of the dilapidated building. Its rusted hood was scattered with fishing gear and bait boxes. I followed T out of the truck and over to where the other guys sat.

"It's 'bout damn time y'all got back with my truck," Clancy said over his shoulder. "Nearly thought 'bout callin' the sheriff." He laughed out loud.

Peabody put down his pole and walked over to the edge of the water. "I thought we'd catch 'em all before y'all got back," he said, bending down to the ground. He lifted a string full of fish out of the water.

"Dang!" T exclaimed. "Y'all have been busy."

"Eighteen cats and four or five crappies," Peabody said.

"Cats?" I asked.

They all laughed. "Catfish," Peabody explained. He slid a fish off the line and held it out toward me. I stepped aside to let the light shine so I could see. The fish was about ten inches long with slick, gray skin and a wide, flat head. The name came from the fact that it had whiskers on either side of its mouth. "Catfish," I repeated. Peabody put the fish back on the string with the rest and dropped the lot of them back into the water.

T poked me in the arm and pointed me toward the gear. He handed me what he called a cane pole and a box of worms, then grabbed some for himself. While we were getting ready to fish, Clancy jumped up from his log and jerked his pole into the air. The pole nearly bent double before he got the line out of the water. A huge fish flopped at the end of the line. It was another catfish, but much bigger than the one Peabody had shown me.

Clancy was grinning from ear-to-ear. "Biggest one yet," he said proudly, holding the fish in the air. "He's AT LEAST a sixteen-incher!"

"No more than a foot," Peabody argued.

"Foot?! Hell. Foot and a half."

"It's grown," T laughed.

"What you think?" Clancy asked, holding the fish out at me.

"Damn big fish is all I know," I opined. Everybody laughed.

"Damn right," Clancy replied.

"You gonna talk about that fish all night, or are we gonna try to catch some more," Peabody complained. "You'd think you'd never caught a fish before."

"Shut up," Clancy defended.

T turned to me and asked, "You gonna act like that when you catch your first fish?"

"Probably."

"First?" Pea questioned. "You mean to tell me you've never caught a fish before."

"Never even been fishin' before," T answered for me. I just shrugged. "Never?"

"Never," I confirmed.

"Yankees don't fish?" Pea asked.

"I'm sure some of us do," I replied. "Just not me!" I said a little more defensively than I had intended.

"Soorrryy," Pea apologized, holding up his arms in mock surrender. "Well hell, let's stop jawin' and get you a line in the water. Can't catch 'em by talkin' about it."

The three of them did their best to explain the basics of what I needed to know. T showed me how to bait my hook and cast the line. I dropped my line out into the water and sat down on one end of a log waiting patiently for something to happen, and praying that I would know it when it happened.

The closest thing to fishing I had ever done was going with Pop to Malone's Fish Market. The first time I remember going, I was barely tall enough to look into the glass case. That first time I stretched up on the tips of my toes to look, I was scared by all those eyes looking back at me. I started to cry. I cried until Pop picked me up and showed me that it was just fish packed in ice inside that glass case. After that, I enjoyed going down to the market on Friday to get a fish for supper, and, by the time Pop died, I was going to the market by myself.

"Eddie, you 'sleep?" T's voice broke my train of thought.

"What?" I started.

"Wake up," he said. "You got somethin' on your line."

"What?"

He pointed toward the water about the time the pole was jerked from my hand. In my scramble to catch it before it slid into the pond, I nearly slipped in myself. I grabbed the pole and lifted it high into the air, bending it double. I lifted the pole as high as I could lift it and still couldn't get the fish out of the water. Someone yelled for me to back up, so I started backing away from the water. Not looking where I was going, I tripped over the log I had been sitting on and fell flat on my back. The others, of course, roared with laughter. T jumped up and grabbed the pole from me to land my catch. I scrambled up from the ground to see my first fish. They laughed even louder when T lifted my trophy into the light of the fire. I flushed with embarrassment and anger when I saw that I had nearly broken my neck for a frog. Granted, it was the biggest frog I had ever seen, over twelve inches with its legs stretched, but it was still a frog.

"You wanna keep it?" T snickered. I just glared at him.

"What's wrong, Cue ball?" Clancy laughed. "Got a frog in your throat?"

"Shut up!" I snapped angrily, but I couldn't help but laugh.

"You don't like frog legs, Cue?" Peabody asked, snickering.

"Not hardly," I snapped back. In spite of myself, I had to laugh along with them.

T unhooked the writhing frog from the line and held it out to me one last time. "You sure?" I just looked at him. He turned and tossed the frog back into the pond. Out beyond the edge of the firelight, it made a huge splash when it hit the water.

"How 'bout catchin' a fish this time," T said, handing back the pole. "Those are the swimmin' things that don't have legs!"

"Funny. Very funny." I baited my hook and dropped it back into the water. I sat back on my log to give it another try. For a few minutes, we sat quietly, then Peabody spoke up and said, "That was a DAMN big frog you caught, Cue ball."

"You ain't kiddin'," Clancy agreed.

"Could we shut up about the frog, already?" I implored.

"Cut the man some slack, y'all," T urged.

"Okay! Okay!" the brothers echoed. With that, the furor over the frog was laid to rest. Except for an occasional "ribit" followed by howling laughter, no one mentioned the frog incident the rest of the night.

I finally landed my first real catch of the night. It wasn't the whopper that Clancy had brought in, but I was proud of it just the same. I was giggling like a school girl when I added it to the string of fish the others had already caught. The others laughed along with me and slapped me on the back when I dropped the stringer of fish back into the water. Once I got the hang of things, I took to fishing like I was born to it.

Before the night was over, we had found what Pea called a "sweet spot". We were bringing in fish as soon as the bait hit the water. Fish after fish was added to our previous catch. By the time our luck ran out, we had filled four stringers with fish and had started filling an old bucket that Clancy had dug out of the barn.

We laughed and joked the whole time we fished. Sometimes we made fun of each other's catch. Sometimes we just made fun of each other. Of course, a lot of the jokes were at my expense, since I was the outsider of the group. My skin color and my accent made me an easy target, and I was enjoying every minute of it. I managed to fire off a few good barbs myself. All the joking and insults were thrown in good fun, and I have to say that it was more fun than I had had in months.

About one o'clock, after fifteen or twenty minutes without a bite between us, Peabody dropped his pole against his log and stood to stretch. After a second or two with his hands in the air, he made a noise that was somewhere between a sigh and a growl. He sat back down and started taking off his shoe. He said, "I don't know 'bout the rest of you, but I'm gettin' damn tired of fishin'." We all voiced our agreement. "How 'bout a swim?" he suggested. The other two quickly agreed.

I was about to protest my lack of swim trunks when Peabody stripped naked and jumped in with a loud splash. T and Clancy, just as naked, followed right behind him, leaving me standing on the bank alone. I sat down on my log and watched the three of them splash around at the edge of the firelight.

It didn't take them long to figure out that I had not followed them into the water. "Yankees can't swim either?" Pea joked.

"I can swim."

"Well, come on in. The water feels great."

"I don't think so."

"What's wrong?" Clancy replied. "You embarrassed that we're gonna see your bare white ass."

I laughed. What I didn't want to do was jump into water where I couldn't see what was swimming around me, especially without my clothes.

T said, "He's a city boy, y'all. He ain't scared of showin' his ass. He scared of gettin' bit on it." Thankfully, in the shadows of the fire, they couldn't see my face turn red.

"Is that it, Cue ball?" Peabody piped up. "You worried 'bout that bullfrog swimmin' up and bitin' you on the balls?" Everyone roared.

"Something like that," I admitted, embarrassed.

"I wonder what ol' Billy would say if he knew you were scared of a bullfrog," Clancy chided.

"I'm not scared of that frog," I protested, "but there are other things swimming around out there."

"There weren't many critters in the neighborhood swimmin' pool, huh?" Clancy continued.

"No."

"Well," Pea conceded, "I guess if he don't wanna swim, he don't have to. He ain't the only one who don't like to swim with the critters."

"Who else?" T asked.

"Our little sister," Pea laughed. "She's three."

"Too bad we didn't bring her along," Clancy suggested. "Then Eddie'd have somebody to play with."

"Very funny," I replied. Being compared to a three-year-old girl was more than I could stand. Reluctantly, I stripped down and waded out into the water. Despite the heat of the night, the water was almost cold. Almost as soon as I was waist deep, something swam into my leg. I jumped and was on my way out until the guys grabbed me and pulled me back. I fought with them, but the three of them were more than I could handle. They picked me up and tossed me out into the deeper water. I just barely got a good breath before I went under. I was mad that they had dunked me, but, by the time I righted myself and made it to a point where I could put my feet down on the bottom, I realized how good it felt to be in the water. It only took me a little while longer to get used to the bumps and brushes that I was feeling below the water.

"If you hadn't come in when you did, we were gonna come out there and drag you in," Peabody said.

"You just about did that anyway," I reminded him. "I didn't appreciate getting dunked like that."

"But don't it feel good now?" Clancy asked.

"Yes," I had to agree, "but I'm still mad. I'll get you back."

"OOh, I'm scared!" Clancy teased.

"You better be," I said, grabbing him by the shoulders and pushing him below the water.

Before he surfaced, he jerked my legs out from under me, sending me under again. I popped back up and grabbed the closest one of them and pulled him under the water. Clancy had moved out of reach, so I had dunked T. He righted himself and wrestled me under. Pretty soon, we were all dunking and splashing each other.

"I thought y'all were out here fishin'," the female voice surprised us. In the confusion of our horseplay, Jenny Besmer had managed to sneak up on us.

"We are," somebody answered.

"Really?" she replied, bending over to pick up a pair of underwear from a log. She lifted them up and stretched the waistband a couple of times, then said, "Exactly what kinda bait y'all usin'?" Everybody laughed, and I'm sure everyone was as glad as I was to be standing in chest-high water.

"Why don't you come in and see?" Peabody teased, boldly.

"Fresh," she playfully scolded. "I came out here to fish," she continued, "but I guess since y'all ain't fishin', I may as well get wet like the rest of you." She sat down on the log and unlaced the boots she was wearing. She stood up and nervously adjusted her clothes. She was wearing a pair of cut-off blue jeans and a denim shirt that she had pulled up and tied at the top of her shorts. She untied the knot and let the tail of the shirt fall down over the shorts. We all stood there and watched her. She looked up at us and grunted, "What am I? Entertainment?" We all looked away, embarrassed. She added, "Go ahead and look. You're gonna see it all in a minute anyway." With that, she unbuttoned her shorts and pushed them slowly to the ground. I don't know about the other guys, but I was then more glad than ever to be under water. She stepped out of the shorts and left them where they lay. She stood there for a moment, toying with the first button on her shirt. Then she shrugged slightly and unbuttoned it and then the one below it. We were still standing still in the water, gawking at her, eagerly waiting for her to open the shirt. She slowly unbuttoned a third button, then, laughing, she turned her back to us. She smiled back over her shoulder at the collective grunt of protest. "Give me a break," she said. "I've never undressed in front of four boys before." She sort of wiggled back and forth as she undid the rest of the buttons. She released the last button and held the shirt open. Again, she looked back over her shoulder, still holding the shirt. She was teasing us. She closed the shirt back and held it close to her body as she turned around. "Y'all ready?" she asked. No one answered. We just stood silently anticipating. She took a deep breath and said, "Here goes nothin'!" She pulled open the shirt and laughed out loud at the audible gasp that came from the four of us. She dropped the shirt to the ground and stood there in a swimsuit. She had been playing with us the whole time. She was a bold one. I had to give her that.

"Jenny Besmer," Clancy laughed, "you are evil!"

"What?" she asked innocently. "What kinda girl do you think I am?" She laughed loudly, then added, "I kinda figured y'all'd get tired of fishin' sometime durin' the night, and, in spite of what y'all wanted, I wasn't 'bout to go skinny dippin' with the likes of y'all."

"Well, what about us?" I asked. "We didn't benefit from your foresight."

"Don't worry 'bout that, Eddie," she replied. "I've got two brothers. You ain't got nothin' I ain't seen before." With that said, she jumped into the water in the midst of us, splashing us all. She surfaced and said, "Now, what were y'all doin' before I got here?" Then she splashed me square in the face. I returned the gesture, but she ducked beneath the water. Before I could get out of the way, Jenny grabbed my legs and jerked them out from under me. I went down fast and grabbed for her. I caught her ankle as she swam away. I pulled her toward me and wrestled her below the water. She wiggled free, and we broke the surface at the same time. She gave me a big smile and said, "That was fun!" She set her sights on T and headed off in his direction. Peabody came up behind me and knocked my legs out from under me. I caught his shoulder as he surfaced and pushed him back under. I pushed off toward where Clancy was standing. He side-stepped out of the way, but I caught him in the face with a big splash of water. Peabody came up splashing from the other side, catching Clancy in the crossfire. He tried to keep up with both of us but had to give it up. He ducked beneath the water to get away. We took off after him. Peabody got hold of his left shoulder and kept him from escaping. I dove under the water and came up under his legs. We lifted him out of the water and tossed him out toward the edge of the firelight. He righted himself and swam back into the light. Peabody and I had stopped to take a few breaths. Clancy stopped beside us to catch his own breath.

In the calm of our rest, we noticed that Jenny and T had disappeared beyond the limits of the firelight. A big smile broke across Peabody's face. He winked at Clancy and me. "Y'all all right?" he called out. T called back an okay, followed by the sound of Jenny giggling. Then it was silent again. Peabody turned toward the two of us and commented about them having found something better to do. We both agreed. I stood for a moment, staring in the direction of their voices. The realization that they could see me snapped me back to reality. I dropped down to my neck in the water and let the water hold me for a moment. Peabody and Clancy were doing the same. We lounged quietly for a while. All of us more than a little jealous, I'm sure.

"When you headin' out again?" Peabody asked, breaking the silence.

"If the rain holds off, I'll probably pull out early tomorrow morning," I answered. "I've been here too long as it is."

"You don't like our company?" Clancy joked.

"That's the problem," I replied. "I like it around here, too much. I can't believe that I've stayed this long. I haven't spent more than one night any place since I left home. Not too often, anyway."

"Ever considered that here might have been where you was headed in the first place?" Peabody asked. I didn't answer. "You know," he continued, "the Lord works in mysterious ways."

"That He does," I agreed. "That He does." This place was beginning to feel a lot like home.

"Enough of this serious talk," Clancy piped up. "I don't know 'bout the rest of you, but I'm 'bout to starve to death. All that wrestlin' done worked me up a helluva appetite. I say we break out some of them sandwiches Mama packed." We both agreed.

"You two want a sandwich?" Peabody called out toward T and Jenny.

"In a minute," T's voice called out.

"Suit yourselves."

The brothers swam the bank and climbed out into the light of the fire. Jenny let out a whistle and a catcall, followed by giggling. Although the need for modesty had been thrown out the window the first time Jenny wrestled me under the water, I was embarrassed at parading around naked if front of her. I took a deep breath and pulled myself up out of the water. More whistling. I felt myself flush. The guys laughed. Peabody had gone over to the truck. Clancy was standing with his back to the water, letting the fire dry his body. I stepped up next to him. I was ready to put some clothes on but not wet. I'd decided to endure a few more minutes of embarrassment. Peabody came back from the truck with a couple of towels. He tossed one to each of us, then pulled on his pants. I dried quickly and grabbed my own clothes. I relaxed a bit once I had pulled on my pants. I tossed the towel across the log and finally turned to face the water. T and Jenny had moved back in the circle of light, heading for the bank to get out. I put on my shirt but left it unbuttoned. I sat down on the log and pulled my boots on my feet. The brothers had dressed and had gone off to where ever they had stashed the food. T climbed out and reached back to help Jenny, but she had already scaled the bank and stood beside him. I tossed them each one of the towels. T pulled his jeans on and sat down by the fire. Even in the heat of the summer night, it was still a little chilly coming out of the water. Jenny draped the towel around her shoulders and sat down beside him on the log. I gave T a questioning glance while she wasn't looking. He just smiled and shrugged.

The others came back with a basket of food and an ice chest full of cold drinks. T looked at his watch as he buckled it on his wrist. A little before three. " 'Bout time for breakfast," he commented. "Your mama pack some bacon and eggs in that basket of y'alls?"

"Nope," Peabody answered. "How 'bout a ham sandwich?" He tossed one to T. He handed out one to the rest of us, while Clancy passed out the drinks.

We ate and talked. Peabody had to recount the story of my frog, at which Jenny nearly fell of the log laughing. She told us about nearly getting caught sneaking out of the house and having to pay her little brother a dollar to keep him from ratting her out. I was really having a great time. I was thinking the whole time about what Peabody had said earlier. It sounded good, but I shrugged it off. My destiny lay in the orange groves of Florida. I set my mind to heading out the next morning, rain or shine. Good times and new friends aside, it was time to get on with it.

"Y'all expectin' anybody else tonight?" Jenny asked through a mouthful of sandwich.

"What?" Peabody asked.

"Company," she replied and pointed at the headlights that were just visible across the field. "Y'all expectin' any more?"

"Jawbone?" I asked.

T shook his head. "Not this late." He stood up and looked across the field, trying to make out who was coming. "It's a pick-up."

"Bobby?" Clancy wondered.

"No way," Peabody laughed. "You know Sister Irene ain't gonna let him out of the house at three in the morning, and it'd be easier breakin' out of prison than sneakin' out of her house!"

"True enough." They all laughed.

When the truck broke free of the tallest of the grass, Jenny said, "Looks like that piece of shit Dodge that Seth Jenkins drives."

"Trouble?" I asked, remembering the name from Carl's warning.

"Naw," T assured me. "Not if it's just the two of them."

It was.

They pulled the truck up right behind Jenny's car. I took the driver to be Seth. He was the first out of the truck. He was a fairly big fellow. Not tall, not quite my height, just big. He was wide across the chest and shoulders. Muscular, except for the paunch that hung over the top of his belt. He looked to be a formidable opponent, but I took T's assurance that they weren't going to be trouble. T identified the passenger as Seth's younger brother, Warren. He was tall and lanky, as tall as Peabody. He stepped out of the truck and stood there in the door for a long minute saying something to his brother. After that moment, he lifted something from the gun rack above the seat. My pulse quickened until he passed the object through the glow of the cab light. A walking stick. He slammed the door and came around to where his brother was standing. He leaned heavily against the cane in his left hand. He limped a step behind Seth as they came around to the front of Jenny's car. We stayed seated where we were. One of the guys tossed a stick into the fire and made it spark and crackle. None of us spoke.

"Evenin', Jenny," Seth spoke with a deep drawl. Warren leaned back against the hood of Jenny's car, taking the weight off his left leg. He nodded to Jenny. They both eyed me curiously. Neither of them acknowledged the others. Seth went on, "What in hell you doin' out here with these niggers?" Clancy tensed beside me, but Peabody put a hand on his shoulder.

"Why? You jealous?" Jenny responded. "Me and the boys here are havin' a mighty fine time tonight." She leaned over and sucked T's earlobe into her mouth. T just smiled. Both Jenkins boys grunted in disgust. I chuckled to myself. She was bold.

Warren spit a long stream of tobacco juice in our direction, then spoke. His voice was weak and raspy. It reminded me of a snake hissing. He said, "Jenny Besmer, I always knew you were a whore, but I never thought you'd stoop low enough to fuck a nigger." That brought T to his feet. Seth stepped forward as if to protect his brother. Jenny stood up and held on to T's arm.

"Better'n any limp dick redneck," Jenny continued. "Y'all just mad 'cause y'all ain't gettin' any."

"Not even on a bet," Seth replied, trying to be clever.

"Oh! Come on!" Jenny laughed. "You and your gimpy brother've been tryin' to get into my drawers since eighth grade." She ran her hand down her belly into the top of her still unbuttoned shorts. "You're gettin' horny now just thinkin' 'bout it, ain't you?" She pulled her hand back out and blew him a kiss with it.

"You slut!"

"You wish!"

"Your Daddy know you act like that?" Seth growled.

"Why don't you ask him? He's right behind you." They both jumped and looked behind them. We all laughed.

"You're one sick bitch, Jenny Besmer," Warren hissed.

"Thank you for noticin', Warren." She smiled coyly. "If y'all don't mind, this is a private party. Why don't you two climb back into that piece of shit you call a truck and go find somebody who gives a damn."

Peabody stepped up and said, "Now."

Seth bowed up and responded, "Who do you think you are? You think you can order me around like a slave?" The word was meant to provoke Peabody, but he kept his calm and looked down into Seth's cold eyes. He quietly said, "You can either drive out of here right now, or they can carry you out of here later. You decide. In case you can't count, there are five of us and only two of you." He paused and looked over at Warren, then continued, "Well, one and a half." The comment stung the younger Jenkins hard. He swung at Peabody with the cane. The blow caught him in the back and jarred him forward into Seth, nearly knocking him down. Before the cane hit his brother, Clancy had jumped the fire and dove at Warren. They collided and rolled over the hood of Jenny's car and hit the ground wrestling and punching.

The cane went flying. Jenny grabbed it and took a swing at Seth. He dodged the blow and shoved Jenny back, making her fall. T came by me and ran hard into Seth, knocking him down. He was back on his feet almost as soon as he hit the ground. He punched T in the stomach on the way up. T doubled over, gasping for air. Peabody got a quick jab to the side of Seth's head while his attention was on T. Seth spun to return the blow and took Peabody's big fist square in the face. Jenny was at T's side.

I stood for a moment, not knowing what to do. I wasn't at all interested in getting involved in the fight, but I couldn't just stand around while my friends were getting beat up. Even Jenny was in the fight. My final decision was made for me. Clancy called my name. On the opposite side of the car from the other melee, Warren was getting the best of Clancy. Still on the ground, he had managed to get his arm wrapped around Clancy's neck and was beating his head against the knee of his good leg. Clancy was batting at his back and the back of his head, but from the position Warren had him, he couldn't get a good blow. They were sitting so that Warren's back was more or less turned toward me. I ran up behind them and grabbed Warren by the shirt collar. I jerked back on the collar, pulling the shirt hard into his throat. He let go of Clancy, and his hand shot to his neck. Gasping for breath, he tried to relieve the pressure on his windpipe. I released his shirt and jerked him up from the ground. I pushed him back into the side of the car and punched him several times in the stomach before he had time to recover. When he regained his composure, he punched me hard in the side and jammed his shoulder into my chest, nearly knocking the breath out of me. I staggered back, letting him push free of the car. With the momentum of his push from the car, he hit me with his shoulder again. This time he knocked me to the ground and landed hard on top of me. In spite of his lame leg, Warren had turned out to be strong as an ox. He straddled me and was punching wildly at my head and chest. My wiggling kept him from landing many good punches, but I did take a couple of hard hits to the face. I could taste the blood that trickled out of my split lip. He had my arms pinned to my sides, but I bucked and kneed at his back as hard as I could.

Clancy had recovered, ran over, knocked Warren off of me, and kicked him a couple of hard times in the ribs. Warren hollered, twisted around, and snatched Clancy's legs out from under him, pulling him down more or less on top of me. I tried to roll out of the way but still managed to take Clancy's shoulder against my already aching ribs. We rolled away from one another and up on one knee. Warren had crawled to Jenny's car and was trying to pull himself up against its side. Clancy was closest, so he jumped and grabbed the foot of his bum leg and jerked him back to the ground. He rolled onto his back and tried to kick Clancy's hand from his ankle. Despite the beating his knuckles were taking, Clancy held on and dragged Warren away from the car. With the two of us between him and anything he could pull up on, Warren's weak leg kept him pretty much stuck on the ground. His inferior position gave us an advantage against his enormous strength. We just stood back from him and taunted him. When he'd try for something to support himself, one of us would grab his ankle and drag him back. He made several attempts to stand on his own, but the weakness of his leg would send him tumbling to the ground. Between attempts to stand, he pelted us with rocks, but he was doing more damage to the paint on Jenny's car than anything else.

It was Jenny's scream that took our attention away from Warren. We both jerked around to see what was wrong. She was screaming because Seth was pulling her hair. T was holding Seth from behind. He had Seth in a head lock and had his right arm twisted behind his back. With his free arm, Seth had managed to grab a handful of Jenny's hair, which he was furiously pulling. She was screaming and punching at him trying to make him let go. She was giving him a pretty good beating. Peabody was sitting in the ground a few feet away, holding his stomach. Seth had apparently got a good shot at him before T grabbed him. He looked to be all right, and, despite Jenny's screams, they had Seth pretty much under control. We figured we would be more help if we kept Warren occupied and out of that fight.

Warren, however, wasn't at all interested in that idea. With our attention on the fight on the other side of the car, he had managed to sneak up on us. Before we knew what was happening, Warren rolled across the ground and into our legs. The unexpected blow knocked us both to the ground. Unfortunately for him, he was not able to get past our legs before we were on top of him. He was kicking and swinging at us as we pounced on him. I misjudged a kick and took his foot to the face. I rolled off to the side, nursing my now bleeding nose. Clancy wrestled with him and managed to get Warren over on his back and was sitting straddle him. He had Warren's arms pinned to the ground with his knees. Warren was kicking and wiggling, trying to get free, while Clancy was giving his head and shoulders a pretty good beating. I sat for a moment trying to get my breath.

Jenny managed to get free from Seth and was standing to the side rubbing her head. T had Seth by both arms, and Peabody was punching him in the stomach. We had finally gained the upper-hand and were giving the brothers a pretty good beating.

The melee was in full swing when the shot of a gun brought everything to an abrupt halt. Everybody's head jerked toward the sound. Mr. Baxter was standing just inside the light of the fire with a double-barreled shotgun pointed toward the sky. Despite the shotgun in his hands, I had to laugh at the knee-length nightshirt he was wearing, but the humor was erased by the tone of his voice. "What the HELL is goin' on out here?" he barked. No one answered. "I think I asked y'all what was goin' on!" he said more calmly than before. While he was waiting for our response, he breeched the gun and pushed another shell into the empty chamber. Still, no one said anything. We just watched the old man's hands as he reloaded the gun. He snapped the barrel back in place and pointed the gun at Seth. "One of you is gonna answer me," he demanded, "and I choose you."

Seth wiped a trickle of blood from the corner of his mouth and said, "Why don't you put that gun down, old man, and go back to bed. You ain't gonna shoot nobody."

Baxter laughed, "You wanna try me, you little shit?" Seth took a step toward him, but he stopped dead when the old man swung around and pulled the trigger, peppering the side of Seth's truck with holes.

"You old son-of-a-bitch, " Seth cried. "You shot my truck." He took an angry step toward the old man.

Baxter swung the gun back around toward Seth and said, "Next time it'll be your sorry ass. Now get back over there before I blow your damn knee caps off!" Seth complied. "Now, let's try this again. What is going on here?" Still, no one answered him. "Y'all can either tell me or we can go up to the house and call the sheriff." He looked right at Jenny and added, "And I'm sure that none of us wants to get the sheriff out of bed this time of night. Do we?" We all grumbled agreement. "Well, then, let's try again. Seth Jenkins, did I or did I not tell you that the two of y'all weren't welcome out here tonight?"

"Yes, sir," Seth mumbled.

"What's that? I can't hear you."

"Yes, sir," he repeated.

"That's what I thought I told you, but you know, I'm gettin' on up in years, and sometimes the old memory ain't what it used to be," he chuckled. "Well, since we both agree that's what I told you, then maybe one of you can tell me what the two of you are doin' out here gettin' the shit beat out of you." When neither of them answered, Baxter shook his head and added, "Could it be that you're a couple of dumb sons of bitches!"

The rest of us chuckled, to which Baxter responded, "What y'all laughin' at. You five are just as much to blame as them. I remember tellin' you," he said, pointing to Peabody, "that you and your brother and Johnson could use the place tonight. Then he drove up with the Yankee, and I figured what harm could that cause. Then I get rousted out of bed by some God-awful ruckus and come out here and find y'all, the Yankee, and the sheriff's half-nekkid daughter wrestlin' with the dumb-ass brothers.

"First of all, I gave y'all permission to fish, not have an orgy. Girl, your mama'd have a duck if she knew you's runnin' around dressed like that in front of all these hard legs. You ought to be ashamed of yourself.

"Secondly, I absolutely despise bein' woke up in the middle of the night. Did you two dunderheads think you could sneak back here without me knowin' it? If you didn't already know it, you drove through my backyard," he said to the Jenkins boys. We all chuckled again. "There y'all go with the laughin' again. Ain't nothin' funny 'bout none of this. A man my age could have a heart attack gettin' jarred from sleep like that. Now, I'm sick of the whole damn lot of you." He motioned to Seth and said, "Why don't you scoop up the gimp and get the HELL out of here!" Seth remained where he stood. Baxter swung the gun around and leveled it on him. Seth scrambled over to where Warren sat on the ground, scooped him up, and half dragged him to the truck. He dropped Warren into the passenger seat and slammed the door. He paused at the front of the truck to say something, but Baxter growled, "Now!" and accentuated his command with a shotgun blast into the air. Seth just grumbled under his breath and climbed on into the truck. He slammed the truck into reverse, spun it around, and sped off across the field.

"Now, as for the rest of you, I think the best thing for y'all to do is pack up your stuff and go on. And for goodness sakes, girl, put your clothes on."

Peabody stepped forward and said, "Mr. Baxter, we're sorry 'bout all the trouble."

"Hell, boy, I know it weren't your fault the dumb-ass brothers showed up. They were out here earlier tonight, but I told 'em to get lost. I ain't ever cared too much for them boys or their daddy either. They ain't got half a brain amongst 'em. I'd let y'all stay on tonight, but I'm afraid they're just drunk enough to come out here again. In a week or two, come on back and try 'er again, but, for now, it's best if everybody clears out." He breeched the gun and pulled the spent shells from the chamber. He tossed them on a pile of trash beside the old barn, then said, "Y'all make sure to put out that fire before y'all leave. Wouldn't want my barn or that fine automobile to get burned up, would we?" With that, he turned and walked back toward the house, chuckling to himself. He stopped just outside the light and repeated, "And for goodness sakes, girl, put your clothes on!" Then he was gone.

Clancy was the first to laugh. He cackled and grabbed his bruised ribs. He echoed Baxter in his best old man voice, "Girl, put your clothes on!" The rest of us roared with him.

"Let's get this stuff together," Peabody said, nursing his rapidly swelling left eye. "I think I've had enough fun for the night. He started gathering up the fishing gear and loading it. He pulled the stringers of fish from the creek and dropped them in a bucket of water in the back of the truck. T and I put out the fire and added our trash to the pile. Jenny put her clothes on.

"Looks like one of us is gonna have to ride in the back of the truck," Clancy said when everything was loaded.

"Huh?" Peabody questioned.

"Well, there's four of us, and I know that we ain't gonna fit, so one of us is gonna have to ride with the fish. Since it's my truck, it ain't gonna be me, so, little brother, you and T and Eddie need to decide who gets the honor."

"Well, I'll be the first one out, so I'll do it," T volunteered.

Jenny spoke up, "There's no need for y'all to drive all the way out to T's place, then all the way back to town. Since T lives out my way, why don't I just take him on home, and y'all can go on into town."

"Sounds like a plan to me," Peabody responded.

We all agreed, and T dropped into the passenger seat of Jenny's Corvair. Peabody, Clancy, and I climbed into the cab of the truck. Jenny pulled out first and we followed her across the field. She emerged into Baxter's yard and disappeared around the house. Clancy pulled through the fence and stopped. He and Peabody jumped out and closed the gate behind us.

 Before they could get back to the truck, Baxter emerged from his back door onto the porch. He clipped the end off of a huge cigar and lit it. After he got it started good, he took it out of his mouth and said, "I expect a plate of them fish when y'all get 'round to cookin' 'em."

"You bet," Clancy agreed. "You'll have to come out to the house for a fish fry. Mama enjoyed you the last time."

"You know, I might just have to do that," he replied. "Your mama knows she can cook."

"Yes, sir. I'll tell her you said that."

Baxter took a long pull from his cigar and blew a ring of smoke into the air. "Y'all have a good night, you hear." He threw his hand into the air and sat down on one of his rocking chairs to enjoy his cigar.

"You, too," Clancy said, returning the wave. Then he pulled the truck in gear and headed out toward town.

Nobody spoke for a while, then Peabody turned and asked, "Cue, you have a good time tonight?"

"Yeah," I answered. "Most fun I've had in a long time."

"Not as much fun as T was havin', I bet!" Clancy suggested.

"Damn, you know it," Peabody agreed.

"What was that all about?" I asked, with just a hint of jealousy. "How long has that been going on?"

Clancy shrugged and said, "Tonight's the first time they actually got together, far's I know."

"What do you mean 'actually'?" I wondered.

"Well," he explained. "T's been in love with Jenny Besmer for as long as I can remember, but I never knew Jenny had any feelings for him. Tonight was a surprise to us, too."

"Really?"

"Yeah!" Peabody replied. "Surprised the hell outta us when they disappeared in the dark like that. I never thought T had a snowball's chance with that girl."

"Wasn't his brother involved with a white girl?" I asked.

"Bloodworth girl," Clancy confirmed. "Over in Smithville."

"Cost the boy his life," Peabody added. "T told you about that, right?"

"Yes," I replied. "It seems that T wouldn't want to get involved in the same thing that killed his brother."

"Like father, like sons, I guess," Peabody mused.

"Yeah," Clancy agreed.

Since I had met T's mother, I was confused by the comment, but they both looked at me like I was supposed to know what they were talking about. I didn't want to show my ignorance, so I sat silently trying to figure it all out. Then like a shot it hit me. "Janie?!" I blurted out. Half asking, half telling.

"Give the man a cigar," Peabody confirmed. "I knew you couldn't be that slow."

"But..." I started, then asked. "Does Mrs. Johnson know about it?"

"Know about it? Hell," Clancy chuckled. "Story is, the two of them shared the man."

"Really?" I replied, shocked.

"Yeah. You've seen that ring on the chain around Janie's neck, right? That's his ring."

"I just assumed that it was her husband's," I said.

"Janie ain't ever been married," Clancy explained. "She'd have married Mr. Johnson if she could've, but things like that just weren't acceptable back then." He paused for a moment, then added. "Hell, ain't acceptable now either, I reckon."

"Does T know?" I wondered.

"He knows," Peabody replied. "Most of our people know."

"What about Janie's people?"

"Who knows?" Clancy said. "That ain't really somethin' the white folks wanna admit. One of their own shackin' up with a colored man."

"T said that Janie was like one of the family, but I never imagined anything like this," I said. Janie just didn't seem like the type to carry on an affair like that. Especially with a married man, but I really didn't really know the woman. I had just met her, and you never know what secrets are hidden behind a person's public persona.

For the rest of the trip to town, the brothers were jabbering about different things they thought I might be interested in. I pretty much sat silently, half listening, commenting when the conversation called for it, but I was thinking about Jenny Besmer and how her relationship with T affected me. I could definitely feel some electricity between us whenever we were together. I knew that I was not deluding myself to believe that the attraction was mutual, and, until I saw them together tonight, I thought that I might have a shot with her. Until the fishing trip, the only obstacles were Jenny's dumb-ass cousin and her mountain of a father. While those were formidable hurdles, at the least, they were conquerable, but this unexpected competition from T complicated things. Suddenly, I had to choose between T and Jenny. Was just the chance at something developing with Jenny worth losing T's friendship, or was it worth walking away from a chance with an amazing girl for a guy I had just met. I finally decided as we pulled up in front of the Wixton Inn that none of it mattered, since I wouldn't be around long enough for any of it anyway. I would just have to add them both to my long list of new friends and put Jenny in my collection of what might have been.

Clancy pulled up to the curb to let me out. "You headin' out today, or you gonna stay a while longer?"

"I'm too tired to go anywhere today but bed. I'll get as much rest as I can today, and if the weather holds out, I'll head out tomorrow," I replied. "Maybe we can all get together tonight sometime."

"Maybe so. Maybe so," he agreed, pulling the truck in gear. He fingered a cut on the side of his face and nodded toward Peabody and said, "But first, little brother and me have a date with a hot bath and a bottle of iodine."

I patted the top of the truck and turned to go inside. I threw my hand into the air and waved as they drove off. I climbed the steps and unlocked the front door with my room key. The lobby was dark, and the door to the apartment was closed. I locked the door behind me and headed up the stairs to my room. My muscles ached from the fight, and the climb was almost unbearable. By the time I unlocked my door, I was about ready to pass out from exhaustion and pain. I peeled my torn, dirty clothes off, threw them in the corner, and fell onto the bed. I was asleep almost before my head hit the pillow.

Chapter Eight

*P*op and I are standing at the counter at the fish market. I am seven, and I am standing on an old soft drink carton so that I can see the fish in the case. It is the first time Pop has let me pick out the fish for supper. I am no longer scared of them. Pop and Mr. Malone are very patient with me as I examine each of the fish through the glass. I finally make my decision, and Mr. Malone takes it out of the ice. He hefts it up and down in his hands a couple of times and says, "Fine fish, son. Fine fish." I turn and grin up at Pop, who smiles and rubs the top of my head to let me know he is proud of me. Mr. Malone cleans the fish, wraps it in newspaper, and hands it to Pop. He looks down at me and asks, "You want to carry it home?" I grin from ear-to-ear and nod my head. He hands the bundle to me, and I tuck it under my arm. He gives Mr. Malone the money and guides me out the door. I step through the door onto the sidewalk.

Suddenly, I feel strangely alone. The normally busy street is deserted. No cars. No people. No sounds. I am scared, and I turn to Pop for comfort, but he is gone. I start to cry. I run back into the fish market, but it is now deserted. I don't see Mr. Malone anywhere. I am alone in the store with all those eyes. I start to cry. I stand in the middle of the floor, clutching the wrapped fish to my chest, and cry, but there is no sound. My chest hurts from sobbing, but there is no sound. I scream for Pop, but there is no sound. Just those eyes! Thousands of them. Black and lifeless. All staring at me.

I turn and run back out the door. I come out the door and find myself on the front porch of the Wixton Inn, looking out over the deserted Main Street. I am no longer seven. As I stand there looking at the empty street, I realize that I am still clutching the fish to my chest. I know that holding onto the fish is a silly thing for me to be doing, but, for some reason, I can't put it down. Finding it suddenly funny, I throw my head back and laugh. The sound of my own laughter echoing down the street is deafening. I turn around and try the door behind me, but it is locked. I search in my pocket for my key, but it isn't there. I begin to bang on the door and call for Joshua and May, but they do not answer. I finally give up and walk down the street to the diner, which is deserted. The tables are covered with partially-eaten plates of food, and a steaming pot of coffee sits on the counter. I call out for Janie, already knowing that she will not answer. I walk over, sit at the counter, and pour myself a cup of coffee from the pot in front of me. I sit with my back to the door, sipping from my cup and cradling the fish.

Behind me, I hear a coin drop into the slot in the jukebox in the corner. I spin around to see who *has played the record, but there is no one there. A cold chill runs down my spine as Hank Williams begins to sing.*

Hear that lonesome whippoorwill.

He sounds too blue to fly.

I am suddenly scared of being alone. I call out for Janie again. Nothing!

The midnight train is whinin' low

Besmer! Nothing!

I'm so lonesome, I could cry.

Hello! Hello! Hello! Nothing! Nothing! Nothing!

I've never seen a night so long.

When time goes crawlin' by.

The moon just went behind the clouds

To hide his face and cry.

I get up from the counter and run to the door. I look up and down the street. No one!

Did you ever see robin weep

When leaves begin to die?

I am standing in the middle of the street calling out.

That means he's lost the will to live.

I run back to the inn and bang on the door. No answer!

I'm so lonesome, I could cry.

I sit on the steps and hold the fish to my chest. I am embarrassed by my fear. I am always alone. Why am I so scared, now? I sit, rocking, holding the fish to my chest, still unwilling to put it down. I close my eyes tightly, willing the loneliness away. Willing myself back to the fish market with Pop and Mr. Malone.

The silence of a falling star

  Lights up a purple sky,

And as I wonder where you are,

I'm so lonesome, I could cry.

I cry.

The sound of the door opening behind me startles me. I jump to my feet and spin around to find Jenny Besmer standing in the open doorway.

"What's wrong, Eddie?" she asks in a voice that weakens my knees. She is dressed only in a man's shirt, her bare legs below it.

My heart is pounding in my throat. I cannot answer her.

She takes a step toward me and reaches for the wrapped fish in my hands. I resist at first, then finally release it to her. She smiles for a moment, looking at the package, then tosses it to the ground. My eyes follow it down and watch it disappear into thin air. "You don't need that anymore. You have me," she whispers. She pulls herself up to me and presses her lips to mine. I step back, breathless from the kiss. She steps back from me and begins to unbutton her shirt. My eyes follow her hands to each button. My mouth is dry with anticipation of what is to come. Two buttons. The curves of her bare breasts tease me. Three. The smooth skin of her abdomen peeks at me. Four. The slight swell of her belly pushes against the loosening shirt. She slowly unbuttons the final one, and the shirt falls open to reveal her naked body beneath it. I stand and admire her beauty as she slides the shirt off her shoulders and lets it fall to the floor.

A voice from across the street startles us. It is Mr. Baxter, in his nightshirt, saying, "For goodness sakes, girl, put some clothes on!" He is gone. We both laugh.

She steps toward me and pulls my mouth down to hers. I reach behind her and pull her to me. I feel the heat from her body through my clothes. I want her. She breaks the kiss and pulls at the buttons on my shirt. "Will you make love to me, Eddie?" she asks. I manage only a nod. Suddenly, I am aware, but uncaring, that we are standing naked on the porch. I am driven only by my desire for Jenny. She lowers herself to the floor and pulls me down to lay beside her. There is now a blanket beneath us. "Make love to me," she says again. I draw her to me and make love to her on the front porch of the inn. After that, we lie together on the blanket, listening to the silence around us.

Our reverie is broken by the sound of a car in the distance. Louder and louder. Drawing closer. Seth Jenkins' Dodge turns the corner onto our street and screeches to a stop in front of us. Warren sits in the bed of the truck, pointing his walking stick at us. "WHORE!" he shouts. They drive away.

Jenny boils with anger. "Bastards!!" she yells after them, shaking her fist in the air.

I draw her to me to comfort her. Before I realize what is happening, she is on top of me. We make love again, more passionately than before.

The doors behind us fly open, and her enraged father bursts through. "What the HELL you doin'?" he shouts, dragging her off of me. "You bastard!" he cries, jerking me up from the floor and throwing me out onto the street. The pavement tears into my bare skin. He follows me down and begins kicking me. Jenny cries for him to stop, but he won't. She pulls on his arm, but he pushes her off and yells at her to put on her clothes. Then he is gone.

I am lying in the street, bruised and bleeding. Jenny kneels beside me and tries to comfort me. She holds me carefully to herself, rocking gently back and forth.

T appears in the center of the street. His face is flushed with anger. Jenny lets go and backs away from me. She stares at her feet, embarrassed by her show of affection toward me. T's stare burns into me. "You bastard!" he yells at me. I do not reply. He turns to Jenny. "I thought you loved me?" he asks.

"I do," she replies.

"Then, how could you?" he asks, his voice trembling from the hurt. He turns and walks away. Jenny runs after him. Then they are gone.

I drag myself up from the street and stagger toward my clothes. Every step is agony. A fit of coughing overtakes me. My side screams with pain. Broken ribs! I clutch my sides, unable to stop the coughing. I taste blood in my mouth. I have to gasp for air. The pain is overwhelming. I fall to the ground.

"What's the problem, Chance?" Billy Watson asks. He is leaning against the porch rail, chewing on a toothpick. He is unusually calm.

I reach out to him and say, "Help me."

"Help you?" He sneers. "Why the hell would I help you, you Yankee bastard? You have the gall to fuck my cousin in the middle of town, and you want me to help you." He walks down to where I am curled up in the road. He kicks me hard in the side. My mouth fills with blood. He keeps kicking me. "Help you!?" he repeats. "I'm gonna kill you, you son-of-a-bitch!" He pushes me onto my back and drops to one knee on my chest. He presses the barrel of his revolver between my eyes. "You like bein' on the bottom, huh?" he demands. He pulls back the hammer. "How do you like it now?" He laughs. In slow motion, I see his finger tighten on the trigger and the hammer fall.

Chapter Nine

My eyes snapped open, and I sat bolt upright in the bed, gasping for air. I was drenched in sweat with my heart pounding so hard, I thought it might jump out of my chest.

"Eddie, you all right in there?" May asked through the door. "That was a frightful sound you just made."

"Yes, ma'am," I replied, realizing that I must have screamed when I sat up. "Just another bad dream. Sorry."

"Nothin' to be sorry about, son." The concern showed in her voice. "Just checkin' on you."

"Thank you," I said.

"You want somethin' to eat?" she asked. "I'm gettin' ready to set the table."

I looked at my watch. Eleven-thirty.

"No, ma'am," I lied. "I don't feel much like eating right now."

"There's plenty," she volunteered. "Come on down when you're ready, and I'll fix you a plate."

"Thank you," I answered. I listened to her footsteps grow fainter down the hallway.

I was really famished. My three-o'clock ham sandwich was most certainly gone, but I needed some time to recover from the dream. My heart was just now starting to slow down, and my breathing was just about normal again. I laid back on the bed and tried to relax, but it was not to be. After a few minutes, sounds from the room above interrupted my meditation. The squeaking bed springs and her cries of "Oh, Frankie!" showed that the new bride maybe wasn't as innocent as she seemed to be. I had to laugh. I felt almost guilty eavesdropping, but I couldn't stop listening. The sounds of their passion brought the images from my dream to my mind. The images of Jenny Besmer. The smoothness of her skin. Her caress. Her kiss. They were so real. So vivid. I lay there listening to the newlyweds and replaying the scenes in my head.

I was almost envious of the young soldier and his new bride. They had found each other and now had someone with whom to share their lives, their love, their bed. I wondered what it would feel like to make love to a woman. To have her scream out my name. I knew there was no call for envy since my celibacy was self-imposed. All through school, I had been picked on by my friends because I was still a virgin. They were always bragging about their conquests and telling me that all I needed was to get laid, but, for me, sex was not something I took lightly. It wasn't as if there weren't opportunities. It was really hard to resist the temptation of Rosalee Bartelli, tight sweater and all, with her tongue in my ear and her hand down my pants, but she was not the girl to lose the battle to. Just about every guy at Harland Gaines High School had been with her, including a couple of the teachers, and I did not want someone like that to be my first. I was waiting until the right girl came along. I had to admit that there had been times when I doubted the rationale of my conviction, and lying there with my fantasies of Jenny on my mind and the moans of passions above me was one of those times. I was just about ready to throw in the towel by the time she screamed Frankie's name for the hundredth time.

I took the hottest shower that I could stand to work the soreness from my bruised body. The marks on my face weren't that pronounced, but still noticeable. I knew Joshua and May would ask. I dressed and headed down the stairs.

Joshua was perched on a stool behind the front desk working on his books. "Mornin', son," he said, glancing up as I came down. "Had a late night last night, huh?"

"Yes, sir," I replied. "I hope I didn't disturb you when I came in this morning."

"Hell, who could sleep anyway!" He grinned and flicked a thumb toward the stairs. I nodded agreement. "They keep you up?"

"By the time I got in, I was too tired to let that bother me," I answered. "I didn't hear them until this morning."

"Little lady's got quite a set of..." He was interrupted by May's emergence from their apartment.

"Joshua Wilson!" she exclaimed. "You ought to be ashamed of yourself!" She laughed.

"Lungs," he proclaimed. "I was gonna say lungs!" He patted her on the rear end as she walked by and added, "You know I've only got eyes for you."

"You just know that girl'd kill you, you old fool."

"But what a way to go," he replied, winking at me.

"You shameless old coot," she grumbled, stalking out around the desk toward the stairs with the bundle of sheets she was carrying.

Joshua turned his attention back to me. "What the hell happened to you?" he asked, the concern showing on his face.

"I got in a fight last night."

"Watson?"

"No. Not this time. Seth and Warren Jenkins."

"You take 'em on by yourself?"

"No. Me, T, and Clancy and Peabody Dupree." I prudently left Jenny's name out.

"I hope y'all put a whoopin' on 'em."

"We did," I said. "At least, we were before Mr. Baxter got there with the shotgun."

"Shotgun?" he questioned. "You seem to invite trouble, boy."

"Seems so," I agreed.

"May said you had another bad dream last night," Joshua changed the subject. "Woke up screamin' again."

"Yes, sir," I acknowledged.

"Anythin' you wanna talk about?" he asked.

I shook my head saying, "Same old. Same old."

"Well, if you need an ear," he volunteered. I nodded.

May came back down the stairs carrying my clothes from last night. "Eddie, what in the world happened to these clothes? They look like they were run over by a truck," she mused, then she got a good look at my face. "Son, you look like you were wearin' 'em at the time. Are you all right?"

"Yes, ma'am."

She held the pants up and looked at the holes in them. "It'll take some doin', but I can save 'em," she announced.

"You don't have to go to all that trouble," I said.

"Nonsense. It ain't no trouble," she assured me. "And, besides, you don't have that many clothes to begin with. You can't afford to lose the ones you've got." I had to agree.

"You ready for that lunch now?" she asked.

I started to protest, but she wouldn't hear it, so I said, "That would be nice." I followed her around the desk and into the apartment. Joshua fell in behind us, deciding to take a break from his bookkeeping.

May lead me to the table and went about the business of preparing my lunch. She placed a heaping plate of food on the table in front of me. She followed that with a basket of biscuits and a pitcher of iced tea. I thanked her and dug into the generous helping of pot roast and mashed potatoes she had provided. I felt a bit self-conscious of eating alone, but I was too famished to worry about it.

Joshua sat across from me at the table and browsed through the Albany paper, occasionally commenting on what he was reading. About the time I began my second plateful, he folded the paper and asked me about the events of the night. I told him about the fishing, the frog, and the fight. Again, I left Jenny out of the narrative. He laughed out loud when I described Baxter with his nightshirt and his shotgun. He loudly expressed his opinion of the Jenkins brothers and their "good for nothin'" father, bringing more than a couple of stern admonitions about his language from May. Those, in turn, brought grunts of protest from Joshua as he continued his rant session. I just sat eating and laughing to myself.

After two platefuls, I was thoroughly stuffed. May offered me another helping, but I couldn't hold another bite. She cleared away my dishes, then offered me a piece of pie. As good as it looked, I had to refuse. "Thank you again for the meal," I said. "Between you and the Besmers, the last couple of days has been the best eating I've done in forever. I never dreamed I'd miss Aunt Liz's lasagna, but after scores of two-bit diners or cold beans from the can, I welcome the home cooking. If you keep this up, I might never leave," I laughed.

"Stay as long as you like, son," she replied. "I like havin' someone else around to cook for besides him." She flicked a thumb toward Joshua. "Someone who appreciates it."

"Speakin' of leavin'. When you plannin' on headin' out again?" Joshua piped up. He stood up from the table and motioned for me to follow him to the living room. He sat down in his worn recliner.

"Everybody keeps asking me that. Are you trying to run me off?" I replied, taking a seat opposite him on one end of the sofa.

He laughed, "Hell, son! We ain't tryin' to get rid of you. I'm just curious as to how long you were gonna be usin' that room up there. I just needed to know so I could get your bill ready." He sat stone-faced for a moment, then broke out in a huge grin. "I was just wonderin' if you planned on headin' out with the weather like it is?"

"I was hoping to head out tomorrow morning early," I replied. "I would have left this morning, if I hadn't been out all night."

"Says in the paper there that we can expect scattered showers through the weekend," he volunteered. "All over Southeast Georgia."

"A little rain shouldn't hurt me, I don't guess."

"Rain's one thing, but lightnin', that's somethin' else again," he said. "I'd hate for you to get caught on the side of the road in a bad thunderstorm and get yourself fried. Y'all took a pretty big chance gettin' in the water last night. It didn't get all that bad here, but they had a helluva storm over in Americus. Two inches of rain. Knocked out the power and the phones. One stray bolt and that's all she wrote."

"That's something to think about," I agreed, "but, like I said yesterday, I'm beginning to like this place a little too much. If I don't head out of here soon, I may never leave."

"Would that be so bad?" Joshua asked.

"No." I thought long and hard for a reason to say yes, but I couldn't come up with anything.

"Place kinda grows on you, don't it?"

"That it does," I answered.

"Well, since you ain't leavin' today, what you got planned?"

"No plans, " I replied. "I may hook up with the guys later."

"If you're interested, I got a proposition for you," he suggested. "How'd you like to eliminate that room bill I was kiddin' you about? You can stay as long as you like, and you don't have to pay for any of it."

"You certainly have my interest," I replied, "but, I'm a little scared to ask what I have to do."

"What'd you think I was gonna ask you to do? Kill somebody?" He laughed, then his expression turned to stone. I didn't quite know how to read his face, and I was becoming visibly nervous when he began to laugh. The tension in my body snapped, and I laughed with him. "I scared the hell out of you, didn't I?" He continued to laugh.

"Yes," I answered. The blood was finally returning from my feet. "You are a hard man to read, Joshua Wilson."

"I'm sorry, " he replied. "I guess that's not the best way to ask you for a favor, is it?"

"Not really," I replied sternly. I sat silently for a moment, letting him stew in his guilt, then I smiled. "But, I'm game."

"Good. Good," he said. "I was afraid for a minute there, that I had joked my way out of some good help."

"You almost did," I agreed, "just because you nearly scared me to death. What is it that you want me to do?"

"When the original proprietor of this place had it built, he had his living quarters on the fourth floor. In this place's heyday, there was a staff that ran it. The owner lived up top, and the manager lived in the apartment back of the lobby. When we bought the place, May and I decided to take the bottom apartment, because we didn't have no manager, and I sure as hell wasn't gonna climb up and down all them stairs when somebody wanted to check in or out in the middle of the night. It's a good thing, I guess. Since I got old, my arthritis has just about stopped me from climbin' stairs at all. I ain't been above the second floor in over a year. May runs up and down these stairs like she's twenty years old, but it damn near takes me fifteen minutes to climb up to the second floor." He paused for a moment to sigh at his infirmity. I just nodded. He continued, "Bear with me, son, there is a point to this story. Anyway, May and I took the bottom apartment, so that left the upper one empty. It's a nice apartment. Four bedrooms, two bathrooms, and a kitchen. Last night, Corporal 'Oh Frankie' and his screamin' bride convinced me to do somethin' I've been thinkin' 'bout since I bought this place. I'm gonna turn that place upstairs into a suite. You know. For honeymooners and the like. It'll give folks a special place to stay if they want it. Anyway, we've been usin' it for storage, and that's where you come in. All the junk we have stored up there is gonna have to be moved down to the basement, and I was hopin' you would do it for me."

"How much stuff are we talking about?" I asked.

"It's not that much at all. Just some boxes and some other junk. I just can't do it myself, and some of the stuff would be too heavy for May to try to carry, " he replied. "If you're interested, why don't we climb up there and take a look at it. If not, I'll let you be."

"I'll be glad to take a look at it, " I accepted. "I have nothing better to do."

"Good," he acknowledged. "You can take a look at it and tell me if you think the job's worth more than I'm offerin' you."

"Let's take a look," I agreed.

He got up and went out to the bedroom where May had disappeared to let her know where we were going. She followed him back out and cautioned him about being careful of the stairs. With a grimace from Joshua, she made me promise to watch out for him. I agreed, and we headed out toward the attic. Joshua stopped outside their door and took the key for the attic apartment from the cubby behind the registration desk.

We then headed up the stairs with him in the lead. I hung back a few steps, giving him time to make his way up to the second floor. As he had said, he couldn't make the climb as fast as I could, and I didn't want to rush him by dashing up to the top ahead of him. At the second floor landing, he paused a few minutes and shook the pain from his legs. "Damn knees," he muttered under his breath. When he was ready to travel again, I fell in beside him, and we made our way to the opposite end of the hall where the stairs to the upper floors were.

Joshua laughed and gestured to the rainbow of doors down the hall. He chuckled under his breath and explained, "Paintin' the doors like this was May's idea. So were these pictures and these flowers and stuff. She said it gave the place a little life. Make people's stay a little more cheery, she says. I can't rightly argue with her, and most of the people who stay with us compliment the decor."

"It's nice," I agreed.

"There you go," he chuckled.

We reached the end of the hall where my room was. He tossed a thumb toward the door and asked, "Your room all right?"

"Best I've had in a long time," I acknowledged, "and I couldn't ask for better hosts."

"Thank you kindly," he accepted.

He passed by my door and stopped at the bottom of the third-floor stairs. He stood with his hand on the banister staring up the steps. Gathering the resolve to make the climb to the next level, I guessed. Finally, he sighed and took to the stairs, muttering and cursing under his breath with each step. I offered to make the climb by myself, but he was unwilling to admit defeat and continued to climb and mutter and curse. I laughed to myself.

About halfway up the stairs, we began to hear the "Oh Frankie" drift down from above. The closer we got to the floor, the louder they became and were, now and then, punctuated by grunts and moans that we couldn't hear from below. We couldn't help but laugh.

"Makes you horny just listenin' to it," Joshua commented. I nodded agreement, with a big grin across my face. "Oh to be that young again," he lamented. "Been a long time since May's screamed my name like that, at least in the throes of passion." He paused and chuckled to himself, then added, "Hell, I don't know if I can even still throw my passion." He threw his head back and laughed out loud. I joined in. He looked at me and predicted, "You laugh like that now, son, but you'll get here one day." I nodded, still grinning.

"I have a question for you," I said as we reached the third-floor landing.

"Good," he said. "Gives me an excuse to rest my knees. Shoot." He sat down on a small bench that sat in the corner of the landing. I sat on the top step.

"I was just wondering, with all these empty rooms, why did you put them right above me?"

"Bathroom."

"Huh?"

"Bathroom," he repeated, then he explained. "Your room and their room are the only two with bathrooms inside the rooms. All the other rooms have to share the bathroom down the hall."

"Why just the two?"

He shrugged. "Don't know. None of the them did originally, but one of the owners past remodeled and added the two in-room baths. He may have intended to add on to all the rooms, I don't know, but all we got were the two, and we ain't had the money to add anymore. So, I always put guests in those two rooms first. Besides, I can charge a little more for the room with a bathroom, and with all the motels popping up along the highways, I need to make a dollar where I can." I nodded understanding. He continued, "Had I known she was gonna do all that caterwaulin', I'da put 'em down at the end of the hall."

"I don't think that would have helped much," I joked.

"You're probably right about that, son. Probably right," he laughed. "At the rate I'm movin', it'll take all day to get to the top," he said as he was getting to his feet. "You ready?"

"When you are," I replied. I stood and followed him down the hall to the stairs to the fourth floor. We passed by the newlywed's room. It was the first on the floor. They were unusually quiet. Exhausted, no doubt. We both chuckled as we continued farther down the hall. Unlike the floor below, which was shortened by the expanse of the lobby, this floor extended the full length of the building, adding four more rooms to the floor. Just like my floor, the doors were each a different color. The stairs to the top floor were at the very end of the hall beyond the last room. I allowed Joshua to take to the climb before me, and we made our way upstairs.

The stairs emerged in the center of the back wall of the floor. The stairwell was enclosed by a waist-high fence that separated it from the rest of the fourth-floor landing, which looked to serve as a sitting room for the apartment behind. It spanned the whole top floor and was at least as deep as it was wide. To the right of the stairwell, in the corner immediately in front of the stairs, sat a piano. A tall upright with cherry finish and a mirrored front. In the opposite corner, to the left of the stairs, was a felt-topped gaming table with four matching chairs. In the center of the room, a pair of long, leather sofas sat opposite one another on a large Persian rug. Behind each sofa was a cluster of four wing chairs, arranged to promote conversation among their occupants. Each quartet of chairs sat upon its own Persian rug. The left wall was dominated by an enormous stone fireplace. In the corner beyond was a large, glass-fronted display case. Its shelves sat empty beside the long, cold fireplace. Along the right wall was a mahogany billiard table. A rack of cue sticks hung on the wall behind it. In the remaining corner was a built-in bar. Floor-to-ceiling, open-faced liquor cabinets were fronted by a marble-topped bar. Everything in the room was covered in a thick layer of dust. Despite its unkempt state, the room had an air of elegance about it.

"This is quite a room," I commented to Joshua.

"They say that Josiah Kenlow, he was the one that built the place, and then his son, Henry, who took over the place when his father died in ought nine, were quite the entertainers. They were notorious for throwin' extravagant parties in this parlor. Lots of booze and lots of women. I hear tell they played host to congressmen, governors, and Henry, as the story goes, even had a president. Can't nobody 'round here recall which one, but the story still gets told." He laughed a doubting laugh. "Course all that was before Prohibition took his liquor, and the Depression took his money. Henry lost his fortune in twenty-nine. Lost his mind soon after. Spent the last years of his life in the state hospital over in Milledgeville. Since he didn't have any family, what was left of his estate, if you can call it that, went to the state. The building was sold at an auction for the back taxes in thirty-three. Bought by a man named Lucas Macabee. I bought it from him, well, his lawyer, in forty-six. Just after the war. From what I gathered from the lawyer, Macabee never set foot in the place." He paused a moment, then continued. "Anyway, back in the day, them Kenlow boys threw a mighty fine soiree." He ran his finger along the dusty banister in front of us and said, "Place was a lot less dusty back then, I'm sure." We both laughed.

He pushed the small gate open before us and motioned for me to step through. The gate swung shut behind us.

He pointed to the far wall, which was broken by three doors. Joshua headed for the middle door, which I assumed led to the living quarters. He slipped the key into the lock and tried to open it. "Damn thing don't wanna open," he said. "Been too long between uses, I suppose."

"Let me give it a try, " I offered. He stepped aside to let me try. The lock protested the turn of the key, but it finally gave to my persistence with a loud click. The knob was more cooperative, and I pushed the door open with the screech of rusty hinges. The air in the small entranceway beyond the door was stale and reeked of old cardboard. We stepped back into the parlor to let the air clear some before we ventured farther in.

"It's been months since anybody was in there. Stayin' all closed up like that, things are bound to be a might musty," Joshua said. "May used to try to keep this aired out up here, but finally gave up on it. Didn't see much need in it." He stepped back into the apartment. "Air's a bit better now. We'll throw open a window or two once we get on back to the bedrooms. Let a little fresh air in." With that, he walked farther into the apartment.

To the left of the entrance door was another door that stood open to reveal a small bathroom. I realized that the left exterior door must lead to this bathroom also. Easy access for party guests. Directly ahead of us was a short hallway lined with doors: bedrooms, all of which stood open. Beyond those, the hall opened into a large room, but I could tell nothing about it from where I stood.

We made our way down to each bedroom. Joshua stopped at each one and opened the window to let fresh air blow through. The rooms were piled with all manner of junk. Hundreds of boxes occupied much of the space between the furniture that remained, but all sorts of other odds and ends were also scattered about. I even saw an old car fender in one of the rooms. Joshua laughed and shrugged his shoulders when I pointed it out to him.

"No tellin' what you're liable to find up here," he offered. "Most of this stuff was already here when we got the place. Some of it we brought up when we cleaned out the rooms before we opened for business. All of it's been sittin' here undisturbed for nearly twenty years. Most of it probably needs throwin' out, and one of these days, when I have the inclination and the energy, I'm gonna sit down and go through it all, but, for now, I just want it all moved outta here."

Once we had opened up all the bedrooms, Joshua lead me on down the hall to the apartment's common area. It was a large room that was divided into three sections. The largest section, the one visible from the hallway, was the den, or sitting area. This room was more intimate than the outer chamber. The furnishings here were less pretentious. The leathers and dark woods had been passed up for floral fabrics and light oak finishes that carried throughout all three sections of the great room.

The section immediately to the right of the hall was the dining room. It was separated from the sitting area by waist-high bookshelves, and from the kitchen beyond it by a short serving counter. The large oak dining table and ladder-back chairs once dominated this middle area, and would have still if it had not been so completely filled with boxes.

The job before me presented itself as quite a challenge, but it was the least I could do after all Joshua and May had done for me. It was obvious to me, and I'm sure to Joshua too, though he made no mention of it, that the work was more than a man could do in one afternoon. As I stood in the middle of the great room and contemplated the hundreds of boxes that would have to be carried down at least four flights of stairs, I guessed that I'd be at it for at least a week. I shrugged at the thought. I really had nowhere to be and all the time in the world to get there, so what would a few extra days matter. Besides, I was having the time of my life with these people.

"Well," Joshua started after I'd had enough time to take it all in. "Whatcha think? You wanna tackle it, or should I look elsewhere?"

"I must admit that it'll be quite a job, but I'd be glad to help."

"Fine. Fine." He was obviously pleased. "Let me show you a couple more things up here, then I'll take you down to the basement and show you where I want it all put." He turned, and I followed him down the hallway. Halfway down, he paused and said, "Leave anything that looks like furniture. Everything else goes." He stopped again at the bathroom door, stepped inside, and flushed the toilet. "The john works, in case the need arises, but you'd better bring up a roll of paper," he suggested. "I know I sure as hell wouldn't wanna wipe my ass with forty-year-old toilet paper!" We both laughed.

Outside the living quarters, he pulled the key ring from his pocket and unlocked the third door. It opened to a large storage closet that looked to run the entire depth of the apartment next door. The shelves that lined the narrow room were surprisingly bare.

"Fill this up first," Joshua said. "It'll hold quite a few of them boxes. Might save your back a bit, the less you have to carry down all them stairs."

"Yes, sir, " I agreed.

"Come on and I'll take you to the bowels of the beast and show you where we're goin' with all this junk."

Back on the third floor, we met Corporal "Oh Frankie" and his wife emerging from their room. No doubt in search of food to refuel. "Good afternoon," he said as we approached.

"Afternoon, son. Ma'am," Joshua responded. I nodded and smiled. "Goin' out about town?" Joshua queried.

"Headed to the diner down the street for a late dinner," he responded.

"Maybe take a walk around the square," she volunteered shyly. "Get outta that room for a while."

Joshua and I grinned at each other. "That's a nice walk, if you can stand this heat," he said.

I nodded knowingly and added, "Town has a nice library a couple of blocks down. I visited there yesterday morning myself."

Once the small-talk was completed, they departed down the stairs with a short look back from her as they disappeared below the floor. When they had been gone long enough to be out of hearing range, we both broke out laughing. "Nice library," Joshua managed to say when he paused to take a breath. We roared again, then headed down ourselves.

"Let's get on down to the basement before these stairs get the best of me. My knees are screamin' at me," he complained.

I followed him back down to the lobby. The door to the basement was hidden in a small alcove beneath the stairs. He unlocked the door and pulled a string just inside it to light up the stairway. He stood in the door for a few minutes and looked down the steps. He shook his head and said, "I just ain't got it in me, son." He stepped back from the door, then continued, "I think I'll let you do this one on your own. I want all that stuff stacked in the room just to the right of the stairs. You can't miss it. It's the room without a door."

"Yes, sir."

Rather than attempt another set of stairs, he decided it was time to get back to his bookkeeping. He handed me the apartment and basement keys and went back behind the front desk and into his own apartment.. I stuffed the keys into the pocket of my jeans and ascended the stairs to tackle the monumental task before me.

"What have I gotten myself into?" I muttered under my breath. All those boxes were going to take me forever to carry down all those stairs. As I made the climb back to the top, I wished that Josiah Kenlow had put in an elevator.

By the time I reached the fourth floor, I had resolved myself to fit as many of the boxes as I possibly could into the closet. Therefore, my first course of action would be to move the few items that already littered the shelves to one place to make room. I found a half-empty box on the floor and was able to pile most of the loose debris into it. I sat it in the far corner on the very top shelf. The rest of the junk I piled next to it as neatly as I could. Then, I checked the stability of each shelf to gauge how much weight it could hold. With that done, I began the arduous task of transferring the clutter from one place to the other.

On my fourth or fifth trip around, I emerged from the closet to find May at the top of the stairs carrying a portable radio. I hurried over and took it from her. "What's this?" I wondered out loud.

"Thought you might like a little music to work by," she answered. "I image it'll get a might lonesome up here without some background noise to keep you company."

"I appreciate that," I replied, "but you didn't have to trouble yourself like that."

"Nonsense. It weren't no trouble, son," she answered. "It's the least I could do after you agreed to help us."

"This is the least I could do after all the kindness you two have shown me."

"Glad to do it. Nice to feel needed again." She smiled.

I set the radio up on the bar and tuned in a clear station. I thanked her again for the radio and said, "This will make the job go a lot better. I was already getting tired of hearing myself breathe."

May was standing in the door of the apartment looking at some boxes I had set in the hallway. "It's gonna be quite a job, ain't it?" she asked, shaking her head. "You sure you wanna get into this?"

"I don't mind," I answered. I considered it for a moment, then added, "Gives me an excuse to hang around."

She smiled and said, "We enjoy havin' you."

"Thank you."

"Well, I reckon I'd better get on outta your way and let you get back to work," she said. "I'll bring you up some lemonade a little later."

"You don't have to go to that trouble," I repeated.

"Nonsense!" she scolded. "You let me worry about what trouble I go to, okay?"

"Yes, ma'am."

With that, she turned and headed for the stairs. "Be careful, Eddie," she warned before she disappeared below.

"Yes, ma'am," I called after her. As I smiled at her concern, I had to believe that my own mother would have been that way.

When she was gone, I decided it was time to get back to work. With the music fromthe radio to liven the mood, I took to the task before me. Box after box after box. I made so many trips back, and forth between the two rooms, the activity became almost unconscious. My mind was set on the one goal of filling up that closet before I quit for the night. I had a lot of boxes to move, and I wanted to get as much of it done before night, because I wanted to meet up with the guys again that night. Clancy and Peabody had said something about maybe going back out to Baxter's place again. Do a little more fishing or shoot bottles in the clay pit. I didn't have a clue about any clay pit, but it sure sounded like fun. I was looking forward to it, but there was a ton of work to do first.

I was about two-thirds of the way down one side of the storage area when I heard the stairwell gate swing shut. "May, is that you?" I called out. I slid the box I was carrying into its place on the shelf and walked back out to see if May had brought up that lemonade she had promised. "May?" I repeated.

"Cue ball, that you in there?"

"Pea?" I questioned, surprised by his voice.

"Who else?" he answered. He and Clancy were leaning against the bar.

"Mrs. Wilson sent up some lemonade for you," Clancy said, indicating a serving tray that now sat on the bar next to the radio.

"She's a sweet little lady," Peabody offered.

"Yeah," Clancy agreed. "She started tryin' to feed us as soon as we came in the door."

"It ain't a wonder you ain't left this place yet," Peabody laughed.

"You may be right," I acknowledged, pouring myself a glass of the lemonade. "Help yourselves. Looks like May sent up enough glasses for the three of us."

"Don't mind if I do," Peabody accepted. "Don't mind if I do."

They both poured themselves some lemonade, and we all took our glasses and went over to one of the chair clusters and sat down. I welcomed the moment of rest.

"What you doin' up here, Cue?" Clancy asked.

"Moving some boxes around for Joshua. He's going to make this place into a suite for special quests. I told him I'd clean the place out for him," I explained. "What are you two doing up here?"

"We came to see what your plans for tonight are," Peabody replied. "See if you were gonna hang out with us or what."

"I figured I'd knock out a big chunk of the moving, then head out to find you guys," I said. "I didn't expect you guys to come by here, especially not this early."

"Didn't plan on it either. Just sorta happened."

"We're headed down to Shaker's to play a game or two of eight ball. We thought we'd ask if you'd like to tag along."

"I'd love to," I admitted, "but I really need to get some more of this done before I quit for the night."

"How 'bout we help you," Clancy offered. "The three of us can knock it out."

"You don't want to do that."

"Sure we do," Peabody assured me. "We ain't in no hurry to get anywhere. Shaker's will still be open when we get there."

"Besides," Clancy added, "it's the least we could do after you helped us with Seth and Warren last night."

"If you insist," I conceded, thankful for the help.

Even with several stops for lemonade, we made quick work of the closet. I stood in the doorway and surveyed what we had done. From floor to ceiling, the room was stacked to capacity. Every space that could hold a box was filled. I considered for a moment, then decided that I had done enough for the night.

"I think it's time to call it a night," I announced my decision as I locked up. "Let's go have some fun."

"Sounds like a plan," Clancy replied.

"Here! Here!" Peabody agreed.

෨෬

The same old man was sitting at the bottom of the steps at the pool hall. The guitar was missing, having been replaced by a harmonica. He was playing a tune that I didn't recognize, but enjoyed. The guys stopped and spoke to him and dropped some change in his box. I pulled a dollar from my pocket and dropped it into the box. The old man smiled and thanked us for our generosity. He put the harmonica back to his lips and blew a long, soulful note. He gave us a wink and broke out into a rousing tune.

The pool hall was just as crowded as it had been the time before. I followed the brothers through the crowd to the same table we had played on that night. Bobby was bent over the table lining up a shot. His opponent, who I didn't recognize, stood off to the side. I looked around for T but didn't see him.

"Bobbeee," Clancy called, dragging out the last syllable. "Mama Irene let you outta prison tonight?"

Bobby didn't acknowledge the crack. He took his shot and missed. "Damn." His opponent stepped up to the table, and Bobby came over to where we were standing. He nodded toward me, then turned his attention to Clancy. "Not without a fight," he finally replied.

"Shame she wouldn't let you out last night," Peabody said. "We sure could have used that left hook of yours against them Jenkins boys. It was a good thing Cue ball was there. He fights pretty good for a white boy." He winked at me.

"And a Yankee on top of that," Clancy added.

"So glad I could help, in spite of my obvious shortcomings," I laughed.

"He don't look exactly white to me," someone said from the crowd.

"Me neither," someone else agreed.

"What are you," the first voice asked, "just a nigger tryin' to pass?"

"Cut it out, y'all!" Peabody demanded.

"Why?" the heckler continued. "He ashamed of what he is?"

"I'm Italian!" I interjected. "My parents were from Italy. I'm not ashamed of it, and I'm not trying to pass for anything. And if you want to talk to me, you come out here where I can see you. Or are you scared?"

"I ain't scared of no wop," he said as he stepped into the open. He was a bull of a man. Not as big as Jawbone, but still intimidating.

"Were you scared when you thought I was a 'nigger tryin' to pass'?" I continued, refusing to show my fear.

"I ain't scared of nobody, you little shit," he barked.

"Leave him alone, Willie," Clancy commanded, stepping between us. "He don't want no trouble, and after what I saw last night, I don't think you want to jump on 'im. You just liable to get your ass beat."

Willie and I glared at each other for a moment. I could see the anger in the veins that stood out on his neck. I damn sure didn't want to fight him, but I wasn't about to back down. We stood our ground, glowering at each other, with Clancy between us.

"Hey, man," Bobby addressed Willie. "Besides that, man, he's on our side. You saw him the other night about to brain Billy Watson."

"Yeah," someone from the gallery called out, "anybody that hates Watson can't be all bad."

Willie's expression softened. I also relaxed and smiled. I put my hand out for him to shake. He looked at it for second, then took it. His grip was fierce. We parted with a mutual respect, but far from friendly. He returned to his game across the room, and I turned back to my friends.

Peabody smiled and shook his head. He said, "Cue ball, you seem to invite trouble."

"Seems that way, doesn't it?" I agreed.

"That may be true," Clancy said, "but I'm still glad he was with us last night."

"Yeah. I heard y'all put a whoopin' on them boys," said Bobby's opponent, who Peabody introduced as R.C. "Them crazy white boys must have been drunk to jump the four of you like that."

"Four?" Peabody questioned. "There were five of us."

"Wait a minute," Clancy interrupted. "Where'd y'all hear about it, anyway?"

"T was tellin' us about it," Bobby answered. "He said the three of y'all and him got in a fight with Seth and Warren Jenkins. He never said nothin' about nobody else. Who?"

"When'd you see T?" Clancy wondered.

"He was here 'bout an hour ago," Bobby answered. "Who else?"

"An hour ago? Where'd he go?" Clancy continued.

"Didn't say. Just said he had to meet somebody. We figured he was goin' over to the Wilson's to meet up with him." He pointed at me. "Who else?"

"He say if he's comin' back?" Clancy asked, obviously intrigued by T's behavior.

"He didn't say," R.C. replied. "Who else was there?"

"Jenny Besmer," Peabody admitted.

Bobby looked at me and asked, "Am I speaking English?" I shrugged. He continued, "He never said nothin' 'bout Jenny Besmer. What was she doin' there?"

"Swimmin'," Clancy offered.

"And gettin' friendlier than I would've expected with T," Peabody added. He then asked, "D'you say T left outta here to meet somebody?"

"Yeah," R.C. confirmed. "He was shootin' pool with Bobby and me. Goin' on about the fight and all that. Then he looks up at the clock over there and takes off like a rabbit. Dropped his cue in the middle of a shot and bolted. Hollered back about the meetin' as he was headed out the door."

"He didn't come after me," I stated. "I haven't talked to him since we left last night. We didn't make any plans."

"I wonder where he's at?" Peabody said.

"I ain't got no idea 'bout where he's at," Clancy admitted, "but I gotta damn good idea 'bout who he's with." Peabody and I looked knowingly at each other.

"Who?" Bobby asked.

"Jenny Besmer," the three of us answered in unison.

"You shittin' me!" Bobby doubted.

We shook our heads and repeated it, then told them the rest of the story about the events of the night before. As we filled in the holes that T had left in his version, I wondered if T had left Jenny out of the story to protect her, as I had done with Joshua, or if he just wanted to hide it for some reason.

I also wondered what they were doing, if they were together. My mind was flooded with images of all the things they could have been doing, as well as images of her and me from my dream. My jealousy flared, and, for a moment, I was pissed off at T, though I had no right to be. I did not want to think about T and Jenny, but the guys wouldn't let the subject rest. As I sat there and listened to their conversation, I became more and more uncomfortable.

"She is damn good-lookin' for a white girl," R.C. opined.

"And y'all didn't see her in that swimsuit last night," Peabody pointed out. "Um! Um! Um! Make you stand up and slap your grandma!"

"Make you stand up all right!" Clancy laughed. "Ain't that right, Cue ball?" I nodded my agreement, not wanting to let them in on my jealous pouting.

"I wonder if she's as good as she looks?" Bobby supposed.

"Ask T," Clancy suggested. "He probably knows."

They all laughed. I laughed half-heartedly along with them. Although I shared their curiosity, I was incensed by their lack of respect for Jenny. Although my own fantasies of Jenny played across my mind, I was disgusted by their vulgar vocalization of what we all were thinking. My hypocrisy was fueled, no doubt, by my jealousy. I didn't know if I were more angered by their verbal treatment of Jenny, or the fact that she was with T and not me. Either way, I had had my fill of the discussion. I knew that, with the mood I was in, I wouldn't have any fun, so I feigned a headache and announced to the guys that I was heading back to my room. After they all tried to talk me into staying, Clancy offered to drive me, but I begged off with a lame explanation that the night air might do me some good. I gave my regrets and left.

At the top of the stairs, I met T coming in. He grinned broadly when he saw me, and I felt a little guilty about being so angry with him. I looked past him, but didn't see any sign of Jenny. I let him speak first.

He asked, "Where you rushin' off to, Eddie?"

"I don't feel well," I lied. "I think I've had too much excitement the last coupla days. I'm going back to my room to lie down."

"You want some company on the walk over?" he asked. "I got somethin' I wanna tell you."

"No," I said a little too abruptly, wanting to be spared the details of his liaison with Jenny. I quickly covered myself by explaining, "They're all waiting for you downstairs. Maybe we can talk tomorrow."

"All right," he accepted, obviously disappointed.

I hadn't really lied. I did not feel well, though I wasn't actually sick, and I damn sure wasn't in the mood to hear any bragging about his conquest. I wanted to be alone to wallow in my own misery. I turned away down the alley and left him standing at the top of the stairs.

Chapter Ten

The walk back to the inn did do me some good. The time alone gave me a chance to clear my head of some of the emotional baggage I had been collecting over the past couple of days. I was letting myself get too attached to the people and the town. The attachments were clouding my mind and distracting me from my purpose. I decided on that walk back that I would finish the job I had agreed to do as soon as possible, then I would leave for Florida. It was time to be moving on.

I was surprised to find the door of the inn still unlocked when I got back. I didn't expect to find Joshua sitting in the lobby when I entered, but he was stretched out at one end of the sofa with a pipe in his mouth and a book in his hand. He jumped a bit when I opened the door, startled by my sudden appearance. He took the pipe from his mouth and said, "You're home awful early tonight, son. The way you and the Dupree boys were cuttin' up and carryin' on when y'all came down while a go, I expected you to be out 'til all hours again."

"I decided to turn in early tonight, so I can get an early start tomorrow. I still got a ton of boxes to carry down."

"You sure you wanna do all that, son?"

"Yes, sir."

"All right, I won't ask you again," he said. "They say it's supposed to be a scorcher tonight, so I put a fan in the room there for you. Won't be much, but it'll at least move the hot air around a bit."

"Thank you," I acknowledged. "Goodnight."

"Goodnight, son."

He went back to his reading, and I headed up the stairs. Before I reached the top, he called out, "Come down in the mornin' before you get started, and May'll fix you some breakfast. It ain't good to go to work with an empty stomach."

"I might just do that," I said. "Thank you."

The fan he had mentioned was sitting at the foot of the bed. I considered it for a moment, then set it on the sill of the open window where it could at least draw in some fresh air. To further combat the heat of the Georgia night, I stripped naked and lay uncovered so the semi-cool air could blow across me.

I closed my eyes and tried to sleep, but every time I would close my eyes, my mind would churn. The images from last night's dream swirled in my head. Graphic images of Jenny and me. Then T standing in the street screaming at us. Then the scene would change. It would be Jenny and T, and I would be screaming at them.

Jenny and T.

Jenny and me.

Back and forth.

The sex.

The hurt.

The betrayal.

Back and forth.

Over and over again.

Finally, I gave up. I was too wound up to fall asleep, and I was almost scared of what my dreams would bring that night, if I did. I lay there in the bed staring at the ceiling, the wind from the fan cooling the sweat that covered my body. I was grateful that, for the moment, the lovers upstairs were quiet. I was in no mood to listen to their lovemaking. I was angry. I was jealous. Jealous of them. Jealous of T. And I was alone. I was surrounded by a dozen people who had accepted me into their lives, their homes, their families, but I felt painfully alone. Before I realized it, the tears were streaming down my face. I sat there cross-legged on the bed and cried.

I didn't know how long it lasted, seemed like hours, but, finally, the tears stopped. My eyes burned. My breath was shallow and labored, and the tension in my back had it tied in knots. Suddenly struck with an overwhelming sense of claustrophobia, I got off the bed and paced the floor. I went to the window, still naked, and stood there staring out at the night. Even that did not help. The darkness that faced me was just another wall that closed me in. I wanted to scream, but I refrained. Like a caged tiger, I longed for a release. Then I saw the keys to the apartment upstairs lying on the dresser. I decided that I would put all that pent up frustration to use. I pulled on my clothes, grabbed up the keys, and headed for the attic.

Everything was as we had left it. Except, apparently, May had come up to retrieve the lemonade service. In its place on the bar was a plate of cookies. Even with the foul mood I was in, I had to smile. She was a sweet lady. Among all the people I had met since my arrival in Wixton, she and Joshua were the ones I knew I'd miss the most. They were like the grand-parents I never had. They had accepted me into their home, and treated me more like their son than just a patron in their place of business. That was the main reason why I didn't mind doing this job for them. I nodded to myself. Yes. I would miss them the most.

I took a big bite from one of the cookies and unlocked the closet door. I was again satisfied that we had put everything we could possibly put in that room without blocking the floor. I mentally patted myself on the back for a good job, then locked the door back.

Joshua had been right. A big part of the boxes had fit into the closet, so what was left wasn't that bad. In order to save my back somewhat, the heaviest of the boxes had been moved first, so what was left was mostly light work and a few oddball items like the car parts. The hardest thing about what was left was that it all had to lugged down four flights of stairs. No use fretting over what couldn't be helped. I had known what I was getting myself into, so I shrugged it off and unlocked the apartment door.

I grabbed the first box I came to and carried it down to the lobby. Joshua had abandoned his reading for the night. The door to his apartment was closed, and most of the lobby lights had been turned out. One small lamp in the corner of the room was all the light there was, but it was more than I needed to find my way around to the basement door. The door was slightly ajar, and I had to push it open with my knee. Thankfully, Joshua had left the light on. I descended the stairs and found the room he had indicated earlier. I sat the box against the wall in the far corner and climbed the stairs back to the top, thus completing the first rotation of the cycle that would carry me far into the wee hours of the morning.

About four o'clock, I paused to take a breather. I grabbed a handful of May's cookies from the tray on the bar and headed back to the great room where I had been working. I said aloud to myself, "Eddie, you keep going like this and you may get it all done tonight." I didn't doubt that I would finish. I had moved over half of the remaining boxes, and I was showing no signs that I was running out of gas. The frustration and tension that had brought me up in the first place were all but gone, having been replaced by determination to get the job finished before I quit. "But first," I said as I stuffed the last of my third cookie into my mouth, "I need to pee."

The master bedroom was the first room off the hallway from where I was. It had its own bathroom, so that's where I went. I laid the cookie I was carrying on the side of the sink. It slipped off the edge and crashed to the floor, crumbling into a dozen pieces. I shrugged, thinking that I'd clean it up after I took care of the business at hand, and turned to the toilet. Out of the corner of my eye, I saw a blur flash from behind the toilet and scurry behind me. I turned to watch the mouse raise up on his hind legs and furiously gobble up the crumb of cookie he held between his forepaws. I stood still for a moment, watching him eat and waiting to see if he was going to be joined by any more. He wasn't. I wondered if he was even aware that I was there. He continued to eat from the pile of crumbs on the floor until I moved my foot a little too close to where he sat. He dropped his cookie and darted toward the corner. I laughed. I figured he didn't realize he was boxing himself into a corner, not that I was going to try to catch him if he did. He surprised me by disappearing through the wall, or so it seemed. He ran to the corner and was gone. I was beginning to wonder if I had imagined the whole thing—lack of sleep hallucinations or something—until I saw the crack in the corner. Barely visible from the angle I was looking at it, the bottom of the wall protruded from its intended position. Just the old building showing its age, I figured, and mice were notorious for slipping through the smallest of openings. I kicked the toe of my boot against the wall in the corner, trying to flush the little fellow from his hiding place. Instead of scaring the mouse, I moved the wall. With the blow from my foot, the whole section of the wall slipped slightly farther into the corner. I studied it for a minute and pressed against the area with my hand. It moved with my touch. Like a partially open door, I realized after a couple of minutes. The section of wall wasn't very wide, about two feet. It extended from the corner to the edge of the recess that housed the bath tub. I assumed that it was just an access panel for the plumbing for the tub, until I noticed that the faucet was on the opposite end.

There was no handle, nor any sign that there ever had been, and there were no visible hinges. If it were a door, someone had done a good job of hiding it. Why, I wondered, and how could I get it open? Around the corner, above the tub, was a built-in linen shelf. I searched it, hoping to find a hidden lever or button like you always see in the movies. There was nothing, of course. I examined the wall itself, looking for something to hold onto. The wall was featureless except for a hole about head-high where a hook was probably hung. There was my door handle, I realized, but the hook was long gone. I needed to find something to pry the panel open. I went out into the apartment to look for a tool of some sort.

I found a serving fork in the back of one of the kitchen drawers and took it back to the bathroom. It was almost too wide to fit in the crack between the panel and the wall, but I managed to insert it enough to pry open the door. It swung open on hidden hinges to reveal a small compartment. Although the door went from floor to ceiling, the area behind it was only about four feet high. Its roof was the bottom of the shelf behind the tub. The cubby was as deep as it was high, extending to the outside wall of the building. At the far side of the recess was a ladder that disappeared through an opening in the floor. I had discovered some kind of secret passage. I wondered if Joshua knew about it. I figured he probably did.

Curiosity got the best of me, and I decided that I couldn't let my discovery go unexplored. I found something to prop open the door. Just in case it closed, I didn't want to take the chance of getting trapped in the hole. Besides, the light from the bathroom would give me some relief from the darkness below.

Not much I discovered. I crawled into the cubbyhole and looked down the hole. Even with the light from outside, I couldn't see much below the floor I was on. I turned around and let my legs dangle through the opening and peered into the darkness. "What the hell?" I said and stepped cautiously onto the ladder. The rung held my weight, and I began my descent into the abyss. About two feet below the level of the floor, I could tell that the area around me opened up. I had passed through to the third floor. Unable to see anything, I continued down the ladder. I assumed that the ladder was just a quick route from the top to the bottom floor, but, after a few more steps down, my foot scraped what turned out to be the third floor landing. Still holding onto the ladder, I tested the floor for stability. Finding it solid, I stepped off the ladder onto it. I stood still for a moment to allow my eyes to adjust to the darkness. I gathered from feeling my surroundings that I was standing in an area much like the one above. Except here, there was no shelf to obstruct my standing fully. I stood on the small landing and tried to get my bearings, but I wasn't familiar enough with the layout of the building to know what part of the third floor was below where I started. I shrugged it off and was about to continue down when a sliver of light suddenly appeared through the wall.

The shaft of light broke the darkness about waist-high on the wall to the left as I stood on the ladder. The light was shining through a gap between the planks that formed the walls. I stepped back onto the landing and crouched down, level with the crack. I put my eye to the hole and looked into the room of the newlyweds. I pulled back from the peephole, but, again, curiosity overcame my reluctance, and I peered through the opening.

I had a perfect view of their bed. A small bedside lamp provided the light that attracted my attention. I could see her in the bed. She was lying on her side with her back to me. The thin sheet clung to the curves of her body. She appeared to be alone at the moment. The sound of water running to my left made me realize that the area I was in was adjacent to their bathroom like the one above, and I assumed the one below, my room. The sound also indicated that he had gone to the bathroom. I heard him bumping the wall beside me, no doubt rehanging the hand towel on the hook there. Next, I heard the bathroom door open. At this sound, she turned my direction. The sheet pulled away from her, revealing her breasts and just a hint of the curve of her hip. My heart skipped a beat. I had never seen a naked women before. At least not really. I had seen pictures in the magazines that Uncle Nico had hidden in the top of our bathroom closet back home, but this was altogether different. She was beautiful. Her rich brown hair fell across her face as she turned, and she brushed it back. She smiled in the direction of the bathroom door. At him. She pulled herself up on her elbow. The sheet slipped farther down past her knee. I could now see she was completely naked. I felt myself flush as my eyes followed the contours of her body. My mind absorbed the vision of things I had only imagined. My heart was pounding in my chest. I was both excited and embarrassed by my invasion of her privacy, but I could not turn away.

"I'm sorry," he spoke. "I didn't mean to wake you."

"I wasn't asleep," she replied. "I was layin' here thinkin' about tomorrow."

"Baby, don't think about that now."

"I can't help it, Frankie. I don't want you to go back."

"You know I have to." The regret sounded in his voice.

"I know."

During the conversation, he had come into view. He was also naked. He sat down on the edge of the bed. She sat up and leaned against her pillow. I felt dirty trespassing on their private moment, but still I watched.

He leaned in, kissed her forehead, and said, "We still got tonight." She smiled. He put his hand behind her head and pulled her toward him. Her lips pursed to accept his kiss. It was a long and passionate kiss that obviously aroused him. Her hand found its way to his lap. He responded to her touch with a moan. I almost moaned with him. I knew I needed to go, but I couldn't pull myself away.

He lay back across the bed. His legs dangled over the side. She continued to hold him but moved up onto her knees. He caressed her hips and moved his hand between her legs. She hung her head back and sighed loud enough for me to hear her. I watched her bend down over him. Her hair fell around her and blocked my view, but I could see enough to weaken my knees. I had to sit down, but still I watched.

His hand still explored regions of her body that I had only dreamed about. She raised up from him, her body writhing against his unseen hand. He sat up and again pulled her to him. He kissed her hard on the lips, then let his mouth drift down the curve of her neck to her chest, then continued across her stomach. His lips and tongue exploring her skin as they passed. She drew her legs apart and his face disappeared between them. She raised up on her elbows, arching her back and thrusting her heaving chest into the air. My own chest heaved as I watched them.

He was now completely on the bed, on his knees, with his face still hidden. She began to moan loudly and cry his name. "Oh Frankie!" she sighed. Louder and louder, with the increased motion of his bobbing head. "Oh Frankie!" She flung her arms out to her sides and gripped the sheets on the bed. Her back was arched as she pressed herself against his hungry mouth. Her body bucked wildly. "Oh Fraaannkieee!" she cried out and collapsed onto the bed. My own body went limp.

Frankie lifted his head up and smiled at her. She smiled back. He crawled up the bed and lay down next to her. He was on his back, and she rolled to face him and lay her leg across him. Her back was to me. I sat and admired her body, while I tried to allow myself to catch my breath. In the light of the lamp, their bodies glistened with the sweat of their passion. My own body was drenched in sweat, but I still sat there in the almost stifling confines of my hiding place, mesmerized by what I saw.

They lay still, embracing each other, for a long while. I decided they were asleep, but then she stirred. She raised up on her knees and straddled him. She rocked back and forth in sync with the rhythm of his gentle thrusting. As the pace of their lovemaking increased, he began to moan. His body tensed, then he fell back against the bed. She lay down across his chest. She kissed him passionately on the mouth and rolled off onto the bed. She snuggled up to him with her head on his chest. He stretched over and switched off the lamp.

The room went black. I could no longer see them, so I turned around and leaned against the wall. I sat there in the darkness long after their lovemaking was over. My body was a bundle of raw emotion. My heart beat fiercely in my chest. My breathing was quick and labored. I needed to regain my composure before I could even attempt to climb that ladder. Even as I tried to relax, my mind worked frantically to make sense of all that I had seen. I thought of how my own fantasies had failed to live up to the reality I had just witnessed. My inexperience afforded my imagination only the basics to work with, but that night as I crouched undetected, a Peeping Tom, I got an education. The two of them had shown me things that I had barely heard of, even in the bawdy locker room recounts of my friends' sexual conquests. I was suddenly embarrassed by my naiveté and eager to explore those newly discovered pleasures for myself.

Although I was emotionally exhausted, I was more wired than ever. I had a hidden passageway to examine, so I took to the ladder and continued down. There was another landing on the second floor level, adjacent to my room. I stepped off onto it and felt around. It was identical to the one above. I wished for a flashlight. It was impossible to determine the purpose of the passage and the small landings in the dark. I pushed against the front wall of the cubicle, hoping for another doorway. There was none. It appeared that the only entrance on the upper end was through the fourth floor bathroom. I was certain there would be an opening of some sort at the other end. Wherever that might be.

When I got to the first level, I stepped off the ladder onto the floor. From the sound of snoring coming from behind the walls, I guessed that I was somewhere inside Joshua and May's apartment. Still enveloped by total darkness, I could not see the space around me, but I could tell that the area was larger than the previous three. It was wide enough for me to stretch my arms out to the sides. I stepped forward to see how deep the room was and almost tripped over a crate of what sounded like bottles or jars. Glass of some kind, anyway. Scared that the glass rattling would wake up one of the Wilsons, I froze until I was satisfied that they were still sleeping, then I crept forward. My feet brushed against several more crates, but I was careful not to make any more noise. I was sure this room would have a door to the outside, but finding it would have to wait until everyone was up.

More intrigued than ever, I pressed on. I took to the ladder again and climbed down to the basement level where the ladder terminated. I fell when my feet hit the floor at the bottom. In the dark, I didn't see it coming, and the jolt startled me. I let go of the ladder and tumbled to the floor, nearly jarring the breath out of me. The pain of my fall made it obvious that the floor beneath me was not wooden like the rest. From the texture, I concluded that it was brick. Since there was no shattering crash when I fell, I assumed it was empty of the crates of glassware.

I caught my breath and stood. Something brushed against my face, and my first image was a big spider. I swatted at the place it had touched me, but there was nothing there. I turned, and it hit me again. I jumped back and batted the air around where my head had been. My hand struck my "spider", a length of string that hung down from above. The sound of metal clinking against glass above me made me realize it was the light switch. I pulled the string, silently praying that light would follow. A small, naked bulb flicked on.

Having been in the dark for so long, my eyes squinted, even against the miniscule illumination the lone bulb provided. When I had adjusted to the change, I surveyed the room around me. It appeared to be identical in shape and size to the dimensions I had determined for the area above. Here, though, the walls and floor were brick. The ladder was at one end and the other end opened into a room of some sort. The light did not extend that far, so I could not see what was out there yet. To the left of the ladder was an opening about four feet high in the wall. It looked to be the entrance to a tunnel. I dropped to my knees and looked into it, but, again, I couldn't see more than a few feet in the dark. I decided to leave it for later and rose to investigate the outer room.

I fumbled around in the dark until I found the light switch and lit up the room. It was obviously a work room. A work bench stood just inside the doorway I had entered. It was bare, save for a basket full of corks. To the left of the table were crates of empty bottles, stacked six high against the wall. Opposite those, stacks of filled bottles lined the far wall. Directly across from the entranceway, four large barrels lay on stands along the back wall. Each had a spigot attached. It was a bottling operation. That was obvious, but for what, I had no idea.

Although I didn't know what it was until later, my answer lay in the contraption that occupied the far corner. It was a large, copper kettle, now green with age, attached to a couple of smaller pots by a series of pipes and a spiral of copper tubing. These were set on racks above a fire pit, and the whole lot of it was sheltered by a sheet metal hood which was attached to a stove pipe that disappeared through a hole in the ceiling. It was an odd-looking thing, and I had no clue what it might be.

After a moment, I turned from the metal monstrosity and looked around the room. I thought to myself that the hidden passage couldn't be the only way into the room. I wondered about the tunnel off the alcove, but I couldn't be sure if it even went anywhere, until I explored it. With that in mind, I surveyed the room around me for the door to the outside. I found it, almost hidden behind the stacks of bottles in the corner. I tried the knob, hoping it would not be locked. After a slight hesitation, it turned, and the door swung open to reveal the backside of the furnace. The area outside the door was a space just wide enough for a man to squeeze through. When I stepped out to look around the furnace into the room beyond, the door swung shut behind me. I turned to reopen it but could not. The panel that was the outside of the door blended into the wall around it. Had I not known there was a door there, I never would have seen it, and, because concealment was the goal, the outer surface had no doorknob. I pushed against the door to no avail. I examined the wall around it for a lever, a switch, or something to open it, but it apparently only opened from the inside. I was locked out. I was disappointed that I could not explore the tunnel, but I wasn't about to go to the top and climb back down again. The tunnel would just have to wait.

My mind was abuzz with a thousand questions, and I was anxious for the answers. What were they bottling? Why had they gone to such lengths to hide it all? Who were they? I wondered if Joshua had something to do with it, but, somehow, I doubted that. Hopefully, he might be able to shed some light on the situation, anyway. I resigned myself to having to wait for the answers, squeezed around the furnace, and headed for the stairs.

After I had returned to the fourth floor to lock everything up, I went to my room to get some sleep. Fatigue was finally creeping up on me, and, although it was morning, I decided it was time to call it a night. I had to shut the curtains to block out the rising sun, so I moved the fan across the room where it would blow across the bed. I stripped naked again and fell across the bed. I was asleep almost instantly.

Chapter Eleven

I *was home. In Aunt Liz and Uncle Nico's apartment. I am in the bathroom, sitting naked on the edge of the bathtub. One of Nico's magazines lies open on the floor in front of me. I look down at the woman in the picture there. It is my favorite one. The redhead. She is so beautiful. Posed on her knees on the bed, she holds her long red hair on top of her head with both hands. Her breasts pushed forward by the curve of her back. Below, a fold in the green silk sheet covers her most private place. I long to see it. I absentmindedly drop my hand between my own legs. I close my eyes and imagine her here with me. The excitement swells in me.*

"You like to watch, don't you?" The voice startles me.

I open my eyes, embarrassed that I have been caught, but there is no one there. I look down the picture. The image has changed. The face that looks back at me now is that of the young bride upstairs in Wixton.

Suddenly, the bathroom disappears, and I am in the room in the inn with her. She is posed like the picture, but alive in front of me. "You like to watch, don't you?" she repeats. "It's okay. Frankie won't mind. He's off playin' soldier somewhere."

I stand and start toward her. She quickly pulls the sheet up in front of her and says, "No. No. You can look, but you can't touch. I'd much rather see you touch yourself, again." I flush with embarrassment. "Don't be embarrassed. Frankie won't do that in front of me. He says he don't do it. But I know he does. All men do. I got four brothers, and I know how y'all act." I say nothing. She continues, "Most women do, too, though they won't own up to it. Ain't lady-like to play with yourself, is it?" I do not respond. She holds the sheet away from her body and lets it fall. "But a woman has needs. Her husband off soldierin' and all." She lays back across the bed and begins to rub her hands across the swell of her belly and below. I start toward her again. She stops and wags her finger at me. "I said you could watch but nothin' else, so go over there and sit down. I know you wanna watch. I know you was watchin' Frankie and me that night. I liked it." I am dumbfounded by her revelation and her total lack of inhibition. I do as she says and sit and watch.

Then:

I am alone, but I am no longer in the bedroom. I am back in the darkness of the hidden passage. I am crouched on the small landing peering through the crack in the wall again. She and Frankie are gone now, though. Instead, I am watching Jenny and T. Their naked bodies glisten with sweat. I want her. I tremble with anger and jealousy, but I am shocked and intrigued by the sharp contrast of his dark skin against the whiteness of her own. I watch. Over and over again, they reenact the scenes of the newlyweds. Again and again, she screams his name. I yearn for her to scream my name.

"You pervert!" Billy Watson says behind me. I spin around to face him, but he is gone.

"You okay in there, Eddie?" Aunt Liz asks.

"Yes, ma'am," I reply.

"You been in there a long time," she worries.

"I'm fine, Aunt Liz," I answer.

I am back in the bathroom where I started. The beautiful redhead stares up at me from the magazine on the floor. She smiles a knowing smile as I discover the stickiness in my hand. I clean myself off with a towel from the hamper, then put my clothes back on. I put the magazine back in its hiding place until next time, and I flush the toilet to uphold the pretense.

I turn the knob to leave, and the room dissolves around me. I am now in the middle of a desert. For as far as I can see, there is nothing but sand. The sun beats down on my bare head. I do not know where I am, so I pick a direction and walk. For days and days, I walk through the desert. My tongue is swollen from thirst, but I do not die. I continue to walk. I pass a skeleton lying bleached white in the sand. It is holding a newspaper in its bony hand. I pick up the paper and read the headline. "What You Standing Here For? This Guy's Dead" it says. I throw it down and try to scream, but my tongue won't cooperate. I walk on.

Miles of endless sand surround me. I am about to give up hope when I see it. An orange tree. In the middle of the desert there is a single orange tree loaded with ripe fruit. Unmoved by the absurdity of the idea, I run to the tree and grab an orange. I fall to my knees as I tear through the rind and suck viscously at the juice inside.

"That'll be a dollar, mister." A girl about nine or ten in a white cotton dress stands beside me. "It's a dollar an orange. Yes, sir. Out here in the desert, it's a dollar an orange." I tell her that I have no money. "Pervert!" she screams and runs off across the sand.

I am confused by her reaction, but I am too thirsty to care. I grab another orange from the tree... and another... and another. The acidic juice stings my parched mouth, but still I lap at it like a stray dog until I am satiated. I collapse against the trunk of the tree in the shade to rest. My face and hands are sticky from the oranges.

After a while, I see a dark spot shimmering in the heat against the horizon. I watch it grow larger as the distance between us narrows. Before long, I can tell that it is a taxi cab, speeding across the sand. It screeches to a stop in front of me. The driver is a burly man in a stained t-shirt and a red stocking cap. He rolls down the window and calls out to me, "You Sam Chance's boy?" I nod. "What the hell you doin' out here? Get in. I'll give you a ride back to the city."

"I don't have any money," I tell him.

"Hell, this one's on me, kid," he offers. "Sammy and me go way back. Damn shame what happened to him." I nod, sadly.

"Sorry, kid," he apologizes. "Didn't mean to open up old wounds."

"It's okay," I let him off the hook as I climb into the back seat.

"You still live at Nico Barboni's place up in the Bronx?"

He pulls away from the tree and starts across the sand. We drive a few feet, and the desertscape *dissolves. I find myself sitting in traffic on the Triborough Bridge, looking out across the East River. Horns honk and brakes squeal around us. I remember why I don't miss the city.*

We ride the rest of the way to the Bronx without speaking, until we pull up in front of Liz and Nico's apartment building.

"Here we are, kid. Home sweet home," the driver announces.

"Thanks," I say as I start to get out of the cab.

"I am sorry about what happened to Sammy," he says.

"Thanks," I repeat and step out.

I shut the door of the cab and turn toward the apartment building, but I turn to face the front of the Wixton Inn. I am back in Wixton. I have come full circle. I shrug and go inside.

Billy Watson and his two henchmen are waiting for me there. Watson meets me half-way across the floor. His goons follow soon after.

"What do you want, Billy?" I demand.

"Shut up!" he growls. "I'll ask the questions? Where have you been?"

"You wouldn't believe me if I told you," I suggest, "but it's none of your business, anyway!"

"Everything's my business."

"What do you want? I'm tired, and I don't feel like dealing with you."

"You're under arrest, Chance."

"For what?"

"Because I don't like you."

"You can't arrest me for that."

"My town. My rules."

"Carl won't stand for this."

"Carl," he spit the word out with contempt, "can't help you anymore."

Before I can say anymore, the two henchmen grab me by the arms. Billy punches me hard in the stomach and my knees buckle. He backhands me across the face, drawing blood. I spit at him, and he slams me across the back of the head with the butt of his pistol.

"You son-of-a-bitch," I manage to say.

He brings the gun down again, harder than before. The pain is intense. My vision dissolves with a blinding flash, and the world goes black.

I awoke with a gasp instead of a scream. That at least was an improvement, but not much. When I finally came back to myself, I realized that I was on all fours on the bed. The jolt that woke me up must have brought me to my knees. I took slow and deliberate breaths, hoping to ward off hyperventilation. My heart beat heavily in my chest, and my sweat-drenched body shivered with the wind from the fan. I lay back down and pulled the sheet up over me.

The room was partially lit by the light seeping in around the curtains. I looked at my watch on the bedside table and groaned. I had only been asleep a little over an hour. I cursed Billy Watson under my breath, buried my head under my pillow to block out the light, and quickly went back to sleep. I dreamed no more.

Chapter Twelve

Just after one in the afternoon, my eyes opened again. I was on my stomach, and I lay there looking across the surface of the bed at tiny particles of dust that danced in a shaft of light breaking through between the curtains. I could have stayed there all day, but my bladder screamed for me to get up. I obliged and crossed the room to the bathroom and relief.

After I peed, I examined the wall beside the tub. Nothing unusual showed from the outside. Nothing indicated that there was a hidden passageway behind the wall. I pulled on the coat hook that hung there and tried to pry the planks apart in the corner, but I came to the same conclusion as I had the night before. The only entrances to the hidden area were the bathroom upstairs, the door behind the furnace, probably the tunnel, and, most likely, somewhere in Joshua and May's apartment. I was anxious to get back downstairs and see where that tunnel went, but, first, I had to talk to Joshua. I wondered again if he knew about the passageway and the hidden chambers. I assumed he must, since he had lived in the building for so many years. How could he not?

I dressed quickly and headed out for the lobby. I was eager to talk to Joshua, and I was famished. I selfishly hoped that May would have something for me. Going to the diner would take too much time. I still had a ton of work to do, and I had a tunnel to explore.

I was somewhat embarrassed to see Frankie and his wife standing at the desk. He was once again in his dress greens, and she wore an unassuming tan dress with a belt that hid the beautiful body beneath it. Her hair was pulled back and tied with a simple white ribbon. I blushed uncontrollably when her eyes found mine, and she smiled. She knows, I thought to myself, although I knew she couldn't really. I was just ashamed of myself.

Joshua was talking to them when I reached the bottom of the stairs. I sat down to wait for them to leave.

"Goin' back to Benning, son?" he asked Frankie.

"Yes, sir."

"What 'bout you, little lady?"

"Goin' home I guess," she answered, with more than a little sadness in her voice.

"Where's home?"

"Arlington," she replied. "My daddy runs a store down there."

"Nice little town," Joshua commented.

"I guess," she reluctantly agreed. "Won't feel much like home anymore, though."

"I suppose not, sweetheart," Joshua acknowledged. "I suppose not."

Joshua thanked them for their business, and they had gathered up their things to leave when May appeared through the apartment door with a package bundled up in a multicolored scarf.

"Wait," she called after them. She offered the package to the young bride. "A wedding gift," she explained. "It ain't much. Just a tin of cookies and a jar of fig preserves. I hope you like them."

"That's very kind of you, but you didn't have to," the young woman thanked her.

"I wanted to," May replied and gave her a short hug. "Good luck," she added.

"Thank you," they both said.

Frankie pulled his duffle bag onto his shoulder and took her suitcase in his other hand. She clutched the gift to her chest and fought back the tears that welled in her eyes. They thanked them again for the hospitality and the gift, then disappeared through the front door.

"Such a lovely couple," May commented. Then, she, too, disappeared through her own door.

Joshua and I both nodded. He said, "It'll be a lot more quiet around now, I 'spect."

"Yes, sir," I agreed.

He turned back to me and asked, "You been 'sleep all this time? You came in awful early last night."

I shook my head and replied, "I couldn't sleep when I came in. I spent the night moving boxes downstairs."

"You moved that junk all night?"

"Until about four, I guess."

"Well, hell, boy, no wonder you slept all mornin'!" he observed. I just smiled. "You get it all done?"

"No," I replied. "I got sidetracked."

"Sidetracked?" he wondered. "By what?"

He sat and listened while I recounted my exploration. He was very interested in my description of the room in the basement and the apparatus in the corner. When I was done, he scratched his chin and said, "I'll be damned. Ol' Henry had himself a still."

"What?" I was puzzled.

"A still," he repeated. I shrugged. "For makin' shine," he tried to explain." I shook my head, still not getting it. He continued, "Shine? Moonshine? Whiskey? That big contraption with the pots and all that is a whiskey still. Apparently, Henry was a bootlegger. Must have started makin' shine when prohibition hit."

As Joshua explained it, I remembered Zachary Brewster talking about "bootleg whiskey" and "moonshine" on the drive down from Macon. I had nodded, but I hadn't really understood much of what he was talking about.

When Joshua finished his explanation, he said, "Well, son, let's get a look at this still of yours."

I laughed and replied, "I guess I'll have to go up and climb down the ladder from the top, because the door downstairs only opens from the inside."

"Didn't you say that there was a way in through our place in there?"

"Seemed to be," I acknowledged, "but I didn't check for a door, because I didn't want to wake you."

"Well, there ain't no need for you to hafta climb all the way up there and back down again. Let's see if we can find that door." He motioned for me to follow him. "Where 'bouts were you last night?"

"I'm not sure where I was in relation to what we see out here," I responded, "but the landings on the upper floors are off the bathrooms. It takes up the dead space beside the tub."

He twisted his mouth to the side and studied the room around us. Finally, he said, "I hate to admit it, but I get disoriented inside a buildin'. I can't tell east for Egypt indoors. You'd think I'd be able to match where we are to what's above us, but damned if I know. I was hopin' you would."

I laughed, "I'm no better than you as far as that goes. All I can tell you is that, when I got to this floor, I could hear somebody snoring."

"Well, you couldn't have been too far from the bedroom, then. May snores loud, but not that loud." He winked at me.

"What lie you tellin' 'bout me?" May called out from the kitchen where she was sitting. "Now, Eddie don't you be listenin' to all that nonsense. I have to stuff cotton in my ears to get a moment's peace at night!" We all laughed.

"Anyway," Joshua continued, "you were close to the bedroom, the way I figure it. Since the door was in the bathroom upstairs, it stands to reason it probably is down here, too. The bathroom's on the same side of the buildin'."

"You sure?" May taunted.

"Hush up, woman!" he scolded, playfully.

The bathroom was in the very back of the house, through the bedroom. I followed him into the tiny room to search for the entrance to the storage closet I had been in the night before, but the layout of this room did not lend itself to the concealment of hidden passages. It was a perfect rectangle. There was no alcove for the tub, which sat on clawed feet in one corner of the room. There was no linen closet, just a freestanding shelf stacked with folded towels in another corner. The toilet occupied yet another corner, and the sink hung on the wall beside it.

"Devil if I know," Joshua conceded, coming to the same conclusion I had. "Thattun upstairs may be the only way in from the outside." I agreed. "Don't make no sense, though. That'd mean somebody hauled them crates of bottles you mentioned up that ladder for no reason."

"Why?" I asked.

"Well, from the description of the operation downstairs, Henry was cookin' shine for more'n just himself. He had obviously set himself up as a supplier. He probably had buyers all over the county and then some. With all his friends in high places, he wouldn't have too much fear of goin' down for bootleggin', but still just enough respect for the possibility to warrant all the secret passages and what have you. He couldn't break the law right out in the open, so he built the set-up you stumbled into. That tunnel of yours likely leads to the garage out back. All the big money orders were carried through the tunnel and loaded on trucks, or the trunks of cars more than likely, parked inside the garage. Cars drive in and out at night, and nobody's the wiser.

"Now all this is pure speculation, but I'd bet money on it. Henry was a resourceful rascal. I can tell you that. That was why it was so surprisin' when he lost his mind after the crash. He'da been back on top quicker than most, if he'd stuck it out.

"At any rate, the big money came in and out the back door, so to speak, but I've no doubt money changed hands across the counter out front on occasion. That's where the hidden closet comes in. Once word got around that there was whiskey to be had, and it would get around, I assure you, there'd be a lot of individuals wantin' to make small purchases. So the desk man would have a stash for sale to the registered guests and the occasional walk-in client. Strictly small potatoes. Certainly nothin' you'd want to jeopardize the big money for. You wouldn't want to have to run down to the basement every time a buyer stopped by. That would increase the risk for detection of the still, besides wearin' out the poor runner. So, you'd need a stash up here, but you would keep it out of the normal places. Even hidden in a closet or a cabinet, it'd be too risky if the revenuers came to call, as I'm sure they did. They'd find it, and that'd be all she wrote, but, if you had your supply hidden in a secret room, that'd be a different story. If your room was hidden good enough, as this one apparently is, the revenuers would leave empty handed, scratchin' their heads.

"So you haul a few cases up the ladder and stack 'em on that little landing you found. When a customer came by, the desk clerk would skeddadle back here, get his stuff, and carry it back out to him in a plain brown bag. Cash on the counter. Everybody's happy." He concluded his supposition with a shrug, then added, "We could stand here all day and argue the existence of the damn thing, but that don't get us any closer to findin' it."

I agreed and was about to offer to climb the ladder from the top again, but I asked, "What's on the other side of this wall?"

"Kitchen," he replied. "The pantry actually." The idea must have struck him about the time it hit me, because we both took out for the kitchen.

The pantry was a huge walk-in closet lined on all four walls with shelves. The shelves, which May had packed with cans and jars, started just below the ceiling and continued to about three feet above the floor.

"It's gotta be in here somewhere," Joshua mused.

"Must be."

The shelving looked pretty solid, not designed to move, but we were sure the door was there. I dropped to my knees and began to examine the wall beneath the shelves. I was on my second pass when I found the latch hidden behind one of the shelf brackets. I pulled the small lever, and a short section of the wall swung back into the hidden room. I bent to crawl in, but Joshua stopped me. He disappeared through the pantry door and returned with a flashlight. I took the light and went in. He crawled in behind me, and I helped him to his feet.

With the flashlight, I was able to find the string to turn on the small light above. The bulb was good and lit the area and its contents. The contents consisted of several crates of whiskey bottles and a stack of empty crates. An old ledger stood on one of the cross beams in the wall. Joshua picked up the book and sent a cloud of dust billowing into the air.

He scanned a few pages and said, "Lots of familiar names here. Lots of locals. Most of them repeat business, from the frequency of the entries. Henry had quite a clientele."

"I never realized stuff like this really went on, and I certainly didn't know it was such a big business," I admitted.

"Quickest way to make somethin' sell is to make it illegal to own it. Everybody wants a piece of somethin' they ain't supposed to have."

"I guess you're right," I acknowledged. "You want to climb down and see the rest of it?"

"I want to see the still," he said, "but, with these knees of mine, you know I can't climb down that ladder. I'll leave that to a young jack rabbit like yourself. I'll go down the cellar stairs and come in by the furnace door. You shimmy down the ladder and open 'er up."

"Okay," I said and climbed down.

"You got quite a bit of them boxes down here," he said, when I let him in the door.

"Yeah," I replied, "until I found all this." I swept my arm around the room.

He looked around and exclaimed, "Woowee! This is some set up! Looks like Henry was cookin' shine for half the state of Georgia." He walked around the still and the work table. He found another ledger that listed all the bulk-order customers. He tucked it under his arm and said, "This'n here and that'n upstairs'll make for some interestin' reading', I 'spect." He went to the barrels at the side of the room and picked up a tin ladle that hung on a nail beside them. He opened the spigot of one barrel and caught some whiskey in the bowl of the ladle. He lifted it up and smelled the liquid, then took a drink. He emptied the ladle and let out a sigh. "Damn, that's smooth. I don't think I've had a drink that good from a store-bought bottle." He held the ladle out to me and offered, "Take a swig."

"I don't think so," I declined.

"Suit yourself," he shrugged, ran a little more out of the barrel, and drank it down. "You sure you don't wanna taste?"

I nodded and asked, "What will you do now? Call the sheriff?"

"I suppose that's the right thing to do. And the smart one, I guess. I wouldn't want somebody else to stumble across this stuff and charge me with moonshinin'. I'll call Besmer Monday mornin' and let him come in here and haul this stuff off."

"Monday?"

"Yeah, he's outta town 'til then. I heard down at the hardware store this mornin' that he got called to Atlanta for some kind of meetin'. Lester Kirkland, he runs the five-and-dime, said he'd heard that sheriffs from all over the state were called up to meet with the governor 'bout somethin', but he couldn't say 'bout what. All that may or may not be true. That bunch of coots that hang out at the hardware store gossip worse than women, but I did talk to Lenora at the courthouse. She didn't say why, but she did confirm that the sheriff had left town early this mornin' and said he'd be back sometime Monday."

I was worried about the prospect of two days without the sheriff around to keep the reins on Billy. I was hopeful that I could avoid him altogether. With Carl out of town, I was sure Billy would be too busy to bother with me. Maybe.

"I'll call then," Joshua continued. "That'll give me time to draw off a bottle or two, or a case, of this." He patted the top of the nearest barrel. He explained, "For special occasions and the like. I'd hate to have all this good whiskey go to waste without somebody gettin' to enjoy it. That somebody might as well be me." We both laughed.

"Why go to the trouble to bottle more with all these already poured up?" I wondered. "Wouldn't it all be the same?"

"No," he replied, "even if it came from the same batch, what's in the bottles wouldn't be near as good as this here. You ever hear people say wine gets better with age? Well, the same holds true of hard liquor, but the process is a little different. Wine ages in the bottle. The longer it sits, the better it tastes. That what they say, anyway. But whiskey don't work like that. You put whiskey in a bottle, and it is what it is. You have to leave whiskey in the barrel to age it, and this here shine has been sittin' down here untouched for over thirty years. Like I said before, this is the best whiskey I've ever tasted, so I'm gonna save me some of it. But that can wait. Where is that tunnel?"

I lead him to the alcove where the ladder descended and the tunnel began. He bent down, looked in and said, "Dark, ain't it?"

"That's why I didn't try it last night," I explained.

"No tellin' what might be down that dark hole."

"I know."

"Well, you got some light now." He indicated the flashlight I had stuck in my back pocket. "You wanna see if it goes where I think it does?"

"You bet," I said eagerly. I switched on the light in my hand and dropped to my knees before the opening. "I'll be back."

With that, I crawled into the mouth of the tunnel. My progress was slow, because it was awkward crawling with the flashlight in my hand. Also, I had to stop after about twenty feet in to rest my knees from the beating they were taking from the brick floor.

"Eddie!" Joshua's voice echoed down the shaft. "You all right in there?"

"Yeah," I called back, "just resting my legs."

"You find anything yet?"

"Cobwebs," I answered. "I'm going to crawl a little farther. See what I can see."

The end of the tunnel was another thirty or so feet beyond where I had stopped. The ceiling at the terminus rose out of sight, and a ladder extended into the darkness above. A small, wheeled cart rested in the corner. From the coil of rope that sat on top of it, I assumed it had been used to pull the cases of whiskey through the tunnel. I crawled up and leaned against the wall beside it, resting my knees before I tried to stand. I pushed against the cart and found that it rolled smoothly even after all those years.

I swept the light around the area above me. Unlike the tunnel, the roof here was wooden. A hinged door centered the ceiling. Two large slide bolts held it closed.

"Eddie, you still with us?" Joshua called.

"Yes," I yelled back. "I found the exit."

"Where'd it come out?"

"I'm not sure yet. I found a trap door, but I haven't opened it up yet."

"Let me know when you do."

I propped the flashlight against the wall beside the ladder and climbed up to the door. The panel was hinged to open downward, so I slid back the bolts and let it swing open. The opening it left was covered with metal grate. Above that I could see the underside of a car bumper and the ceiling of the building that housed it. I tried the grate. It gave to a push and rose out of the frame that held it. I shoved it to the side and climbed all the way out. A blue and white Biscayne hardtop sat in the garage where I emerged. The Wilson's car, I assumed.

The car jogged my memory, and I leaned over the hole and called out to Joshua. I had to call several times before he heard me. I told him where I was and about the car, and he confirmed that I was in their garage. With that mystery solved, I climbed back down the ladder and pulled the grate back into place. After I secured the trapdoor, I climbed to the floor of the tunnel and crawled back to where Joshua waited.

"Any problems?" Joshua asked as he helped me to my feet.

"Other than killing my knees, " I replied, "No."

"You say there's a trapdoor that leads up to the garage?" he asked. "Comes out under that drain grate in the floor, don't it?"

"Yes, sir," I replied.

"I'll be," he commented. "I've always wondered why there was a drain in the garage floor."

"The metal grate covers the trapdoor. The door itself can only be opened from the bottom. It's latched shut." I told him about the cart, and he agreed with my theory of its use.

He stepped back into the bottling room and looked around. After a moment, he shook his head and said, "I can't believe that all this has been down here all these years, and I didn't know it. I 'spect the folks in town that did know it was down here are few and far between."

"What about all the local people that you saw in the ledger upstairs? They knew," I suggested.

"Probably not," he supposed. "All they knew was that this was the place to get a bottle of hooch. They probably even figured that Henry had a still somewhere, but I doubt they knew where it was. Henry was too smart for that. Kept 'em guessin', I'd bet."

"That makes sense."

"Well, now that that's over with, what're your plans for the rest of the day?" he asked.

"I guess I finish my moving," I replied.

"You ain't gotta waste your day like that."

"I don't have that much more. I can knock it out pretty quick."

"Suit yourself," he conceded. "You ain't had anything to eat today have you?" I shook my head. "Well, let's go on up and see if we can't rustle up some grub for you. We can't be havin' you workin' on an empty stomach, can we?"

"I am hungry," I admitted, "but I don't want to put you to any trouble."

"Ain't no trouble, son. When you gonna get that through that head of yours? Now come on. Before we go, I want to prop this here door open so I can get back in without havin' to climb that ladder." I pushed a short stack of bottle crates over in front of the door, then he lead the way upstairs.

After May had fed me two generous platefuls of fried chicken and potato salad, Joshua asked me to move everything from the room behind the pantry down to the basement. I made quick work of that and headed for the fourth floor. Joshua stayed in the basement and set about his bottling. He said he'd get me to move his private supply into the room when he got it poured up.

Because of the beating my knees had gotten from all the crawling, the stairs were a little harder to climb, but I was able to get the last of the boxes moved down by about eight o'clock. When the final box was dropped in place, I went back to the distilling room and carried Joshua's whiskey upstairs to his hiding place. He had decided on two cases. He said that as little as he drank, those sixteen bottles would last him the rest of his life and then some.

I stopped by the Wilson's apartment on my back to my room to let Joshua know that I had finished. He thanked me and offered to dance at my wedding. I laughed at that. It was suppertime, and May tried to feed me, of course. I declined and explained that I wanted to get out for a little while, so I was going to grab some food at the diner. Maybe visit with Janie, if she was there that late. May wrinkled her nose at the mention of diner food, but she didn't try to argue. We said our goodnights, and I went up to take a quick shower.

Chapter Thirteen

The diner was busier than I had expected it to be at ten o'clock. Friday night, I guessed. Janie and another waitress were busy tending to several groups of customers that sat about the diner. Janie looked up and smiled when I came through the door. The other girl looked my way and grinned. She was a pretty girl, about twenty-one, twenty-two. She had her blond hair pulled up in a bun with a pencil stuck down through it.

"Evenin', stranger," Janie called out and waved me toward the counter. "I'll be with you in a jiffy."

I took a stool at the counter next to an old man who sat reading the newspaper and nursing a beer. He looked up at me and nodded when I sat down, then flicked the ashes from the stub of a cigar that sat in the corner of his mouth.

Janie soon appeared around the end of the counter. She stopped in front of Mr. Cigar and asked, "You ready for another beer, sweetie?"

"You know two's my limit."

"Piece of pie?"

"No, ma'am. I reckon I ought to be gettin' on to the house. It's gettin' close to my bedtime." He drained the last of the beer from the glass in front of him and threw some money on the counter next to the empty mug. "Keep the change, baby," he said as he stood to leave.

"Thank you, honey," Janie called after him. "You come back now!"

"You know I will." He threw up his hand and was out the door.

Janie came down to me. "I was 'bout to think you had left town on me, but I was sure you wouldn't have took off without stoppin' by to say goodbye."

"I'm still around," I stated the obvious. "I've actually been busy."

"Yeah, I heard you was cleanin' out the old Kenlow place for Joshua."

I grinned. Small town grapevine. "Yeah," I confirmed. "It was quite a job."

"I talked to T this mornin'. I stopped by out there to check on Miss Grace, and he said you were under the weather last night. Everything all right?"

"Yeah," I said, then lied. "Just tired last night, I guess. Too much work and not enough sleep."

"He said y'all had been out fishin' the night before 'til all hours. Well, anyway, I'm glad to hear you're okay," she said. "You in for dessert? We got some hot apple pie. Max just took 'em out the oven."

"Maybe later," I decided, "but I want to start with a hamburger."

"On a bun this time," she laughed. "The bread truck finally came. Fries? Water again?"

"Coke."

"Will do." She scribbled it all down on her order pad and dropped the slip on the ledge of the small window that led to the kitchen. "Ticket down!"

Max appeared in the window, scooped up the paper in a shovel of a hand, then disappeared again. Less than a minute later, he reappeared to set a plate of food in the window. "Karen! Order up!" he yelled and was gone again.

The other waitress retrieved the plate from the window and hurried off to deliver it. She returned shortly and whispered something to Janie that made her frown and look past me into the room behind.

Janie stood from the huddle and called out to a lone man who was standing to leave. She said, "Evenin', Sim. You callin' it a night?" He mumbled something I didn't understand. She continued, "Chloe still down to Preston at her mama's?"

"Been two weeks," he admitted.

"Gettin' a might lonely, I suppose," Janie guessed. She elbowed the girl beside her softly in the ribs. They giggled. Sim blushed beet red, then hurried toward the door. "Come back now!" Janie invited as the screen door slammed shut.

The other waitress shook her head and said, "Ought to be ashamed of himself. With his wife gone to see 'bout her sick mama."

"He ought to be glad you told me and not your daddy," Janie stated. "He'd a done more than embarrass him."

"That's for sure," the girl agreed. "Now you gonna introduce me to your friend here?"

"Karen, this is Eddie Chance. Eddie, this is Karen, Max's daughter.

"Pleased to meet you," she said, extending her hand.

"Likewise," I replied, taking it.

Karen was Max's youngest daughter, I found out. Her three older sisters had married and moved away. She was a junior at the university but was home for the summer. She was cute, but I had already sworn off one girl. I didn't need another. Besides, Janie mentioned that Karen had a boyfriend back in Athens. A football player.

The three of us made small talk while I waited for my food. Occasionally, one or the other of them would dart off to help a customer.

"Janie! Order up!" Max yelled and sat my hamburger in the window. He looked the situation over and said, "Karen, you gonna stand around all night jawin'? How 'bout refillin' the table setups."

"Yes, sir," she huffed. "I guess I gotta get back to work. See ya around?" She bent under the counter and came out with a basket that held giant containers of salt and pepper and a bundle of paper napkins.

Janie set my plate in front of me. "Don't mind him," she nodded toward the kitchen. "He's a bit overprotective of his baby girl." She reached beneath the counter and pulled out a bottle of ketchup. "Enjoy." She set the bottle down and went out to check on her other customers, leaving me to eat my supper.

The food was as good as I remembered it to be. Not as good as May's home cooking, of course, but still very good. About halfway through the meal, Karen came by and refilled the glass I had emptied. I thanked her with a smile that she acknowledged with a wink and a smile of her own.

"My pleasure," she said, leaned against the counter, and dropped her voice to whisper. "Sorry 'bout Daddy. He still thinks I'm a child. Thinks I need protectin'." She nodded toward the kitchen. "He'd probably shit a brick if he knew I wasn't still a virgin!"

I nearly choked on the bite of hamburger in my mouth. I coughed and drank down the remainder of the Coke she'd poured me, trying to regain my composure.

She reached across the counter and hit me on the back and said, "You okay? I didn't mean to shock you. It's just that he makes me so damn mad sometimes. Thinks I can't take care of myself. Thinks every boy that talks to me is tryin' to get in my pants, and I don't have sense enough to keep my knees together. Sends me off on some bullshit job to get me away from you." She shook her head in disgust, then continued, "Like he thought I was just gonna hike up my skirt and straddle you right here at the counter!"

I was stunned by her bluntness, but I had to smile. "He means well," I defended. "At least he loves you."

"Yeah, I know," she nodded. "He could be one of those fathers that don't give a damn. I just wish he didn't worry so much."

"At least you have a father to worry about you." I let the statement hang in the air without explanation. Small town being what it was, I figured she would find out about me sooner or later, if she didn't already know.

She nodded, "I guess you're right. I should be thankful. Another Coke?"

"Please."

She refilled my glass again and went off to tend to her other customers. I looked up at the kitchen window. I nearly fell off the stool when I came across Max's face framed in the opening. I was worried for a moment until a smile spread across his stern face. He mouthed, "Thank you."

I nodded and returned his smile. He tipped his cook's hat to me and disappeared from the window. I sat there and wondered how much of the conversation he had heard. More than Karen would have wanted, I was sure.

I shrugged it off and finished the last of my hamburger. I pushed the empty plate away and took a long swallow from my glass. I turned around on the stool and leaned back against the counter to look around the room. As I watched Karen clear the empty dishes from a vacant table, the picture of her straddling me at the counter flashed through my mind. I smiled again at the thought, but quickly pushed it from my head. I already had enough images to deal with. I didn't need any more.

I sat for a long time and watched the other patrons. Nearly all of them had long since finished eating and were just talking amongst themselves. One table was playing cards. With the departure of Mr. Cigar and Sim the Cheat, I was the only lone diner. Most of the crowd was the same as when I arrived. Several people had left, but only one group had come in while I was eating.

A quartet of teenagers had taken up residence in the big corner booth. They were each eating a piece of Max's apple pie and seemed to be having the time of their lives. The boys were trying hard to impress their dates with their masculinity, and the girls giggled and whispered. The whole group laughed and joked with each other, completely oblivious to what was going on around them.

Although they couldn't have been more than a couple of years younger than me, I felt decades removed from them. The events of the past couple of years had aged me beyond my years and had separated me from them by a chasm of experience. They, no doubt, had homes to go back to and parents that loved them and took care of them. Of course, I had family, but a terminally depressed aunt and a perpetually drunk uncle, who hated my guts, were a far cry from loving, caring parents; my home was the road or wherever I chose to lay my head.

I longed for the stability that they most certainly had, and I was beginning to wonder if I would ever have it again. I had started to believe that I was destined to drift through life alone and wandering, with no place that I could or would call my own.

"...sweet potato."

"What?" I asked, shaken from my musing.

"I was just askin' if you was ready for that pie now? We got apple, of course, and sweet potato. You want a piece?" Janie explained when she had my attention.

"Apple," I accepted.

"Ice cream?"

"That would be nice."

" 'Specially with this heat," she said as she cut a slice from the apple pie that sat beneath the glass dome at the end of the counter. She added a scoop of vanilla ice cream from a small freezer in the corner. "Here you go, sugar."

Karen plopped down on the stool next to me. "Man, I'm beat," she sighed. "I wish these folks would hurry up and leave, so we can go." She and Janie explained that on Friday and Saturday nights, Max kept the place open until the last customer left, and they were both ready to call it a night.

While they waited, we sat at the counter and talked. After a while with no new orders, Max shut down the grill and joined us, so we moved from the counter to a table. Janie had been right. Max was a pretty nice fellow. Although I was sure I had helped my cause during my conversation with Karen earlier, he seemed genuinely interested in the stories I told. More than once, a hint of fatherly concern played across his face as I told them about my life. Although she had never indicated that she knew anything of my past, Janie did not seem at all surprised by my narrative. I assumed that T had already told her most of what I was saying. She, as well as Karen and Max, expressed sorrow over the losses that I had endured. At some point Karen reached across the table and put her hand on her father's. I think she appreciated what I had said earlier, since she learned the truth behind my words.

About ten to midnight, the last of the crowd, the four love birds, decided to head home. The girls waited by the door while their dates took care of the bill. From the conversation the boys were having while they waited for Janie to ring them up, I concluded that they were brothers, and the younger of the two was on his first date. Their dates were the older brother's girlfriend and her cousin from Albany. The younger brother had been enlisted to accompany the visiting cousin so that the girlfriend could come. He admitted after Janie had given them their change that he'd had a good time.

Max followed them to the door and locked it behind them. He turned back toward me and asked, "You don't mind if I lock up, do you? If I don't lock it while I got the chance, somebody else is bound to wander in, and I'll be stuck here all night." He came back to the table and sat down next to me. He glanced over his shoulder at Karen, who was clearing the dishes from the big booth. He leaned in and said, "Thanks again for what you said to Karen while ago. She thinks I'm meddlin', but I can't help worrin' about her."

"She knows you care about her. She just wants you to realize she's an adult."

"She's got a mind of her own. That's for sure. Got that much of her mama in 'er," he acknowledged. "That's probably why I worry so much. She's always been one to jump before lookin'. Been known to stir up a hornet's nest for the hell of it, too. I just hate to see her get hurt."

"Sometimes you just have to let your children make their own mistakes," I suggested. "We appreciate the advice a lot more if we ask for it, rather than having it thrown at us."

"How old d'you say you are?" he laughed. He pushed back from the table and said, "I'd better help them get the place buttoned up for the night. I think we're all ready to get outta here. It shouldn't take long to wash up the last of the dishes and sweep up. You can stay as long as we stay, if you like, and help yourself to another piece of that pie. Whatever's left will just go to waste. I make 'em fresh every day."

"Don't mind if I do," I accepted. I went to the counter and cut myself a generous piece of the apple pie, and he disappeared into the kitchen.

After a while, I began to feel guilty watching them work, so I volunteered to help put the chairs up on the tables so Karen could sweep. Max and Janie worked in the kitchen, while we finished up out front. With the four of us doing our part, it did not take long to finish. Just past twelve-thirty, Janie flicked the dining room light off with the switch by the front door.

"I don't know 'bout you folks, but I'm tired," she sighed. "These late nights are gonna be the death of me."

"Ain't neither one of us as young as we used to be," Max observed. "I don't know how much longer I'll be able to do this myself."

"I don't know about gettin' old, and no offense intended to y'all," Karen laughed, "but I'm damn glad that I ain't gonna have to do this for the rest of my life."

"I'll remind you of that next time you call home with talk about quittin' school," Max chided.

"You don't have to worry 'bout that," Karen assured him. Janie had told me that Karen was the first of the family to go to college, and she had hopes of going on to medical school.

"I hope not," Max smiled.

"Listen, folks," Janie interrupted. "Y'all can have this family moment at the house. I just stood here and said I was tired, and I'm sure Eddie ain't interested."

"I have nowhere to be," I said.

"You ain't helpin', honey," Janie replied.

Everyone laughed, then Max unlocked the door and ushered us through. Janie made me promise to stop in again before I left town, and Max and Karen wished me luck with my plans. We said our goodbyes, and they walked toward the alley where their cars were parked. I headed for the inn.

The lobby was dark when I let myself through the front door. Joshua and May had long since gone to bed. I climbed the stairs to the second floor. The hallway lights were not burning, and, rather than search for the switch, I made my way to my room in the dark. My upstairs neighbors were gone, so the building was deathly quiet. Coupled with the darkness, that was enough to spook me before I could unlock the door and get inside the room. I had to laugh at myself when I realized that I was breathing heavy. I felt silly letting myself get scared like that.

I was no less relieved that the light was still on in my room. I locked the door behind me and threw the key onto the dresser. Next to it, I emptied the contents of my pockets, then went to the bathroom to empty my bladder. I stripped naked and piled the clothes in the corner of the bathroom.

As I had done the night before, I moved the fan into the open window. I pulled back the covers on the bed, but again lay down on top of them. I must have been more tired than I felt, because I quickly fell asleep.

Chapter Fourteen

I am sitting at a table in Max's Diner. Across the room, Karen is bussing the big corner booth. She is leaning way over the table to reach a dish. Her skirt has ridden up her thighs, and I can see the tops of her stockings and the straps of a garter belt peeking out beneath the hem of her uniform. She continues to reach, and the skirt slides farther up her leg. She doesn't seem to notice or doesn't care.

"You gonna eat that?"

"What!?" The question startles me.

"You gonna eat that?" repeats the little girl in the white cotton dress, pointing to the untouched slice of apple pie on the table in front of me.

"No."

"Can I have it?" she asks. I recognize her but can't remember from where.

I push the pie toward her. She grabs the plate and quickly disappears into thin air. The other diners do not seem surprised by the child's sudden departure, so I shrug it off.

I turn my attention back to Karen, but she has finished.

"Daddy'll kill you if he catches you lookin' up my skirt like that," Karen says from behind me.

"I... I..." Embarrassed, I am unable to respond coherently.

"It's okay, sugar. I don't mind. Lookin' never hurt nobody." She bends down close to my ear and whispers, "I'm not wearin' any panties." Then she is gone.

The diner is gone.

I am sitting in the dark. Pitch black darkness so deep that I can't see my hand in front of my face. Without seeing, I know that I am in the tunnel beneath the inn. The brick floor beneath me is cold and hard, and the air reeks of stale whiskey. I start to crawl. I crawl and crawl, for hours it seems. I come to a fork. I cannot see it, but I know it is there. I am confused. There were no forks in that tunnel. From the inn to the garage. That's all. No forks. No branches. Something is wrong. I am frightened. Frightened of the darkness, the enclosure, the uncertainty of the fork. I begin to cry.

"Find your way, son," my father's voice says from the darkness.

"Pop!" I cry out. "Where are you?"

"I am here, Eddie. I'm always here."

"I'm scared."

"That's okay. Fear just means you're cautious. But you've got yourself into a mess haven't you?"

"I'm lost."

"You're not lost. You've just misplaced yourself."

"Help me. Show me which way to go."

"I can not. You must find your own way, son."

"I can't!"

I sit for a long time waiting for him to respond to me, but he does not. I know he has gone. I miss him so. His words echo in my head. I must find my own way. I take a deep breath and plunge ahead into the branch of the fork that I hope will lead me to the outside. The tunnel twists and turns around me. Time after time, I am faced with the choice of directions. After hours, maybe days, of crawling alone in the darkness, I begin to fear that I am destined by some wrinkle of fate to wander aimlessly through this labyrinth of stone and earth. A man-sized mouse in a man-sized maze.

I have nothing to eat or drink, but I have no need for these things in the maze. I do not sleep either, but the hard floor batters my knees, so I stop and rest sometimes. On one of these rest breaks, I am sitting in a corner staring into the perfect blackness ahead of me. I wonder if I'll ever see the light of day again. I find that I have forgotten what sunlight looks like. I close my eyes to the reality around me and try to remember. I search my mind for memories of the times Pop took me to Coney Island. The memories are there, but they are incomplete. I can hear the constant chatter of the barkers calling for challengers for their games of chance. I hear the screams of the passengers on the roller coaster. I feel the rush in my head as we top that last hill. I smell the hot popcorn and the aroma of the hot dogs cooking.

The sounds.

The smells.

The sensations.

But no sights.

Just the same awful blackness that surrounds me now. I scream in despair and curl into a ball on the floor of my prison. I have no hope of ever being free again. I lie there and wish for death.

"Hello, Eddie," a woman speaks.

"Who's there?" I ask.

"I am here, Eddie." The voice is the most beautiful sound I have ever heard. The voice of an angel, I am convinced.

"Who are you?" I ask. "Are you my guardian angel?"

"No, but I do watch over you," she responds.

"Have you come to help me out of here?" I hope.

"I can not do that, Eddie. You must find your own way out. I am just here to let you know that you are not alone."

"Who are you?"

"You know who I am. You just haven't realized it yet."

I am perplexed by her answer. I do not recognize her voice. I am sure I have never heard it before, but, still, there is something familiar about it.

"I can't see you," I said. "I can't see anything. I can't even remember what seeing is like."

"Darkness can be frightening."

"I am scared."

"I know, Eddie, but fear is good sometimes. Fear just means you're cautious."

"My Pop told me that."

"I know. I taught him that. Years ago. Before we came to America."

"What?" I am confused, then I realize. "Mama?"

"Yes, Eddie."

"Is it really you?"

"Yes."

"How? Why?"

"I came to tell you that I am proud of you. I always have been. The Lord saw fit to take me away before I got to know you, but I have watched you grow. I know you have turned out to be a fine young man."

"I wish I could have known you."

"Me too, but Sam did a pretty good job raising you."

"Yes, ma'am. I miss him."

"He misses you, too."

"You are with him?"

"Finally."

"I'm glad."

"I have to go now, Eddie."

"Don't leave me alone."

"You're not alone. We are always here, but you have to do this on your own."

"But it's too hard."

"Nonsense. Adversity builds character. When you get where you are going, you'll be a better man for the journey. I must go now."

"I love you, Mama." I wait for her response, but it never comes. "Mama!" I call into the darkness.

"Who you talkin' to, Chance?" Billy Watson asks from somewhere in the darkness. The voice is coming from everywhere and nowhere at the same time.

"Watson!" I spit. "Leave me alone."

"I can't do that," he argues. "I'm here to fulfill your wish."

"What wish?"

"To die."

I feel the air around me change. Suddenly heavy with moisture. In the distance, I hear a faint rumble. I can feel the floor vibrate beneath me. I am terrified.

"See you in Hell, Chance."

"Hold your breath, Eddie!" my mother cries out to me.

I obey just as the water hits me. I am slammed into the roof of the tunnel so hard I almost lose consciousness, but I fight to stay awake. I push hard against the wall and kick furiously against the water, swimming for my life. I am driven by my need for air. My chest burns. I have tapped the last of the oxygen from the breath that my mother commanded me take. The breath that, thus far, has saved my life. My back scrapes against the roof of the water-filled tunnel. I pray frantically for an air pocket, but find none. I swim. My muscles ache and burn from the exertion and the lack of oxygen. Still, I swim as hard as I can.

The tunnel turns gradually upward, until I am swimming vertically. The tunnel maze has become a shaft. I kick as hard as I can for what I hope will be freedom. Higher and higher. My lungs burn. I can feel my heart pounding in my head, and my chest feels as if it will explode if I don't take another breath.

Then I see it. I see what I have longed for. In the gloom above me, I see a circle of light growing larger with each kick. The surface! AIR! I kick harder. The circle of light above me grows closer. So close that the brightness of it burns my eyes, but I don't dare close them against the pain. I fear that I will die if I lose sight of the surface. I pray that I do not go blind before I reach the top.

Just as I reach the last of my endurance, as the pain in my chest rises in my throat, as the over-powering hunger for breath reaches the breaking point, I breach the surface, and I'm flying. Or falling. The air in my lungs explodes from my mouth in a shout, and I slam into the hard ground.

The fall to the floor woke me. My thrashing and flailing had thrown me from the bed. My chest burned with each breath, and I wondered if I had really been holding my breath. My body was soaked, and I was convinced for a moment that the dream had been real, then I realized I was wet with sweat. I tried to stand, to return to the bed, but my legs were too weak to support me. So, I sat where I had landed, gasping for air and sobbing.

"Eddie?" Joshua called through the door. As before, he didn't wait for my response. That was just as well, because I did not have the composure to speak. "Another dream?" he asked, opening the door.

"Good Heavens!" May exclaimed at the sight of me trembling naked on the floor. I was too distraught to be embarrassed.

Joshua pulled the spread from the bed and draped it across my shoulder. May disappeared into the bathroom and returned with a cold washcloth. She knelt on the floor beside me and mopped the sweat from my forehead.

"Another dream?" Joshua repeated.

I nodded, still unable to speak. The sour taste of bile suddenly filled my throat. I swallowed hard to fight the urge to vomit, but I couldn't hold it back. I scrambled across the floor into the bathroom, barely making it to the toilet before I emptied the contents of my stomach.

They followed behind me. May again mopped my forehead and let me wipe my face with the cold cloth. Joshua helped me to my feet. My legs shook when I took my first cautious steps, but they held. I felt surprisingly better after vomiting, though my throat burned from the heaving.

"Drink?" I finally managed to say.

May returned to the bathroom for a glass of water. I drank it quickly and asked for another. Then another. And another, until my thirst was quenched.

"I'm sorry," I apologized, my breathing having finally returned to close to normal.

"No need to apologize, Eddie. We told you that," Joshua scolded. "We're just concerned about you."

"You hollered like you had been hit by a truck," May added, "and then there was that crash."

I managed a smile. "I fell off the bed," I explained. "I'm sorry about not having on any clothes. The heat. I hope I didn't embarrass you."

"Can't embarrass me, son," she laughed. "I raised two sons and a husband. You ain't got nothin' I ain't seen before." We all laughed.

"Still," I responded, "I'm sorry."

"It's okay," she assured me.

"What time is it?" I asked.

"About four," Joshua answered, then added, "It's okay that you woke us up, so don't apologize. This'n must a been a doozy. Threw you out onto the floor and all."

"Yes, sir," I replied. Although they had not asked this time, I felt compelled to tell them about it. A catharsis of sorts. Cleared my mind of the aftermath of the horrors I had seen. I was relieved to find that, when they had gone, I was able to fall asleep rather quickly.

Chapter Fifteen

P eals of thunder jarred me awake later that Saturday morning. Rain fell in sheets out-side my open window, and I halfway wondered if God were trying to make me stay in Wixton. As I watched the torrent through the turning blades of the fan in the win-dow, I decided, for another day, at least, I would stay.

My mouth was like cotton, so I stumbled on still-shaky legs to the bathroom to drink water from the sink. Since Joshua had put the fear of lightning in my head, I decided to skip the shower and just pulled on my clothes. With no desire to get soaked to the bone and no plans, I figured that I would hang out inside for the day, maybe see if Joshua had anything he wanted me to do for him, and hopefully, see if May had something for me to eat.

I was relieved, in a way, to find the Wilsons sitting in the lobby when I came down. I would have felt too presumptuous to have knocked on their apartment door and ask for food. Joshua was reading a soggy copy of the Albany paper, and May was reading the Bible. They both smiled when they saw me on the stairs.

"Good mornin'," May said, placing the open Bible on her lap. "You look much better than you did the last time we saw you."

"Yes, ma'am," I replied.

"Couldn't look much worse," Joshua piped in. We all laughed.

"Feel much better, too."

"If you feel better," May said, "you probably feel like eatin'. How 'bout some breakfast? You hungry?"

"Yes, ma'am," I answered, "but I don't want to be any trouble."

She rolled her eyes and scolded, "Nonsense! I've told you time and again that you ain't no trouble. Besides, I ain't havin' you traipsin' off to that diner in this rain and catchin' your death of cold. I kept somethin' warm on the stove for you. Now sit down here, and I'll go fix you a plate. You can eat out here, if you like."

She hurried off to get my breakfast, and I sat down on the end of the sofa to wait. I still felt guilty about putting her out, even if she insisted otherwise.

"She enjoys havin' you around, you know?" Joshua said, as if reading my thoughts. "And she must like you. She ain't let me eat out here in years. Help yourself to the paper. Be careful, though, it's a mite damp this mornin'."

I almost took him up on the offer, but May returned with my food. While I ate, they returned to their reading so they wouldn't disturb my meal. Although May had piled on enough food for three people, I was famished and had no trouble cleaning the plate.

"More?" she asked.

"I couldn't." I patted my bulging stomach and said, "I'm stuffed."

"If you say so," May conceded, taking the empty plate from me.

While May was gone to the kitchen, Joshua looked over the top of the paper and said, "Look's like you're stuck with us another day."

"Yes, sir."

"You got any plans for the day?"

"No," I replied. "You have something else you want me to do for you?"

"Oh! No!" he explained. "Nothin' like that. I was just wonderin'."

"No," I repeated. "I had intended on leaving this morning, but not now."

"You know you're welcome," May said, returning to her chair.

"That room up there is yours as long as you want it," Joshua added.

"Thank you," I replied.

"After all that work you did upstairs," Joshua continued, "we owe you that much..."

"...and then some," May finished the sentence.

"I'm glad I could help, and I enjoyed the adventure of it. Finding the still, the tunnel, and all that, I mean."

"Too bad you didn't find a stash of money," Joshua laughed.

"Could be some here somewhere," May offered. "Ain't no tellin'. I wouldn't doubt anything after the last few days." We all laughed.

May fingered the open Bible she had replaced on her lap. "Eddie," she finally said, "I noticed you had been readin' from that Bible in your room the other night."

"Yes, ma'am," I replied.

"You read it much?"

"Try to."

"You a believer?"

"Yes, ma'am," I answered. Although there were certainly aspects of my life that weren't as they should be, I had made my decision for Christ a long time ago.

"When's the last time you went to church?" she asked.

"My father's funeral," I admitted. "Pop didn't care for church, so we hardly ever went. He said that most of the people he knew went to church to be seen, not to worship, and he couldn't stand pretentious people. He loved God and taught me to, but he just didn't believe in congregating. We went on Easter a few times, but not much more.

"Pop said he'd rather spend time with God one-on-one. Said it was more personal that way. I'm like him, I guess. I have never found a church where I was comfortable."

May considered everything I had said, then announced, "You just haven't been to the right church, yet."

"Probably not," I shrugged.

"How 'bout comin' with us tomorrow?"

"To church?" I asked. "I don't know. I think I would feel out of place, and, besides, I don't have clothes to wear to church."

"Nonsense! " May exclaimed. "First of all, you won't be out of place, you'll be among other believers, and I'm sure everyone will make you feel at home. Second, if you got clothes on, you got clothes to wear to church."

"These clothes aren't good enough to wear to church," I debated.

"It don't matter what you wear, as long as you're there," Joshua announced.

"I would feel under-dressed," I argued.

"Nonsense," May countered. "We're simple people. Folks come to Sunday services in everything from suits to overalls. You'll fit right in."

"Brother Radley would love havin' a new face in the crowd," Joshua observed.

"He'll be tickled pink," May confirmed.

"Hold on here!" Joshua exclaimed. "May, don't you have somethin' for Eddie?"

"My goodness!" she cried. "I completely forgot." She jumped up and hurried to the apartment. She returned a few minutes later carrying a large box wrapped in bright paper. She handed the box to me and sat down again.

"What's this?" I asked.

"Open it," Joshua laughed.

I tore open the wrapping paper and lifted the top from the box. Inside were clothes. Two pair of pants and two shirts. "What's this?" I repeated, surprised by their generosity.

"I looked at those torn clothes of yours," May explained, "and didn't see any way to salvage 'em, so we decided just to buy you some more."

"You didn't have to do that," I said.

"We know," they answered in unison, "but we wanted to."

"You admitted yourself that you can't afford to lose what few clothes you got," Joshua reminded me.

"Yes," I acknowledged, "but..."

"But nothin'," he interrupted. "You needed 'em. We got 'em. And that's the end of it."

"I already feel like I'm taking advantage of your kindness," I explained.

"Nonsense!" May exclaimed. "We ain't done nothin' for you that we haven't wanted to. I'd like to hope that somebody'd take care of my boys like this if they ever needed it."

"Now don't let me hear another word about you bein' trouble," Joshua scolded, again.

"Okay," I agreed.

"Look here," May said, reaching for the box in my lap. She pulled a pair of tan pants from the box. "These are to replace the ones you made a mess of. Next time you go fishin', don't wear your good pants. Just like a man. Wear a suit to dig a ditch if we didn't tell you different." She rolled her eyes and laughed. "And these others," she continued. "We figured you could always use a pair of jeans."

"Yes, ma'am," I agreed. "Thank you."

"You're very welcome, son," May accepted. "Wish we could do more."

"You've done more than you needed to as it is," I said.

"Nonsense."

"Them tan ones there," Joshua indicated the pants May was holding, "look good enough to wear to church. Don't they?"

"Yes, sir."

"Then you ain't got that excuse no more, do you?"

"No, sir."

"Well, then, how 'bout it?

"Okay," I gave in. "You've convinced me."

"Hallelujah!" May exclaimed, clapping her hands.

With that settled and the rain still pouring outside, I settled back to enjoy the day. Joshua had discovered, through some of our conversations, my love of chess. Teaching me how to play was the only positive thing Uncle Nico had ever done for me. Behind alcohol, chess was his passion, and in spite of his nearly constant drunkenness, he was a damn fine chess player. Liz didn't have the mind for the game. She occupied her time reading romance novels, when she wasn't crying, so Nico taught me. Anyway, Joshua knew about my affection for the game, so he challenged me to a match, which took up the rest of the morning. His announcement of "Checkmate!" came just before May called us in for lunch. I took two games in a row in the afternoon before we decided to retire the board for the day.

I really enjoyed the time I spent with the Wilsons that rainy day. May commented more than once that Joshua and I were like two schoolboys. She said one would never guess that there was nearly fifty years difference in our ages. She, of course, took every opportunity to overfeed me. One thing I could say about her and all the southerners I had had the pleasure of eating with, they were not stingy with food.

I went to bed that night stuffed and more relaxed than I had been in a long time. I took some time at the end of that day to, again, thank God for everything good in my life, and I read more from the Bible by my bed. I was both nervous and excited about going to church Sunday. Like I had told May, it had been two years since I had been, and, even before that, I could probably count the times I had been on one hand. I wanted to feel at home in church and hoped that the people would accept me there. Joshua and May had assured me that I was worrying about nothing, but I needed reassurance from the One in charge, so I prayed. When I finally rolled over to go to sleep, I felt an unusual calm about me, and for the first time in almost a week, I slept without dreaming.

Sunday morning came quickly. Before my pillow had time to lose its fluff, or so it seemed, I was awakened by Joshua's knock on the door. He announced through the door that May would have breakfast on the table shortly. I thanked him for waking me and loped to the bathroom for a shower. I dressed in new clothes, grabbed the Bible from the bedside table, and headed downstairs to breakfast.

My nervousness returned when I climbed out of the backseat of the Wilson's Biscayne in the parking lot of the Wixton Baptist Church. The lot was full of cars and scattered with small clusters of people. I scanned the groups for anyone I knew. I caught sight of Janie across the way, but she did not see me. She was involved in a conversation with an older couple and a man I had seen in the diner the night before. Farther down the lot, I saw the Besmers. Carl, of course, was absent, but the rest of the family was there. Taking Carl's place was a tall, rugged looking man who was holding Norma Jean's hand. J.R. was the spitting image of his father.

Jenny saw me and broke out in a huge grin. She waved at me across the parking lot, then leaned over and said something to Joanne. Joanne looked my way, waved, and nodded to Jenny. Jenny jumped and ran toward me.

"Mornin', Eddie, Mr. and Mrs. Wilson," she called when she got close enough. We all returned the greeting. When she had gotten all the way over, she kissed my cheek and said, "Guess what?" She didn't leave me time to respond before she answered herself, "Mama said I could sit with you durin' preachin', if you don't care? You don't care, do you?"

"No, that would be nice," I lied. Trying to get over her would not be easy with her sitting beside me, and having her that close to me would not be conducive to my listening to the minister, but I couldn't tell her no.

"Is it okay with y'all?" she asked the Wilsons.

"Of course," May replied.

The four of us headed into the church. We stopped several times to speak to other people who also were making their way to their seats. Joshua introduced me to everyone. Most of them were happy to have me, and those who weren't hid it pretty well. Church was no place for that.

May made a point to introduce me to the minister. "Brother Radley," she said as we approached him.

He extended his hand to shake hers and said, "Miss May, how're you this fine Sunday mornin'?"

"Wonderful."

"Praise the Lord!"

"Brother Radley, I want you to meet someone. This is Eddie Chance. He's been stayin' with us over at the inn."

Brother Radley was a rotund man who was nearly as wide as he was tall. His balding head was already slick with sweat. "Mr. Chance," he said, extending his right hand toward me. His left hand rested against his chest, gripping the lapel of his jacket. "So you're the one I've heard so much about?"

I shook his hand and replied, "Good, I hope."

"Most of it," he answered, matter-of-factly, then he laughed, heartily. His belly was still shaking when he added, "I'm just ribbin' you, son. Most of what I've heard was from Miss May, here, and Miss Jenny's daddy. And I can tell you, both of 'em think mighty high of you." He looked at his watch and announced, "It's time I got up front. I see Brother Lowell's tappin' his hymnal against the leg of his chair. He does that when I'm takin' too long to get to the pulpit." He leaned toward me and whispered, "Drives me crazy." We both laughed. He shook my hand again and waddled toward the front of the church.

Jenny took me by the arm, and we followed May to the pew where Joshua had taken residence. Everyone around us settled into their own seats and pulled the red hymn books from the racks on the backs of the pews. Jenny pulled one and opened it. She whispered, "He always starts with this one."

The man Brother Radley had identified as Lowell stepped to the pulpit and cleared his throat. The congregation quieted, then he said, "Good mornin', folks. Let us praise the Lord with song this mornin'." He called out the number of the page that Jenny had selected, bringing a smile to her face.

After the song, still holding his lapel, Brother Radley took his place at the pulpit. He stood smiling while he waited for the crowd to quiet again. His hand dropped from his lapel to pull his jacket back into place by tugging on the hem. Returning the hand to the lapel, he looked out over the congregation and said, "Dearly beloved, we are gathered..." He paused, leaned over, and examined the area in front of the alter, then asked, "Where'd they go?" He paused, letting the question hang for a moment before he bellowed with laughter. The congregation laughed with him, but it was a subdued laugh for a joke that I guessed was too often told. As he laughed, Brother Radley, again, tugged at his jacket hem and replaced the hand back to his lapel.

"Mornin'," he greeted us. "Let us open this mornin' with a word of prayer." We dropped our heads. "Heavenly Father, bless this gatherin' of Your people in Your house. May their ears and minds be open to the message I bring to them this mornin' from Your Word. Lord, use me as Your instrument to touch the lives of each and everyone here. Lord, bless us and guide us. In Jesus' name I ask. Amen."

"Amen," the congregation responded en masse.

After another song, Brother Radley, tugging his jacket hem, stepped forward again and said, "I'm pleased to see all of you here this mornin'. Always good to have a full house. I see we have some familiar faces missin' this morin'. Brother Sim, Miss Chloe's mama still under the weather?" Sim nodded. "Sorry to hear that. We'll keep her in our prayers. Miss Joanne, the good sheriff must still be out of town. He is certainly missed." She confirmed it. "I guess young Watson must be out on patrol in his absence," he added with a hint of sarcasm in his voice.

"Out causin' trouble mor'n likely," came a call from somewhere among the crowd.

"Amen," someone agreed.

"Now folks," Brother Radley interjected, "talk like that don't belong in the church."

"It's true," someone protested.

"I didn't say it wasn't true. I said it didn't belong in church."

The remark brought uproarious laughter from the congregation. Brother Radley was obviously pleased with the laugh, but he quickly changed the subject. He looked my way and said, "You've probably noticed that we have a new face in our crowd today. We want to welcome Mr. Eddie Chance to the Lord's house. Eddie comes to us from New York, by way of the Wixton Inn." A few of the people sitting near us turned and offered their hands and welcomed me to the church. Brother Radley continued, "Eddie, I have a good mind to call you up to give your testimony. From what the Wilsons have told me, you have quite a story to tell." I just nodded. "But I won't put you on the spot like that. You stay with us long enough, and I'll do it." He tugged at the hem of his coat, then returned his hand to his lapel. He glanced behind him, then said, "I guess I'd better get a move on before Brother Lowell knocks the leg off his chair!"

The congregation roared, and Brother Lowell turned three shades of red as he swapped places with Brother Radley. The minister patted him on the back and whispered something that made the song leader smile. He led us in another song, then called upon a member of the congregation to pray. Offering plates were passed through the church by a quartet of ushers, then Brother Radley stepped forward to deliver his sermon for the day.

Despite his comical manner and the constant lifting and tugging of his suit coat, he was a highly polished orator. Save an occasional "Amen", the congregation sat in awed silence while he delivered an impassioned plea against becoming a complacent Christian.

About halfway through the sermon, I felt Jenny press a folded piece of paper into my hand. I looked at her, and she smiled. I opened the note and read, "I need to talk to you."

I pulled one of the little green pencils from the slot in the back of the pew in front of me and wrote a reply. "About what?" I passed it back to her.

She read it and wrote, "Not here. Come home with me. Eat lunch. Talk after. IMPORTANT!"

I was curious to find out what she wanted to talk about, but I did not need to get involved with her. Even if it turned out to be nothing, I didn't need any more baggage where she was concerned. I thought for a moment, then wrote, "I can't. Helping Joshua today." I felt guilty about lying to her, especially in church, but I felt it was best. I refolded the paper and laid the note on the open Bible in her lap. I watched out of the corner of my eye as she read it. A look of disappointment played across her face, and she frowned.

"Please," she mouthed.

I leaned over to whisper in her ear. She smelled incredible. I wanted to bury my face in her hair, kiss her neck, taste the salt on her skin, but I bit my lip. Knowing that I was leaving in the morning, I said, "Maybe tomorrow." By the time she realized that I had stood her up, I would be long gone. It would be better that way. Better for me, anyway.

When the service was over, I hoped Jenny wouldn't press me to come with her, and I prayed she wouldn't mention anything to Joshua. She didn't. With a hint of sadness in her voice, she said, "See you tomorrow?" I nodded. She kissed me lightly on the lips and hurried off to join her family.

I looked toward Joshua, who cocked an eyebrow and smiled. "Pretty girl," he observed.

"Yes, sir."

Several people came by to speak to me before leaving. I guessed having the minister's endorsement gave me validation. All that came by shook my hand, wished me luck, and offered prayers. I accepted all that was offered. I needed all the help I could get.

"You fellas ready to head home?" May asked. "I got dinner to get ready." She shooed us toward the car. "That chicken's not gonna fry itself, you know."

Over that fried chicken, I assured May that I had enjoyed church, and I promised her that I would try to go more often. After the meal, I went up to my room to try to relax. Rest up for Monday. I fell asleep.

Chapter Sixteen

My sleep was interrupted by someone knocking on my door. "Who is it?" I asked when I had mind enough to form the words.

"It's Jenny," she called back.

"What?" I asked, more out of disbelief than misunderstanding.

"Jenny," she repeated. "Jenny Besmer. Can I come in?"

My body tensed. I took several deep breaths to relax myself before I got up to unlock the door. She had traded her church dress for a pair of blue jeans and the denim shirt she had worn the night of the fishing trip. Her hair was pulled back in a ponytail the way it was the day we met. "Hello," I managed to say, trying to hide the quiver in my voice.

"Can I come in?" she asked again. Not waiting for my response, she pushed past me and plopped down on the bed. She ran her hand over the bed, feeling the warmth where I had been. With sarcasm and a bit of anger in her voice, she asked, "Mr. Wilson needed his bed held down?"

I blushed, caught in the lie. I stammered, "I...I...don't know what to say."

She smiled and let me off the hook. "I don't care why you lied to me. I'm sure you had your reasons, but I couldn't wait until tomorrow." She became visibly nervous. She continued, "Come and sit here and let's talk." She patted the bed beside her.

I sat next to her, and she leaned over and laid her head against my chest. I started to pull away, but she put her hand around my waist and held me still. "Don't get up," she whispered. "Hold me for a moment."

The look of defiance that usually burned in the back of her eyes was replaced by a vulnerability that I had not seen nor expected in her. Cautiously, I obeyed her, touched by the longing in her voice. Her tone and demeanor made me so nervous about what she was about to say that I could not enjoy the feeling of her body against my own.

"Eddie," she began after a heavy silence, "I think I love you."

The words hit me like a bolt of lightning. "What?"

"I love you," she repeated. "I want you. I want you to make love to me." She rose to her knees and kissed me passionately. She pulled back and said, "Now."

I pulled away and stood up. My thoughts were clouded by my desire, but I considered my response to her revelation as carefully as I was able, then said, "I'm flattered and, certainly, tempted, but you don't love me."

"Yes, I do," she protested. "I can't stop thinkin' 'bout you. Dreamin' 'bout you. Sexy dreams."

"That's not love. That's lust. To be honest, I've had those same thoughts and dreams about you. That's why I lied to you today," I confessed. "My desire for you was starting to cloud my purpose and starting to interfere with my friendship with T."

"T?" she repeated. "What's T got to do with anything?" The mention of his name relit the fire in her eyes.

"I was, am, jealous of the relationship the two of you have."

"Really?"

"Really. Look, Jenny, I can see the way you look at him. That look in your eyes, just now, when you heard his name. I saw it that night at your house, but I didn't recognize it until later, after I had seen the two of you together. You don't have that look when you look at me. You don't love me. You just want me because I'm like the forbidden fruit. Mysterious drifter. Unknown. Maybe a little dangerous. But, from the look of things, I think you have enough forbidden fruit in your basket."

She sat in silence while I spoke and for a long while afterwards. She was considering everything I had said. "I do love him," she finally admitted, "but it's hard. Talk about forbidden fruit. No one would understand. Not even Daddy. He's no bigot, but he'd have a hard time accepting this. And Billy. God only knows what he'd do, though it's none of his damn business. I don't know what to do. I guess I was trying to use my attraction to you as a way to get out of the mess I'm in."

"Like I said, I'm flattered, but I couldn't do that to T, to you, to myself. It wouldn't be fair to any of us," I explained. "If you and he are meant to be together, you'll find a way to work it out."

She came to me and hugged me. She kissed me lightly on the lips, a friendship kiss. She began to cry. "I'm just scared that T might end up like his brother, and I couldn't live with myself if anything happened to him because of me."

I didn't know what to say to that, so I just stood there and held her while she cried. She needed comfort, a shoulder to cry on, and I was the only one in town that would hear her out without passing judgment on her.

"Eddie!" May's shout and her banging on the door startled us. "Open the door, quick!"

The urgency in her voice alarmed me, and I flew to the door.

"May, what's wrong?"

She looked over her shoulder as she hurried in and closed the door. She addressed Jenny. "Billy Watson's downstairs lookin' for you, and he's madder than a wet hornet. I overheard him yellin' at Joshua and ran here to warn y'all."

"How'd he know I was here?" Jenny wondered. "I parked down at the courthouse and took the long way around here. Told Mama I had to get somethin' I left in the mailroom."

"I don't think he does, yet, " May informed her. "From what I could gather, he don't know where you are. He's just speculatin'. He was rantin' about searchin' the whole buildin' if he has to."

"Bastard," Jenny grunted, then apologized to May.

"He is what he is," May acknowledged, "but, if he finds you up here, there'll be hell to pay for the both of you." We agreed.

"Is there a back way down from here?" I asked.

"No."

"That ain't good," Jenny observed.

"No," I agreed, "but we have to figure some way to get you out of here without him seeing us."

"I don't rightly see any way," May said. "Only way out is through the lobby."

I spotted the keys to the upstairs apartment lying on the dresser. "I may have a way, but, Jenny, you have to keep a big secret."

May followed my eyes to the keys and smiled.

"You're not afraid of the dark, are you?" I asked Jenny.

"No."

"Can you keep a secret for a little while?"

"Yes," Jenny answered, confused.

"May, do you mind if I drive your car?"

" 'Course not."

"Okay, here's what we do," I said, then explained my plan to them. May was to go down the stairs and stall Billy long enough for Jenny to get upstairs. I told Jenny about the hidden door, the passageway, and the tunnel. She assured me that she would be waiting for me at the car. I was to follow shortly behind May to confront Billy in the lobby. If Billy insisted on searching the building, he wouldn't find Jenny.

May hurried off, and Jenny and I went to the third-floor stairs. I handed the keys to her and said, "Lock the outer door behind you, and make sure you're careful on the ladder. I don't know how long it'll take for me to get away from Billy, but sit tight. I'll be there."

"I know," she replied. "My hero." She kissed me again.

"You'd better stop doing that, before I change my mind about turning down your offer." She giggled and hurried up the stairs.

I rushed back toward the lobby stairs and met Billy and May on the way up. Joshua followed behind them cursing Billy, the stairs, and his knees the whole way up.

Billy stopped me at the top of the stairs. "Where you goin', Chance?" he asked angrily.

"Down," I said smugly.

"Don't get smart with me."

"Why?" I asked. "You afraid you won't be able to keep up." I heard Joshua snickering behind Billy. I continued, "Do you want something?"

"You know damn well why I'm here," he barked. "Where's Jenny?"

"How would I know?" I lied. "I haven't seen her since church. We missed you, by the way."

"You're lyin'."

"No, really, we did miss you, " I teased him, "but Brother Radley asked about you."

"You know what I mean." The anger boiled in his face. He grabbed my shirt collar, pulled me close to his face, and growled, "Where is Jenny?"

Not pulling away, I took hold of his wrists and replied sternly, my voice not much more than a whisper. "I told you I don't know, and if you grab me one more time like that, I'm going to kill you. Slowly and painfully." I smiled.

He snatched his wrists away from me and stepped back. He shouted, his voice quivering with fear, "Don't threaten me, boy!"

"Then don't touch me," I said matter-of-factly.

Joshua stepped forward and put his hand on my chest. He looked at Billy and said, "Look, Deputy Watson, we already told you Jenny Besmer ain't here, and she ain't been here. And I'll be damned if you think you're gonna search this buildin'. If Eddie here wants to let you take a look in his room, as a gesture of goodwill, I think that ought to satisfy you." He winked at me.

I stepped aside and said, "Be my guest."

He searched the room, the closet, the bathroom, and under the bed. When he was sure she wasn't there, he announced, "I know she's here somewhere, and I plan to prove it. And when I do, you'll all be sorry. I'll be watchin'. She's gotta leave sometime." With that, he turned to leave.

Before he got out of hearing distance, May asked, "Eddie, can you go out to Nate Pomeroy's place out on the highway and pick me up a mess of greens for supper. The ones I have spoiled." I had told her to find some excuse to ask me to leave in the car. She continued, "You can take our car. I'll write down the directions, and I'll call Nate and let 'im know you're comin'."

"Sounds good," I played along. "Give me a chance to get out of here for a while."

Billy had heard her request, then descended the stairs. When she was sure he was far enough away, May whispered, "If he's plannin' on watchin' the comin's and goin's, it'll be better if you do go get the greens after you drop Jenny off. I will call Nate Pomeroy and tell 'im to get me up a mess." She looked over her shoulder at the stairs and added, "I hope Billy or one of his boys don't follow you."

"Me too," I agreed.

Down the stairs, we found Billy sitting in one of the armchairs reading Joshua's newspaper. "Y'all don't mind if I sit here a while do y'all?" he asked smugly.

"Suit yourself," Joshua said.

We went to the desk, and May jotted down the directions to Nate Pomeroy's. I tucked the paper and the money she gave me into my shirt pocket, got the keys to the Biscayne, and headed out to the garage and Jenny. I went out the front door and found Dick Brinson leaning against the building across the street. I nodded to him. Farther down the road, Dan Sims sat on the hood of a big black car. He was carving on a stick with a big pocket knife. I threw up my hand to him, and he just spit a stream of tobacco juice in my direction. Neither of them spoke, nor did I expect them to.

I went around the building and into the side door of the garage. I locked it behind me, and called Jenny's name. When she didn't answer, I worried that one of Watson's flunkies had gotten to her, but I realized that I would have heard about that by now. Billy would have relished rubbing our collective noses in our lie. I was scared. Something had happened to her on the climb down. She had fallen, broken her neck. A hundred horrible things ran through my mind as I jerked the grate from above the trap door. I was thankful to find that the door could be opened from this side. I popped the latch and let the door swing down. I had hoped Jenny would be waiting below, thinking that maybe she hadn't been able to unlatch the door, but she wasn't there. I was afraid to yell too loudly, for fear of attracting attention, so I dropped down into the tunnel and called her as loudly as I dared. No answer. My only choice was to crawl through. No problem. I had been through it before.

I dropped to my knees and crawled a few feet into the darkness. I was seized by an unbearable panic. I tried to take a breath but couldn't. The walls of the tunnel closed in around me, and I couldn't move. I tried to call Jenny, but the shout died in my throat. With all the will I could muster, I scrambled back into the exit shaft and the light from above. I sat in the corner and breathed. My heart pounded in my throat. The dream had come back to haunt me. I was scared to go into the tunnel, afraid to get lost in the darkness, but Jenny needed me. I tried again to enter the tunnel, but the panic gripped me again. I scrambled back to my corner.

Find your way, son. My father's voice spoke in my head. That girl needs you.

"Pop?"

I knew he wouldn't answer, that he wasn't really there, but he was right. Jenny needed me. I took a deep breath and stared into the tunnel. I couldn't bear to crawl into that darkness. Then an idea struck me. I grabbed the cart from the other corner and pushed it into the mouth of the tunnel. I could not avoid going into the darkness. I could not risk exposing myself or May or Joshua or Jenny to Billy. The cart wouldn't protect me from my fear, but it would get me through it as fast as possible. I untied the rope and pushed it away to make room for me on top. I lay across the cart, pulled against the floor, and propelled myself into the tunnel. The panic grabbed for me. My arms were like jelly. I couldn't coax the strength to move the cart again. I prayed and reached for the floor before me. With all the force I could command, I pulled against the bricks beneath me. The cart sailed down the lightless shaft. Another stroke before the momentum was lost carried me farther in. Soon, the light from the alcove at the other end became visible. With a final burst of energy, I burst from the tunnel and found Jenny pacing furiously in and out of the bottling room.

She ran to me and hugged me. "I was worried that you wouldn't know to come after me."

"What happened?" I asked.

"I got scared," she admitted. "I couldn't go through there alone."

"I can understand that," I said, "but, right now, we'd better get a move on. Billy's boys are going to get suspicious if I don't drive out of that garage soon."

I lay back down on the cart and she lay on top of me. I pulled us through the tunnel as quickly as I could. After we had climbed through the trapdoor, I pulled it shut and dropped the grate into place. Jenny hid under a sheet in the back floorboard. I lifted the garage door, then drove the car onto the street right by the watchful eyes of Billy's cronies. I was relieved when neither of them made motion to follow us.

I began to follow the directions that May had given me, but a few blocks down, I doubled back on a back street and stopped a block over from the courthouse to drop off Jenny.

She paused before she stepped out of the car to say, "Thank you... for everything."

"You're welcome," I answered. I reached out and brushed the stray hair out of her face, letting my fingertips rest against her cheek. She was so beautiful. I knew I didn't love her, that she wasn't the one, but I could have spent hours just holding her.

She leaned over and kissed me deeply. After several minutes, she pulled away, leaving me wanting more. "I've gotta go," she announced. "If Billy's been lookin' for me, he may have told Mama that I wasn't at the courthouse." She slid out of the seat and closed the door behind her. Leaning back in the window, she said, "Promise me that you won't forget me, Eddie Chance." Somehow, she knew that I would be leaving before I saw her again.

"Never," I assured her. She laughed, then she was gone.

With the taste of her lips still on mine, I drove to Nate Pomeroy's place, which was a tin-roofed shack off the Cordele Highway. I pulled into the yard, sending several dogs running for cover. Pomeroy turned out to be an elderly white man, who was sitting in a rocking chair on his front porch. He was standing at my door before the car stopped rolling.

He extended his hand through the open window and asked, "Eddie?" I shook his hand and confirmed my identity. He went on, "Miss May called and told me you was comin'." I started to get out of the car, but he protested, "You sit still. I done bundled up some greens for you. Let me grab 'em off the porch there. 'Sides, you get outta that car, one of them mutts might take ya leg clean off!" He threw his head back and howled. He hustled to the porch, scooped up two bundles of "greens", and deposited them on the back floorboard.

I gave him the money May had sent. He thanked me, jogged back to the porch, and plopped back down in his chair. He threw up his hand up and waved when I backed out of the yard. I returned the gesture as I drove away.

Back at the inn, I was only half-surprised to find Dick and Dan still at their posts but was relieved to find that Billy had long since gone. He had left the boys outside on the slim chance that Jenny might still come out. I had to laugh. They would be waiting an awfully long time.

"They still out there?" Joshua asked as I came through the door.

"Yes," I confirmed. "How long did Billy stay?"

"Not long," he replied. "Left right after you did."

"Just talking big," I observed. "Jenny was scared he'd call her mother. Get her in trouble."

"She called, by the way," Joshua remembered.

"Jenny?"

"Her mama," he corrected.

"Her mama?"

"Called to see what the hell you were doin' to her daughter."

"Huh?" I sweated.

He grinned. "Scare you?"

"That ain't funny!" I scolded.

"Ain't?" he questioned.

"Seemed appropriate," I explained. We both laughed.

"Really," he said, "Jenny called to let you know she got home and to thank us for helpin' keep her out of trouble."

"I appreciate you and May going out on a limb for us like that," I thanked him.

"Glad to help, son," Joshua replied.

"There's no telling what Billy would have done if he had found Jenny in my room," I surmised. "Even though we weren't doing anything wrong."

He smiled, knowingly, and said, "Eddie, I don't know, and I don't care, what you kids were doin' up there. Ain't none of my business, but it damn sure ain't none of Billy Watson's. And he ain't got no right to storm in here and tell me what I am and ain't gonna do in my own home!"

I was a little angry at his accusation but thought better of trying to defend myself. I changed the subject instead. "Did May really need those tonight?" I asked, pointing at the two bundles that I had placed on the counter.

"Nope," he grinned.

"Thanks," I repeated.

"Chess?" he asked.

"I don't know."

"Come on now," he pleaded. "You got me down by a game. At least give me a chance to even things up."

"Okay," I agreed.

"You boys 'bout ready to eat?" May called us to supper later that evening.

"Not yet," Joshua protested. "I've just about got him this time." He captured my rook with his queen. "Check!" he exclaimed.

I surveyed the board for a moment before reaching for my bishop, which had been waiting patiently on the outskirts of our current skirmish. Joshua's eyes followed my hand to the forgotten piece.

"Damn!" he complained when I captured his queen.

Two moves later, my remaining rook captured his knight and trapped his king behind his unmoved pawns.

"Check," I announced, "and mate."

"Damn! Damn! Damn!"

"Joshua Wilson," May scolded. "What did I tell you about your language? Now you two put that infernal game away and come to the table. The food is gettin' cold."

"Yes, ma'am," we answered simultaneously.

As usual, the food was unbelievable, and I ate more than I should have. Although I hadn't even left yet, I was already missing May's cooking, and I told her so. She said she was flattered and piled another helping onto my plate.

"So you really leavin' us tomorrow?" Joshua asked.

"Yes," I replied. "It's not supposed to rain tomorrow, so I plan to head out first thing."

"I wish you'd stay with us a while longer," May implored.

"I've been here longer than I intended now. Just planned on staying overnight. Tuesday will be a week, so I really need to get going."

"We'll miss you," they said together.

"Me, too," I replied, swallowing the lump that was rising in my throat.

The ringing of the desk bell, thankfully, interrupted our moment before we were all reduced to crying.

"Someone checkin' in this time of night?" May wondered.

"Wouldn't surprise me," Joshua said, getting up from the table to go see. He went out to the lobby, returning a moment later. He announced, "Eddie, you got a visitor."

"Who?" I wondered, afraid of what he might say.

"Don't worry," he assured me. "It's T Johnson.

The statement only made me feel marginally better. I was relieved that it wasn't Billy, but I wasn't sure I was ready to face T after the fool I had made of myself the other night.

"I invited him to come on back, but he said he needed to talk to you alone," Joshua continued, adding to my anxiety.

I took a deep breath and went to face him. Joshua, probably sensing my apprehension, patted me on the back as I walked by him.

"Evenin'," T greeted.

"I didn't expect to see you tonight," I said.

"Didn't expect to come here, either, " he replied. "I got the feelin' the other night that you didn't care to talk to me."

"I'm sorry about that," I apologized. "I had some issues I had to work out."

"I know. Jenny told me about your conversation this afternoon," he explained. "That's why I'm here. I want to thank you for what you did."

"It's okay," I said. "I was glad to help her, and I enjoyed putting one over on Billy."

"Not that. I do appreciate you keepin' her out of trouble, but I was talkin' 'bout what you said to her. Thank you for convincin' her not to give up on us," he explained. "Heaven knows we have enough obstacles without throwin' you in the soup."

"Hey, man," I said, "I admit I was having a hard time for a while. I could tell there was something more than admiration in your voice the first time we talked about her, and then, like I told Jenny, when I saw the two of you together, I knew it. I was jealous, and I shouldn't have been. Somehow in my mind I got the idea that I had to choose between the two of you, so I chose neither. Jenny helped me realize that I didn't have to choose. I could have you both... as friends."

"Thanks," he repeated.

"One day maybe the two of you can love each other without worrying about the consequences," I suggested.

"Maybe," he doubted, then changed the subject. "Jenny said you were leavin' tomorrow."

"Yeah," I confirmed. "I need to get back on the road. I've got a promise to keep."

"Yeah," he repeated, sticking out his hand.

I took the hand, and he pulled me to him and gave me a one-armed hug. He thanked me again for my help and made me promise to keep in touch. I made him promise not to give up on him and Jenny, and I told him to tell the rest of the guys goodbye for me. We hugged again, and he left.

I went back into the Wilson's apartment to let them know that I was going upstairs to pack and, maybe, get a jump start on sleep. I planned on putting some miles behind me the next day, and I needed all the sleep I could get.

Packing didn't take long. When you can carry all your possessions in an old duffel bag, stuffing them all back in is not a timely process. When it was finished, I took my battered atlas and sat on the bed to plan my route south. I was somewhere on Highway 27 just below Bainbridge, when I was jolted from my concentration by a knock on the door.

"Chance!" Billy Watson yelled through the door. "Open up!"

"Go away!" I barked.

He pounded on the door and shouted again, "Open this damn door!"

"I told you already," I growled, "go away!"

"You open the door, Chance, or I'll break it down!" From the sound of the impact, I knew he had thrown his shoulder against the door.

To prevent any more of the nonsense, I decided to open the door. "Hold on," I called to him.

He stormed into the room before I got the door open all the way. He was nervous as a cat, and, from the smell of him, I could tell he had been drinking. I looked into the hallway, as he passed, for Dick and Dan, but they weren't there. If he had brought them, they must have waited downstairs. More than likely, he had greased his courage with enough liquor to come alone.

"What do you want, Watson?" I snapped. "I'm busy, and I don't have time to fool with you."

He looked around the room at the map that lay open on the bed and the duffel bag that leaned against the dresser by the door.

"You finally leavin' town?" he asked.

"Maybe, maybe not," I replied, "but I don't see where that is any of your business."

"I told you once," he snarled. "Everything that goes on in this town is my business."

"Look, Watson," I said, taking a step toward him, "I know you didn't come up here to ask me about my travel plans, so get to the point or get out!"

"Don't order me, you son-of-a-bitch," he hissed. "I'll kick your ass!"

"You have been threatening to kick my ass since I got here. If you think you can, go ahead, because I'm getting damn tired of you." I bowed up at him and almost laughed out loud when he shrank back from me. "Now, what do you want?"

"I don't know how you got her out of here," he started, "but I know Jenny was here this afternoon."

"Did you see her?"

"You know I didn't, but she was here."

"I told you then, and I'm telling you now. She was not here, and I have not seen her since church," I repeated. "So why don't you go home and sleep it off?" I opened the door and motioned toward the hall.

"I know she was here, and I want to know why," he demanded.

"Even if she had been here, it wouldn't be any of your damn business!" I growled.

"So she **was** here."

"I didn't say that," I corrected. "I said if she had been here, I wouldn't tell you why."

"Listen, asshole," he spit, "you just admitted she was here, now you're gonna tell me why. What were you doin' with my cousin?"

"I said she wasn't here, and I can't help it if you don't believe me."

"Damn right! I don't believe you," he retorted. "Why was she here?"

"Get out!"

"I'm not leavin' 'til I get the truth!"

I was growing very tired of the exchange. Billy wouldn't know the truth if it kicked him in the balls. I got right up in his face, almost gagging from the smell of bourbon on his breath, and screamed, "You want truth? I'll tell you the truth. Yeah, she was here." I paused for a moment to let him gloat, then I dropped his jaw with, "And I fucked her!" It took a second for what I had said to sink in. "She was damn good, too," I embellished the lie. The anger boiled on his face. I poured it on thicker. "Best piece of ass I've ever had." I felt a little guilty talking about Jenny that way, but she would never know, and it was worth it to see the contortions of Billy's face. Finally, I hit him between the eyes with, "Then she sprouted wings and flew out the damn window!"

"Huh?" he grunted. My last statement caught him off guard.

"I said she sprouted wings and flew out the window," I repeated. "That's why you couldn't find her."

"What?" He was confused. The alcohol was clouding his already slow mind.

"If you'd close your big mouth and open your ears, you might hear me! I did not see her, I did not have sex with her, and you are a dumb son-of-a-bitch! Now get the hell out of here!"

I don't think Billy knew how to react to what I had said. His booze-dulled brain couldn't process the sarcasm. Watching the internal struggle play out in the expressions on his face was almost comical. If I hadn't been so mad, I would have been bent double laughing.

"Stop fuckin' with me, Chance," he snorted, finally realizing that I was jerking his chain.

"There's somethin' damn funny goin' on between you and Jenny, and I don't like it, and I bet her daddy won't like it either."

"You're not going to tell Carl about any of this," I informed him.

"Like hell I'm not!" he argued. "He'll tear you a new one when he hears what you said 'bout his little girl, and I'm gonna enjoy watchin' it."

I leaned as close to him as I dared and quietly said, "I said you aren't going to tell Carl anything, because, if you do, you'll have to admit that you thought Jenny was up here in bed with me." I poked him in the chest, then added, "And he'll tear you a new one, as you say, when you look him in the face and call his daughter a whore." I poked him in the chest again. "Got it?"

He stepped back and rubbed his chest. As he considered what I had said, his face did its dance again. This time, I did laugh. I believed I had him, and, after a moment, he confirmed it.

"Damn you," he fumed, accepting defeat. "I don't know what went on here this afternoon, but I'm gonna get to the bottom of it."

"You do that," I approved, "because this time tomorrow, I'll be gone."

"See that you are."

I motioned toward the open door and said, "Goodnight, Billy." He stalked out.

The argument with Billy left me exhausted, so I stuffed the atlas back into my bag and got ready for bed. I bowed my head and asked God for a safe journey, then lay down to try to get some sleep for the big day ahead of me.

Sleep came quickly.

Chapter Seventeen

*R*inging church bells awaken me. I get off the bed and look out the window. The street is full of people. Everyone is dressed in black, and all walking in the same direction. No one speaks. Even the children in the crowd are deathly quiet. I stand in the window and wonder who has died.

"Where's everyone going?" I call down to a passing man.

"The wedding's today. I thought everybody knew that," the man replies. He looks nervously at his watch, then dashes off.

"What wedding?" I call after him, but he is already gone. No one else pays any attention to me.

The door to my room opens and Joshua enters carrying a tuxedo. "Eddie, you better get dressed. You're gonna be late for the weddin'."

"What wedding?" I demand.

"What weddin'?" he repeats. He throws his head back and laughs. "What weddin'?" I hear him mumble as he leaves.

I follow him out the door into the hallway to demand an explanation, but the hallway isn't there.

I find myself in the sanctuary of the Wixton Baptist Church. I am standing alone at the altar looking out at the crowd. The pews to my right are filled with somber-faced white people, all dressed in black. Joanne Besmer sits on the second bench wiping tears from her eyes with a red handkerchief. With her is Jason, J.R, and Norma Jean. Jenny and Carl are nowhere to be seen. Their absence brings the meaning of all this to my mind.

I turn to the other side of the church for confirmation. These pews are filled with black people. Mirroring their white counterparts, they are all dressed in black and sitting stone-faced as the soft sound of organ music drifts about the room. T's mother sits in her spot at the front. Janie is also there, but between them sits a large, handsome black man I do not recognize. I notice that he is holding both Mrs. Johnson and Janie's hands. T's father, I realize. On the other side of Janie is a younger black man. He is the spitting image of T. Ray, I suppose. With him is a very beautiful and very pregnant white girl. Leslie Bloodworth. Beside her is a white man in uniform. He is holding a blond-haired little boy in his lap. Blond hair, like his mother, Leslie. The soldier is Leslie's husband.

I am confused by the presence of the two dead men and Leslie's family, but the purpose of the gathering is clear. The townspeople, black and white, have come to see Jenny and T married, and none of them seem to be very happy about it.

T bursts from one of the side doors, nearly at a run. "Where have you been?" he calls to me. "We've all been waitin' for you." He ushers me toward the center of the church as Brother Radley joins us.

The first chords of "Here Comes the Bride" echo through the church. The congregation stands and turns toward the back of the church. The little girl in the white cotton dress steps into the aisle. She waves at me, then prances down the center of the church, dropping orange blossom petals along the way. Carl is the next to appear. Dressed in his uniform, he steps into the small portico and holds his arm out for Jenny.

She follows her father from the small side room where they have been waiting. She is breathtaking in her long white gown. The sheer veil obscures her face but doesn't hide the huge smile on her face. She takes Carl's arm. The pianist taps out the cadence for their march down the aisle.

T beams as he watches her approach the altar. He nervously rocks back and forth beside me. I place my hand on his shoulder to reassure him.

"She's so beautiful," he whispers.

"Yes," I agree.

Carl and Jenny stop before us. He releases Jenny's hand to T, then goes to sit by Joanne.

"Dearly beloved," Brother Radley begins, "and barely departed." He laughs wickedly at his own joke. No one else does, so he continues, "We are gathered here in the sight of God and these witnesses to join these two young folks in the state of holy, albeit unusual, matrimony. I ask you now, who gives this woman in marriage this day?"

Carl stands to his feet and announces, "Her mother and I do."

"Is there anyone here who can give any reason why these two should not be joined in marriage..." A muffled roar spread through the crowd. "...let him speak now, or forever hold his peace."

The front doors of the church explode inward with a great rush of wind and heat. The murmur of the crowd escalates to panicked screams from both sides of the sanctuary as everyone scrambles for cover. When the smoke clears, Billy Watson stands in the shattered doorway holding a lit stick of dynamite.

He screams, "Ain't no kin a mine gonna marry a..."

Billy continues to scream, but I cannot hear him. A terrible pressure like an invisible hand grips my throat, cutting off my air. I claw at my throat in a vain attempt to free myself of the unseen assailant.

A few seconds passed before I realized that the pressure on my throat was real, that someone was choking me. My eyes snapped open to the face of Dan Sims. He was standing over me with a sadistic smile on his face and his hand around my throat. I grabbed for his wrist. I was unable to move his hand. He loosened his grip but did not remove the hand. I hungrily gulped for air.

"What do you want?" I whispered, unable to coax any volume from my aching throat.

"Billy sent me," he confirmed what I already knew.

"Why?"

"He wants me to punish you," Sims explained.

"For what?"

"For fuckin' Jenny Besmer."

"But I didn't."

"I know that, but Billy don't."

I was about to defend myself when what he said sank in. "You know that?" I asked. "How?"

"'Cause I been followin' her," he admitted. "I seen her fuckin' that nigger friend of yours. At Newbern's Oak. Down from her house. Straddled him on the hood of that little convertible of hers."

Although I had come to terms with my feelings for Jenny, hearing the words stung me. "You watched them?"

"Damn right," he smiled. "They put on a hell of a show. I'd love to get my hands on that hard little body of hers." He saw the disgust wash across my face. He laughed. "You can't tell me that you ain't wantin' it." I didn't deny it. "That's what I thought," he said.

He released me and stepped away from the bed. I sat up and rubbed my neck. I thought of tackling and choking him, but I remembered Jawbone's warning. I remained seated and waited for him to speak.

When he didn't, I finally asked, "If you saw them together, why did Billy send you after me?"

"I told him it was you."

I was shocked by his revelation. Why in the world would he have lied to Billy. Certainly not to protect T. I figured Dan Sims for one of the last men who would care about a black man, especially with him in Billy's back pocket.

"Why?" I wondered.

"'Cause I wanted to," was the only reason he gave.

"Fine," I huffed. "Don't tell me, but tell me this. If you know Jenny was with T, then why are you here?"

"I want you to tell your friend to stay the hell away from Jenny Besmer," he commanded.

"Why don't you tell him yourself?"

"'Cause you gonna tell him," he replied. "I don't want nobody to know 'bout all this. If I went bustin' in on them niggers, all hell'd break loose, and everybody'd know 'bout Jenny and the Johnson boy. I don't want nobody to know, least of all Billy."

"But you don't mind if Billy comes after me."

"I don't give a rats left nut 'bout you," he admitted. "Billy can piss in your pocket for all I care, but I don't want him anywhere near the Johnson boy."

I was more than a little confused by what I was hearing. I could not image any reason for any of it.

He added, "So that's why you gonna tell him to stay away from Jenny Besmer!"

"Why do you care so much about T Johnson?" I wondered aloud.

"It's none of your damn business!" he barked.

"None of my business?" I growled. Before I thought about the consequences, I sprang from the bed and grabbed his shirt. "When you broke in here and nearly choked me to death, you made it my business!"

He pushed me away from him, but he didn't hit me. "That took balls," he said. "Been a damn long time since anybody stood up to me like that."

"So I got balls," I remarked. "So tell me." I was relieved that the big man didn't kill me. "Janie is my sister."

I didn't realize for a moment who he was talking about. "Janie? From the diner?" I realized.

"Yeah," he confirmed. "I don't give a shit 'bout T Johnson, no more than I give one 'bout you, but Janie loves that boy like a son. She 'bout died when the other one was killed. Somethin' happens to this one, and it'll hurt her bad, and I'll do whatever it takes to keep her from gettin' hurt." He pushed me backward, causing me to fall on the floor. "You tell the boy what I said, you hear." Before I had a chance to get back up, he left.

I sat, stunned, on the floor for a long time processing all that I had heard. I wondered if Sims knew why his sister cared so much about T's family. I assumed he did, but he probably wasn't happy about it. I considered my options. If I went to Besmer about the threats, I would betray Jenny and T, so I concluded that I had no choice but to talk to T. He needed to know that his relationship with Jenny was no longer secret, and he needed to know about the threat. I would call him first thing in the morning.

I finally dragged myself up from the floor and stumbled to the bathroom to look at my neck in the mirror. Two purple bruises had already formed on the sides of my throat. Maybe, I thought, leaving wasn't such a bad thing after all. I took a long drink of water from the tap, then went back to bed.

My hopes of a restful night's sleep disappeared with Dan Sims, and I tossed and turned for the rest of the night. With the first hint of daylight, I gave up the effort and went downstairs to call T.

Joshua was sitting in his usual spot in the lobby. He looked over the paper he was reading and greeted me, "Mornin', son. You leavin' already?"

"Not yet," I replied. "I just couldn't sleep." I saw no reason to tell him about my late-night visitor.

"You still leavin' us today?" he asked.

"Yes," I answered. "I just need to talk to T before I go. Can you get him on the phone for me?"

He got up from his chair and went to the phone in the corner. He put the receiver to his ear and said, "Mornin', Ramona. Early? Yes, ma'am. Can you..." He rolled his eyes at the interruption. "He's still with us." He listened. "Probably later today." He looked at me and shrugged his shoulders. "Listen, Ramona, would you like to talk to him? He's standin' right here." He paused for a moment for her answer. A smile broke out on his face, and he said, "Sadie Johnson's place." He put his hand over the mouthpiece and whispered, "She's doin' it." He handed the phone to me and went back to his newspaper.

I had to laugh at the exchange, but I realized, as I listened to them, that I could not tell T what I had to tell him over the telephone... not with the chance of Ramona listening. I let the phone ring through and planned to ask T to come to town to talk to me.

"Hello," T came on the line.

"T?" I confirmed.

"Eddie?" he verified. "I thought you were leavin' this mornin'."

"I am," I answered, "but I need to talk to you about something." I hesitated, then added, "But it can't be on the phone."

"I understand," he acknowledged, "but I'm stuck here until mama gets home from the gin."

"The gin's running again?" I asked.

"Naw," he laughed. "They ain't no cotton to gin this early, but mama works out in the warehouse. They got a buildin' full of it to move out before the harvest comes in. Early bloom this year, you know."

I didn't know, but I didn't see the need in admitting it.

He continued, "Anyway, mama's got the car at the gin, so I ain't got no way to get to town. Besides, I can't leave Grandma, anyway." He paused, then asked, "You got any way of gettin' out here? Janie might let you borrow her car again."

I looked over my shoulder at Joshua. "Hang on a minute," I told T. I called out to Joshua, "Can I borrow your car?"

"You tired of walkin'?" he laughed.

"I need to run out to T's." I offered no further explanation.

Joshua furrowed his brow as he considered the request, then he pulled the keys from his pocket and tossed them across the room to me. "Don't run off with it, you hear?!" he laughed.

"I'll be out there as soon as I can," I said to T, then hung up the phone.

I thanked Joshua for the car and headed out the door for the garage. I was not surprised to find Dan Sims sitting on the hood of his car down the street from the inn. He was carving in a piece of wood and spitting tobacco juice into the street. I threw up my hand at him. He nodded in response. He nodded again, spit a long stream of tobacco in the direction of the car, but made no motion to move from his perch when I drove by him. He must have assumed I was delivering his warning, so he felt no need to follow me.

I was surprised to find a car parked in the yard in front of T's house when I arrived. It was a white Ford station wagon with "COUNTY HEALTH SERVICES" stenciled in red letters on the door. My first thought was that something had happened to T's grandmother. I jumped from the car and rushed to the porch, afraid of what I would find inside.

T met me at the door. "We'll have to talk out here," he said, pulling the door closed behind him.

I nodded toward the door and asked, "Something wrong?"

"Oh no!" he exclaimed. "County nurse is here."

"County nurse?" I repeated.

"Yeah," he answered. "She comes out twice a month to check on Grandma Grace. She surprised me this mornin'. Drove up right after I hung up with you. She normally comes on Tuesday, but she says she's got some meetin' or somethin' to go to in Macon tomorrow. Any way, she's in there with Grandma Grace, so we have to talk to out here. Mrs. Abernathy has got big ears and an even bigger mouth."

I quickly told T about my confrontation with Billy and about my late night visit from Dan

Sims. He was dismayed that Sims knew about him and Jenny, and he was angered by the ultimatum. He was unsure what he was going to do about it all, but he admitted that he would have to talk to Jenny as soon as possible. We both supposed that she would explode.

The door opened behind T, and a short, heavy-set woman in an ill-fitting white dress stepped out onto the porch. She gave me the once-over, smiled, but did not speak to me. Instead, she turned to T and said, "Theodore, Gracie's doin' quite well for a woman her age."

"Yes, ma'am."

"I noticed a sore on the back of her left foot," she continued. "Probably from layin' in the bed all day. I put some salve on it, and I left the jar on the dresser there. I'll get Doc Lang to leave a prescription for it and some antibiotics down to Brown's. Y'all need to keep the ulcer greased up 'til it heals up good, and put some of that salve on any more sores she gets. We don't want to have to take her foot off, do we?"

"No, ma'am," T responded.

"You tell your mama I said hello," Mrs. Abernathy said as she descended the stairs for her car. She backed the big wagon from the yard and threw up her hand before she drove away.

"You wanna come in now?" T asked.

"I really need to go," I responded. "I just wanted to give you the heads up on Dan Sims and put you on notice about the warning. I just want you and Jenny to be careful."

"Scares the hell out of me," he said. "I thought we were pretty safe. Pretty well hidden. I can't help but think about what would have happened if it had been Billy himself that had seen us." He paused for a moment and considered the possibility, then he added, "I'd probably be dead right now."

I agreed.

He again invited me inside, but I begged off with the excuse that I had to get Joshua's car back to him, and I had to get on the road. I planned on putting some miles behind me before dark, but I had a couple more stops to make before I left town. I wanted to say goodbye to Carl Besmer, and I had to stop by the diner to see Janie, Max, and Karen.

T reluctantly accepted my rejection of his invitation with a shrug. He thanked me again for the warning and the information about Sims. I thanked him for the friendship he had shown me and wished him luck with his relationship with Jenny. We hugged again before I left him standing on the porch and returned to Joshua's car.

He called after me, "Hey Eddie!"

"What?" I answered.

"Don't forget 'bout us po' folk when you get rich, you hear?" he laughed.

"Funny," I responded. "Funny."

I glanced at T through the rearview mirror. He stood on the front porch watching me drive away. He was still standing there when I turned the last corner that took me out of visual range. I did not envy his position. He was separated from the woman he loved by a barrier which, in 1963, was not easily crossed. It was a barrier that crossing could leave him dead. I was cut to my very soul by the looks of hurt, anger, and sadness that played across his face as I relayed Dan Sims' message, and it was that final look of painful resignation that haunted my thoughts as I drove back to the inn. I prayed that their love for each other that so obviously glowed in their eyes was strong enough to defeat the hatred and ignorance that fought so hard to keep them apart.

It was also that look on T's face that fueled my own hatred for Billy Watson. To me, he symbolized the ignorance that placed the wall between T and Jenny, Ray and Leslie, Janie and T's father, and others like them. There were people like Billy, small-minded bigots, on both sides of the fence, but he was the one that was right there throwing his stupidity in my face. He was the one who looked at me and hated me for what he saw, rather than what I was, and I hated him for that. I hoped for a day when people like him were dinosaurs, driven to extinction by their inability to adapt, and I prayed that we would all live in a society where everyone could look past our differences to realize that we were all the same.

By the time I got back to the inn, I had worked myself into a controlled rage. If I had seen Billy Watson, I probably could have killed him with my bare hands. It was hard enough driving by Dan Sims, who was still at his post, still carving, and still spitting. I did not acknowledge his gesture when he nodded at me as I passed. Instead, I stared straight ahead of me until I pulled into the garage. I almost thought of going in through the tunnel to avoid seeing him again, but, I had to laugh at the absurdity of the idea. The laughter lightened my mood, but I still didn't acknowledge Sims when I went around front to enter the building. I didn't even look his way.

"Thought I might have to call the sheriff out after you," Joshua laughed as I came through the door. I handed him his car keys and thanked him again for the favor. "Don't mention it," he insisted.

May had joined him in the sitting area of the lobby while I was gone. She was working, again, on the knitting I had seen her doing before. She looked up from her needles and said, "You're out and about awful early. Joshua told me you had some business with T Johnson this mornin'. I hope his folks are doin' good."

"Yes, ma'am," I answered.

"His mama still work out at the gin?" Joshua asked.

"Yes, sir," I replied.

"The sheriff came by a little while ago lookin' for you," Joshua changed the subject. "I told him you'd run out to the Johnson place. He said he'd check back a little later."

"Did he say what he wanted?" I wondered if it were all about to hit the fan.

"He just said he'd heard from Jenny that you were leavin' today, and he wanted to see you before you run off."

"His office was my next stop," I explained. "I wanted to say goodbye and test the waters."

"He didn't act like he knew anything about it," Joshua assured me.

"We'll see," I said. "I'm going to go over there now, then go down to Max's to see Janie and get some breakfast."

"What?" May piped in.

I repeated what I had said, knowing full well that she had heard me.

"Nonsense!" she exclaimed. "You'll so no such thing. You can go see the sheriff and Janie and whoever else strikes your fancy, but you'll do it after you've had a proper breakfast."

"But..." I began to argue.

"But nothing," she stopped me. "I've got breakfast on the stove waitin' on you. Now come on. Let's sit down and eat it."

I looked to Joshua who was laughing at the whole exchange. He shrugged his shoulders and said, "Don't look at me. She wouldn't let me eat a bite 'til you got back, so I'd be much obliged if you'd do what she says, so I can eat. I'm starvin'."

After breakfast, I walked across the street to the courthouse. The sheriff's car was parked alone at the curb, so I was pretty confident that Watson wouldn't be around. I was certainly not ready to face him yet. As mad as I was at him, I was afraid I might do something I would regret.

I climbed the steps and pulled open the heavy door. Zeb was on his bench down the hall. I waved as I stepped inside. He quickly turned away. I laughed out loud. I left him to his embarrassment and stepped toward the open door to the sheriff's office. Lenora was sitting behind her desk stubbing out a cigarette into an already half-filled ash tray. She was already lighting another by the time I stepped to the counter.

She looked up at me and asked, "You here to see the sheriff?"

"Yes, ma'am," I answered.

She rolled back in her chair and banged on the closed door to Carl's office. Without waiting for him to answer, she called out, "Carl! That Chance boy is here to see you!" She turned back to me and said, "He'll be right with you."

Not long after Lenora's knock, the door opened and Carl stuck his head out of it. He smiled when he saw me. "Eddie," he said, "Come on back." He stepped back from the doorway to allow me to enter. He addressed Lenora, "If Billy comes in, tell him I'm not here."

She furrowed her brow and replied, "Carl, he'll know you're here. Your car's outside."

"I don't care." He stepped into the office and shut the door. He motioned me toward one of the gray padded chairs that sat before the desk. He plopped down in the leather chair behind the desk, propped his feet on one corner, and took a drink from the large, red and black coffee mug that sat on the opposite one. "Coffee?" he offered, pointing to the pot on the hot plate in the corner of the small room. I shook my head. "Suit yourself," he shrugged and took another pull from his own cup. "Takes the edge off the mornin'." He set the cup down, pulled a small folding knife from his pocket, and began to clean under his fingernails.

We sat in silence for a few moments while he scraped his nails. Something about his demeanor, the quiet, and the presence of the knife, made me extremely uneasy. I sat nervously and wondered if the rumors about Jenny and me had made it back to him. I was sure that Billy hadn't told him, and I didn't figure Sims or Brinson for the kind to go blabbing to the sheriff, but I had no way of knowing who they had told. A knot formed in the pit of my stomach as I waited for the explosion that I had convinced myself was coming. It didn't.

"Jenny told me you were leavin' today," he announced, breaking the awkward silence.

"Yes, sir."

"Stay on with us," he offered, putting me at ease.

"I can't say that I haven't thought about it," I replied. "The Wilsons have been trying to convince me to stay just about since I got here."

He laughed. "I know. I think May would adopt you if she could. She thinks a lot of you."

"I think a lot of them, too," I said. "They're like the grandparents I never had."

"You could do worse."

I agreed.

Once my anxiety was relieved, Carl and I had a good visit. He talked about his trip to Atlanta, and I told him about my proposed route south from Wixton. He offered a couple of changes that would keep me away from places he knew would be trouble. He also offered to make some calls, to make things easier for me. He was friendly with a lot of the lawmen in the area, and with every town we mentioned he had a story to tell.

I heard so many stories about this sheriff or that police chief that I lost count, and I also lost track of the time. Before I knew it, it was nearly ten o'clock. I must have jumped when I noticed the time on the clock on the wall behind the desk, because Carl jumped and nearly spilled the cup of coffee he was holding.

"You sure I can't persuade you to stay?" Carl asked as he walked me out of the courthouse.

"I'm sure," I repeated. "But I appreciate the invitation. You don't know what that means to me."

"You're good people," he said, "and I'm glad I got the chance to know you."

"Likewise, Carl Besmer," I replied.

I extended my hand to him, and he grasped it firmly. "You take care of yourself, Eddie," he advised as he released my hand, "and if you're ever in this neck of the woods again, stop by and holler at us."

"I will."

Leaving a place had never been this hard before. With each goodbye, the lump in my throat grew bigger. I still had two sets of people to see before I left for good, and I was worried that, by the time I was done, I was going to choke to death. At the bottom of the courthouse steps, I cleared my throat and wiped the moisture from the corners of my eyes.

I steeled myself against the hardest one to come and walked across the street to the inn. Thankfully, the lobby was empty when I came in, so I was able to get upstairs to get my things before I had to face anyone. I wanted a few minutes to prepare myself for the emotions that I was sure would come.

That did not go like I planned it. When I unlocked the door to my room, I saw that May had already been there to straighten up and make the bed. In the center of the bed was a small wrapped box with a large red bow on it. I sat down on the bed and held the box, unopened, for the longest time. There was a small card attached. In May's handwriting, it read, "For the road. Love, May." Inside the box was a tin full of cookies. Tears blurred my vision.

"You always seemed to enjoy the ones I left for you," May said from the doorway. I was so moved by the gift that I had not noticed when she had opened the door. Joshua stood just behind her in the hall. "I figured you could use a few on your trip. To keep your energy up, you know." She was no longer able to fight back the tears in her own eyes. They came into the room, and May sat on the bed beside me. Joshua sat on the arm of the chair across from us.

"Thank you," I managed to choke out. I wiped the tears from my eyes and said, "You didn't have to go to all that trouble."

"Nonsense!" she exclaimed. "What have I told you about that?"

"She would've baked you a peck of 'em if you'd had room to carry 'em," Joshua interjected with a quiver in his voice.

"I don't know what to say," I shrugged.

"Done said all you need to say," May replied. "Ain't no need to say no more. Just enjoy the cookies."

"I will do that," I assured her.

"You dead set on leavin' us?" Joshua asked.

"I guess so," I answered.

"You don't sound too fired up about it," he commented.

I laughed without much conviction, then said, "I've made a lot of friends here, more than anywhere else I've been, and I'll miss you all."

"We're gonna miss you, too," May sniffed. "I kinda got used to havin' you around."

"Yeah boy," Joshua agreed. "You know you could stay with us and hire on as a hand. I can always use a strong back around here."

"I'd love to, but I got a promise to keep," I reminded him.

"I understand," he said, "but the offer stands."

"Thank you."

May broke the uncomfortable silence that settled between us. She put her hand on mine, which was still holding the tin of cookies. She indicated the cookies and said, "I put in a few oatmeal raisin, but mostly they're chocolate chip."

"My favorite," I smiled.

As much as I hated to leave, I felt it was time to go. I stood up from the bed and picked up my bag from its place by the door. I untied the drawstring and placed the can inside. I heard a sniff from May as I drew the bag closed again and pulled it onto my shoulder. The weight was foreign to me at first. It would take a day or so to get used to it again.

Joshua stood to see me out. He made no more mention of my staying, because he knew that my mind was set on leaving. He offered his hand to shake, but he laughed when I took it and pulled me into a big bear hug.

May was close behind him. She embraced me, gave me a peck on the cheek, and made me promise that I would write. She smiled, but tears streamed from her eyes. She patted me on my arm and reminded me to enjoy the cookies. I assured her I would.

The three of us stepped from the room into the hall. May stopped just inside the doorway and flipped off the lights. She pulled the door closed. I stopped and fished the room key from my pocket and handed it to her. She looked at the key in her hand and said, "The place seems empty already." The statement hung in the air between us.

Joshua broke the silence. He turned to May and said, "Mama, we ain't doin' nothin' but hinderin' the boy." I started to protest, but he interrupted, "Don't try sayin' we ain't. You know we'd keep you here all day, if you'd let us, but that ain't fair to you. Now you take care of yourself out there, and remember, you're welcome here anytime. If you ever want it or need it, you got a home with us. Always."

"Always," May repeated.

I tried to thank them, but I couldn't speak. I was too choked up by their kindness to form the words, so all that came out was a labored sob. Tears poured down our faces as we all gave in to the emotion of the moment. May put her arms around me and held me while I sobbed against her shoulder. I was all but a stranger to the Wilsons, but they had taken me into their home and made me feel like a member of their family. I had not felt love like that since my father died, and I was overwhelmed.

Several minutes passed before I regained my composure. I stood up from May's shoulder and wiped my face on the back of my hand. "I'm sorry," I apologized.

"It's all right," May assured me, wiping away her own tears.

Before we had a chance to yield to our emotions again, I started down the stairs to the lobby. Joshua and May followed me down and out onto the porch. We embraced one last time, and I descended to the sidewalk. I turned and waved at them before they disappeared through the front door. I stood for a moment and looked at the front of the inn. It felt strange to be walking away from the place I had begun to consider home. Oddly enough, I regretted leaving the Wixton Inn and the Wilsons more than I had regretted leaving Liz and Nico two months ago.

I took one last look at the bright red doors and the sign that hung above them. "You're no stranger here," I whispered to myself. I took to heart the truth in those words. I gave the place a final wave, shifted the heavy bag on my shoulder, and headed up the street to the diner and my final goodbye.

Chapter Eighteen

The diner wasn't that crowded. With just over an hour until noon, the lunch crowd was just beginning to trickle in. Before long, the place would be filled to capacity, about seventy-five people. Janie had told me that the lunch crowd was about more than the two of them could handle. I hoped to have said my goodbyes and be long gone before the bulk of the rush hit.

Karen was refilling the napkin holders for the lunch crowd, and Janie was taking an order at the big corner booth when I arrived. They looked my way and waved when they heard the screen door slam. Both frowned when they noticed the bag on my shoulder. I waved back and shrugged. Janie waved me over to the counter, then turned her attention back to the men at the table. I took a stool and dropped my bag to the floor beside me.

Karen was the first to come over. Having finished the napkins, she came around the end of the counter and placed the big basket underneath. Janie came around close behind her. She dropped the order ticket in the window and called, "Ticket down!" Max appeared in the window for the order. He threw up his hand to me and smiled before he disappeared. Janie then joined us at the counter.

"Are you really leavin' us?" Janie asked, pointing toward my bag on the floor.

"I'm afraid so," I answered. "I figure it's time I got back on the road."

"Well, we sure hate to see you go," Janie said.

"Yeah," Karen agreed.

"You want some lunch before you head out?" Janie asked.

"No, thank you," I replied. "May cooked a big breakfast this morning."

"You gotta at least have a piece of pie for the road," Karen offered. "You won't find a better pie than Daddy's anywhere."

I thought for only a moment before I accepted, "Pie sounds good."

"Ice cream?" Karen asked.

"Just pie."

She stepped away to get the pie, leaving Janie and me alone for a moment. She leaned in and whispered, "I talked to T this mornin'. He said you had a run-in with Danny."

Danny? I almost laughed. I was surprised that T had mentioned it to her at all, and I was curious about the extent of what he had told her, but I didn't ask. I thought it best to just acknowledge the confrontation. I replied, "Yes."

She frowned and said, "I'm sorry 'bout that. Danny's a good kid, most of the time, anyway, but sometimes he gets a little carried away. And hangin' around with Billy Watson don't help matters. I ain't sayin' Danny's an angel. Lord knows, he's always had a bad temper, and Watson, the bastard, plays on that, and Danny's misguided loyalty." She sighed and said, "Anyway, I'm sorry 'bout him botherin' you."

"It's not your fault," I assured her.

"I know," she sighed again.

I didn't know how to respond.

Karen, who had been intentionally standing to the side while Janie and I talked, took the uncomfortable break in the conversation to return with my pie. She winked at me when she set the larger than usual wedge of apple pie on the counter in front of me. "Enjoy!" she instructed. "On the house." I started to protest, but she cut me off. "Goin' away present."

"Thank you."

I dug into the pie while Janie and Karen tended to the growing crowd. Before long, the two of them were too busy to stop and chat. A moment here and there, to rest their feet, was all the break they got. Since they were too busy to talk, after I had eaten the pie, I decided it was time to go. I caught Janie's attention and announced my intention. She shook her head at me and pushed another slice of pie in front of me. I didn't even think of declining.

By the time the big, yellow clock that hung on the wall behind the counter said it was 12:30, the dining room was completely filled, and I was well past my intended departure time. I sat at the counter and watched how Janie and Karen worked the crowd. I was amazed by the banter they exchanged with the diners. They talked about the weather, jobs, sick family members, or whatever the situation called for. They knew so much about everyone that they could move from one table to the next like they were at a family reunion.

Taking a short break, Janie came and sat beside me at the counter and asked what my plans for the day were. Before I had a chance to tell her anything, Max set a plate of food in the window and called, "Order up! B.L.T. on wheat! Hash browns!"

"That's mine, sugar," she sighed, patting me on the arm. "Time to get back to work." She sighed again, then went to collect the plate from the ledge. "I'll be back in minute, honey," she called out as she rounded the counter. "Just let me give this to Mr. Parker."

Janie took care of a couple more customers after dropping Mr. Parker's B.L.T off at his table. Karen passed by while I waited for Janie's return and sat a third piece of pie on the counter in front of me. She winked when I looked up at her. I looked down at the pie and thought that I was going to be too sick to go anywhere if I continued to sit at that counter and let the two of them push that pie in my face. I thought momentarily of leaving the pie untouched, but the sweet smell of the apple filling changed my mind. I picked up my fork, scooped up one of the warm, syrupy apples, and savored it.

I was about halfway through that third piece, and Janie had not yet returned to finish our conversation. I was thoroughly enjoying the pie, although I was beginning to feel a little nauseated from eating nearly three-quarters of a pie by myself. I laid the fork down and took a long pull from my neglected glass of Coke. Karen came by, so I got her to refill my glass, then I pushed the pie away and drank several swallows of Coke in an attempt to settle my stomach. While I waited for the wave of nausea to pass, I heard someone whistling over the noise of the diner. I turned toward the sound and found that it came from a table occupied by a quartet of the local "good ol' boys", as Janie called them. Three of them were strangers to me, but the fourth was Dick Brinson, who had whistled. The four of them were looking toward the door. Brinson whistled again, and his buddies whooped and hollered. I turned to the door to see what was causing all the commotion.

The what turned out to be who. A young woman stood just inside the door in front of the big, plate-glass window. I was stunned, to say the least. She was one of the most beautiful women I had ever seen, and certainly the most beautiful woman in Wixton, Georgia. She glanced in the direction of the catcalls and whistles, and dismissed the lot of them with a look of pure disgust. Not giving them a second look, she came toward the counter where I was sitting.

I did not want to stare at her, but it was hard not to watch her walk across the room toward me. Back lit by the big window, the curves of her body were silhouetted against the thin cotton fabric of the simple white dress that she wore. She was stunning, though she wore no make-up and her long red hair fell carelessly across her shoulders and down her back.

I was afraid that my staring would warrant me the same look that Dick and his friends had gotten, but, instead, she smiled at me as she dropped the shopping bag she was carrying onto the floor and took a seat two stools down from me. I smiled back, calmly, but inside I was melting. I had never believed in love-at-first-sight, but I knew that if it could happen, it must have felt a whole lot like what I was feeling. I was about to introduce myself when Janie walked up to her.

"What can I get for you today, sweetheart?" Janie asked.

"A hamburger and a Coke," she said, then pointing over my way, she added, "and a piece of that apple pie." She winked at me, not appearing to be put off by my staring.

I blushed but managed to smile and say, "It's good."

"That's good to hear," she replied, then turned away from me to wait for her food.

Janie brought over her hamburger and Coke and set them down on the counter in front of her. She thanked her, then bowed her head and asked the blessing. I smiled to myself. A beautiful, God-fearing woman. What more could a man ask for? I watched her as she prayed, and when she opened her eyes, she looked right over at me. I quickly turned my head down to my pie, but, out of the corner of my eye, I could see her smiling. Uncontrollably, I smiled back without ever taking my eyes off my plate, and, although I was still slightly nauseated, I scooped up a forkful of pie and ate it. I just sat there eating pie I didn't really want and watching her out of the corner of my eye.

While I was trying to muster the courage to speak to her again, I wondered what I was doing. The day was half over, and I was still in Wixton. Every time I thought about getting on the road again, something would happen to stop me, and, as I glanced at the flame-haired beauty beside me, I wondered if I was ever going to leave.

I was so enraptured by her that I did not notice the diner had grown strangely quiet. When I became aware of the change, I forced myself to take my eyes off of her and looked over my shoulder. To my dismay, I saw that Dick Brinson had left his table and was headed toward us, or toward her. I'm sure he was paying no attention to me. He had a big smile on his face, and all his buddies were snickering and waving him on.

Although she never looked back at him, she must have sensed trouble coming, because the tension in her body was visible, and the smile disappeared from her face. Even after Dick reached the counter and sat down on the stool on the other side of her, she still didn't look up at him. She kept her eyes on her plate and took another bite of food.

"Well, hello, Miss Lucy," Dick said. She grimaced when he said her name. He went on, "Been a long time since I seen you in town. I figured you was thinkin' you too good to come down here amongst us common folk." I could tell by the expression on her face that she was getting angry, but she did not acknowledge him. She just kept her eyes on her plate. Dick continued, "I sure do love seein' you, though. You and all that red hair of yours." He reached out and touched her hair. She flinched as if he'd hit her, but did not speak. He added, "My daddy always said that a redheaded woman's got a passion in her."

One of his buddies cried out, "Red on top! Fire in the hole!" The other two roared with laughter.

Dick glanced over his shoulder at the table and chuckled, then asked, "You know what I've always wondered, Red? You don't mind if I call you Red, do you?" She didn't answer. "One thing I really want to know, Red. Is this here red natural? What I mean is... If I were to... What I want to know is... is this red the same all over?" He grinned. His buddies laughed again. "Yeah boy! I sure would like to get a look at the rest of it. You know... for curiosity's sake."

She continued to ignore him. I started to get up and put an end to it, but Janie put her hand on my arm and stopped me. I reluctantly stayed seated.

Janie said, "Dick, why don't you go sit back down? I'll bring you out a fresh cup of coffee."

Dick ignored her and continued his torment, "You need to loosen up, Red. I bet you ain't been laid since Rooster left, have you?"

"Dick Brinson!" Janie exclaimed. "Watch your mouth! Go sit down!"

He paid no attention. "That's what you need, sure enough. Every hen needs a good lay every now and then." He looked over his shoulder at his buddies, who laughed heartily at her expense. Dick went on, "Your Rooster done gone off and left you without a cock around. That's what you need, ain't it, Red, a cock in your henhouse?"

One of Dick's buddies crowed like a rooster, and Dick and the rest of them cackled with laughter. She closed her eyes, took a deep breath to calm her nerves, and continued to eat. I noticed that her hands were shaking when she put the hamburger to her mouth to take a bite. As I watched her chew the food, I caught the glint of a tear on her cheek. Anger boiled in me, but Janie put her hand on me, again, and whispered, "He'd kill you." She was probably right, but I was so mad I could have killed him with my bare hands. Only the look in Janie's eyes kept me seated.

"Dick, leave Miss Brewster alone and go sit back down!" Janie commanded.

Dick turned to her and barked, "Why don't you shut up, bitch?" His buddies gasped at the statement, and, from the look on Dick's face, I guessed he wished he could have pulled the word back in his mouth. Dan Sims, no doubt, flashed through his mind. Knowing he had no way of going back, Dick turned back to Lucy and continued his taunting. "Yes sir, a cock in your henhouse. A good lay, that's what you need." He paused for a moment, then said, "Maybe I got you all wrong. Maybe you ain't a layin' hen. Maybe you're a settin' hen. Is that it? You a settin' hen? Why don't we go on back to your place and you can set on my face!" He laughed. His buddies whooped and hollered. "You ready to loosen up, Red, and use that fine body of yours for what God intended?"

She still refused to acknowledge him. She finished her food, looked to Janie, and asked for her check.

"On the house," Janie replied, adding a whispered, "I'm sorry."

"Thank you," she smiled. She shrugged her shoulders and said, loud enough for nearly everyone in the tomb-quiet diner to hear, "Men with the smallest cocks always have the biggest mouths." The crowd roared with laughter. Several of the women in the crowd, though red-faced, clapped.

The smile disappeared from Dick's face. Anger seethed in his expression, while his brain search for a rebuttal. He barked, "Listen here, woman, I got more cock than you've ever had before."

I noticed that the tears I had seen in her eyes earlier had been replaced by a flicker of defiance, and, for the first time since he approached her, she spoke to him. She said, "Well let's see it."

"What?" he stammered, caught off guard.

"Let's see it," she repeated. "You seem awfully proud of it. I want to see it. You were all fired up about wantin' to see if I'm natural or not, and I want to see this fabulous cock you say I need. I'll show you mine, if you show me yours."

Dick smiled, "Hell, Red, you do got a fire in you. Let's go home, and I'll give you the time of your life."

"Uh-uh," she replied.

"Uh-uh?" he questioned. "You just said you wanted it."

"You want it, too, don't you?" she asked.

"Hell yeah!" he replied.

"How bad you want it, Dick?" The way she spit out his name, it was obvious that she meant it more as label than an address. She didn't wait for his reply. She continued, "You want it more than anything right now, don't you, Dick? It's startin' to hurt, you want it so bad."

I was shocked at her behavior. I couldn't believe that the woman who had been on the verge of tears just moments before was coming-on to her tormentor. It didn't make sense, and it didn't fit into the impression that I had formed of her in my mind, but, like everyone else in the room, I sat there and watched it happen.

She reached over and rubbed her hand across the front of his pants. "My goodness. You are a big man, ain't you?" She continued to rub him, while sweat puddled on his forehead.

He was about to the breaking point, and so was every other man in the room, more than likely. Myself included. "Pull it out, Dick," she requested.

"What?"

"Pull it out," she repeated.

"What?"

"You hard of hearin', Dick?" she asked. "You heard me. Pull it out. I said I'd let you see mine, but I gotta see yours first."

"Here?" he asked, stunned.

"It's here or nowhere," she announced. She jerked her skirt up to her lap and said, "You want to fuck me so bad, drop your pants and do it! Right here! Right now!"

Gasps of disbelief erupted from the crowd. Wives and girlfriends tried, in vain, to cover their partners' eyes.

I laughed out loud, because I realized that she had been playing him. Dick was right about one thing. She did have fire in her. I looked over to Janie, who was laughing, too. She stood beside Max, who had stepped from the kitchen to see what the commotion was about. Neither he nor anyone else made any motion to stop the spectacle that played out before us.

Dick's eyes grew wide. I don't know if it was because of what he saw or the boldness of her action, but he stood bug-eyed and silent. The hesitation seemed to infuriate Lucy. She dropped her dress back in place, jumped to her feet, and got right up in Brinson's face. She yelled, "What's wrong, Dick? What happened to that big talk? Cock in the henhouse. Good lay. More than I've ever had. Huh? Where is it? What's wrong? You ain't man enough, huh?" She never let him respond, not that I really expected him to. He was too stunned by her tirade. She continued, "Let me tell you somethin', Dick, you ain't half the man Rooster was, and I wouldn't fuck you on your best day. And my name is Lucy, it ain't Red, so don't ever call me that again. You hear me? Huh? And if you ever touch me again, I'll cut off that cock you're so proud of and shove it down your throat." She drew back and punched him in the face. He recoiled from the blow as if it had come from a prizefighter rather than the petite spitfire who threw it. She didn't wait for a return punch. She stormed out of the diner, apologizing to the other diners as she went. Many of them cheered her, and others just sat open-mouthed in shock.

Dick wiped the trickle of blood from the corner of his mouth and growled, "Bitch!"

"I done told you once to watch your mouth," Janie scolded. "Why don't you take that herd of coffee-swilling morons you call friends back there and get the hell out of here, before I pour this pot of coffee down your pants. We'll see how much the big man can do with his crotch on fire."

He ignored her. He had noticed the bag that Lucy had left on the floor next to where she had been sitting. "Looks like she left in such a hurry that she forgot to get her stuff." His voice was full of false bravado that he hoped would mask the embarrassment he surely felt. "Looks like I got a reason to see her tonight. I guess I'll just have to drive out to her place tonight and give it to her."

"I don't think so," I said as I took the bag out of his hand. Trying to keep my fear of the big man from showing in my voice, I calmly directed, "You stay away from her."

"What the hell business is it of yours, Chance?" he asked. "I figured you was too busy ballin' the sheriff's daughter to stick your nose in my shit." Although I ignored the comment, it brought another gasp from the crowd. Dick said, "Where do you get off tellin' me what to do? I'll snap you in half."

"Maybe. Maybe not," I replied with a little bravado of my own, "but you don't have the right to treat a lady like that."

"Lady?" he questioned. "Shit. She ain't no lady. I don't care how much money she's got. Rubbin' all over me like that. She ain't nothin' but a whore!"

"From where I was sitting, it looked to me like you were enjoying that rubbing she was doing. What does that make you?" I asked. "It looks to me like you're just mad because she made a fool of you. I have to admit that her methods are a bit unorthodox, but the result was just the same. You picked on her, she made a fool of you, and we all got a good laugh. Seems to me like the whole mess was your fault."

"You son-of-a-bitch," he growled. He reached out to take the bag back from me.

I caught his wrist and said, "I said no!" He jerked his hand away from me with the rage building in his eyes. I tensed up for the punch that I knew he was going to throw, but it never came.

"Dick," Janie said, "I told you once to get out of here, and I meant it. Get on out of here. Now!" Max stepped up behind Janie and gave Brinson a hard stare.

He just sneered and said to me, "I'll take care of you later." Then he walked back over to his buddies at the table. I didn't wait around to see if he left. I scooped up my bag, took her bag, and went out to see if I could find her. She was pretty angry when she left, and I wanted to make sure she was okay.

I looked up and down the street but didn't see her anywhere, so I decided to walk up town. I walked up and down the street for about ten minutes before I spotted her sitting on the ground under a tree on the corner of the courthouse square. She was leaning against the tree hugging her knees to her chest and rocking back and forth. She was staring at the ground in front of her. She didn't look up at me when I walked up and set the bag next to her legs.

"Miss Brewster?" I asked timidly. She looked up at me as she wiped the tears from her eyes. She smiled.

I continued, "You left this back at the diner, and I knew you wouldn't want to come back and get it."

"Thank you. There's no way I'm going back in there as long as that jackass is in there. Sometimes I wish he'd die. I can't come into town without him or one of his buddies, or that damn Billy Watson, givin' me a hard time." She paused, then added, "But why am I telling you this? I don't even know you."

I stuck out my hand and said, "My name is Eddie Chance. Nice to meet you, Miss Brewster."

"Lucy," she corrected. "Nice to meet you, too." She laughed and took my hand. "Would you mind helpin' me up?"

I was so overwhelmed by the fact that she was holding my hand that I nearly didn't respond to what she said. Finally, I said, "Oh, yeah," as I stood up and pulled her from the ground. "My pleasure."

"Thank you," she said, "and thank you again for bringin' my bag."

"Once again, my pleasure. That was some show you put on back there."

She blushed. "I went a little overboard." She put her hands on her head and shook it. "I can't believe I pulled my skirt up like that."

"Nobody else can either. When I left, all the women were scraping their jaws up off the floor and poking their husbands eyeballs back in their heads." She laughed. I added, "I would have been out here sooner, but I had to find my own eyeballs before I could come." She blushed again.

"You're sweet," she said as she leaned over and kissed me on the cheek. My knees went to jelly, and I knew that I was glowing bright red. I also knew that, with that kiss, she had taken a hold of my heart. "I'm sorry," she said, "I didn't mean to embarrass you."

"Let me take you to dinner tonight to make up for it," I said.

"Are you hittin' on me?" she asked, coyly.

"If you can't tell, I must be doing it wrong," I answered.

"Tell you what. I never had that piece of pie back there. I've got a strawberry cake at the house. It's not nearly as good as Max's apple pie, but it'll do. How 'bout we go back to my place and have a piece, then I'll take you out to dinner tonight for bringin' me my stuff. Deal?"

My stomach churned at the thought of cake, but I wouldn't have turned her down for anything in the world. "Deal," I replied. She leaned over and kissed me again. Then I added, "But you'll have to stop kissing me like that. My knees are so weak now that I'm about to fall down, so, unless you want to carry me, you'll have to stop." I laughed. She kissed me again and winked.

"You know what, Eddie? I just met you, but I feel really comfortable with you, and I haven't felt comfortable in this town for a long time. Maybe I'll tell you about it, but, first, you've got to tell me what a guy like you is doin' in a place like Wixton. You look to me like someone who's a long way from home." She took my hand to lead me down the street. I was in heaven. She added, "Maybe Dick Brinson finally did somethin' good for a change."

"What do you mean?"

"If it hadn't been for him, I may have never met you."

Chapter Nineteen

I followed her to her car. She deposited the shopping bag she was carrying into the already crowded cargo area of the black Chevy Nomad. I put my duffle bag in the back seat and took my place next to her in the front. She pulled away from the curb and drove north, away from the courthouse, out of town. We had ridden several minutes before she turned to me and said, "I live about ten miles above town. Just this side of the county line."

"I came down this way when I first came to town. I rode down from Macon with the foreman of a big plantation out this way. He dropped me off at the front gate. I don't think I ever saw the name of the place, but his name was Zachary."

"Angel L."

"What?"

"Angel L. That was the name of the plantation."

"Yeah, that was it. Do you live near there?"

"Somethin' like that," she confirmed. "I own it."

"What?" I questioned. At first, I thought she was kidding me, but I remembered Dick Brinson's comment about her having money.

"I'm Angel L. Well, at least, I'm L. It's named after me. Daddy bought it when I was three months old, and, when he died in fifty-eight, I inherited it."

"I'm sorry about your father," I offered. I was more moved by the loss of her father than by the revelation that she was wealthy. "What about your mother?" I wondered.

"She died when I was six, givin' birth to my little brother. He died two months later of pneumonia. After that, it was just Daddy and me. Now, it's just me and the Angel L." A tear rolled down her cheek.

"I'm sorry. I didn't mean for you to drag up painful memories."

"It's okay. Sometimes it's good to talk about it."

By this time, we had reached the gate of the Angel L. Lucy turned into the driveway, stopped to check the mail, then drove on toward the house. The driveway up to the house was lined on both sides by a white, wooden fence. As we drove on, the fence was replaced by pine trees that continued almost all the way to the house. The road turned this way and that for almost a mile, then it emerged into a large, grassy area that surrounded the enormous, beautiful house that I had seen the week before. We drove by the house and pulled into the garage that sat back away from the house, connected by a breeze-way that passed by a pool. Lucy pulled the car into its space between a new Cadillac and a beat up pick-up truck. Another truck, which looked like the one that brought me down from Macon, and another car, that was covered by a tarp, occupied two other spaces in the huge garage.

We were unloading the packages from the trunk of the car when Zachary walked into the garage from outside. "You need any help with those things, Lucy?" he asked, not seeing me bent over getting my bag out of the backseat.

"No, thanks, Zachary. Eddie's helpin' me."

"Eddie?" he questioned. I stood up and said hello. He smiled and said, "Mr. Chance, I figured you'd be in Florida by now. What in the world are you still doin' in these parts?"

"I like it around here. I met a few nice people in Wixton, and I thought I would hang around a little while. I was headed out of town, but I got side-tracked."

He raised an eyebrow at that, but said, "Well, it's nice to see you again, and since you two seem to have everything under control, I got some work to do. We just about got the hole in the back fence patched up, but we still ain't got word on where Dusty got off to, though."

"He'll turn up," Lucy said hopefully, then she turned to me and explained, "Dusty's my horse. The storm blew an old, rotten pine over on the back fence. It knocked about ten feet of fence down. Dusty found the hole before we did." She laughed, half-heartedly.

"You'll find him," I assured her.

"I hope so, Eddie. I sure hope so."

Zachary disappeared through a door in the back of the garage, while Lucy and I gathered up the packages from the car and went out the side door toward the house.

"This is a beautiful place," I said as I looked around the grounds. "How much is there?"

"All together there are eight thousand acres. Zachary and his two sons oversee the four hundred acres inside the fence that make up the house grounds, and we have a crew that farms the three thousand that we call the Angel L. The rest is leased out to other farmers in the area."

"Wow!" was all I was able to say.

She laughed. I guess because I was walking around with the awed look of a five year old in a candy store. I couldn't help myself. I had never been around such wealth before. In a way, it all worried me. I wondered if I had a chance of anything with Lucy. Could a woman like her fall for a kid from New York whose fortune consisted of about eight hundred dollars, three suits of clothes, and a crazy dream of growing oranges for a fruit stand that had been torn down two years ago. I could only hope. She led me into the house via an enormous kitchen. Like everything else about her, it was beautiful. Once again, I was five years old. The kitchen was almost bigger than the apartment that Pop and I had lived in.

"Mama loved to cook, so when Daddy had the house built, he built her a kitchen she would enjoy cooking in."

"It's great," I replied. "I love this floor," I said, pointing down to the polished marble. "This is a wonderful house, and it's so big."

"Yeah, I can get pretty lonely here sometimes. Let's put this stuff down, then we can get a piece of that cake I promised you. I'll tell you all about how I ended up alone in this big house, and you can explain what Zachary meant by that Florida remark. Besides, all I know about you is your name and that you are one of the sweetest men I have ever met. I must hear more about who you are and where you came from. Okay?"

"Okay," I replied as a smile took over my face. We put the packages on a corner table, then Lucy lifted the cover off the cake. It looked delicious, but I was still reeling from all the pie. I had hoped she would forget about it, but, as she pulled a cake knife from a drawer, I was convinced I would have to force down a piece. However, she gave me an out. "How big a piece do you want?"

Although I didn't want to make her mad, I replied, "To be honest, I don't think I could eat a bite." She looked disappointed, so I explained, "That pie I was eating when you came in... that was my third piece."

"Well, no wonder. I'm surprised you're not sick already." She cut herself a piece and re-placed the cover. "Maybe later." She picked up her plate and moved to the kitchen table. She motioned for me to follow, saying, "While I eat, you come sit down over here and tell me about yourself."

"Where should I start?"

"Well, it's obvious from the way you look and talk that you are not from Wixton, Georgia. I want to know where you came from and what you're doin' here now."

"That's fair enough," I replied as we sat down across from each other at the kitchen table. "Like I told you in town, my name is Eddie Chance. My full name is Oliver Edward Chance. I was born in New York and lived there with my father, Sam Chance, until he died when I was sixteen. He ran a produce stand on the corner in front of our building. One night, two punks tried to rob him, but the stubborn old man wouldn't give them the cash box. They shot him twice in the chest. He died in my arms."

"Eddie, I'm sorry."

"Thanks. Like you said, I've learned to deal with it now. My mother died when I was born, so I never knew her. When Pop died, I moved in with Mama's sister Liz and her husband Nico. She was a good woman. He was a bum who was rarely sober. Aunt Liz cried all the time because of the way he drank. The two years that I lived with them were like hell on earth.

"When I turned eighteen in April, I withdrew the money Pop had put away for me. When Nico found out about the money, he started ranting about repaying my debt to him. He and I had a big fight, and I took off. Headed south to find my fortune."

She interrupted me, "Did you say you turned eighteen in April?"

"Yeah."

"I didn't realize that you were so young. I figured you to be closer to my age."

"How old are you?" I asked.

"Twenty-three," she admitted. "Go on."

I continued, "Since Pop ran a produce stand, I spent most of my life around fruits and vegetables, so I decided at six that, when I grew up, I was going to move to Florida and grow oranges for Pop to sell. At eighteen, I was old enough to get the money he had left for me, so I hit the road."

"You still goin' to Florida? Even though...?" she hesitated, not knowing how to ask the question.

I took her off the hook, saying, "Yeah, even though." She smiled. I explained, "To honor his memory. Anyway, I've been wandering around the east coast. Taking my time. Seeing what I can see. I met Zachary last week in Macon, and he brought me here. Dropped me off at the front gate out there, and I've been in town ever since. I finally made up my mind to leave today, but now I'm not so sure I'm in a hurry to go." I winked at her and smiled.

She blushed. "Why's that?" she asked. I just smiled. She then added, "This is movin' pretty fast, don't you think?"

"What is 'this'?" I asked.

"I'm not sure, but it feels kinda good, don't it?" she asked, then added, "Eddie, I've known you less than an hour, but you make me feel like I haven't felt in a long time. I'm in no hurry for it to end."

She leaned across the table to kiss my cheek again. Her hair brushed across my face, and the aroma of apples filled my nostrils. As her lips touched my cheek, I turned into her and pressed my lips to hers. She met my advance and pulled me hungrily to her. For several seconds, we were joined in a passionate kiss that left a bit of longing in my heart. Logic told me that I really had not fallen in love with her in an hour, but I knew, with my entire being, that I didn't have far to go.

Still stunned by the intensity of our connection, I managed to say, "Since we seem to be planning our futures together, you have to tell me more about yourself. I've poured myself out before you. Now it's your turn."

"That's fair enough," she agreed. "Where should I start?"

"I'm dying to find out what Dick Brinson was running his mouth about."

Her expression grew dark for a moment, but then she smiled and said, "That's really the end of the story." She paused for a moment before continuing. "First, let me fill in the holes in what I've already told you. I was born in Atlanta in June of forty. The twenty-seventh. To Richard and Rebecca Marlow. October of that year, Daddy bought this land because Mama didn't want to raise me in the city. He bought the eight thousand acres and named it the Angel L.

"When we entered World War Two, Daddy joined the Army as a fighter pilot. He was shot down in forty-three. He lost his left leg in the crash. He was discharged and sent home. He was a stranger to me for a long time, because I was so young when he left, but it didn't take long for me to accept him and love him as a father.

"Like I said before, my brother was born when I was six. Mama died due to complications of the birth. Matthew died two months later of pneumonia. I had a hard time acceptin' that Mama was never comin' home again, but Daddy did the best he could to make me understand that she and Matthew had gone to be with God, and that we could see them again one day. That helped a lot, but I still missed her.

"I finally got used to her absence and moved on with my life. Daddy put me in school, a private school in Albany. I was a very good student. I graduated in fifty-eight. Valedictorian. Scholarship to the University of Georgia. I had already enrolled at Athens for the fall when Daddy was killed. He was thrown from a horse. The fall broke his neck. In a way, his death was both easier and harder to accept. By that time, I understood death and what it meant, but he had been all the family I'd had for so long. I didn't know what I was going to do without him. Of course, college would have to wait, because I was now the owner of a plantation, several textile mills, and a candy factory in Atlanta." She paused to take a breath.

"Wow!" I said, taking the opportunity to comment. "That's a lot of responsibility for an eighteen year old!"

"You better believe it. I had suddenly become the owner and president of three major operations. Thankfully, Daddy had good judgment in the people he hired. Everyone who worked for him was like family, so they were quick to accept me and my ignorance of the business world. They all took me under their wings and helped me learn the ropes, and none of them ever tried to take advantage of me.

"Today, five years later, the factories are producin' well and turnin' a profit, and, as you can see, the Angel L is thrivin' under the supervision of Zachary and his two sons. I still have overall control of the businesses, but each operation has a great administration team that runs the day-to-day."

"Wow!" I repeated. "All this is a lot for a poor kid from the Bronx to take. Here I am, practically homeless, sitting across the table from a millionaire head of an empire!"

"I'm just like you, Eddie!" The anger flared in her voice. "I've been through the same things, the same heartaches, and I tell you, all this damn money doesn't make it any easier to face the pain."

"Lucy, I'm sorry." Realizing I had hit upon a sore subject, I wished I could take the words back. I tried to smooth it over. "I didn't mean anything. Believe me, I know the pain you've been through. I was just saying that your world is a lot different from what I'm used to."

"It's just bigger and more complicated."

"I'm sorry," I said again. "I didn't mean to upset you. Can we get back to the story?"

She smiled, letting me off the hook. "I'm sorry for blowin' up at you like that. I know you didn't mean anything." She put her hand on mine and continued her story. "Like I was sayin', Daddy was dead, and I was head of Marlow Industries. After several weeks of meetin's with the company lawyers and the individual administration teams, I felt comfortable with everything and everyone, so, like Daddy had always done, I left the corporate office in Atlanta in the hands of my vice-president, Mitch Patterson, and came home. I am the president and absolute head of the company, but, if someone has business with the company, Mitch is the man to see about it. If he feels the need, he consults me.

"Anyway, I came back here and settled into bein' alone. I threw myself into the Angel L, tryin' to get my mind off Daddy's death. I worked alongside Zachary and his sons, Mickey, Steven, and Rooster."

"Rooster?"

"Rooster was Zachary's youngest son, Phillip," she explained. "Rooster was a nickname he got workin' on his grandparents' chicken farm in Alabama. His buddies called him Rooster, because he spent all day in the henhouse." She laughed, but I could see the pain in her eyes. She wiped a tear from the corner of her eye.

"You don't have to go on if you don't want."

"I'm okay," she said, wiping away another tear. "Anyway, he was a couple of years older than me, but we practically grew up together. We were inseparable right up until he graduated from high school in fifty-six. He got a job drivin' a truck for a freight company out of Columbus, so he was on the road most of the time. I only got to see him every now and then. It was after he was gone all the time that I realized how much I loved him.

"When Daddy died, Rooster took leave from work to come home and be with me. His bein' here made it easier to accept that Daddy was gone. Rooster gave me a shoulder to cry on. We decided to get married that February. He put his job on hold, and we set up housekeepin' here. Everything was great for a little while, then Rooster got stir crazy. After two years on the road, he didn't take to the homebody routine, so we decided that he would start drivin' again. He took a job drivin' for Gwinnett Trucking. Some weeks he was home every night, and, sometimes, he was only home on the weekend. Anytime he was gone longer than that, I went with him.

"January of sixty-one, Rooster stopped by on a run from Atlanta to Orlando to tell me that, on the way back, he had to run over to Panama City to pick up a load of painted sand dollars to take to Chicago. He left Tuesday and said he'd be back Wednesday evenin' to pick me up for the trip to Illinois. He left..."

Her story was interrupted by the ringing of the telephone. "Hello," she answered. "Speakin'. You did?! Is he okay? Thank goodness! I'll be there as soon as I can." She hung up the phone. Her face was lit up with her beautiful smile. "That was the foreman from the Twin Pine. They found Dusty grazin' in a pasture a little while ago. You want to ride with me to get him?"

"Sure."

"I'll need my saddle," she said, heading toward the back door. She stopped and spun around, nearly running into me. She indicated the dress she was wearing and said, "I need to change my clothes. I can't ride like this. I'll be back in a minute." She disappeared through the kitchen door, and I heard her climbing the stairs. A few minutes later, nearly running, she reappeared wearing jeans, a t-shirt, and a pair of well-worn boots.

"You ready?" she asked. "Would you mind drivin' back so I can ride him home?"

"No problem," I answered, following her out the back door and across the yard to the garage.

She passed through the garage and disappeared into the room that Zachary had gone into earlier. By the time I caught up to her, she already had her arms full and nearly knocked me down on her way back out. I had just enough time to look around the tack room. Racks and shelves filled with saddles and various other riding paraphernalia lined the walls. The room smelled of old leather. It was a good smell.

"Grab that key with the blue chain," she said, motioning to the key rack hanging just inside the door.

I grabbed the key and headed toward the pickup, but Lucy was headed to the front of the garage.

"We taking the truck?" I asked.

"Nope," she called over her shoulder. She was headed for the tarp-covered car in the first space. She set the saddle down and grabbed the corner of the tarp. "You mind helpin' me with this?"

I grabbed the opposite corner and helped her uncover the car. The red and black two-seater looked like nothing I had ever seen before. It was narrow, barely wider than the two seats, and low to the ground. It was not shaped like any other car I had ever seen. It wasn't shaped like a car at all. It was nearly flat to the ground, as flat as it could be and still carry passengers. It was shaped like a teardrop, wide and round at the back and pointed at the front. The rear wheels where completely hidden in the body of the tear, while the front wheels sat at the ends of narrow arms, like a dragster. The passenger compartment was open. I saw no sign of a top, and no doors to speak of. As a matter of fact, the whole body seemed to be one continuous piece with no seams visible.

"Do you mind holdin' this stuff on the way over?" she asked. "There's no trunk. I know the pick-up would be more practical, but this'll get us there a lot faster. The Twin Pine is about twenty-five miles away by road. That'd take a half hour by truck. We'll get there a lot quicker this way. You mind?"

"No, I don't mind," I answered, not really knowing if I minded or not. "Twenty-five miles?"

"Yeah, thereabout, by car, anyway. We meet back-to-back through the woods, but the entrance is nearly around to Jones Hollow."

I nodded as if I knew what she was talking about, then I climbed into the passenger seat. Like I said, there were no doors, so I had to literally climb in.

"You'd better put on that safety belt," she said, "just in case."

I obliged, then took the saddle and other things she was carrying into my lap. She took the key and settled in behind the wheel. She quickly snapped her own safety belt and turned the ignition. The car's engine roared to life behind me.

"Engine's in the back," she volunteered, reading my mind. I just smiled. She revved the engine, but gave it little time to warm up before she dropped it into reverse and backed out of the space. We were still rolling backwards when she pushed the gearshift up into first. She let go of the clutch and floored the accelerator. The force of the takeoff pushed me hard into the seat. I remained that way for the rest of the trip.

We had topped seventy-five by the time we reached the highway. She had to slow to make the turn. Slowed barely, I should say. The rear end of the car slid around on the sand where the driveway met the road. When the rubber of the back tires grabbed the asphalt, we were sling-shotted forward. Lucy slid through the gear changes with the speed and precision of a stock car driver. She leveled off just above a hundred, then turned to me and said, "Some ride, huh?"

"You're not kidding!" I replied. "This is some car. What is it?"

"The man who built it called it 'The Stinger.' It was specially built by a man outside Detroit. Rooster brought it home from a run to Canada. The man designed and built cars by special order. If you could pay his price, he'd build anything you wanted. He told Rooster that this car was commissioned by an Air Force test pilot, but he crashed into the mountains in Colorado before he was due to pick it up. His family didn't want it, so they told the builder to sell it. Rooster said he got a good deal on it, but he never did tell me how much he paid for it. I never asked. He got whatever he wanted."

"It's the fastest thing I've ever seen," I said.

"You've got that right. I have no idea how fast it will actually go. The speedometer registers one-sixty, and she'll do that with pedal to spare. The man that built her claimed she'd top two hundred, but you'd have to be a fool to drive it that fast. Rooster set out to try several times, but he'd always chicken out when the numbers gave away."

About six miles north of the gate of the Angel L, we came to a crossroads. An old, abandoned store building sat in the north-east corner. The other three corners were empty. Lucy slowed just enough to cut the corner between a fence post and the stop sign. Dust and rocks were flying everywhere. I coughed.

"I'm sorry," she said once we were back on the road. "Slowin' down takes too much time."

"No problem. I'm having the time of my life."

She laughed, then said, "That was Cooper's Junction."

"What?"

"The crossroads," she explained. "It's called Cooper's Junction. J. S. Cooper ran a store there for over seventy years, and for forty of those years, that store served as the regional transfer station for the Merriwether Bus Line. Anybody who went anywhere in this part of the country on a Merriwether bus spent some time at Cooper's Junction General Store.

"My parents met there... back in '36. She was eighteen. He was twenty-one."

"Sort of like us," I interrupted.

She just smiled and continued her story. "Mama was takin' the bus from Savannah to visit her grandparents in Dothan. Daddy was on his way to see his older brother in Bainbridge and had stopped at Cooper's for gas.

"He saw her through the bus window when it pulled into the station. She waved at him as she passed by. 'She was beautiful,' he said. He said she looked just like me with light brown hair. His was black. Who knows where this stuff came from?" she said, running her hand through her red hair.

"I like it," I replied.

"Thanks. I never have. Anyway," she continued, not missing a beat, "he wanted to meet her. When the bus stopped, he was standing at her window. They introduced themselves. The bus had a half-hour layover, so he asked her to have a cup of coffee with him at the store's snack counter. She wanted to, but she had broken her leg the week before and couldn't get off the bus easily." She paused. "I'm sorry. I'm probably borin' you to death."

"No, it's all pretty interesting, but you never did finish telling me about Rooster."

"Okay. Okay. Let me tell you the rest of this story, then I'll tell you about Rooster."

"Okay," I answered. How could I argue? I would have sat there and listened to her recite the alphabet, just to be close to her.

"Like I was sayin', Daddy asked her to have coffee, but she couldn't get off the bus. They decided that he would get the coffee and sit on the bus with her until time for it to leave. Problem was, the bus driver wouldn't let him on the bus without a ticket, even after Daddy explained the situation to him. Daddy finally gave in and bought the ticket. He and Mama sat on the bus and talked for the rest of the half hour. They exchanged addresses and phone numbers and promised to keep in touch. He said it broke his heart to see her ride away on that bus down the highway. He called her in Dothan the next day and asked her to a movie... Dothan and Bainbridge are only about sixty miles apart. She agreed, and they had their first date. For the next two years, Daddy drove from Atlanta to Savannah every weekend to see her. He proposed in April, and they were married June 15, 1938. I was born in 1940, and you pretty much know the rest."

She sighed, then added, "Incidentally, Daddy ended up givin' the ticket he had bought, and a hundred dollars, to a young black man who was at the station tryin' to bum a ride to Birmingham to see his mother in the hospital. He was Mitch Patterson."

"Your vice-president?"

"Yep. Daddy gave him a business card and told him he could pay him back when he was able. About six months later, Mitch showed up at Daddy's office with the money, askin' for a job. He has been with the company for twenty-seven years. Been vice-president for eight."

"I guess it was a good thing your mother had a stubborn bus driver," I joked.

"Guess so," she laughed. "Hang on, we've got another turn to make."

I braced myself. She laughed. "Do I drive that bad?" she asked. I just smiled. We were almost on top of the intersection, and she hadn't even begun to slow down.

"We're turning here?" I asked nervously. I knew we were going to flip, so I tensed up and waited for the crash.

She laughed at me. "Calm down, Eddie, you're gonna live." She punched the accelerator and cut the wheel hard to the left. The rear end slid around on the pavement. Lucy's feet danced on the pedals, and she flung the wheel from left to right until we were straight in the road again. She was an amazing driver.

"Where did you learn to drive like that?" I asked after I had untied the knot in my stomach.

"Rooster taught me. He could drive anything," she explained, smiling. I could tell that she had loved him. She added, "We've got about six or seven more miles to go. I guess we'll have to put the story on hold until we get back to the house." I nodded.

She slowed as we approached the entrance to the Twin Pine. The gate was spectacular. A huge marble arch spanned the drive, connected at the ends to brick columns that flowed out along the driveway toward the road, then wound around to encircle the two evergreen trees that sat on either side of the drive. The black, wrought-iron gate was pulled open and held that way by chains that were hooked over the upturned trunks of a pair of marble elephants that flanked the drive just inside the arch.

"This is some gate!" I said, as we turned.

"This is as good as it gets," Lucy replied.

"What do you mean?"

"You'll see."

I did see as soon as we passed through the stand of trees and shrubs that obscured the view of the house from the road. Well, actually, there was no house, at least not much of one. In the distance, I could see the burned out shell of what had been the main house. Its massive structure was burned nearly to the ground. All that remained was the foundation and a section of the outside wall here and there. The rest was just piles of debris scattered about. To the left of that was a group of mobile homes in a semi-circle.

"What happened to this place?" I asked.

"Burned down in fifty-eight. It's been like this ever since. The place is owned by a ninety-three-year-old widow who just happens to be loonier than a betsybug. She's in a home up in Macon. Her son controls the property and all the money, and he won't pay to have the house rebuilt or even the old one cleaned off. His father put it in his will that, in order for the son to get the money, the plantation was to stay in the family. The boy couldn't care less about the condition of the place. All he cares about is the money. He hasn't even set foot on this property since the house burned."

"That's a shame," I replied.

"Yeah it is. The foreman, Red Sparks, lives in that first trailer. He's the one who called," she said as we pulled through the fence that surrounded the mobile homes.

A tall, heavy-set man in muddy jeans and an unbuttoned flannel shirt stepped out onto the porch of the trailer as we stopped out front. "Howdy, Miss Brewster," he said, spitting tobacco juice into the dirt off the edge of the porch. He wiped the leftover trickle of spit away from his mouth with the back of his hand, which he promptly wiped on his pants. He was disgusting. He looked over at me but didn't acknowledge my nod of greeting. Over his shoulder, I could see three faces peering out from behind the curtain of the front window. Two of them belonged to small boys, but the third was the face a teenage girl, who grinned as we pulled to a stop in front of her house. Her face, framed by curly blond hair, looked familiar, but I couldn't place where.

We climbed out of the car and met him at the bottom of the steps where he shook Lucy's hand. I extended mine, but he ignored it. I shrugged it off and put my hand back in my pocket. I looked over his shoulder again. The girl I had seen through the window was now standing in the doorway. She looked to be about fourteen and was very pretty. She smiled at me when she noticed that I was looking at her.

She smiled and asked me, "D'you find the post office t'other day?"

That's when it hit me. She had been the girl reading the story to the children at the library. "Yes, ma'am," I answered.

Red glared at me, then turned around to her. "Get back in the house, girl," he screamed at her. "You ain't got no business out here."

She didn't move. "Daddy!" she said, defiantly. "I just wanted to say hello to Miss Lucy and her friend."

I smiled at her and took a step to shake her hand. Red stepped over between us and glared at me. He then turned to her and barked, "Amber Lynn! I done told you to get back in the house! Now do like I told you, or I'll tan your hide."

Amber Lynn gave him a dirty look, then stepped back through the door. She winked at me before she closed the door. I just smiled, but that was enough to set Red off. He stepped closer to me and said through gritted teeth, "You better back off, boy. Stay the hell away from my daughter!" I stepped forward and looked him square in the eye. I just stared for a moment before I replied, "Listen, Mr. Sparks, I was just being friendly. I have no interest in your daughter." The scowl on his face told me that he was unconvinced. I took another step toward him, glanced over my shoulder at Lucy, leaned into Red Sparks, and said, quietly, "Why would I want your daughter, when I have that." I nodded toward Lucy, who stood a few steps behind me, looking anxious.

Red looked over my shoulder at Lucy. I watched his eyes walk up and down her body while he considered what I had said. I looked back at Lucy, who was giving me a disapproving look. I shrugged apologetically. I regretted the comment, but it worked. When Red had finished drooling over Lucy, he looked back at me, cocked an eyebrow, and said, "Hell, boy, I guess you got a point." He halfway grinned, then the smile disappeared. He leaned in and said, "Still. I catch you lookin' at my girl again, I'll skin you alive. You got me?"

"Yes, sir," I replied.

"Red," Lucy interrupted. "You said on the phone that you had Dusty. Please take me to him."

"Yes, ma'am. He's out in the barn."

I grabbed the saddle and fell in beside Lucy. She looked at me and winked. I smiled a confused smile, glad that she was not mad at me.

Red lead us between the trailers and through the gate out back to the barn. He was walking several steps ahead of us but looked over his shoulder several times to make sure we were following him. When he stopped to open the barn door, he turned to Lucy and said, "Massey found him out on the back pasture, grazin', and brought 'im to me. I recognized 'im right off, so I called you."

"I sure do appreciate you callin'. I've been worried sick about him since he went missin'."

By that time, Red had the barn doors open, and Lucy went straight to a beautiful, smoke-gray horse that was tied to the center post of the barn. She hugged him, and he rubbed his head against her shoulder. "You had me worried sick," she said to him as she looked him over to see if he was hurt in any way. "Are you ready to go home, boy?" she asked. He nudged her shoulder again. She took the saddle blanket from me and laid it across Dusty's back. Then she placed the saddle over the blanket and fastened everything. When she had put the bridle on him, she turned to Red and asked, "How much do I owe you puttin' him up?"

"Not a thing. It was a pleasure to take care of such a beautiful animal. The livestock 'round here ain't been worth a damn since the old man died. That two-bit son of his won't spend a dime on the place. The only reason I'm still here is the share of the crop that I get 'cause of the will. If he was havin' to pay me a salary to work the place, I'da been out on my ass a long time ago." The contempt is his voice was extremely evident.

"It's a shame he's let the place run down like he has," Lucy replied. "Are you sure I can't pay you somethin'?"

"I won't take a penny."

"Do you mind if I ride him home across the woods? I didn't want to take the time to hitch up a trailer, and the trip by road would be too hard on him."

"That'd be fine," he replied.

Lucy took Dusty's reins and led him outside. She said, " Do you think you can find your way home, Eddie?"

"It didn't look too hard. I just have to remember where to turn. I'll manage."

The three of us walked in silence back to the car. I climbed in, and Lucy climbed onto the horse. "Thanks again, Red. You let me know if there's ever anything I can do for you or your family," she said to him, then she turned to me and said, "I'll see you at the house. Be careful drivin' back. She has a tendency to try to run away with you."

"I'll remember that," I said as I fired up the engine. "I'll see you in a while, and you be careful going home, too."

I watched her ride out the gate and back toward the barn before I pulled out and headed home. The Stinger drove wonderfully, and I knew that the trip home was going to be an experience. I took it easy out to the road, but when I hit the pavement, I gunned her and held on for dear life. I leveled off at about eighty and relaxed my grip on the steering wheel. Nothing in my life had given me the rush that driving that car did. The sheer power of it was invigorating, almost addictive. I could see why Rooster had wanted it, and I could see why he had fallen in love with Lucy. I could only imagine what it was like growing up with her, but after only spending a few hours with her, I was already dreaming about what it would be like growing old with her.

I was at my first turn before I knew it, but, unlike Lucy, I wasn't good enough behind the wheel to take the turn without slowing down. If I had tried what she did, I would have flipped, and I didn't want to take that chance, so I slowed enough to make the turn, but I punched it on the way out of the turn and shot forward like a rocket. I was at a hundred before I knew it, and since the road was straight for several miles, I didn't let off the pedal.

I climbed to one thirty-five before I leveled off. The road began to rise and fall with the surrounding hills, but there were very few curves to speak of, and none were sharp enough to slow me down, so I held my speed and enjoyed the thrill of the ride. My enjoyment came to an abrupt end when I topped a hill to find a truck pulling a trailer loaded with hogs sitting across both lanes of the road. My first thought was that I was about to die, and I said, "God, help me!" He did. I didn't even think about what I did next. Instead of slamming on the brakes, which would have been a fatal mistake, I held the pedal and aimed for the ditch. I flew past the truck, hogs and all, without so much as a bump, but the car began to slide on the grass of the shoulder. I was completely sideways when I slid out of the ditch onto the highway. I slung the wheel hard to the right to get her straight on the road. I went into the ditch on the other side, but not before I had the car pointed back in the right direction. I pulled back onto the highway and took my foot off the pedal. When I stopped rolling, I planned to get out, get on my knees, and thank God for saving my life, but, unfortunately for me, the whole episode had been observed by Billy Watson, who just happened to be on his way out to help get the load of hogs out of the road. He hit the siren and pulled up in front of me when the Stinger finally came to a stop.

"What the hell are you doin', boy?" he yelled at me as he ran up to the side of the car. He grabbed my shirt and tried to pull me out of the car.

I shrugged his hand off and said, "I'm getting out!" I climbed out of the car. I knew that he had me this time. He had been looking for something that would give him the chance to throw the book at me, and now he had it.

He slung me face down on the hood of the car, then said, almost joyfully, "I got you this time, Chance! How fast were you goin'?" He paused and looked at the car. The hint of recognition played across his face, but he asked, "Where'd you get this car, boy?" When I didn't answer, he pushed my head against the car and screamed, "D'you steal it?"

"I didn't steal anything," I yelled back, pushing against his hold on me.

"Don't fight me, asshole." He pushed harder. "I'd sure hate to have to shoot you for resistin' arrest, " he laughed. "That'd be a damn shame, wouldn't it?"

Billy was just stupid enough to think he could get away with shooting me, so I relaxed my body. "Okay. Okay. But I didn't steal the car. I have permission to drive it."

"What kind of fool do you take me for? I think you stole it." He kicked the back of my legs and hit my head on the car again. "Who you know's got a car like this?"

"Lucy Brewster," I said.

"What?"

"The car. The car belongs to Lucy Brewster."

"Lucy Brewster?" he growled. "How the hell do you know Lucy Brewster?" He banged my head into the car again.

He was making me madder and madder. I pushed against him again. That time he wasn't ready for me, and I broke his hold. I jumped up and spun around. He stumbled back, fumbling with the strap on his gun belt.

"That's it, punk! I'm gonna blow your damn head off," he screamed.

I jumped at him and grabbed for the gun, which he had halfway out of its holster. He punched at me with his free hand. It was an awkward punch, causing him to stumble. I took the opportunity to push him to the ground, but I lost my balance and tumbled down on top of him. We wrestled on the ground, both of us clutching onto the gun. He thrashed from side to side, trying to break free of my hold on him. Billy twisted and rolled until he got his gun hand free from mine. He pushed himself over on top and shoved the barrel of the pistol under my chin. He smiled an evil smile and said, "I got you this time, Chance." He pushed the barrel harder. "I'm tempted to blow the top of your head off." He pulled the hammer back, and I tensed up, waiting to die. The old saying that your life passes before your eyes is not true, at least not for me. All I could see was Billy Watson's ugly, grinning face. I didn't want to die, but it looked inevitable. I closed my eyes and shut out everything around me. I had long ago prepared to die, and now all I could do was wait for it to happen.

Suddenly, I felt Billy's weight lift off of me and heard a voice say, "What the hell are you doin'?" The voice belonged to Carl Besmer. He had driven up just seconds before, but I was so worried about the gun to my throat that I didn't hear the car. He and the driver on the hog truck had dragged Billy off me. "Answer me!" he yelled into Billy's face.

"He was resistin' arrest!" Billy lied. "He tried to jump me."

"Resistin' arrest?" Besmer questioned. "Nigel here says you just jerked him out of the car and started beatin' his head into the hood. I would have resisted that too. Go sit in the car. I'll deal with you later."

"But..."

"I said get in the car!"

Billy walked toward his car, but stopped before he got in to say, "You just wait, Chance. Your time's comin'."

"Billy, shut up and get in the damn car!" Carl yelled, then he turned to me and asked, "You okay, Eddie?"

"Yeah," I said, rubbing the bruise on my neck. I could feel the trickle of blood on my nose. I wiped it with the back of my hand.

"Nigel said he saw the whole thing, from the time you came over the top of the hill. Just how fast were you goin'?"

"One thirty-five. I guess you're going to throw the book at me, as they say."

"Not this time. I've driven that car, and I know how addictive it can be. I'm gonna let you get away with it this time, but I suggest you take it slower from now on, okay?"

"You don't have to worry about that. That fool car almost cost me my life twice in less than fifteen minutes. Once I get back to Lucy's, I don't know if I'll ever want to drive it again." He laughed and helped me to my feet.

"I thought you were leavin' town," he questioned. "What're you doin' way out here in this thing?"

"I seem to keep getting sidetracked."

"I see that," he observed. "I heard about the excitement at the diner. Folks in town say Lucy put on quite a show. Several ladies in town are screamin' for me to haul her in for indecency. I think they're just jealous." He laughed. "Dick's a son-of-bitch, anyway." He shrugged and blew an aggravated breath, then added, "I guess you'd better be gettin' this rocket on wheels back to the Angel L? Lucy's bound to be wonderin' where you're at."

"You're right about that," I agreed. "Thanks for your help just now," I said as I climbed into the car. I looked over at Billy. He glared at me. I mockingly waved at him, then drove away. Carl was right. Lucy was probably thinking I had run off with her car, but I wasn't going to be in any hurry to get home.

I met Lucy riding Dusty down the driveway when I pulled in. I stopped where we met, and she climbed down off the horse. "Where have you been? I've been about to pull my hair out worryin'. I've ridden up and down the road a hundred times lookin' for you."

"It's a long story," I said, then told her what had happened with the car, and the hogs, and with Billy Watson.

"I hate that no-good creep," she said furiously, then added, "I'm glad you're okay. I guess I need to retire that thing before it gets somebody killed. I can't afford to lose anybody else." She paused, then climbed on the horse and said, "Let's get the car put away, then get you in the house where I can see about all those cuts and bruises. I bet you need a shower. I know I do."

"Is that an invitation?" I joked.

"Watch it, Buster," she replied. "I never shower with anyone on the first date."

We both laughed, then went to put the car in the garage. We put the cover back on the Stinger, and she put the keys in a locked cabinet in the tack room so the temptation to drive it wouldn't be so great. When we were done in the garage and had put Dusty in the barn, we walked to the house where we sat down in the kitchen while she took care of the cuts on my face and hands. She said that there wasn't much that could be done about the big bruise under my chin where Billy had hit me with the barrel of his gun.

"You feel like that shower now?" she asked.

"Nothing would feel better," I replied.

She took me by the hand and led me upstairs to the master bedroom. "You can use my bathroom. The place where we're goin' tonight is kind of fancy. Would you mind wearin' a suit to dinner?"

"No, but I don't have a suit to wear."

"That's no problem, if you don't mind wearin' one of Rooster's. The two of you seem to be about the same size."

"I can do that," I replied, then asked, "You sure you don't mind dating a charity case like me?" I laughed.

"I don't mind, as long as you don't mind me showerin' you with free food and my dead husband's used clothes," she shot back.

"Do think he'd mind?"

"They're not doin' him any good. He never liked to wear them, anyway. He was more comfortable in jeans and a t-shirt."

"So am I, but I'd wear anything for you."

"Well, thank you, sir. I have a dress or two that might fit you."

"Well, almost anything." We both laughed. "Now that you've tempted me with the shower, are you going to let me take it?"

"Certainly, my lord," she said with a British accent, curtseying as she said it.

"You never cease to amaze me."

"I'm a lady of many talents. Now, go bathe. It's a while before we need to get dressed for dinner, so I'll leave you somethin' on the bed to put on in the meantime. You can just throw those clothes in the hamper in the closet there, and I'll wash 'em for you."

"That'd be great," I said as I walked into the bathroom. She told me where the towels and things I would need were, then went downstairs. She said that she had a few more things to take care of in the barn while I took my shower.

The warm water felt good on my aching muscles. I stood under the hot spray, letting it massage me. I thought about Billy Watson. I hated the man as much as I could hate anybody. I was relieved that Carl had shown up when he did. Either he had not heard the rumors about Jenny and me, or he didn't believe them. Either way, I was thankful he was still on my side.

After my shower, I felt much better. The warm water had loosened my tight muscles, and the time had relaxed my nerves. I found a towel in the linen closet and dried myself. I wrapped it around my waist and peeked out the bathroom door into the bedroom. It was empty, so I went out to get dressed. Lucy had left a bathrobe lying on the bed for me. I dropped the towel and put on the robe. Before I tied it closed, I looked at myself in the mirror. The scuffle with Billy had left me pretty well bruised all over. I closed the robe and turned to go find Lucy. I about jumped out of my skin when I found her standing in the doorway when I turned around. I felt myself turning red.

"How long have you been standing there?" I finally managed to stammer.

She smiled and answered, "Long enough to admire the view. If I had known there was goin' to be a floor show, I'da come back sooner."

The red glow of my growing embarrassment had now taken over my entire body. I smiled and finally said, "It's not nice to spy on a man when he's getting dressed."

"Hey, buddy, it's not my fault you were standin' here stark naked with the bedroom door wide open. You should be more careful."

"I'll have to keep that in mind. When are we leaving to eat?"

"In about an hour or so. I still have to shower." I smiled. She added, "Don't get your hopes up. I've got sense enough not to go paradin' around naked with a strange man in the house. Feel free to look around, or you can sit out on the balcony. It's through the double doors at the end of the hall. The afternoon breeze'll help relax you. That's where I go when I'm uptight."

"Thanks," I said. "I could use a little relaxation right now."

"There's a pitcher of lemonade and some glasses out there. If you're thirsty."

"That would be nice," I replied, then left for the balcony. She closed the door behind me. I walked down the hall through the open doors onto the balcony and looked out over the pool. From the balcony, most of the backyard was visible. The garage was to the right, and farther out past it was the barn and stable where Dusty and Lucy's other horses were housed. Zachary and a younger man, one of his sons, I assumed, were at the barn unloading wood from the back a pick-up. I looked around from side to side for a minute, then poured a glass of lemonade and took a seat on one of the lounge chairs. I took a few sips of my drink before I set it down and closed my eyes. A breeze blew gently across me as I let the exhaustion of the day overtake me and drifted off to sleep.

Chapter Twenty

I awoke to the gentle pressure of Lucy pressing her lips against mine. It was a short kiss, just enough to wake me. "Wake up, sleepyhead," she whispered, then I felt her hand brush softly against my thigh. Her touch was electrifying through the thin fabric of my robe. I reached out and pulled her lips back down to mine. I kissed her firmly, but gently, as I stroked her still-damp hair. I stood up from my chair and backed her against the balcony rail. I ran my fingers up and down her back, caressing her through her identical robe. I continued to kiss her as my fingers explored the curves of her back. She moaned as I kissed across her chin and down the smooth skin of her neck. She rubbed my back as I kissed her. The loosely tied belt slipped free and my robe fell open. I paid no attention to my exposure. I continued to kiss her, pulling her body against mine so I could feel the heat of her body through the single sheet of silk that separated us. She quivered as I kissed up and down her neck, pausing to nibble on her soft earlobe. She moaned. She moved her hand inside my robe and was massaging the small of my back. The electricity of her fingertips against my bare skin was incredible. I longed to make love to her, but I stopped. It was too soon for that. I kissed her one last time on the lips, then held her to me.

"What's wrong?" she asked with disappointment in her voice.

"We should wait," I said. "It's too early for this. The time's not right."

"Eddie, it's been a long time since I've had a man touch me the way you just did." She squeezed a little tighter and added, "Physically and emotionally."

I stepped back and took her by the hands. "You've touched something in me, too. Everything that I am wants to make love to you right now, but I have waited all my life for the right time, and I don't want to give all that up in a momentary fit of passion. If it's right for us, it'll happen, eventually."

We stood silently and held each other. She laid her head against my chest. I stroked her hair, and she rubbed her hand up and down my back.

"Do you believe in love at first sight?" she finally asked.

"Not before today," I answered.

"Me, too, " she answered quietly. "After Rooster died, I never thought I could ever love anyone again, but, when I saw you sittin' at the counter at Max's, you touched a spot in my soul that hasn't been touched in a while. I know it's crazy, but in the few hours that we've spent together, I honestly think that I have fallen in love with you."

"I have never felt about anyone the way I feel about you." I responded. I thought about all the girls that I had thought I was in love with. I thought about Jenny Besmer. There had been feelings there, I know, but nothing I had ever felt made me feel the way I did at that moment, standing on that balcony holding her to me. I said, "Being with you brings a happiness to my life that I haven't had since Pop died. I think I love you." I hugged her tightly, then kissed her.

She stepped back from me and said jokingly, "Hey now, don't start that again. I don't know if I can stop a second time!" Me either, I thought.

A smile played across her face as she stood there looking at me. I reached out and ran my hand through her long, red hair. The image of the picture from Uncle Nico's magazine flashed in my mind. I grinned.

"What's so funny?" she wondered.

"Just thinking," I answered.

"What about?" she asked.

"Nothing," I replied.

"Somethin'," she giggled.

"What?"

"Somethin'," she repeated. "Nothin' don't look like that."

I became acutely aware that I was standing there almost completely naked. I pulled the robe closed. "Admiring the view?" I asked, repeating her comment from before and trying to mask my embarrassment.

"You bet."

"You like what you see?" I asked, smiling.

"Uh-huh!" she confirmed. "Hope to see more." She winked at me and started into the house. "We need to get dressed," she called over her shoulder. I followed her inside.

She pointed me toward the door of the bedroom across the hall from her own, then closed her door behind her. She had laid out one of Rooster's suits on the bed and had brought my bag up from the kitchen. I dressed quickly, anxiously anticipating spending more time with Lucy and replaying the events of the balcony in my mind. For the second time in less than a week, I began to second guess my abstinence. I had to push those thoughts from my mind and focus on getting dressed for our big night out. The suit she had brought me, a dark gray three-piece, fit pretty well, but the pants were a little long. Rooster was apparently taller than me, but he must have had tiny feet, because the shoes she brought me were much too small. I was resigned to wear my boots.

Lucy was still shut in her room when I came out. I knocked on the door and called to her. "You decent?" I asked.

"No, but I'm dressed," she laughed. "Come on in."

I pushed the door open to an empty room. "Lucy?"

"In the bathroom," she called through the half-open door. "Have a seat. I'll be out in a minute. I'm tryin' to do somethin' with this mess on my head." I sat down in the chair in the corner of the room. I fidgeted with a loose thread on the arm of the chair, trying to forget how nervous I was. I was studying the thread when I heard the bathroom door swing open. I looked up, and, for the second time in a day, she took my breath away. The silk robe had been replaced by a strapless green dress. My eyes followed the curve of her body, sheathed in skin-tight fabric, to the slit that exposed her stockinged leg halfway up her thigh. She stepped into the room and spun around. "What do you think?" I couldn't speak. I just stammered something unintelligible. "That good, huh?" I nodded. "Good. How 'bout the hair?" She had her hair pulled up on top of her head and held in place with a big silver clip.

"Beautiful," I finally managed to say.

"Why, thank you," she accepted my compliment, then added, "You clean up pretty good yourself."

"Thank you." I blushed

"I see that Rooster wasn't too much taller than you." She looked down at my boots and frowned. I felt bad until she said, "But he did have small feet. The shoes didn't fit, did they?"

"No," I replied. Not even close, I thought.

"I didn't figure they would," she said. "I didn't look at your feet, but I somehow got the idea they'd be big." She winked. I blushed. She grinned, then went to the dresser and rummaged through the jewelry box on the corner. Coming away with a string of pearls, she held them out to me and asked, "You mind?" Of course not, I thought. She handed me the necklace and turned around for me to latch it. After the pearls were in place, I paused to smell her hair. Apples again, but this time it was mixed with perfume.

"You smell good," I said. I nuzzled her neck. She leaned into me. With my hand around her waist, I pulled her against me. I kissed the soft skin behind her ear, then across her freckled shoulder.

"We need to go," she sighed, breaking my embrace. She turned to face me. Her face was flushed. "We need to go," she repeated. She took my hand and led me downstairs and out to the garage.

"Where are were going?" I asked. I had not seen, nor could I imagine, any place in Wixton that would have warranted the fancy clothes.

"Albany," she announced while she retrieved the keys to the Cadillac from the rack in the tack room. "One Eyed Jack's."

"Where?"

"Albany," she repeated. "You know, I mentioned it earlier. It's a little bit of a drive, but Jack's is fantastic. It's my favorite place in the world to eat, but I haven't been down since... well, since Rooster died. He never cared too much for the place—too fancy for him—but he'd go 'cause I wanted to. Besides, Jack's has the best steak this side of Texas." She paused for a moment and lost herself in the memory. "You drive," she instructed, not waiting for me to protest. She pushed the key chain into my hand and climbed into the passenger seat. I wouldn't have protested anyway. I would have walked through fire for her, so driving the big, fancy car wasn't much of a chore.

Other than her giving me direction to aim me toward Albany, we rode in awkward silence. I was thinking about the confessions we had made about our feelings for one another, and I couldn't help but hope that she was doing the same. I was confused about where it all was leading. I thought about everything that had happened, or almost happened, on the balcony. I kept running everything over and over in my mind, trying to decide if stopping had been the right thing to do. I thought about the taste of her kiss, the smoothness of her apple blossom skin, and the feel of her body against mine. My body was telling me I should have gone for it, while my mind was reminding me that the thing to do was wait. If Lucy was the girl I had been waiting for, and there was a voice in the back of my mind telling me that she was the one, I wanted our relationship to grow before we made love. I had to know that what I was feeling was genuine and not just a response to the incredible physical attraction I had for her.

While my mind and body waged war over the fate of my virginity, my heart was torn between my newly discovered feelings for Lucy and my commitment to fulfilling my promise to my father's memory. I wondered what Pop would think, what he would want me to do. I wished so much that I could ask him what to do, but I knew the decision was mine alone. I did not want to think about it, so I tried to push it out of mind and enjoy myself.

Finally, Lucy broke the silence. "Eddie?" I glanced at her. In the afternoon sun, her hair glowed like fire, and the freckles on her shoulders and arms stood out against her creamy skin. She smiled when I looked and asked, "Whatcha thinkin' about?"

"Nothing. Everything. I don't know."

"Me, too," she admitted. "It's all crazy, ain't it?"

"Where's this going?" I asked, scared of her response.

"Hell if I know," she laughed, "but I think I want to find out."

"Me, too," I agreed.

After a few more minutes of silence, I said, "You never finished telling me about what happened to Rooster. You feel up to it?"

She sighed and began to tell the story. "Rooster left Wixton for Orlando on Tuesday. Wednesday mornin' about three, the phone rang. You know that sinkin' feelin' you get when the phone rings in the middle of the night?" I nodded. "Well, anyway, the phone shook me awake, and I knew what it was before I picked it up. I knew he was dead." She started to cry. I felt guilty and tried to persuade her to stop. She assured me that she was okay and continued. "It was the Florida Highway Patrol. Rooster had made the trip back from Orlando to Panama City and was crossin' St. Andrew's Bay on the Hathaway Bridge. There was a heavy rain that night, and visibility was low. Just over the crest of the bridge, there was a stalled car in his lane. He didn't see it until he was nearly on top of it, but, by then, it was too late. He swerved to avoid the crash, lost control of the truck on the wet pavement, and crashed through the railing into the ocean. Divers pulled Rooster's body from the wreckage. He had drowned, tryin' to get out of the ruined truck." She stopped and held her head in her hands. I wanted so badly to hold her, to comfort her.

"Lucy, please," I insisted, "you don't have to..."

"It's okay," she said, wiping the tears from her eyes. "I'm sorry I keep cryin'."

"I'm sorry I asked you about it," I replied.

"Don't be. Sometimes it's good to talk about it." She smiled, weakly. "Anyway, he saved 'em."

"Saved who?"

"The people in the car. Travis and Lanie Goodson. Young couple. Hadn't been married quite a year. She was eight weeks pregnant. Rooster did the right thing. I know he did, but I miss him so much." The tears came again. I reached over and put my hand on hers. "I'm sorry," she said again. "You don't want to hear that, do you?"

"Baby, I know you loved Rooster, and I hope you always love him, but he doesn't have anything to do with us. If we're meant to be, we'll be." She didn't say anything. She just lifted my hand to her lips, kissed it gently, held it to her cheek, and took complete control of my heart.

"...next light."

"What?"

"Turn left at the next light," she repeated.

I followed her directions through Albany until I arrived in front of One Eyed Jack's Steak and Spirits. The restaurant was housed in the ground floor of an unassuming brick building not too far from downtown. Though it was still fairly early, cars were already lined up along both sides of the street out front. I found a space a block over and pulled in between a big Mercury coupe and a convertible Cadillac, much like ours.

Before we got out of the car, Lucy leaned over and kissed me. "I'm glad you're here, and I hope you enjoy supper."

"I will," I assured her. Because I'm with you, I added to myself.

We got out of the car, Lucy took my arm, and we walked down the street to the restaurant. Under the large green and white awning that fronted the building, several groups waited for tables inside. Everyone turned to look at us as we approached. I could see the envy of the men in the crowd as they watched me walk by with Lucy on my arm. Their dates, on the other hand, eyed the whole lot of us with contempt. I just smiled. We passed by them all and entered the restaurant.

The hostess was a diminutive brunette in a black, sequined evening gown. She stood behind a small podium just inside the entrance. Lucy paused while the woman checked the reservation list for the party of four ahead of us. After a seater was dispatched to take them to their table, the hostess looked up at us. Her face lit up with recognition. "Lucy!" she exclaimed, as she came out from behind her stand to hug Lucy. "I haven't seen you in forever. Not since..." Her smile vanished. "I'm sorry. I didn't mean to..."

"I know, Maggie. It's okay," Lucy assured her.

"How you been?" Maggie asked sheepishly.

"Well as can be expected, I guess," Lucy replied, then quickly changed the subject. "Maggie, this is Eddie Chance."

"Nice to meet you," I said, offering my hand. She shook it nervously.

"You too," she replied, uncomfortable with my presence.

Lucy took us both off the hook. She asked, "Do you have a table for us?"

"Of course," Maggie replied. She left the hostess stand and led us to our table. Before she left us, she and Lucy embraced again. "I'm sorry about Rooster," she said.

"Thank you," Lucy replied.

Unsmiling, Maggie glanced my way one final time, then returned to her place by the door.

I helped Lucy with her chair, then took my own seat across from her. "She doesn't like me very much," I observed.

"I'm sorry 'bout that," Lucy replied. "She's probably just shocked to see me with someone besides Rooster."

"It's okay," I assured her. "You and he must have come here a lot."

"Nearly every week," she confirmed, "even though he was like a fish out of water."

I tugged at the tie around my neck and said, "Feeling a little dry myself." We both laughed.

Dinner was nice. The food was excellent, and the company was even better. While we ate, we made small talk about growing up, about our families, and about the incredible differences in our lives.

When the meal was over, Lucy paid the check, gaining me a disapproving look from the waiter, who was another friend of her and Rooster. Like Maggie, he did not give any indication that he cared for my presence in Rooster's place. Lucy gave me an apologetic look. I just smiled.

On the way out, Lucy stopped by the hostess stand to say goodbye to Maggie, who made her promise not let so much time pass before her next visit. I was surprised by a slight smile Maggie aimed my way, when Lucy agreed that we would.

Back on the street, Lucy turned to me and said, "I'm sorry, again, about the cold shoulder in there."

"I told you it was okay," I said. "I understand. It's always hard for old friends to accept the new people in situations like this."

"I know, but I just wish they hadn't been rude to you," she replied.

"It's okay," I repeated. "Don't worry about it."

We walked hand-in-hand to the car. I took my place behind the wheel, and she slid in beside me. I started the car and pulled away from the curb.

"You remember the way home?" she asked.

"No problem," I answered confidently.

I reached for the knot of my tie and asked, "Mind if I take this thing off now?"

"Of course not," she laughed. "Do you mind if I take these off?" she asked, indicating the stockings she was wearing.

My jaw dropped, again, when she reached under her dress and undid her garters. I nearly ran off the road when she began to roll the first stocking down her leg. "Hey now!" she giggled. "Watch the road." I turned back to the road, but continued to watch her out of the corner of my eye. I had a hard time concentrating on driving, as she rolled the hose down her thigh. I bit my lip and tried not to look. I failed. Since the dress was split only on the left side, she had to twist to reach her other stocking. I turned to look across at her, and she caught me looking. I jerked my head back forward. "I thought I told you to watch the road, buddy," she scolded. "You're gonna get us both killed tryin' to cop a peek at my panties or somethin'."

"Or somethin'," I teased.

She hit me on the arm and said, "You had your chance."

"So did everyone else in Wixton," I shot back. We both laughed hysterically. I almost had to pull off the road.

She slid across the seat and leaned against my shoulder. I put my arm around her and pulled her up close. Her body felt good against mine, and I didn't want that feeling to end. Thankfully, it didn't. For the rest of the drive back to the Angel L, I held her to me, gently stroking her hair.

It was just after ten when we got back to the house. After we had put the car away and had shut up the garage for the night, Lucy took my hand as we walked to the house. We paused by the pool and stood watching the slight breeze push ripples across the surface of the water. She tossed the high heels she was carrying onto one of the deck chairs, pulled her dress up to her knees, and dipped her foot in to the pool.

"Water's warm," she announced. "Water's always warmer at night. Growin' up, I'd sneak out here in the middle of the night and swim. Sometimes for hours, until Daddy would wake up and catch me. Caught me skinny dippin' a time or two. He'd fuss, then send me back to bed. He's worried I might drown, I guess." She waved her foot back and forth in the water for a moment, lost in thought. "You know. I had my first kiss out here."

"Rooster?" I asked. She smiled and nodded. "That's probably what your father was worried about."

She laughed, "More than likely." She stepped back from the pool, still laughing. "He'da been worried 'bout you, too, I think."

"Why?"

"Because of this." She pulled me to her and kissed me. She broke the kiss and looked at the watch on her arm. "The night's still young, " she observed. "You wanna take a dip?"

"I don't think so," I declined, not really knowing why.

"Okay," she accepted, without the slightest hint of disappointment. "You're not sleepy are you?" I shook my head. "Well, whatcha wanna do?" she asked.

"First thing is go upstairs and get out of these clothes," I said.

"Oh?" She raised an eyebrow.

"You know what I mean," I replied.

"Can't blame a girl for hopin'," she laughed. "Come on then. We can get comfortable, then we can sit out on the balcony and talk some more. If that suits you."

"Sounds good."

She lead me upstairs to my room and disappeared into her own. I changed out of Rooster's suit into my own jeans and a t-shirt. I draped the clothes across the foot of the bed and sat down beside them. About twenty minutes later, Lucy appeared at the door in a pair of cut-off jeans and a baggy t-shirt. Like me, she was barefoot.

"You ready?" she asked. I stood to follow her outside. "You sure you ain't ready to go to bed?" I gave her a coy smile. "I meant to sleep," she clarified, hitting me on the arm. "I don't wanna keep you up, if you're sleepy, you know. I'm a bit of a night owl. There're nights I don't go to sleep at all. Been that why all my life, I suppose. Reckon that's why Daddy caught me in the pool all them times. Got too cold to swim, I'd go out to the barn and sit with the horses." She paused, tugging nervously at the tail of her shirt. "You don't care 'bout all that, do you?"

I would listen to you read the dictionary, I thought. I said, "Go ahead. Getting to know you."

"Whatever cranks your tractor," she replied, then changed the subject. "You want, I'll go make some more lemonade."

"I'm fine," I passed.

"Maybe later."

There was a porch swing on the balcony, overlooking the pool. We sat there. Lucy leaned against me and curled her legs up onto the seat. I pushed, absentmindedly, with my legs to keep us in motion while we talked. Lost in conversation, we did not notice the time slipping away, but, after a while, the lateness of the hour, and the gentle swaying of the swing began to lull us to sleep. My eyelids grew heavy, and she began to drift into periods of silence when she was speaking.

After one of those silences, she patted me on the leg and said, "I guess I'm more tired than I thought. Why don't we call it a night. We can get back to this in the mornin'."

"It is morning," I observed, looking at my watch. "It's nearly five."

"Well, why don't we call it a mornin' then." We both tried to laugh, but we were too sleepy for much more than a chuckle.

Inside, we stood in the hallway between our bedrooms and said our goodnights.

"Goodnight," she said, taking my hand in hers.

"Goodnight, Lucy," I replied. Not wanting to let it end, even for the night, even for a moment, I pulled her close to me and breathed deeply, hungrily, of the air around her. I lost myself in the smell of her hair, of the traces of perfume that lingered on her skin. I kissed her neck, felt the rapidness of her heartbeat against my lips. She sighed, and I knew that she was the one I had waited for, but not then, not with the exhaustion of the day weighing so heavily upon us. We kissed one last time, then separated.

In my room, I knelt by the bed and thanked God for bringing me to this place. I thanked Him for the opportunity to meet someone like Lucy, and I prayed that He would show me what I should do about Florida and my promise to Pop. I stayed on my knees for a long time, running it all over in my head, waiting for a sign, I suppose. Finally, I climbed into bed and fell quickly to sleep.

I am sitting at the counter in Max's diner. I am alone, except for a little girl in a white cotton dress.

"You gonna eat that?" the little girl asks, pointing at the untouched pie in front of me. I do not respond. I just push the pie toward her. "Thanks, Daddy!" she exclaims, grabs the pie from the table, and disappears into thin air.

"Wait!" I call after her. "Who are you?"

She reappears, her face smeared with pie filling. She studies my face for a minute, then says, "You really don't know, do you?"

"No," I answer.

"I'm your daughter!" she announces and disappears again.

"Wait!" I call. "My daughter? What do you mean? Who are you?"

"She's gone, you know," a voice from nowhere says.

"Who is she?" I ask.

"She told you."

"How can that be?"

No answer.

"Hello!"

No answer.

"Hello!"

"Eddie, who you talkin' to?" Lucy asks. She is sitting on the stool next to me. She was not there before.

"The little girl. Did you see her?"

"What little girl?"

"In the white dress. She took my pie."

"What are you talkin' about? I took your pie."

"No," I protest. "She took it and disappeared."

"Disappeared? Eddie, are you okay?"

"I don't know anymore."

"Eddie, who you talkin' to?" Janie asks from behind the counter as she sets another piece of pie in front of me.

"Lucy." I point to her, but she is not there anymore.

"Lucy? Lucy Brewster? She's gone. She left with Dick Brinson."

"Gone? When?"

"Just now. She was hangin' all over Dick. I ain't ever seen nothin' like it."

I jump from the stool and run to the door. I crash through to the sidewalk, but I am not on the sidewalk. I find myself standing in the middle of a country road surrounded by hundreds of hogs. I am in the middle of nowhere. There is no one anywhere to be seen. I am alone. Just me and the hogs.

The sounds of their grunts and snorts is all the sound I can hear. Each time I try to escape from their midst, they close in around me. They gather in around my legs, bumping me, pushing me down the road, leading me somewhere. When I try to resist, the pigs bite at my pants. I feel the scratch of their teeth against my skin. I kick at them and try to run. They crowd me, preventing me from moving. They bite and push. Bite and push. Still leading me down the road. We walk for miles. My legs ache with every step. My pants hang in tatters around my bitten and bloody legs. Miles and miles.

Finally, I stop and scream at the top of my lungs, "LEAVE ME ALONE!"

The pigs squeal and open a circle around me. Although I am still surrounded, still trapped, the pigs have moved back away from me several feet. They all stand perfectly still, staring at me and grunting. I walk toward the edge of the opening, but the pigs move in unison with me. No matter which way I step, the distance between me and my living prison stays exactly the same.

I throw my head back and scream in frustration.

"Them hogs got a mind of they own. I can tell you that." Nigel, the pig farmer, stands at the edge of the sea of hogs. He smiles a toothless smile as he wipes sweat from his brow with a stained bandana. "I ain't got no idee 'bout where they takin' you." He spits a wad of phlegm to the ground.

"Can't you help me?" I scream at him.

"Don't rightly see how." He spits again. "I done told you they's got they own mind."

"Nobody can help you, Chance!"

"Where are you, Watson!?" I call out, recognizing the voice.

A loud, cackling laugh fills the air around me. "I'm over here!" I turn toward the sound. He is standing just outside the circle of pigs, opposite Nigel. "You stay away from Lucy Brewster. She's mine, you hear!"

"She doesn't want you," I call back. "You stay away from her."

"She's mine, I tell you. MINE!" He shakes his fist in the air. "MINE!"

"You're a pathetic fool," I say. "She loves me."

"You son-of-a-bitch!" he screams.

He pulls his gun from its holster and shoots into the air. The explosion scares the pigs. In an uncontrolled stampede, the animals rush away from the sound. The wave hits me and knocks me to the ground. I feel hundreds of hooves trampling me into the ground. Everything goes black.

Suddenly, I feel a hand reaching through the blackness. Strong fingers close around the collar of my shirt and jerk me away from the rush. I feel myself being dragged through the air and crashing onto the road. The blackness that had surrounded me slowly fades, and I find myself lying in the middle of a bridge. The roadbed around me is damp from a recent rain. Kneeling beside me is a young man in jeans and a plain white t-shirt. His clothes are soaked.

When he sees that I am aware of his presence, he smiles and says, "Hell of a mess you got yourself into there, partner. Them hogs damn near trampled you to death." I watch his face as he talks. He is the spitting image of Zachary. Rooster, I realize. "Couldn't have that, you know. Lucy sure thinks a lot of you." He smiles. "I miss her," he says thoughtfully.

"She misses you, too," I inform him.

"I know," he frowns. "I'm glad she thinks about me, but I hate seein' her sad like that. That's why I couldn't let the hogs get you. You make my baby happy, and I ain't lettin' that son-of-a-bitch Watson take that away from her." He stands and helps me to my feet. He extends his hand. I shake it. His skin is clammy. A shiver runs down my back. "You take care of her. You hear?" Before I can answer him, he runs to the side of the bridge and dives into the dark water below. I run the rail, calling his name.

"Eddie, who you hollerin' at?" Lucy asks.

I find myself standing on the balcony of her house, looking out over the pool. I am dressed in a silk robe. A glass of lemonade sits on the railing near my hand. I turn to Lucy. She is dressed in a matching robe. I look into her beautiful eyes and say, "Nobody. I was just thinking out loud."

"You scared me."

"I'm sorry."

"It's okay."

She comes to me at the rail. I pull her to me and kiss her passionately on the mouth. The smell of apples fills my nostrils as I run my fingers though her freshly washed hair. My hands caress the curves of her body through the thin fabric of her robe. She does the same to me. She tugs at the belt of my robe and lets it fall open. She rubs her open palms across the skin of my exposed chest while my hands grope for the belt of her robe.

"Get your damn hands off her!" Billy Watson orders from behind us.

"What the hell are you doin' in my house?" she screams at him. "Get the hell out of here!"

"What's he doin' here?" Billy asks. "What are you doin' with him?"

"What business is it of yours?" I ask.

Billy ignores me. He looks longingly at Lucy. "I thought you were my girl," he says, sadly.

"Your girl?" she barks in disgust. "I wouldn't be your girl if my life depended on it!"

"But..." he says with hurt in his eyes.

"But nothin'," she cuts him off. "I am not your girl, and I never will be! I am with Eddie now." She pulls me to her. "Now get out of my house!" she orders, then kisses me hard on the mouth.

"Whore!" he screams. He pulls his gun and fires.

Lucy screams and grabs her stomach. Blood stains her robe and spills over her hands. "Eddie!" she cries. She stumbles to the rail and falls over.

"Luuucceee!" I scream, diving frantically after her. "Luuucceee!"

"Eddie! Eddie!" Lucy's voice drew me out of the nightmare. She was sitting on the edge of my bed, gently shaking my shoulder. She smiled when I looked up at her, but there was no joy in her eyes.

"What?" I asked. "Did I wake you?" I had told her about the nightmares, but I did not know what had brought her to my room.

"You were screamin' my name," she explained. "It just scared me a little."

"I'm sorry."

"Don't..." she started. She reached across and wiped the sweat from my brow. "You all right?" The concern, again, showing in her eyes. I nodded. I didn't want to speak, for fear that my labored breathing would betray me. She saw through my lie, anyway, and leaned down and kissed my forehead. "Anything I can do?" she asked. She sat silently for a moment. "You called my name. Was I in your dream?"

"Yes," I answered. Feeling myself relaxing, I sat up in the bed. I looked at her for a moment, before continuing. She waited patiently, while I collected my thoughts. Although the dream was not the worst I had had, and not even the worst I had had since coming to Wixton, the image of Lucy bleeding, falling and dying, pierced me to the deepest part of my heart. I wasn't sure I wanted to inflict those images on her, but I could see the curiosity in her eyes, so I took a deep breath and began to relay the dream to her. She sat quietly and listened to the narrative. By the time I finished, tears streamed down her face. I regretted subjecting her to it.

"I'm sorry I told you," I said.

"No. I wanted you to," she assured me. "I'm just sorry for you." She bowed her head against her chest and sobbed. "I feel responsible." She cried harder.

"Hey," I said as I put my arm around her shoulder and pulled her against me. "The dream wasn't your fault. Why would you think that?" The tears poured down my own face.

"You called me," she sobbed. "The pain in your voice."

I held her closer. "Baby." The term of affection seemed natural on my lips. "Hey, it's nobody's fault. It was just a dream."

She sobbed, more quietly, against my shoulder. "But..."

"Hey, look at me." I put my hand on her chin and lifted her face toward me. She was so beautiful. My breath caught in my throat as looked into her big, wet eyes, and I almost couldn't finish my thought. "These dreams were a part of me long before I met you. You have become part of my life, so you have become part of the dream. That's all." I lifted her chin a little higher and kissed her tenderly on the lips. "The only pain you could cause me is seeing the hurt in your eyes."

"I'm sorry," she apologized.

"Silly," I laughed and kissed her again.

I laughed and hugged her. "Hey now," I began, "you're supposed to be here to comfort me. Not the other way around." She smiled and started to apologize, but I placed my finger on her mouth and said, "Don't." I removed my finger and replaced it with my own lips. I drew back from the kiss and asked, "Are you okay?"

She nodded. "Yes," she said. "If you are."

"I am. Since I'm with you."

She snuggled against my shoulder. "Can I lay with you for a while?"

Until then, she had been sitting on the edge of the bed with her feet still on the floor. I slid over and made room for her beside me. Still on top of the covers, she moved farther onto the bed. It was then that I noticed what she was wearing. Her light blue nightgown barely reached the top of her thighs. As she slid across the bed against me, it slipped enough to reveal the white silk panties she wore underneath. I bit my lip to counter my excitement, but I felt myself growing hard beneath the covers. I was still sitting on the bed, leaning against the headboard. She cuddled up to me, laying her head on my chest and her leg on my leg.

We lay like that for a long time. The pressure of her body against mine was comforting. I could tell by her breathing that she had fallen asleep. Although I was exhausted, I was too wired to sleep. Instead, I lay there in the light of the bedside lamp and watched her. The way her head rested upon me, I could not see her face, but the top of her head was only inches away from my lips, so I leaned down and kissed it. The smell of apples still clung faintly to the fiery strands that cascaded across my chest. Her hair tickled my face, but I did not pull away. I lingered there, drawing deeply of her scent.

She shifted her leg, drawing my eyes down her body. Her gown had ridden up above her underwear, showing just a hint of skin at the small of her back. I could not reach it, though I wanted more than anything to run my fingers across its silky contour. My eyes continued over the curve of her hip to her long leg, which lay across me. Like her shoulders, her leg was covered with freckles. Every patch of skin that I had seen, even the sliver of her back, which I was currently desiring, was covered in freckles, and I looked forward to finding out if the rest of her was, too. I closed my eyes and tried to imagine her naked. The image from Uncle Nico's magazine, the red hair, the freckles, the fold of sheet that taunted me, filled my mind, but the face that looked back at me from the glossy page was Lucy's. With the fantasy, I felt myself begin to rise again. I turned my body to keep from pressing into Lucy's leg. I moved carefully, but the motion was enough to wake her.

"What's wrong, baby?" she asked, groggily.

"Nothing's wrong," I whispered. "I just had to move a little. My back's beginning to hurt." It wasn't a lie, my back did hurt, but it wasn't exactly the truth, either.

"I'm sorry," she said, swinging her feet off the bed and sitting up.

I was afraid that she was leaving me, going back to her own bed for the night. Even though my nerves were calm again, I didn't want her to go. I wasn't ready to be without her.

I was surprised, however, when she asked, "Can I sleep here the rest of the night? I don't feel like bein' alone." Not waiting for my answer, she pulled back the cover and slipped beneath. She rolled toward me and, being naked, I did try to turn to conceal my still-evident erection, but she placed her leg directly against it. I shuddered at the sensation of her bare skin against me, but she did not acknowledge the contact. Instead, she kissed my chest and said, "Goodnight, Eddie." Within minutes, she was asleep again. I, too, finally gave in and drifted back to sleep, lying there with the woman I loved in my arms.

Chapter Twenty-one

Tuesday morning, before I was fully awake, I realized that I was alone in the bed. I rubbed the sheet where she had slept. The bed was cold to my hand. Apparently, she had been gone for a while. I pulled her pillow toward me and laid my head on it. It smelled of her. As I lay there holding the pillow, the shadow lifted, and the room brightened. I looked toward the window. The drapes were drawn, but the light poured in around the edges. I could tell that the sun was high in the sky, and the clock which sat atop the chest-of-drawers across from the bed said that it was just after eleven. It was well past time for me to get up.

I found Lucy outside at the stable. She was brushing Dusty when I entered the barn. She looked up at me when I came through the door, and a huge grin broke out across her face. "Good mornin', sleepyhead," she giggled. "You decided to rejoin the livin'?" I grinned, embarrassed.

"You been up long?" I asked, trying to save face.

"An hour or two," she answered. "I took Dusty for a ride. Gave him a good brushin'." She held up the brush she was using, then hung it on a hook on the wall. "I didn't want to wake you. You were sleepin' so peaceful. After that scare you gave me, I thought you needed the rest."

"Thanks," I answered. "I'm sorry that I woke you, and I'm sorry I scared you."

"It's okay," she replied, then changed the subject. "You 'bout ready for lunch? I ate a couple of strawberries on the way out here, but that's all, so I'm starvin'. I've got some turkey in the fridge. We can have a sandwich."

"Sounds good." I would have eaten anything she offered.

"Let me put Dusty away, then we can go eat." She unhooked the reins from the ring on the wall and led the horse deeper into the stable. We passed several horses in the stalls that lined the way. There were six in all, not counting Dusty. They all snorted and huffed as we walked past. The big animals made me nervous for some reason. I couldn't image climbing on top of anything that big that had a mind of its own. I voiced this to

Lucy, and she laughed and promised that she'd change my mind. I eyed the closest one and doubted it. I looked back to Lucy, who winked at me, and I knew that I didn't have a chance to resist. I grinned.

Lucy walked Dusty into his stall and closed the half-door behind him. He quickly turned and stuck his head out through the opening. Lucy patted him on the nose and let him nuzzle her neck. "I'll see you later, boy. I gotta go spend some time with this other fella over there." She tossed her thumb my way and giggled. "Now, you behave yourself while I'm gone, you hear?" Dusty blew loudly and pulled his head back into the stall.

Lucy came back to me, took my hand, and said, "You ready for that lunch now?" She grabbed my hand and led me outside. Just outside the door, she stopped and kissed me hard on the mouth. "Good mornin'," she said when she finally released the kiss.

"I thought you already said that," I wondered.

"Not properly," she said and kissed me again. "Dusty can be a little jealous sometimes." I thought she was joking, but from the look on her face, I could see that she was serious. She continued, "He'll learn to love you, too." I made a face that she ignored. "He's already depressed about havin' to stay cooped up inside. We normally let the horses run free in the back pasture durin' the day, but Zachary wants to check the whole fence before we let 'em loose again. We don't want anymore breakouts." She tugged on my arm and said, "Enough about that. Let's eat."

As we were crossing the yard, a white station wagon appeared from behind one of the out buildings and barreled along one of several rutted paths that criss-crossed that part of the yard. Startled by the sudden appearance, I jumped back, sure it was going to hit us. Lucy laughed and held onto my hand to keep me from running. The car sped toward us and came to a screeching halt in front of where we stood. When the dust cleared, I was looking down into the face of a pretty Asian woman. Two children watched us through the rear window. The driver smiled at me, but addressed Lucy.

She said, her accent weighing heavy on the words, "Hey, Lucy. Sorry." She looked my way and added, "Stevie told me you had company up here." She looked me over and observed, "He's cute." I blushed. Without waiting for any response from Lucy, or me, she declared, "Jr. has a dentist appointment, and I'm running late. Katie poured juice down her dress as we walked out the door. Put us way behind. Talk to you later, sweetheart." She gave me a curt smile before she sped away.

"Who was that?" I asked, although I had a pretty good idea.

"Hurricane Sandy," she laughed. "She's Steve's wife."

"Steve is Rooster's brother, right?"

"Yeah," she confirmed.

"She's not from around here, is she?" I laughed when I asked it.

"Not hardly," she joined my laughter. "She's Korean. She came home with Stevie after the war. She's somethin' else. Does everything wide open."

"I see," I said, adding, "She's very pretty."

"Watch it, buster," she warned, grinning.

"Not as pretty as you, of course," I amended.

"That's more like it," she replied, "but you're right. She is very pretty. She's turned more than a few heads in town. I can tell you that." She paused, then added, "Took people a while to accept her, but none of them could deny her looks."

"They live here?" I asked, wondering about the direction from which she came.

She pointed down the dirt track that Sandy had driven down and said, "Steve and Sandy have a log cabin on the backside of the property."

"A log cabin?"

"Yep, Steve built it himself. Cut the trees right there in the woods. But don't let the name fool you. The place is huge, and beautiful. Sandy is a fantastic decorator. I'll take you back there to see it sometime."

"I'd like that."

"Mickey and Lacy live in town. Her granddaddy left her a place in town. Big ol' house. Dates back before the war."

"The war?"

"Civil War."

"Oh."

"Anyway, the house is huge, nearly as big as this one, and since they had five kids at the time, got six now, they moved off the Angel. Zachary hated to see them go, but, at least, he still works out here."

"Zachary live here?"

"Yeah, Zachary lives down the road, back toward town," she said, pointing in the direction of town. "I'm sure you saw the house. Green two-story with the pond in the front yard." I confirmed that I had seen it. She continued, "That's the house the boys grew up in. Zachary talked about movin' out when Ann died. Too many memories, you know, but all those memories ended up keepin' him there."

"Ann was Rooster's mother?"

"Yeah. I'm sorry," she apologized. "I forgot you're new around here. Ann was Rooster's mother. She died two years before Daddy did." I didn't know if a response was appropriate, so I stayed quiet.

By then, we had reached the house. Lucy led me through the mudroom off the kitchen where she pulled off the battered boots she was wearing. Although my boots weren't muddy, I pulled then off as well. I had put them on with no socks, and Lucy laughed at my bare feet. She couldn't explain why, but she thought it was funny. She rubbed her foot across the top of my foot and giggled, then she pointed me toward the kitchen and went down the hall to the bathroom. While she was gone, I went into the kitchen and began getting the food out of the fridge.

She returned shortly, and we ate. When we were finished, I helped Lucy clear the dishes and put the food away.

"What you want to do today?" she asked. I shrugged. "How 'bout we start with a tour of the rest of the house. I'll show you around down here, and, later, after our food has a chance to settle, maybe we can go in the pool." Where we were standing in the kitchen, we had a great view of the pool through the trio of French doors that took up the back wall. "You swim?"

"Yeah, but I don't have a suit."

"So." She tossed her hair over her shoulder and winked. Rather than protest, I just cocked an eyebrow and smiled. "You ready for that tour?" I nodded, and she led me toward one of three arched doorways that led out of the kitchen. There were eight exits all together—the three arches, the three doors to the pool, the mudroom door, and, opposite the mudroom, there was the corkscrew staircase. We left the kitchen through the arch nearest the stairs. We paused at the door directly across the hall. It was the dining room. I was able to get just a peek at the enormous table before Lucy was off down the hall. She tossed her thumb at the mouth of a perpendicular hall and said, "That cuts across to the other side. Hall just like this one down that side. We'll cross over in a minute, when we come back around, but let me show you this, first." She continued toward the front of the house to the next door along the hall.

"This was Daddy's study," she informed me. "I call it the library now."

The big room was divided into three sections. The section nearest the door was the study, as she had called it. A large desk centered the space atop a beautiful Oriental carpet. The middle section was a small sitting area. A sofa and three chairs were arranged about a second carpet. A door to the outside broke the wall behind the sofa. Its window looked onto a small flower garden. Against the wall opposite the exit was a large cabinet filled with all sorts of weapons.

"This is something else," I admired, stopping to examine the display.

"Yeah," she replied, "Daddy was a collector. There are more upstairs, but these were his favorites." She swallowed hard at the memory.

"Quite a collection of books you have here, too," I observed, trying to move to a less painful subject. My plan backfired.

She looked sadly at the rows of bookshelves that occupied the last third of the room. She sighed and smiled, recognizing my intent. "The books were Mama's passion."

"More upstairs?" I asked, still trying to lighten the mood.

"Yeah," she laughed. It was a beautiful sound. "Come on. There's more to see." She took my hand and pulled me back toward the door. "You ain't seen the best thing yet."

"I have," I argued, pulling her to me and kissing her.

"I meant the house." She playfully slapped my shoulder. "Silly."

"Oh."

"Come on." She took my hand again and directed me down the hall to the foyer.

I knew immediately what she had meant when I stepped into the entranceway. It was breathtaking. The ceiling rose twenty feet above the polished marble floor. An enormous brass and crystal chandelier hung from a thick brass chain in the center of the room. Twin staircases curved from the center of the space around the edges of the room to come together at the second floor landing. Between the staircases, I could see into the house's great room, which filled the center of the floor. Through a doorway across the room, I could see all the way into the kitchen.

"Wow!" was all I could think to say.

"Ain't it, though," she laughed.

Entering the room, we had passed under one of the majestic staircases, and the opposing hall passed below the other. After giving me a few minutes to appreciate the beauty of it all, she pointed me toward that opening.

The first room off the foyer was a music room. The center of the floor was filled by a white grand piano. The top was propped open, giving an elegant look to the instrument. Scattered around the room were several other instruments, including a violin on a shelf and a cello on a stand in the corner.

"You play?" I asked.

"The piano, yes," she admitted, "and the violin, a little. The cello was somethin' Mama bought in an antique store in Charleston before I was born. She couldn't play it. Like me, she was a pianist."

"Did your father play?"

"I don't know," she replied. "He never came in here. The music room was Mama's. After books, it was her second passion. After she died, he never came here."

"He listened to you play?"

"Only in the other room," she explained. "We have another piano in the great room. It's black and not nearly as big as this one. This was Mama's favorite. Until she died, it sat where the black one is now. Daddy had it moved the week after her funeral and never saw it again. He said it was just too painful."

I shook my head and said, "This house, your family, has seen a lot of sadness."

She nodded slowly and replied, "Maybe that has changed." She squeezed my hand a little tighter.

"Will you play for me?" I asked hopefully.

"Later," she promised. "Come on." She pulled me down the hall. "You ready to go swimmin'?"

"Sure," I replied. "What about a suit?"

"Suit?" She laughed. "I'm sure there's one in the pool house that you can wear. Let's go see."

We started down the hall, but were stopped by loud knocking at the front door. "Now who is that?" she wondered. She went back to the foyer and pulled back the curtain on the sidelight window. "What the HELL does he want?" she grumbled. I looked out the other side at Billy Watson. I reached for the doorknob. "Wait," she asked, "let me handle this. I don't want you two gettin' in another fight. He ain't worth all that." I gritted my teeth and stepped aside. She unlatched the door and instructed me to stay inside. She opened the door and stepped out onto the porch. I watched the exchange through the narrow window.

Billy had retreated down the steps to stand beside his car. He was visibly nervous, wringing the brim of the hat he was holding in his hands. Lucy walked to the edge of the porch and stopped.

Billy spoke first. He half stammered, "Afternoon, Lucy."

"Billy," she addressed him with contempt. "Can I help you?"

"I was just out this way, " he began, "and I thought I might need to check on you."

"Really? Why?"

He shifted nervously from foot to foot, before he answered. He finally said, "I was just worried 'bout you. You know. All alone out here."

"I appreciate your concern, Deputy, but I'm just fine," she informed him. "Goodbye." She turned back toward the door.

"Lucy! Wait!" he called. He took a step toward the porch.

"What, Billy?"

As much as his presence angered me, I enjoyed seeing him fumble around for words. "I was wonderin'… kinda hopin'… I don't know… I thought maybe, you'd go out to dinner with me tonight."

"I'm sorry," she declined, "but I've got company."

"Company?" he repeated, looking over her shoulder to the house. "Anybody I know?" His curiosity was getting the best of him.

"Goodbye, Billy," she said and turned away from him.

"It's Chance, ain't it?"

"What?"

"Your company. It's that drifter, Eddie Chance. I saw him yesterday in that fancy car of Rooster's."

"Goodbye, Billy."

He ran up the steps onto the porch and growled, "He's bad news!"

She turned away from him and repeated, more forcefully, "Goodbye, Billy!"

He stepped forward and grabbed her arm. I was out the door before he said another word. "Get your damn hand off her, Watson!"

He scowled at me and screamed, "What the fuck're you doin' here, Chance? I told you to stay away from her!"

The statement made Lucy angry. She wrenched her arm from Watson's grip and got up in his face, screaming, "Who the HELL are you to be tellin' anybody to stay away from me? I don't know what kinda twisted shit you got goin' on in that warped head of yours, but you ain't my daddy, and you damn sure ain't my boyfriend!" She poked him in the chest with her finger to emphasize each word. He grabbed her hand to stop the assault. "Ow!" she cried.

That was all I was going to take. I stepped between them and pushed Billy away from her. He stumbled down the steps and landed on his back on the driveway. Before he had a chance to get up, Lucy said, "Goodbye, Billy," and we turned and went back into the house, slamming the door behind us. "Son-of-a-bitch!" She pounded the back of the closed door. "The nerve!" She threw her head back and bellowed, "Uuurrrgggh! He makes me so damn mad!"

I was standing at the window watching Billy. He had picked himself up from the ground and just stood there staring at the front of the house with a dumb look on his face. I couldn't tell if he could hear her tirade, because his expression never changed. After several minutes, he spat a stream of saliva at the porch and left.

"He's gone," I announced.

"Good," she snapped. "I'm sorry. I didn't mean to snap at you."

"I know," I replied. "He makes me mad, too."

"The gall of some people," she grumbled. "Really!"

For some reason, we both broke out in uncontrollable laughter. We were interrupted, however, by knocking at the door. Lucy abruptly stopped laughing and flew to the door. She jerked the door open and barked, "What?"

"Whoa! Little lady," a startled Zachary asked from the porch. "What's the matter?"

"Zachary, I'm sorry." She blushed with embarrassment. "I thought you were Billy Watson."

"I kinda figured that," he explained. "I saw his car leavin'. What'd he want?"

"Spy on me," she fussed, "and to ask me out."

"What?"

"He saw Eddie drivin' the Stinger yesterday. He came out here today to see if Eddie was still here," she explained. "And he asked me out. Do you believe that?"

"That boy ain't right," Zachary laughed. "I saw him leavin' in a hurry, so I decided to stop to see what was up. I'm goin' over to Americus for the afternoon. I gave the boys the rest of the afternoon off. The fence is okay, so we let the horses out of the barn. Steve and Sandy took the kids down to Albany to the movies, but he said he'd be back in time enough to get the horses up for the night."

"You drive careful now, you hear?" She kissed him on the cheek. "Sorry 'bout hollerin' at you before."

"It's all right, baby doll," Zachary assured her. "Watson's enough to make anybody holler. You kids behave yourselves." With that, he walked away.

Lucy turned back to me and the fit of laugher overtook us again. She came to me while we laughed, and we embraced. The embrace ended in a kiss. She broke the kiss and said, "You still feel like that swim?"

"You bet," I said.

She leaned in and kissed me again. She cocked an eyebrow and said, "Looks like we've got the whole place to ourselves for a while. Wanna skinny dip?" I shook my head. She shrugged. "Oh well. Come on." She took me by the hand and led me toward the pool.

The pool house was on the other side of the pool. The squat block building was on the edge of the patio. It was really nothing more than a changing room with a sofa, and a bathroom with a shower.

Lucy rummaged through a battered chest-of-drawers for a suit for me. She pulled a pair of red trunks from the drawer and tossed them to me. "Try these on for size." I examined them and decided they would do. She plucked a blue bikini from the drying rack in the corner of the small room and headed to the bathroom. "I'll be back," she announced, then closed the door behind her.

I quickly changed into the trunks, which were a little loose, and sat on the sofa to wait for Lucy to emerge from the bathroom. Dressed in only the blue two-piece suit, with her hair falling across her bare shoulders, she was unbelievable. My eyes walked over her from head to foot, lingering longest on the thin line of fine red hair that ran from her navel to the top of her suit. The breath caught in my throat, and I struggled to swallow. The magazine picture, again, flashed in my mind. Just as I had longed to see behind that fold in the sheet, I wanted, much more, to see what was hidden by the cobalt blue bikini bottom.

She caught my eye and winked. "You ready to get wet?" She grabbed two towels from a shelf by the door, grabbed my hand, and trotted to the pool. She tossed the towels onto one of the patio chairs and dove in. She surfaced, brushed the wet hair from her face, and said, "You comin'?" She licked the water from her top lip.

"I don't dive," I confessed. I was scared to death of diving head first into the water. I don't know why, but the idea of trying frightened the hell out of me. I walked to the edge of the pool and sat down, dangling my feet in the water. The water was colder than I expected, but I pushed off the deck and sank into the water up to my waist. The cold shocked me, but I dropped down up to my neck.

"Feels good, don't it?" she wondered.

"It's a little cold, though."

"You'll get used to it."

She swam to me and tugged me into deeper water, where we could stand beside one another and still be below the water. She pulled my body close to hers and whispered in my ear, "I'll warm you up." She nibbled my earlobe. My body shivered, but not from the cold. She released my ear and hunted my mouth with her own. Our lips joined, and I felt her tongue probing my mouth. I explored her mouth with my own tongue. As quickly as she had kissed me, she pulled away and swam to the far corner of the pool.

"Why'd you do that?" I asked.

"Gettin' too steamy on that end. Thought I'd better come down here," she replied. "Come and get me."

I pushed off from the bottom, jackknifed, and submerged. I could see her blurry form through the water as I kicked across the pool. I arched toward the bottom of the pool and came to her from beneath her. As I rose along her body to the surface, my face brushed against the smooth skin of her belly. I broke the surface inches from her face. I quickly closed the gap and pressed my lips to her neck, just above the surface of the water. I flicked the wet skin with my tongue. She moaned. Her hands played up and down my back, while I sucked gently on her bottom lip. She wrapped her legs around me and clutched me to her. I had no chance to hide my obvious excitement. All I could do was hold onto the side of the pool to keep us both from sinking below the water.

When she released me from her leggy embrace, she pulled me to her with an arm behind me. As she had done on the balcony the day before, she massaged the small of my back. She brought her other hand up and pulled my head to hers to bring our lips together. Her hand held my head, while her lips moved hungrily over mine. Her other hand moved up and down my back, her fingers walking along my spine beneath the water. She brought the hand around in front of me and rubbed my chest. She lay it against my pounding heart, then moved down across my stomach. I was surprised when she slid her hand past the waistband of my trunks, while our tongues danced between our mouths.

I was shocked by her aggressiveness, although it went along with what I had seen of her personality. The way she had teased and embarrassed Dick Brinson, without so much as a blush, should have told me that her passion matched her hair.

I began to wonder if it was a Southern thing. Of all the girls I had dated, only Rosalie had been the aggressor, but the women I had met since coming to Wixton were different. I had watched the young bride take control of her soldier husband. I had been propositioned by the sheriff's daughter, and I was being seduced by the beautiful woman who was about to take me farther than I had ever been before.

My body responded to every move of her hand. I broke our kiss and threw my head back with a moan of ecstasy. When she released my head, she dropped her hand to my waist. She grasped my shorts and began to push them down. I realized what she was doing and pulled away from her.

My sudden motion startled her. She released me and pulled her hands away. A look of realization flooded her face. "Oh, Eddie, I'm sorry." For a minute, I thought she was going to cry. She dropped her eyes from mine.

I treaded water and stoked the side of her face. "Hey." I lifted her face so I could look into those gorgeous blue eyes. "Hey," I repeated. "It's okay, Baby. I'm ready."

"What?" she asked, not believing what she was hearing.

"I want you to be my first," I explained. "I want to make love to you, but not here. Not like this. Not in the pool. I want my first time to be special. Romantic."

"You sound like a woman," she laughed. I laughed with her. She put her arms around my neck and brought her face very close to mine. "It'll be special for me, too." She kissed me, then thought for a minute. She said, "Give me a half an hour, then come to me, in my room." She kissed me again, then swam to the ladder and climbed out of the water. I started to get out, but she stopped me. "No," she said, "you stay in 'til I'm gone."

"Okay," I agreed.

She grabbed her towel and disappeared into the pool house. She returned after a few minutes with the towel wrapped around her. "A half an hour," she repeated as she walked around the end of the pool to the house. She paused about halfway across the deck and called to me over her shoulder. "Hey, Eddie!" When she was sure I was still watching, she undid the towel and let it fall to the floor. "Don't be late."

"Don't worry," I assured her, as I watched her naked back as she crossed the final distance to the house. Only after she was gone from my sight did I realize I was holding my breath.

As she instructed, when she was gone, I swam to the ladder and climbed out of the water. My legs shook so much with anticipation that I almost didn't make it up the ladder. I went into the pool house, not really sure what to do. I was nervous. I looked at the clock on the wall. I still had over twenty minutes to kill. I would have thought, for sure, that it was almost time. I stripped off the wet swim trunks and hung them on the drying rack next to her suit. I decided to take a shower, and, since I was still pretty excited from our time in the pool, I left the water just as cold as I could stand it. I toweled off but couldn't decide what to wear when I went to her. Should I be fully dressed, or should I go just wrapped in a towel? I decided the towel wasn't very romantic, and, since I was the one who wanted romance, I pulled back on all my clothes, except my shoes, of course, which were still in the mudroom. Fifteen minutes. I paced. My whole body crawled with anticipation of it all. I was excited, and scared to death, and worried that I would disappoint Lucy, somehow, since she was experienced. I wondered if I could live up to Rooster's legacy. Twelve minutes. I left the pool house and walked out into the sun. I stood with my face turned to the heat. I checked my watch. Ten minutes. I went to the kitchen. My mouth was dry, so I poured myself a glass of water from the pitcher in the refrigerator. I gulped down two glasses, but still felt as if I had cotton in my mouth. Five minutes. I started for the stairs in the corner, but changed my mind. I thought about those old movies about the Antebellum South. The hero dashes up the majestic staircase and sweeps his lover off her feet to make mad passionate love to her. Two minutes. I ran from the kitchen to the foyer. I climbed the stairs two at a time. By the time I had reached the second floor, I was winded. I leaned against the railing to regain my composure before I went to her. Thirty minutes after I had seen her last, I stood before her closed bedroom door. I took a deep breath and knocked.

"Come in," she called.

I wiped the sweat from the palm of my hand and turned the knob. Nervously, I pushed open the door.

The lights were low. Lucy was sitting on the bed, propped against an oversized pillow. Dressed all in white, she looked like an angel in the light from the single bedside lamp. The silk robe she wore was tied at the waist, but it lay open around her stockinged legs. "Hey," she said.

"Hey," I replied. Unsure what to do with my hands, I moved them nervously in and out of my pockets. She smiled.

"Nervous?" she asked. I nodded. "Me, too," she admitted, but I would have bet that she wasn't nearly as nervous as I was. She slid to the edge of the bed and stood up. She untied the belt and let her robe fall open. Underneath, she wore a white lace teddy over silk panties and a garter belt. Her breasts were visible through the sheer fabric of the negligee. I bit my lower lip to keep my mouth from dropping open. She shrugged the robe off and let it fall to the floor. As before, my eyes caressed her every curve. She smiled at my attention, but grew impatient. "You gonna stand over there by the door and gawk at me all day?" I was rooted to the floor by the fear that my quivering legs would desert me if I tried to take a step. "Come here," she commanded. I obeyed. Meeting me halfway across the floor, she took hold of my hands, but I resisted, convinced that if I gave in to her, I would be burned up by the heat that rose off her body. She leaned in and whispered, "Kiss me." Her breath tickled my ear. Just a gentle brush of her lips on mine, and I melted into her, surrendering to the passion. I could feel the heat, but I welcomed the touch of her body against mine. I tried to pull her to me to prolong the contact, but, this time, she pulled away. She stepped back and began unbuttoning my shirt. My already weakened knees began to wobble more. With each button, I grew more unsteady. She must have noticed, because she stopped and asked, "You okay, baby?"

"Just nervous," I replied.

"I won't hurt you." We both laughed, breaking the tension some. She unbuttoned the last button. Rubbing her hands across my chest, she pushed the shirt over my shoulders and down my arms. Her hands traced circles around my chest and stomach, then dropped to my waist. She leaned in and kissed my neck, while she continued to undress me. She undid my pants and slid her hands inside. She pushed the pants down, freeing me from their confines. She took me in her hand again and rubbed me. I tilted my head back and moaned. Still holding me, she pulled me toward the bed. I stepped out of the jeans that sat bunched around my ankles and followed her. She stopped at the bed and said, "My turn." She released me and lifted her hands above her head.

I removed her teddy and dropped it on the floor beside her robe. I brought my hands up to cup her breasts. I bent and kissed each one. I kissed across the curve of her breast to her neck, then to her mouth.

She pulled away from me and sat down on the bed. She leaned back on her elbows, thrusting her breasts forward. She lifted her foot between my legs and caressed me. I wobbled. "Easy, big fella," she laughed. "Don't fall out on me, now. You've got things to do." She leaned farther back and raised her foot to my chest. "I saw how much you liked watchin' me take these off last night. I thought you might want to help this time."

I lifted her foot to my mouth and sucked her big toe through the silk. "Oh, yeah," I answered.

She unhooked the garter belt from the stockings. I ran my hand down her leg to the top of the stocking. I took hold of the edge and pulled it slowly toward her foot, taking time to feel the smoothness of her skin along the way. When I pulled the stocking from her foot, I paused to suck her now bare toe into my mouth, then I teased the bottom of her foot with my tongue. She giggled as she tried to pull her leg away. I resisted for a moment, then let it go. I moved on to the other leg. When both stockings were crumpled on the floor, Lucy pushed the garter belt to her thighs, then wiggled it down her legs and kicked it off. She propped back up on her elbows, looked down at her underwear, then back to me. "Well?" she asked. When I didn't move to remove them, she started to.

"No," I stopped her, "let me. I've been waiting all my life for this."

She was lying across the bed with her legs hanging off. I moved to her and lay my hand on her warm stomach. It rose and fell with her breathing. I rubbed across the swell of her belly to the top of her underwear. I took a deep breath, then moved my hand across the silky fabric, feeling the texture of her body underneath. Moving back to the waistband, I hooked just the tips of my index fingers under the thin band of elastic. I slid my fingers around to her sides and pulled slowly toward me until just a hint of red peeked out. My heart pounded in my chest. I took another deep breath and held it. I grasped the panties and pulled them quickly down her legs, exposing her completely to me. I let the breath I was holding out in an audible gasp. Lucy giggled. I blushed and pulled back from her.

Realizing she had embarrassed me, she quickly sat up, grabbed my hands and said, "I didn't mean to laugh at you."

"I know," I answered. "I'm a little self-conscious, I guess. I'm sorry."

"Don't be sorry." She pulled me close and laid her head against my stomach. I could feel her hot breath on my skin. "I think it's sweet," she said.

"I don't want to be sweet," I explained. "I want to be sexy."

"You are," she assured me. She ran her tongue around the perimeter of my belly button, then said, "Make love to me, Eddie."

"Not yet," I said, smiling at the look of surprise on her face. I pushed her back on the bed. "What?"

"Shhhhh," I whispered, laying a finger across my lips.

I dropped to my knees in front of her and placed my hands on her thighs. I pushed her legs apart, then pulled her body to the edge of the bed. I lowered my face to her. I brushed my face across the triangle of red between her legs. Kissing along its edge, I let the soft hair tease my face. She sighed as my tongue teased the soft skin at the crease of her leg then moved below. Our bodies quivered together. Unlike the young bride I had watched a few days before, Lucy didn't scream as the excitement built within her. Instead, she moaned quietly, and, finally, with a gasp, she brought her legs together against my head, forcing me to pull back from her.

She lay still on the bed for a few minutes. I leaned back on my feet and watched her. Neither of us spoke, but the heaviness of our breathing was audible in the quiet room. After a moment, she sat up on the bed and asked, between labored breaths, "You sure you haven't done this before?"

"Why?" I asked. She did not reply. She just sighed heavily and smiled. I smiled back, and said, "I'm glad you enjoyed it." She pulled me to her and kissed me hard on the mouth.

She released me and crawled back onto the bed. She lay back against the big pillow and motioned with her curling finger for me to follow. I stood from the floor and moved above her. She spread her legs to accept me as I lowered myself to her. Because I was unsure of myself, my movements were awkward and slow. Scared to proceed, I sort of hovered above her. I felt myself brush against her inner thigh. I sighed loudly, frustrated by my hesitancy. She placed a reassuring hand against my cheek. "Bear with me," I asked. "I'm new at this."

"Relax," she whispered. She reached down between us and guided me into her.

She raised her body to meet me, taking me inside. As our bodies joined together, my awkwardness all but disappeared, and I yielded to the rhythm of our lovemaking.

Sooner than I wanted, I felt myself building toward orgasm. My body began to shake, sweat broke out on my forehead, and I cursed to myself. Unable to control myself any longer, I exploded. With my energy expended, I collapsed against her, feeling the heat of her naked flesh against my own.

She kissed the top of my head and ran her hand down my sweat-slick body. I rolled onto my back beside her on the bed. She rolled against me and snuggled close. She was the first to speak. Placing her hand on my chest, she said, "Your heart's beatin' pretty fast."

"Uh-huh," I managed to reply.

"You okay?" She hugged me tightly.

"Uh-huh," I repeated.

She giggled.

"Well?" she asked, still giggling.

"Unbelievable!" I exclaimed. "I'm sorry…"

"You did good," she assured me.

"You're sweet," I said, sure she was lying to spare my feelings.

"I mean it," she said. "You were wonderful. Really."

"Thank you," I accepted, still wary.

"No," she replied. "Thank you." She pulled up and kissed me. "I think you're jerkin' my chain about bein' a virgin. I think you just told me all that to get me horny."

I couldn't read her. By the expression on her face, I was afraid that she really thought I was lying. I started to argue, "I…"

She interrupted me, laughing. "I'm just messin' with you, baby. You just surprised me, that's all."

"Surprised you? How?"

"I wasn't…" she fumbled for the words. I thought it was funny that a woman who would yank up her dress in a crowded restaurant would have trouble talking about sex. She decided on, "Let's just say that, for somebody who just got to town, you sure seem to know your way around." I laughed. "You sure you haven't done that before?" she asked again.

"Positive."

"Well, you're damn good at it," she complimented. With a short laugh, she said, "Surprised the hell outta me when you pushed me back on the bed like that. I didn't know what you were fixin' to do. I guess I figured you'd be naïve about stuff like that."

I was naïve and wouldn't have had any idea about "stuff like that" if it hadn't been for Corporal "Oh Frankie". The technique was all my own, but the idea was all Frankie's. I was glad she had enjoyed it, because I had been scared to death the whole time.

"Where'd you learn… how'd you know…" she fumbled her words again, "…what to do, I mean?"

I told her. I admitted that I had watched the newlyweds through a crack in the wall. I waited for her to recoil from me in disgust, but she surprised me.

"You watched 'em?"

"Yeah," I replied. "I shouldn't have, I know, but I couldn't help myself."

"Tell me about it."

"Huh?"

"Tell me what you saw," she clarified. "Everything."

"Really?" Would she ever cease to amaze me?

"Really."

I laughed, but only to release the tension in my body. Although I was lying naked in her arms, I was suddenly shy. It was hard to find the words that didn't embarrass me. Finally, I took a deep breath and began the story. Unable to look at her while I talked, I stared at the ceiling. She was still snuggled against my side. Recounting the intimacies of their sex excited me, and, from the way Lucy squirmed against me, I knew it was having the same affect on her. She rubbed her legs together, nervously. I felt her hand slide between our bodies and between her legs.

I rolled toward her and said, "Let me."

She rolled onto her back. I kissed her hungrily. Her mouth. Her neck. Her breasts. I rubbed down her body, until my hand brushed the silky carpet below. I continued down and placed my hand on top of hers. Together, we probed the soft flesh beneath our hands. After a moment, she moved her hand away.

She gasped, "Tell me the rest."

I continued talking, while my hand coaxed tremors from her body. By the time I was finished with my story, she was squeezing my hand with her thighs trying to make me stop.

She pulled my hand from between her legs and kissed it. "That was incredible," she complimented. "You are incredible."

"I learn fast."

"Uh-huh!"

"Make love to me again, Eddie," she whispered. "I want you inside me."

Although the excitement coursed through me like an electrical charge, my body wasn't responding. I pulled back from her.

"What's wrong?" she asked, reaching for me.

"I don't think I can do this," I admitted. "I can't… I mean, I'm not…"

"Oh," she said, noticing my condition. "We can fix that. I think." She pushed me against the bed. "Lay back," she ordered.

She reached down and took hold of me. My body quaked with her touch. She kissed down my neck and across my chest to my stomach, pausing just a moment to tease my navel with the tip of her tongue. She then crawled down the bed and took me in her mouth. The sensation was phenomenal. I raised up on my elbows so I could see what she was doing to me. I moaned as I came alive in her mouth. When I was fully aroused, she pulled away. I grunted in protest.

"More of that later, maybe, but now…" She didn't finish her sentence. At least not verbally. She climbed on top and lowered herself onto me. I slid inside her and could not suppress a cry of pleasure. She giggled. I was no longer embarrassed by it. I was too involved in the swirl of sensations I was experiencing to be embarrassed. She could laugh all she wanted, as long as she kept doing what she was doing. I closed my eyes and enjoyed the ride. Her slow, deliberate motion drew me toward my second orgasm. Although I lasted longer that second time, the end came much sooner than I wanted. The release was intense, almost painful, happening so soon after the first. My body jerked as I emptied myself inside her, and I fell back against the bed, exhausted. She leaned down, kissed me, then moved to lay beside me on the bed.

She placed her head against my chest. I put my arm around her and pulled her up close to me. I wanted her as close to me as I could get her. We stayed like that for nearly an hour. Neither of us spoke. We just lay with our naked bodies pressed together. Silent.

I was first to speak, this time. "I'm hungry," I announced.

"Me, too," she agreed. "I'm famished."

"Let's get something to eat," I suggested.

"I want to take a shower first," she informed me. "I feel a little sticky." She climbed from the bed and started toward the bathroom. "You want to join me?" I nearly beat her to the bathroom door.

"Wait a minute," I said. "I thought you said you didn't shower…"

She cut me off, saying, "Second date."

"Oh," I acknowledged.

After the shower, dressed in matching bathrobes, we went back to the kitchen.

"You want me to cook somethin'?" she asked.

"Sandwich'll be okay with me," I said. "No point in going to any trouble."

"No trouble," she assured me. "But I could go for a sandwich, just as well."

We finished off the rest of the turkey we had had at lunch and drank an entire bottle of wine. Already buzzed with the excitement of making love for the first time, the wine left me giddy. I found myself smiling incessantly and laughing at everything Lucy said. She thought that was funny, and that made me laugh even harder.

After we ate, we went to the music room where Lucy played the piano for me. We sat together on the bench while she played her favorite songs. I didn't care what she played, as long I was there beside her. She was very good, and I told her so. She told me that her scholarship to college had been for music. Her goal was to play professionally, and her dream was to play with an orchestra at Carnegie Hall.

"Why don't you do it?" I asked.

"What?" she wondered.

"Play Carnegie Hall."

"Play Carnegie Hall?"

"Why not?"

"I'm not good enough to play Carnegie. Besides, you can't just walk in and say, 'I'm here to play. Where's the stage?'," she laughed.

"Of course not. Where would you carry the piano?" I joked. We both laughed. "But, really, I mean, do what you planned. Go to the university. Pursue your music. Pursue your dream."

"I can't go to school now," she argued. "The business. The Angel L."

"You said yourself, Mitch Patterson takes care of the business, and it looks as if Zachary has things around here under control. You wouldn't be doing anything any different than you do now, you'd just be doing it from Athens instead of here."

"I hadn't ever thought about it that way before," she admitted.

"Well, think about it," I suggested. "You have a talent that shouldn't be wasted.

Maybe you'll never make it to Carnegie Hall, but maybe you will. You'll never know until you try." I let that sink in, then added, "I bet your father wouldn't want you to let his death stand in the way of your dream."

"You're probably right," she agreed.

"Hey," I laughed. "I know all about following dreams."

"I guess you do." She leaned over and kissed me. "At any rate, I'm not gonna make any life-changin' decisions right now, but I'll think about it. I promise."

She put her hands back on the keyboard and played a soft lullaby. I closed my eyes and let the music draw me in. By the time the final notes faded into silence, I was so enraptured that I didn't hear her suggest that we go outside by the pool.

"Eddie!" she had to call to get my attention. "You want to go outside? By the pool?"

"Huh?… What?" I stammered.

"You still with me?" she asked.

"I'm sorry. I lost myself for a moment," I explained. "Got carried away by the music."

She smiled. "Do you want go outside and sit by the pool?" she repeated.

"Outside would be nice," I finally answered her.

"Come on, silly." She grabbed my hand and pulled me toward the door.

She had switched on the pool lights as we passed through the kitchen, and the light from beneath the water cast an almost ethereal shimmer about us as we embraced by the water's edge. Lit from below by the faintly moving light, Lucy, as she had so many times in the past two days, took my breath.

"What you thinkin' about?" she asked, catching the expression on my face.

"You," I admitted

"What about me?" she questioned.

"I just can't believe how beautiful you are."

Even with the rippling shadows, I could tell she had blushed. "You're just sayin' that because I had sex with you," she joked, trying to cover her embarrassment. I didn't acknowledge her silliness. I just leaned in and kissed her on the forehead. "You're sweet," she said. This time, I didn't mind.

We sat together on one of the chaise lounges there on the pool deck. Unaware of how long we'd been there, we just sat and enjoyed each other's company. Swapping stories about our lives, we passed the time cuddled together in the moonlight.

At some point in the night, the light at the stable came on. The light remained on for about half an hour. When it had been off for several minutes, Lucy pulled away from me and stood. She laughed at my surprise, slipped off the robe she was wearing, and dove naked into the pool. She had been waiting for Steve to put the horses away for the night before going skinny dipping. Less chance of getting caught, I guess.

"You comin'?" she asked.

I stripped off my own robe and followed her into the pool. I was pleasantly surprised to find that the water was warmer at night. She swam away from me when I approached her.

"You didn't have enough of that already today?" she kidded.

"I was just… I only wanted…"

"I know what you want," she laughed. She swam in a quick circle around me as she talked, then, in a flash, she was streaking across the pool away from me.

I swam after her, and we began a clumsy game of cat and mouse. We criss-crossed the pool, coming together occasionally to kiss.

Eventually, when the periods of kissing began to last longer than the periods of swimming, we left the pool for her bedroom where we made love for the third time that day. For the third time in my life. When it was over, both of us were drained, and we drifted off to sleep.

Chapter Twenty-two

Our sleep was interrupted the next morning by the ringing telephone. Lucy groaned loudly when she stumbled out of bed and staggered to the phone.

"Hello," she said, sleepily. "Speakin'." Her brow wrinkled. "Am I sure? Well, if I ain't her, I'm wearin' her underwear!" She looked down at her nakedness and nearly burst out laughing. "Can I help you?" she said. "Yes, I'll hold."

"Who is it?" I asked.

She put her hand over the mouthpiece and said, "It's Mitch's office. Some new girl. Asked me if I was sure I was Lucy Brewster." She laughed at the absurdity of it. She started to say something else to me but spoke instead into the phone. "Mitch? Hey, honey. It's too damn early in the mornin'." The bedside clock read eight-fifteen. "Uh-huh. Who was that girl that called? She asked me if I'm sure I'm me. Where's Carolyn? Really? What was it this time? I bet Syd is fit to be tied. What's this make? Five girls? Six, really? They better quit while they're ahead." She made small talk for only a few more minutes, then said, "Okay, Mitch, I know you didn't run me out of bed this mornin' to chit-chat. What's up?" She listened for a few minutes, then said, "He won't take your word for it? I've told him repeatedly that you have full authority. I know. I know. He's a hard-headed old coot. All right. Get Miss 'Are you sure?' to set up the meetin'. Say, tomorrow lunch? We can take him to that place you like so much. What's the name? Yeah, that's it. Get her to make reservations for one, lo-cal time, and book me a flight out of Atlanta for first thing in the mornin'. You flyin' out today?" She looked at me on the bed and added, "Make that a flight for two. First class. Yeah, I said two. Never mind. I'll explain it when I get to Dallas." She hung up the phone with a curse.

"What was all that about?" I asked. "Did you say Dallas?"

"Yeah, Dallas," she confirmed. "We're in the middle of a buy-out of one of our competi-tors, and he's wafflin' on the terms we agreed to. Mitch had already negotiated the changes he wants, but the old man wants to hear it from me." She grunted in frustration. "To top it all off, he wants to meet with me face-to-face. Says he won't trust a deal made over the phone. Do you believe that?" She shook her head. "The stubborn old fool upsets the apple cart, and now we have to fly to Dallas tomorrow."

"We?" I asked, unsure if she was referring to her and me or her and Mitch.

"Yeah, silly. You didn't think I was gonna fly halfway 'cross the county without you, did you?"

I didn't quite know how to respond. I was already caught up in a whirlwind of emotions without throwing Dallas into the mix. I was trying hard to come to terms with my feelings for Lucy and my commitment to my original goal. Our conversation at the piano had really sent my mind reeling. There I was telling her to follow her dreams, when I was contemplating giving up on my own. I thought I would have a few days to decide what to do, but then Mitch Patterson had called, and, suddenly, I was out of time.

My feelings for Lucy were genuine, and I didn't want to cheapen the love we had shared, had made, by walking away, but I had an obligation to myself to finish what I had started long ago with the childhood promise to my father. Or did I? I almost couldn't comprehend leaving the woman that I knew I loved for something that might never be.

We had given ourselves to each other completely, having shared the most intimate parts of our lives and our bodies. She had not hesitated to include me in her travel plans, which told me that she considered me part of her life. How could I walk away from that? I wrestled with the decision that faced me. What was I going to do?

My answer came with her next statement. She climbed back into bed beside me. I relished the feel of her skin against mine. I convinced myself that I belonged with her, but then she said, "If we're flyin' to Dallas tomorrow, we need to take you shoppin'."

"What?" I said, taken by surprise.

"You need a suit or two that fits you," she explained. "And a decent pair of shoes."

A decent pair of shoes! The remark cut me, and made me acutely aware of the difference between us. Lucy had said, before, that we were just alike, but we weren't. She was money. She was big business. She was fancy restaurants, fancy cars, and fancy clothes. No matter how down-to-earth she seemed to be, she was out of my class. Or I was out of hers. I was poor. I was blue-collar. I was greasy spoon, city bus, and borrowed suits that didn't fit quite right. But, most of all, I was dirty, worn, second-hand boots.

Although I'm sure she meant no harm by her comment, it hurt me just the same. I didn't belong in her world. I didn't want to be an embarrassment. If I weren't good enough for her, I needed to go. But how to tell her?

"I'm gonna take a shower," she announced. "You want to join me?"

"Not this time," I declined.

"Suit yourself." She climbed from the bed and disappeared into the bathroom.

I got up and went about the business of collecting my things. I dressed in the clothes that I came to her in yesterday. They lay where they fell when she undressed me. Tears streamed down my face when I sat down in the chair in the corner and pulled on my boots, which I had retrieved from downstairs.

I was still sitting in the chair with my duffle bag at my feet when she emerged from the bathroom. Her eyes grew wide when she spotted the bag.

"What's this?" she asked.

"I need to go. I think."

"Go? Eddie? What are you sayin'?"

"I don't belong here, Lucy," I tried to explain. "You don't need me around to embarrass you."

"Embarrass me? What in hell are you talkin' about?" She was on the verge of tears. "I thought... I thought you loved me. What about last night?"

"Last night was wonderful, and I do love you," I said, "with all my heart and soul, but I don't belong here. You're ashamed of me."

"Ashamed? What are you talkin' about?" she questioned.

"My clothes aren't acceptable. My shoes aren't acceptable. I'm not acceptable."

"I don't care about all that. I care about you," she sobbed. Tears poured down my own face.

"What about suits that fit and decent shoes?"

"I didn't mean you were... Eddie, I love you! I wasn't tryin' to put you down. I just meant..."

"I know what you meant," I interrupted. "I really think you love me, but I don't fit into your world. I should have realized that the other night. You were scared to death that someone would notice my shoes, or realize that Rooster's suit didn't hang quite right." She started to argue, but I cut her off. "You didn't say it, but I could see it in your eyes. The whole time we were talking to your friend Maggie, you kept looking down at my feet. I didn't think much about it then, because I was too caught up in being with you, but now I realize you were worrying that she might look down." She didn't deny it. Couldn't deny it. "Baby, I love you, and I'm ready to spend the rest of my life with you, but I can't be what you want me to be. You can put all the spit and polish on me that you want, but all I'll ever be is a dirty old shoe."

"Eddie, I'm sorry," she cried. "Please don't go."

"I have to, baby," I crossed the floor to her. I put my arms around her and said, "I love you, but I can't stay. If we're meant to be, we'll find each other again." I pulled her close to me and kissed her deeply.

She clung to me, not wanting to let me leave. "Eddie, I love you," she said, "and I'm sorry. Please don't leave."

"I have to."

I left her standing in that same spot, sobbing. She did not try to follow me. I don't know if I would have changed my mind if she had, but she didn't. I walked down the hall, down the majestic staircase, and out the front door. I could barely see my way for the tears in my eyes.

Leaving her that day was the hardest thing I had ever done, but I did what I felt I had to do. With all the strength I could summon, I walked out of her life and pointed myself, body and mind, to the south. My heart, I left behind.

The next afternoon, I stopped at a small roadside store for something cold to drink. I was sitting on the ground under a large tree at the edge of the gravel parking lot. Although the shade of the tree gave little relief, and the bottle in my hand added not much more, I sat for a long while trying to escape the heat of the afternoon. When I finished the last of the Coke, I looked at my watch. Two o'clock. I thought about Lucy, and a lump formed in my throat. At that moment, she was at the meeting in Dallas, the meeting at the restaurant that Mitch Patterson liked so much, the meeting that had put the wedge between us, the meeting that had sent me back on the road. I cursed to myself and threw the empty bottle I was holding at the trashcan which sat a few feet from me. The bottle struck the side of the barrel and shattered.

"You know you coulda turned that in and got your deposit back." The speaker was a dusty, old farmer driving an even dustier pick-up truck.

I stood from the ground and glared at the old man for a second, then snarled, "Who the fuck cares!" I instantly regretted snapping at the man, but I was angry, and he just happened to be convenient. I slung my bag onto my shoulder and stalked down the road. I barely heard the call of "Bastard!" that followed me away from the old man.

For two days, I walked aimlessly south. After leaving Wixton, leaving Lucy, I had lost my direction. I couldn't have cared less about Florida, or oranges, or anything else. I had miles to go, but the joy I had once found in the trip was gone.

Chapter Twenty-three

By lunchtime Friday, I was sitting at a table in a small truck stop just west of Bainbridge, Georgia eating, of all things, a piece of apple pie. Karen was right. Good as it was, the pie couldn't touch Max's. I chuckled to myself at the thought, but then Lucy came rushing into my mind and the chuckle faded away. I had been trying, without much luck, not to think about her, but not an hour went by that I hadn't thought about her, thought about going back to her. I pushed the thought out of my mind, for the moment at least, and tried to enjoy my pie.

The truck stop was crowded. Truckers were constantly in and out of the place. Most were grabbing a quick bite to eat or a shower before heading out on the road again. Some were just killing time between loads.I was trying to find a trucker who was heading south, who was willing to give me a ride.

Earlier that morning, I had realized that I was tired of walking. I was ready to get where I was going. Where ever that might be. I was sitting beside the highway on an old tree stump when the revelation came to me. My first thought was to buy a ticket and ride the bus to south Florida, but, since I wasn't anywhere near a bus station, or a town, or even a house, I put my thumb in the air and hoped someone stopped.

I hiked for an hour or so, before a trucker pulled off the road ahead of me. I jogged up to the cab and climbed up the side. Through the passenger window, the driver, a middle-aged man with a huge eagle tattooed on his upper arm, asked, "You need a ride, son?"

"Yes, sir," I answered.

"Where you headed?"

"South."

"Where 'bouts?"

"Just south."

He laughed. "Well, I'm headed south as far as Bainbridge. You're welcome to ride 'til then."

"Thank you," I said as I climbed into the passenger seat of the big truck. I stuck out my hand and said, "Eddie Chance."

He shook the hand and identified himself, "Buddy Williams. Glad to have you along. You welcome company sometimes."

I nodded my head in agreement. I knew that too many hours on the road alone could make a man stir-crazy, but I could only image what being stuck in a little metal box for hours at a time could do to your mind.

Buddy talked almost constantly for the entire ride. I didn't mind. It helped to get my mind off Lucy, for a while at least. He told me he was hauling a trailer full of corn to the feed mill in Bainbridge, and, after that, he was going to be "bob-tailin' it" to Dothan, Alabama to pick up a load of roasted peanuts for a grocery store chain in Akron, Ohio. He talked about his family, a wife and two sons, back in Montgomery. Of course, he asked about my family. I gave him the short version. Orphaned at sixteen. Left home at eighteen. Headed south to find my fortune. Like everyone always did, he wished me luck.

The miles to Bainbridge passed quickly. He dropped off the trailer, then stopped at the truck stop to eat. I bought him lunch to repay him for the ride. He wished me luck again, and headed out for Dothan.

Before Buddy left, he and I put the word out that I was looking for a ride. No one was headed my way, so I was eating a piece of pie and waiting.

As I finished the last of the pie, a lanky driver came in and sat down a couple of tables over from me. He looked my direction when he took his seat. He gave me a quick smile, then motioned for the waitress.

She hurried over. "Jackson! How's it hangin', cowboy?" she asked.

He swatted her on the rear and replied, "Low and lonely, sugar."

"Jackson, you're too much," she batted his hand away and giggled. "What's your pleasure?" He cocked an eyebrow. She slapped his shoulder and amended, "To eat?" He grinned. "Jackson! Are you gonna order somethin' to eat, or not?"

"Chili dogs. Three of 'em. And fries."

"Comin' up."

"Maybe later."

"You wish."

"Every day."

"You're too much." She turned his order in and came back to his table while she waited for it. "Where you headed?" she asked.

"Orlando."

My luck is changing, I thought to myself. I started to go over and plead my case, but the waitress beat me to it.

"Hey, Jackson, how'd you like some company on the run?"

"You finally come to your senses, honey?" He reached for her.

"Stop that," she reprimanded, batting his hand away. "Seriously. Eddie, over there, is lookin' for a ride."

"Eddie?" he questioned, looking my way, again.

"Yeah, Eddie. Buddy brought him in. Picked him up near Albany somewhere. Said he was a good kid."

I was feeling awkward listening to them talk about me, so I started to go over and introduce myself. Before I could get up, he pushed back from the table and announced, "I gotta pee like a Kentucky racehorse." He shot a look toward the kitchen and added, "Them dogs 'bout ready?" She hurried away to check on his food, while he went to the back to the restroom.

When he came back out, he came to my table instead of going to his own. Approaching me with his hand extended, he asked, "You Eddie?"

I stood to meet him and took his proffered hand. "Yes, sir. Eddie Chance," I answered.

"Jackson Pickett," he identified himself. "Hear you needed a ride."

"Yes, sir," I confirmed. "I'm going to work in the orange groves." I didn't offer any further explanation. I was sure the story would get told eventually.

"Well, I'm goin' to Orlando. You're welcome to ride."

"Thank you."

"I'm headin' out in about half an hour. All right with you?"

"You're the boss."

"Good then. Let me eat, and we'll hit the road."

He went back to his table. I noticed that, while he ate, he kept watching the door. When he took the last bite of his third chili dog, he became visibly nervous. He was looking back and forth between the door and his watch.

I was rethinking the ride, when then door was opened by a squat man in a uniform. He surveyed the room, letting his eyes come to rest on me for a second before he walked to Jackson's table. He bent over the trucker, who whispered something to him. The officer shot me a quick glance, then started my way.

My body tensed in preparation of the confrontation to come. As he approached, I could clearly see the deputy badge that hung off his pocket. I steeled myself for another Billy Watson. I saw that the name on his other pocket was Howard. I leaned back in my chair and took a long drink from my watered-down Coke.

Howard stopped across the table from me. He hitched up his pants, pulled a mangled toothpick from his mouth, and asked, "You Eddie Chance?"

"Why?" I snapped.

He broke into a slight grin. "Carl said you'd say somethin' like that."

"Carl?" I wondered. "What's Carl got to do with anything?"

"He said I was to bring you back to Wixton."

"Why?" A million things were running through my mind, but I couldn't imagine why Carl would have sent this guy after me. And I couldn't comprehend how he had found me. I looked past the man to Jackson, who refused to meet my eyes, and realized that he was responsible for the presence of Deputy Howard, though I couldn't imagine how.

"The man said find you and get you back to Wixton, ASAP, and that's what I aim to do."

"Am I under arrest?"

"If you have to be."

"What charge?"

"I'll think of somethin'."

"I'm not going anywhere until you tell me what's going on."

"Look, Chance," he said, "I don't have time for this shit. All I know is, Besmer has every lawman from Wixton on down lookin' for you. He said, if you gave any trouble, to tell you Lucy needs you."

The name pierced my heart. Why did Lucy have Carl hunting me down? "What about Lucy?" I demanded.

"That's all I know," he answered. "Now, are you comin'?"

I was confused and, suddenly, scared. What about Lucy? My first, horrible, thought was that something had happened to Lucy, and they thought I did it. But that couldn't be it. He said Lucy needed me. I didn't understand. Why? How did she need me? Surely, she had not enlisted Carl and all the lawmen in Georgia just to find me because she wanted me to come back. She was rich enough to do something like that, but I knew that was not her style. Something was dreadfully wrong, and I needed to go to her.

"Let's go," I stood from my chair, threw what I hoped was enough money to cover my check onto the table, and followed the deputy to his car out front. I gave Jackson one last look, and he gave me a shrug.

"Deputy Howard?" I began, once we were underway.

"Call me Jacob," he instructed.

Okay, Jacob," I corrected. "How did Jackson know to call you?"

Under flashing lights, he pushed the car as fast as he dared northward. Once we reached the open road, he began his explanation. "Sheriff Besmer, or really Lenora, same difference, I guess, called our office this mornin' and asked us to keep a peeper open for you. She gave us a description of you. A pretty good one, I gotta admit. She said 'he sticks out like a sore thumb'." I had to laugh at that, even though my heart was being torn apart with worry. He continued, "Anyway, she said you were a suspicious one and passed on Carl's instructions about Lucy." He paused for a minute, then said, "I don't know exactly what's goin' on up there, but I hope everything's all right. I saw the pain in your face when I mentioned her."

"Thank you," I answered. "You really don't know what this is all about?"

"Just what I told you," he replied. "Anyway, though Lenora said she was gonna call around to several towns they thought you might pass through, we put the word out on the radio. Since we knew you were thumbin' it to Florida, we figured that truckers are just about the only one's who'll pick up a hitchhiker, especially one looks like you, no offense, so we put the word on the common channel for anyone comin' across you to call. We hit a bit of luck, with ol' Jackson goin' to Orlando. When Cindy told him your name, he red flagged, and called our office to let us know where you were."

"He know why you were looking for me?"

"Naw, we didn't tell 'im that," Jacob admitted. "All he knows is you're wanted." That's why Jackson was so nervous, I assumed.

I sat and listened to Jacob describe the manhunt that lead to his finding me, but my mind was miles away. Lucy. What was so wrong that Carl needed to chase me down, and what could I do? A knot had formed in the pit of my stomach. As the deputy droned on beside me, and the miles to Wixton clicked away, I worried about Lucy.

Although the trip from Wixton to Bainbridge had taken me two days, even with the help of Buddy Williams, the trip back took less than an hour at the breakneck speed at which we drove.

Just south of town, Jacob picked up the radio mike and announced our arrival. He said, "Decatur unit three to Wixton Dispatch. Over."

The radio, which had, before, been nothing more than occasional background noise, squawked to life. A voice I did not recognize responded to his call. The response was, "Acknowledge Decatur Three. You have Chance with you? Over." The mention of my name made me sit forward in my seat.

"Affirmative. Over."

"What is you current location? Over."

"About three miles south of town. Please advise. Over."

"Barricade is north of town. Approximately ten miles. Over.

BARRICADE!!!! The word stabbed me in the heart. What was he talking about? "What the hell is going on?" I growled. I snatched the microphone from Jacob's hand. He tried to hold onto it, but nearly lost control of the car. He cursed me under his breath. I screamed into the mike, "What's going on? Where's Lucy? What's wrong with her?"

The voice spoke back, "Who is this? Chance?"

"Yes," I barked. "What is going on? Where is Carl? Who are you?"

"Sergeant Miller. State patrol," he responded. "Sheriff Besmer is presently at the scene of the barricade. Over."

"What barricade?" I screamed at him. "What's going on?"

"I'm not at liberty to release that information," he responded, then addressed Jacob. "Deputy? Please continue on your present…"

"Answer me, you son-of-a-bitch!" I interrupted.

He ignored me. "…course. Someone at the property entrance will advise further. Over."

Jacob held out his hand for the microphone. I handed it to him and slumped back in the seat. He pressed the talk button and responded, "Yes, sir. Over."

He placed the mike in its cradle and glared at me. He did not speak, but the anger showed in his face. I turned to the window. I was angry, too, and I was scared, and the knot from my stomach had moved to my throat. We rode the rest of the way in silence.

Chapter Twenty-four

We topped the last hill below the house, and I was stunned by what I saw. The whole place appeared to be under siege. The yard in front of the house was filled with police cars. Even in the distance, I could see that dozens of people, who I assumed were cops, were crouched behind the dam of patrol cars.

By the road at the entrance to the plantation, two cops stood leaning against the side of a car marked Dougherty County Sheriff. One of the men stepped out into the road as we approached and held up his hand. Jacob pulled to a stop beside him. The uniform he wore identified him as a Dougherty County sheriff deputy. The man behind him wore the uniform of an Americus policeman.

The deputy leaned down to the window and asked, "You got Chance?" He looked past Jacob to me.

"I am Chance," I answered.

He didn't acknowledge me, but said to Jacob, "You just might have driven all this way for nothin', hoss."

"What?!" Jacob and I exclaimed in unison.

A humorless smile played across the other deputies lips. He explained, "F.B.I." He let that sink in, then continued, "They got some big time hostage negotiator up there runnin' the show. He says Chance'll hinder rather than help. Says he's gonna talk Watson out without givin' in to his demands."

My mind screamed the word he was saying: Hostage! Watson! Suddenly everything was becoming clear. Somehow, Billy Watson had taken Lucy hostage and was demanding to see me. I did not even want to think about the possibilities of what had happened, was happening. My hatred for Billy Watson hit its highest level as I sat there and listened to the deputy tell me that some F.B.I negotiator was saying that I couldn't be any help in saving the woman I loved from the monster that had her. I decided at that moment that Billy Watson would die before the day was over.

"Why are we still sitting here in the road?" I demanded. "Let's go!"

Jacob pulled the car into gear, but the man beside us didn't move from the window. He said, "Hold up, hoss. I got orders to keep Chance away from the front line. You want to go up there, that's your call, but he stays here." He held firmly to the side of the car.

I looked at the name tag on his shirt. His name was Lincoln. I leaned over Jacob and said, "Look, Deputy Lincoln, I don't know who you got orders from, but there ain't no way in hell that you or anybody else is going to keep me from going up there. If Watson wants me, he's got me, and he's going to regret it. Now, if you don't mind, get your damn hands off this car so we can go."

"No, you look, punk. I don't know who you think you are, but you ain't shit to me. The man said to keep you away, and I aim to do just that. And if you talk to me like that again, I'll rip your damn head off. Got me?" The anger boiled in his eyes. "Get out of the car!" he commanded.

I ignored him. "Jacob, please." I pointed toward the house.

Jacob looked at Deputy Lincoln, then at me. He shrugged and said, "Eddie, if the guy said it was better for you to stay out here, then maybe we ought to hang tight here for a while."

"Whatever," I barked. I got out of the car and slammed the door. "You do what you want. I'm going." I started down the driveway.

"Chance!" Lincoln called. I ignored him. "Chance! Where the hell you think you goin'?"

I never looked back. I just walked farther up the driveway. The impact of his body against mine caught me by surprise. The wind left my lungs, and I felt the sting of the dirt surface as it cut into the side of my face. In spite of gasping for breath, I started up as soon as he released me. I was on my knees when I felt the barrel of his gun against my temple.

"I done told you once," Deputy Lincoln growled. "The man said you ain't wanted, so you ain't goin', and I aim to do that any way I have to. You get it?" I heard him pull the hammer back.

"Deke!" said a voice I didn't recognize. "Bragg said detain 'im, not kill 'im!"

"Hell of a lot a help you been," Deke snapped at the other cop. "What were you gonna do, just let him just waltz up there and fuck everything up?"

"No," the cop answered, "but I ain't plannin' to shoot nobody, and neither are you. Now put that gun down!" The gun didn't move. "He's not the enemy here, man. He's one of the good guys."

"Yeah," Jacob piped in.

"I don't like him," Deke muttered.

"So," the other law men said in unison.

"Look, Deke," the Americus cop spoke, "I called Besmer. He's comin' down here to talk to him. We'll lock him in the car until the sheriff gets here."

The pressure of the gun disappeared. He took my arm and jerked me to my feet. My side screamed where his shoulder had connected when he tackled me, and his jerking my arm sent needles of pain through me. With my free hand, I swung at him. The punch connected with the side of his head, but did little but make him angrier. He punched me hard in my already bruised ribs. I doubled over and waited for the next blow. Thankfully, it did not come. Jacob and the other cop pulled Deke away from me.

"Hang tight, Eddie," Jacob recommended. "Sheriff Besmer's comin'."

The other cop held my shoulder. I tried to shrug his hand off and said, "I'll wait for Besmer. You don't have to hold me."

"You gonna behave yourself?" he asked. I nodded. "All right." He let go, and I bolted. I took about five steps before he caught me. "You're a stubborn one, ain't you?"

"Let me go, damn it," I protested. "Lucy needs me."

"Listen to me," he said. "Bragg said lettin' you up there could put the girl in danger."

"Who's Bragg?" I demanded.

"F.B.I.," he explained. "Hostage negotiator." I tried to break free of his grip again, but he held tight. "Quit that, now. You ain't goin' nowhere."

"I won't run again," I assured him.

"You done lied to me once," he said. He lead me to the patrol car, and put me in the back seat. "Besmer'll be here in a minute. Until then, you can cool your heels in here, 'cause I don't trust you as far as I can throw you." He slammed the door behind me.

I sat for a moment in the confines of the patrol car, trying to catch my breath. The smell around me was the stale stench of sweat and old cigarettes. It made me gag. I was determined to get free. I looked around for a way out. The door and window handles were missing, and the metal screen that separated me from the front seat wouldn't budge. I lay down across the seat and began to kick against the window. I was still kicking when I heard Carl's voice outside.

"What in hell is goin' on?" he demanded. "Let that boy out of there."

"No, sir," Deke Lincoln resisted. "This punk assaulted me and is my prisoner."

"No, sir?" Carl repeated. "What do you mean 'No, sir'? I gave you an order. Now do it."

"You can't order me," the deputy argued. "You ain't my boss." He stepped between Carl and the car door.

"Listen to me, shit head." Carl leaned in and was screaming in his face. "I may not be your boss, but I am a hell of a lot bigger than you." He took another step closer to Lincoln, who was pressed against the side of the car. Carl stopped screaming. He spoke so softly and slowly that I almost couldn't hear what he said through the car window. He said, "I don't know what your game is, son, but, 'round here, I make the rules. If you don't move outta my way, you're gonna know what it feels like to be assaulted. Now, you're gonna open this car door, let that boy outta there, and then you're gonna get in this shit pile and drive your sorry ass back to Albany where somebody gives a shit about what you think. You got that, deputy?"

Deputy Lincoln fumbled behind him for the door handle. He found it, and the door released. I pushed so hard against the door that I nearly knocked the man down. He recovered and started toward me.

"Lincoln!" Carl barked. "What did I tell you?"

"But..." Lincoln protested.

"But nothin'," Carl interrupted.

Deke lowered his head in defeat, then skulked around the car. He gave me a final glare over the roof of the car and nodded toward the house. A thin smile formed on his lips. Somehow sensing my affection for Lucy, he chose his words solely to torture me. He said, "I hope Watson enjoyed her." I lunged toward the car, but Carl caught my arm.

Still holding my arm in a grip like a steel vise, he addressed Lincoln, "I hope you enjoyed bein' a cop, Lincoln, 'cause as soon as I get this shit up there straightened out, I'm gonna come down to have a talk with you boss." Lincoln looked unaffected by the threat until Carl added, "Did I mention that he and I were in the same unit in W.W. Two?" Lincoln's expression fell. The smile on his face faded. Carl commanded, "Now, get the hell outta here."

"Son-of-a-bitch!" I called after him, as he spun a tire to get away.

"Let it go, son," Carl said to me. Then he said to the two remaining law men, "Would one of you explain what was happenin' here? Why was Eddie locked up? Why wasn't he brought to me, as soon as he got here?"

"Bragg said to keep him down here," the officer from Americus explained. "He said bringin' him in was a bad idea."

"Bragg is a son-of-a- bitch," Carl responded.

I butted in and asked, "Carl, what's going on here? What has Watson done to Lucy?"

Carl frowned. "We don't know," he said. "All we know is that he and Dick Brinson have had her locked up in that house since early this mornin'. He's been taking pot shots at the cars out front and demandin' to see you. He says he'll kill her unless he talks to you. That's why I sent out word to find you and bring you back here." He stopped and turned to Jacob, saying, "You Howard?"

"Yes, sir," Jacob answered.

"Good job," Carl said, shaking the deputy's hand. He turned back to me. "I wanna talk to Bragg about givin' the men orders without talkin' to me. F.B.I or not, I don't like him. Let's go." We climbed into the car. "When we get in sight of the house, you better hunker down in the seat there. There is a chance that Billy just wants to get you back up here just so he can shoot you. I want to keep you out of sight for that and until I can find out what Bragg was talkin' about." I agreed.

"Is Lucy okay, Carl?" I asked.

"I don't know, son. I just don't know," he answered. "I know Billy's been in love, if you can call it that, with her for as long as I can remember. I wouldn't think he'd hurt her, but, of course, I sure as hell didn't expect him to flip out and take the girl hostage neither. He sure hates your guts."

I didn't respond. I was too torn up to form the words that expressed my anger and my fear. I was more determined than ever that Billy Watson was going to die. If he had hurt Lucy in any way, he'd die slowly and painfully. Besmer left me to my thoughts, so we rode in silence the rest of the way to the house.

With me curled into the floorboard of the car, Carl pulled in behind the other patrol cars. A shot rang out before we even stopped rolling. Carl said, "Damn Brinson." I rose up and caught a glimpse of Dick Brinson sitting in an upstairs window with a rifle. I didn't see Watson, but I only got a brief look before Carl pushed me down. "You raise up like that again, you might get a bullet in your head. Dick Brinson may be a dumbass, but he can put a bullet up a fly's butt at two hundred yards." I didn't raise up again. "I'll be back for you," he said before exiting the car. Another shot rang out.

I sat still in the floor of the patrol car, helpless. It was an eternity before Besmer came back for me. The passenger door opened to Carl's crouching figure. He said, "Come on, Eddie. Brinson's gone from the window for now. Let's get you out while the gettin's good. Bragg wants to talk to you."

I climbed out and followed him, still crouching, to a small group of men off to the left of where we had parked. All but one were in uniform. The odd man, dressed in a dark blue suit that looked entirely out of place, was Bragg. The uniformed officers parted for Carl and me to pass through to him.

Bragg was the first to speak, "You Eddie Chance?" I nodded and extended my hand. He ignored it. "I've already told Sheriff Besmer, and now I'm tellin' you, you are not welcome here. I didn't want you here. The last thing we need to do is give in to the taker's demands. If he sees you here, he knows he's won. See? So, I'm not overjoyed that Besmer went against my instructions and brought you up here, but, since you are here, maybe you can shed a little light on why Watson took this Lucy Brewster hostage to get to you. Sheriff Besmer has filled me in on the animosity that developed between you and Watson since your arrival in Wixton on Tuesday of last week. Would you describe your relationship with the man as combative?"

"Yes, sir," I answered. "He…"

Bragg continued without regard to my response. "The sheriff has also told me that you have bested Watson on more than one occasion. Is this true?"

"Yes." I did not try to elaborate. Bragg wouldn't have listened, anyway.

Bragg nodded his head. "That establishes the cause of his dislike of you. He perceives you as a threat and seeks to eliminate that threat by eliminatin' you, even though you had already done that for him by leavin' town. Possibly, he felt the need to best you one last time, so he needed to draw you back to enact his revenge upon you. Since he knew Besmer would do what he felt was necessary to protect a hostage, Watson and this fellow, Richard Brinson, took control of this residence, then made the demand for your return." He paused, then added, "What I don't understand was his choice of a hostage. In my opinion, the more obvious choice to inflict pain on you, as well as obtain his goal, would have been the Wilsons, with whom I've been told you resided during your stay here. Is that right?"

"Yes."

I was going to explain the connection that I had with Lucy, but Bragg cut me off, again. He continued his dissertation, "Sheriff Besmer told me of the altercation you had with Watson on Monday. He said Watson attacked you in response to a traffic violation. Is this true?"

"Yes, but…"

Bragg kept talking. "Said traffic violation was committed while drivin' a vehicle owned by Ms. Brewster, but she was not present. Is that correct?"

"Yes," I responded. He was about to interrupt me again, but I cut him off. "Agent Bragg!" I said, sharply. "If you would shut up for just five seconds, maybe I could 'shed a little light', as you say, on this situation." I relished the look of surprise on his face and the smile on Carl's. I continued, "As you said, Billy has had it in for me ever since I came to town, but his jealousy of my relationship with Lucy is his motivation now. All Carl knew was that I was driving Lucy's car Monday when Billy jumped me, but he didn't know that I spent the night here that night. Billy showed up here Tuesday morning pretending to check up on her. He asked her out. When she turned him down, he got mad, but he really exploded when he saw that I was still here. I don't know if Carl told you that Billy has been obsessed with Lucy for several years, and seeing me with her pushed him over the edge. He left that day with his tail between his legs, but must have stewed over it until this morning. He may not have been aware that I wasn't here anymore. Lucy had to fly to Dallas yesterday, so she hasn't been home. Billy probably thought that, wherever she went, I went with her. I'm guessing he showed up here this morning looking for me to get that revenge you talked about. When I wasn't here, he freaked and took her hostage." I paused to take a breath. Agent Bragg started to speak, but I cut him off. I said, "Seems to me that, the more time we sit and analyze, the more time Billy has to do God knows what to Lucy. When are you going to actually do something to get her out?"

His eyes narrowed with anger. He growled, "I've been doin' this longer than you've been alive. Whatever he is gonna do to her, he's more than likely already done. My job is to get her out of there alive, and that's what I'm gonna do. What you need to do is shut up and let me do this my way. Got it?"

He tried to stare me down, but I wouldn't be intimidated. "Carl was right. You are a son-of-a-bitch." Bragg looked at Carl, who gave him a nervous grin. I continued, "You can sit here with your thumb up your butt if you want to, but I'm going to do something useful."

I started to stand, but Carl put his had on my shoulder and held me down. In a commanding tone, he said, "Sit still and let the man do his job."

I glared at him and said, almost on the verge of tears, "Let me go, dammit! I am going in to get that bastard!"

The sheriff squeezed my shoulder and replied in a fatherly voice, "Don't be a fool, Eddie. He'll kill you, and that damn sure won't help her. Now, sit down and let the man handle this." He released his grip on my shoulder and pushed back against the car. I sat stunned for a minute. With every passing second, my hatred for Billy Watson grew inside me. I reached a point where I wanted to kill him just to see the look on his face as he died. I sat under Besmer's watchful eye, boiling in my hatred. I made a silent vow that I would make Billy pay for what he had done to Lucy, but, for the time being, all I could do was sit there and wait for Bragg. To do what, I had no idea.

Chapter Twenty-five

We waited for what seemed like years, then Billy appeared in the window. I tried to raise up to get a better view, but Carl pushed me back.

"You still out there, Bragg?" Billy called from the window.

Bragg picked up the megaphone from the ground beside him and answered Billy. He responded, "I'm here, Watson. You ready to come on out now?"

"You're a funny man, Bragg," Billy laughed. "You got Chance yet?"

"We're workin' on it," Bragg lied. "We got everybody out lookin' for him. He's a hard man to track down." He gave me a sideways glance. I rolled my eyes at him.

"Carl," Billy called, "you there, too?"

"I'm here," Carl called back.

"Carl, you ain't found your buddy yet?" Billy asked. "He is your buddy ain't he, Carl? You know what, Carl? When Chance gets here, there's somethin' I want to ask him?"

"What's that, Billy?" Carl played along.

"I just wondered if he enjoyed Jenny!" He gave a demented laugh. I tried to get up again, but Carl still held me down. Billy went on, "You didn't know that, did you, Carl? You didn't know he was fuckin' your little girl, did you?" Carl glared at me.

I shook my head and whispered, "He's lying, Carl. I swear."

Carl looked unconvinced.

Billy ranted on, "That's right, Carl. Your little girl. Your blood. My cousin. My blood." He raved like a lunatic. "Then he took my girl. My girl, dammit! Lucy is my girl, but he took her. He used her. She should love me. ME! Not Rooster. Not Chance. MEEEE!!" He pulled his pistol from its holster and shot toward us. The windshield of the car we were hiding behind shattered, raining glass around us.

"Dammit!" Carl cursed.

Bragg grabbed the megaphone from Carl. He called to Billy, "Watson?"

"That you, Bragg?" Billy answered. "What you want?"

"How is Lucy?" Bragg asked. "I mean, is she hurt?"

"Hurt?" Billy acted as if the question stung him. "I wouldn't hurt her. I love her!"

"Does she love you, Billy?" It was the first time I had heard Bragg call him by his first name. He was trying to establish a rapport with Billy. "Billy?" he called. "Does Lucy love you now? I bet she's scared, isn't she? I bet she'd like to talk to somebody out here, wouldn't she? You know, just to let us know she's all right. Can you do that for me, Billy? Can you bring her to the window and let me talk to her?"

"You get me Chance," Billy commanded. "You hear!"

Watson disappeared into the house. Several minutes passed without sign nor sound from him. Whirlwinds of thoughts of what he could be doing ravaged my mind. With each image of him and Lucy, my rage increased. I decided that I couldn't take waiting anymore.

Finally, Besmer got so caught up in his conversation with Bragg that he turned his attention away from me for a moment, giving me the break I needed. Neither of them noticed when I crawled away. I hoped to make it into the house before Carl discovered that I was gone. None of the other officers paid any attention to me when I slipped around the end of the line of cars and dove for the bushes that ran along the side of the house. Watson obviously wasn't watching, because he had a clear shot at me for the split second that I was out in the open.

I crawled along the house behind the bushes to the opening for the library door. I tried the knob, but it was locked. I cursed to myself. I moved to the dining room window, but it, too, was locked. I considered breaking the window and climbing through, but I caught sight of Billy walking through the kitchen. He passed by the hall doorway, followed by Dick Brinson. I couldn't hear them, but I could tell by the exaggerated hand motions they were both making, that they were having a pretty heated argument about something. I thought I could use that to my advantage. As long as they were occupied with their argument, I was less likely to get caught. If I could find a way into the house, I could find Lucy and get her out, but finding a way in wasn't going to be easy. To get to the other side of the house and possibly an open window, I had to cross the patio in full view of the kitchen.

I had to try. I crawled around the end of the house to the edge of the doors. Careful not to expose too much of myself, I leaned in so I could get a good view of what was happening in the kitchen. Billy was standing at the kitchen counter, facing the pool. As long as he stood like that, even preoccupied by his conversation with Brinson, I had no chance of making it across the patio unnoticed. He was leaning against the counter drinking from a coffee cup. Across the room, a half-empty whiskey bottle sat on the table next to Billy's pistol. I thought briefly of crashing through the window and jumping him while he was separated from his weapon, but Brinson's presence in the room negated any possibility of success. I dismissed the thought. Although I could better make out the sound of their voices, it was impossible to tell what the argument was about. Brinson was punctuating his every thought with a stabbing finger in the air. As I watched the exchange, I became aware of the absence of Dan Sims. I realized that neither Carl nor Bragg had mentioned his name. I hoped that he wasn't hidden in the house, unknown to the police out front. The last thing I needed was to stumble across him. My only concern was that, while Billy and Dick were in the kitchen arguing, he was guarding Lucy. I would cross that bridge when I came to it. My first order of business was getting into the house. Until I could figure something out, I was, again, forced to wait.

After several more minutes of arguing, Billy pointed toward the staircase in the corner.

He said something that Brinson didn't like, and took another swallow of the whiskey in the cup he was holding. Brinson threw up his hands in resignation and stalked to the stairs, disappearing from my field of vision. Less that five minutes later, I heard the first of several rifle shots. He had retaken his position in the front window, and I was glad. As long as he continued shooting, I could keep track of where he was. So, as long as Lucy wasn't being held in that room, and Dan Sims wasn't somewhere in the house, Billy offered my only obstacle.

I prayed for a revelation. I prayed for a miracle. Since Brinson was gone from the kitchen, the thought of bursting into the room and jumping Billy resurfaced. He was still half a room away from his sidearm, and his reflexes were bound to be dulled by the half a bottle of whiskey he had drunk. I looked around the patio for something I could use as a weapon, and I saw my way in.

At the edge of the patio across from me was an ivy-covered trellis that extended from the ground to the balcony above. From where I crouched, it looked sturdy enough to support me. I could climb up to the second floor and go in through the balcony door which I knew was never locked. I was confident that neither Billy nor Dick had considered the unlocked door as a threat, if they had even considered it at all.

All that stood in my way was about twenty feet of windows. To get from where I was sitting to the trellis, I would have to cross in front of the kitchen doors, which were glass from top to bottom. I peeked around the corner at Billy. He had moved from the counter to the table. He was pouring himself another round. Sitting at the side of the table, he was no longer facing directly out the windows. That was good. But he had his gun well within reach. That was bad. Even with his side to the door, a mad dash across the expanse would have been suicide, but I had to try something. It was time for that miracle.

I lay out flat on the patio and began to pull myself along the concrete just below the steps. Moving inch-by-inch on my belly, the distance seemed to grow from feet to miles. Halfway across, I stopped to catch my second wind. My bruised ribs screamed with each labored breath. I silently cursed Deputy Deke Lincoln. Every minute that I lay exposed on the ground, I prayed that Billy wouldn't notice the movement, or worse, walk over to the window.

Finally, reaching the other side, I squeezed by the trellis and sat in the shadow of the house while I steeled myself for the climb to the balcony. When the pain in my side was bearable enough, I took to the trellis and climbed to the second floor.

The door was unlocked, as I knew it would be. I opened it slowly on an empty hallway. The report of Dick Brinson's rifle filled the space. Relieved that he was still in place, I made my way into the house. I knelt by the opening of the kitchen stairway, listening for confirmation of Billy's whereabouts. His drunken voice, half talking, half singing, drifted up from below. He didn't sound as if he would be coming up any time soon, and, if he did, the squeaking of the metal staircase would alert me of his approach.

Since her bedroom door was closed, I assumed that Lucy was being held there. I ran to the door, hoping that it was not locked. The knob turned in my hand and relief flooded my body, but the relief was replaced quickly by anger without measure when I opened the door.

Lucy was there, and the sight of her broke my heart. She was handcuffed to the bed.

Completely naked, her body was splotched with bruises. Her hair was matted to her head around her tear-streaked face. The left side of her face was bruised and swollen. Tears welled my eyes.

"Eddie!" she cried when she saw me come through the door.

I motioned for her to be quiet as I rushed to her side. I took her in my arms and held her. "Lucy," I whispered. "I am so sorry." I raised up and gently brushed the hair from her damaged face. "I am so sorry," I repeated.

"It's not your fault," she assured me. "He's crazy, Eddie."

"He hurt you," I said. "Did he…" I couldn't bring myself to finish the question, but she understood.

A smile tried to form on her mouth, but she winced from the pain of her swollen lip. "He tried, I guess," she explained, "but he couldn't." Again, she tried to smile. "I was gettin' out of the shower when he busted in. He grabbed me and kissed me, then he came in his pants. He couldn't handle it, I guess. I laughed at him, and he hit me across the face with his gun. Then he handcuffed me to the bed and hasn't been back since."

"What about Brinson?" I asked.

"He comes by every once in a while to gawk at me." She tried to laugh, but the sound came out as a whimper. "I guess he finally got his answer." I smiled, amazed at her ability to joke.

While she talked, I studied her restraint. Her hands were cuffed together around one of the spindles of the headboard. The wood was gouged and worn from Lucy's attempts to free herself. "Let's get you out of here, before one of them comes back," I said. I pulled against the rail, but it was too strong to break by hand. I kicked it several times before I heard it crack. The sound carried like one of Brinson's rifle shots, and I was sure it would bring Watson. I held my breath for a second, but no one came.

When Lucy was free from the bed, I went to the closet to get her some clothes. I helped her into her pants, but with her hands still cuffed together, I couldn't get her shirt on. I tied a blanket around her as best I could.

"Where are your father's guns?" I asked, wanting a weapon in case we were discovered.

"What?"

"Your father's guns," I repeated. "You said there were some up here."

"In the front room," she said.

"Which one?" I asked.

"Across the hall," she clarified.

"Damn!" I cursed. "That's where Brinson is. We'll have to take our chances."

She grabbed my arm with her cuffed hands and giggled, "I've got mine." The woman was amazing.

"I love you," I had to tell her.

"I love you, too," she replied.

I crept into the hall with Lucy close behind me. The door to Brinson's room was ajar. We could see him sitting in the window. We moved quickly across the hall to be out of his line of sight if he happened to turn around. I whispered for Lucy to stay put while I checked on

Billy. I knelt by the stairwell to listen for him. He was still in the kitchen. Still singing. Still talking to himself. He was very drunk. I went back to Lucy and led her toward the front stairs. I hoped that Billy was still in the same place at the table, because he would be unable to see us going down.

Down the stairs. Out the door. Home free.

We didn't make it. As we hit the bottom of the stairs, Billy's voice filled the foyer. "Stop!" he screamed. We froze. He was standing in the middle of the great room, pointing his pistol out in front of him. "Move and I'll blow your damn head apart." To emphasize the threat, he pulled the trigger, and the banister knob beside me shattered. Lucy screamed. Even drunk, he was dangerous with the gun. Probably more.

"You two ain't goin' nowhere!" he yelled. He took several steps toward us. A smile broke across his face. "'Bout time you got here, boy!"

"Why, Billy?" I asked. "Why do all this?" I got an idea as I waited for his answer. I began to look past him. I made sure he watched my eyes as they darted over his shoulder, hoping to prey upon his paranoia. "Tell me, Billy," I taunted him, knowing full well that it could get me shot. "What are you getting out of this?" A quick look over his shoulder.

"I get to watch you die," he laughed.

"Why drag Lucy into this?" My eyes darted past him. "Why hurt her?" A look and a slight shake of my head.

He began to fidget nervously. I was getting to him. "I don't want to hurt Lucy, but she hurt me." He addressed her, "I love you, Lucy. Why don't you love me? Why him? Why?" He was on the verge of tears. The gun in his hand was beginning to shake.

I looked quickly over his shoulder, and gave a pronounced nod. He took the bait. "What the fuck you lookin' at?" he demanded. He turned to look behind him.

As soon as Billy took his eyes off of us, I grabbed Lucy's hand and pulled her toward the hallway. With no chance to get out the front door before Billy recovered, I headed for the library. I pushed Lucy into the room and slammed the door shut.

Outside, Billy realized he'd been duped. "Shit!" he yelled, then he called for Brinson.

I barely got the door locked before Billy slammed into it. "Chance! I'm gonna kill you! Chance!" He rammed the door again. The lock held, but the wood creaked with the impact.

I went quickly to the side door, but I couldn't open it. Because of its window, it was locked with a double-keyed bolt. "Where's the key?" I asked Lucy.

"In the desk somewhere," she shrugged.

Billy hit the door again, and the frame began to crack. Knowing I did not have time to search for the key before Billy got through, I grabbed a floor lamp and smashed it through the glass of the door window. "Help us!" I yelled through the hole while I cleared the broken glass from the frame. No one responded to my calls.

"Shut up, Chance!" Billy screamed through the door.

He slammed the door one last time and the wood splintered apart. The door flew open, and Billy tumbled through onto the floor. I threw the lamp at him. He cursed me and took a shot at us. I grabbed Lucy and dove for the cover of the bookshelves.

"You can't hide, Chance," Billy told me. "You can't get away."

Crouching behind the stacks, we watched him search for us among the books. The area was only so big, and it was only a matter of time before our paths crossed. Lucy seethed as Billy dragged her mother's books onto the floor. I searched for an opportunity to get past him to the door. Making a break for the exit would have certainly brought us a bullet in the back.

Our chance finally came. Billy was standing on the opposite side of the wall of books we were hiding behind. I mouthed an apology to Lucy, then heaved my weight into the shelf. My blow wasn't enough to topple the heavy rack, but it shook it enough that most of the books rained down on Billy, who fell to the floor cursing under the avalanche.

"Go," I commanded Lucy.

I put her ahead of me in case Billy managed to get a shot off, and we bolted for the door. We were stopped by the appearance of Dick Brinson. He was standing in the doorway, blocking our only escape with his bulk and his deer rifle.

"Where y'all think y'all goin'?" he demanded. He looked past us into the room and called, "Billy, where you at?"

I decided to make a break for it. Praying that Brinson wouldn't have the guts to shoot us, I shouted, "Out the window."

By the time we reached the exterior door, Billy had dug out of his book pile and caught us before we could even attempt the window.

"Don't try that shit again, you hear?" he barked. He turned to Brinson. "Why didn't you come when I called you? They damn near got away," he growled.

Brinson flashed an embarrassed grin, then pulled earplugs from his ears. "Damn rifle gives me a headache," he explained.

Billy rolled his eyes in disgust. "What's been goin' on outside?"

"Not much a nothin'. Best I can tell," Brinson replied. "Most of 'em don't even flinch when I shoot anymore. Pisses me off."

"What about Besmer? Or Bragg?" Billy asked. "What they doin'?"

"They been arguing hot n' heavy 'bout a half an hour. 'Course I couldn't hear 'em, but they's goin' at it. That's for damn sure." He paused and looked over at me, then said, "Probably 'bout him, huh? How'd he get in here, anyway? I thought Bragg said they couldn't find 'im."

Billy didn't acknowledge Dick's questions. He was afraid that they were mounting an attack. I got the feeling that he somehow believed I was sent in to get Lucy so they could come in and kill him. Why he thought the police would have sent in a untrained civilian, I'll never know. I'm sure his mind was clouded by the alcohol, the paranoia, and just plain stupidity. He ordered Dick to check on the current status. When the big man was gone, Billy shook his head and muttered under his breath, "Dimwit." I almost laughed out loud. Talk about your pot calling the kettle black.

"Billy?" I asked.

"What?" he barked.

"Why don't you just let her go? You got me. That's what you wanted. Let her leave. I don't care what you do to me, but she doesn't deserve this," I pleaded.

"She turned her back on me," he argued. "She could have loved me. Could have been with me, but she picked you. I hated you the first time I saw you. Everybody likes you. Hell, Carl likes you more than he ever did me, and I'm blood. I don't know how much he thinks of you now that I told him you been fuckin' his little girl. What'd he say 'bout that? I'da loved to see his face when I told him 'bout that."

"That's a lie," I said.

"What is?"

"About me and Jenny," I said. "I was never with her."

"You're lyin'," he snapped. "Dan saw you. He told me."

"He was lying." I corrected, "It wasn't me she was with, it was…" I took a breath before I finished the sentence. Would T and Jenny forgive me? I knew in my heart that Billy wouldn't live to see either of them again, and I longed to see the look in his eye when I told him. "…it was T Johnson."

He lunged for me. "You lyin' bastard. Ain't no kin of mine no nigger lover." He slapped at me with his gun hand. I tried to knock the gun away from him, but I was blinded by a flash of light as the barrel caught me in the temple. I stumbled back, stunned. He reared back, preparing to land another blow, but Lucy hit him between the shoulder blades with her interlaced hands. The force of the blow knocked the wind out of him, but he slapped her hard across the face, reopening the cut on her lip.

I leapt for him, but he caught my movement in the corner of his eye. He spun to me with a quickness I wouldn't have expected considering the alcohol in his blood. He brought his gun around and fired two quick shots. The first bullet hit me in the thigh. A fire like nothing I'd ever felt spread from the wound, but it was the second shot that brought me to the floor. I cried in a shriek that I couldn't believe came from my mouth, as that second bullet shattered my shin bone. My ruined leg betrayed me, and I crumpled to the floor. Lucy screamed and hit Billy again. He backhanded her and grabbed her elbow to stop the attack. I tried to get up, but the pain overwhelmed me. My head spun, and I tasted the bile rise in my throat. I swallowed hard against the urge to vomit as the tears streamed down my face. I screamed in agony, both from the excruciating pain, and the realization that Billy had won. I lay helpless on the floor, completely at his mercy.

The gunshots, like the one earlier that destroyed the banister knob, did not lure the small army of policemen into the house. I wondered, as I lay there on the floor bleeding to death, if they could even hear them. The shots did draw Dick Brinson back into the room, and I thought for a moment that he was going to be our salvation.

He burst into the room and shouted at Billy, "What the hell you doin', man? You didn't say nothing' about shootin' nobody for real. You just said we was gonna come up here and have a little fun with Red."

"Shut up!" Billy growled.

"You never said nothing' 'bout all these police, and you damn sure never said nothin' 'bout killin' nobody," Dick shouted back. "You done gone too far, man. It's time to give up this shit before we get killed."

He took a step toward Billy, but it was a mistake. Before he had made the second step, Billy brought the pistol up and shot him between the eyes. The big man stood there several seconds, already dead, but refusing to fall. Finally, he tumbled to the floor, and his blood be-gan to soak into the oriental carpet.

Lucy screamed. "Shut up!" Billy ordered. He pushed her, half stumbling toward the sofa. Knowing what was coming, I tried to get to me feet, but I was too weak to raise myself onto my one good leg. I fell back to the floor with a cry that brought a laugh from Billy. I cursed him with all the energy I could muster. I closed my eyes and waited for death, but Billy would not let me go out that easy. He came to me and gave me a quick kick in the leg. I screamed. "You scream like a woman," he laughed.

"Fuck you," I growled through clenched teeth.

He bent over me and whispered, "You ain't gonna die just yet. You tried to take my woman. Now I'm gonna take her back, and you're gonna watch." I spat at him. He kicked me in the leg again. I screamed. He reached down and pulled at the hair on the back of my head. He bent right down on my face. The smell of whiskey on his breath burned my nos-trils. He said, "If you close your eyes, I'll kill her."

Lucy fought him. Trying to force her down on the sofa, hold the gun on her, and keep his eye on me, he wasn't accomplishing much of anything. With no fear of the gun at her throat, Lucy pounded his head and shoulders with her fists and the handcuffs that bound her. He jerked the blanket away, and groped clumsily at her bare chest. I turned my eyes away and prayed for the strength to get off the floor and help her. "Turn around, Chance!" he yelled. "I told you, you were gonna watch." I turned back, but I caught sight of something I hoped, I prayed, I could use. I was lying on the floor at the base of the gun cabinet. The weapons inside were locked up tight out of my reach, but there was a cane leaning against the side of the cabinet. Hoping that he was distracted enough that he wouldn't notice the movement of my hand, I grabbed the stick and brought it down to me. Concealing it with my body, I waited for the moment to strike. Praying that my effort wouldn't get Lucy killed, I drew on every ounce of energy that I could muster. My body felt as if it were made of bags of wet sand, but I pushed it up and toward Billy. Ignoring the fiery knives of pain stabbing my shattered leg, I leaped from the floor and swung the cane at his head. He must have caught my movement out of the corner of his eye, because he jumped away from Lucy and brought the gun around.

The third bullet caught me in the stomach. I recoiled from the impact and folded to the floor. The pain was indescribable, and was the final blow to my damaged body. The fire of the initial impact flashed quickly away and was replaced by a relentless, unnerving cold. The world around me faded to black, as the trauma overwhelmed me, and I lost consciousness.

∞∝

When Billy pulled away from her, Lucy clambered over the back of the couch and thumped to the floor. She was hiding there when the last bullet brought me down. Through the space under the furniture, she saw my limp, bleeding body fall to the floor. She muffled a scream, not wanting to draw Billy's attention back to her. Sure that I was dead, she lay there trying to figure what her next move would be. Any attempt to escape would bring her a bul-let in her back. She did not want to die by his hand, but she couldn't bear to remain and be violated and tortured.

Billy was bent over my motionless body. She didn't want to watch whatever he had planned. She pulled herself to her hands and knees, and braced herself for the break for the door. In the shadow of the couch, she noticed the cane lying a few feet from her, where it had flown from my hand. She knew it well. It was the cane that her father had carried with him for her entire life. It was as much a part of him as the limp that necessitated it. She remembered, as a little girl, making up stories about the shiny brass horse that capped the dark wood. She also remembered its secret. The memory brought a change to her plans. She grabbed the cane and pulled the horse from the shaft. She lay prone on the floor, concealing the cane head beneath her body. She would wait for Billy.

Either too drunk or too stupid to check my pulse, he kicked me in the side to confirm my death, then went to look for Lucy. "Where'd you go, bitch?" he called. Lucy remained motionless. Billy came around the end of the couch and saw her on the floor. "Get up!" he ordered. "Got business to finish." She did not move. He nudged her with his toe. "Get up, I said," he repeated. When she didn't respond, he dropped to his knees and shook her. "What's wrong with you?" he asked. He grabbed her and rolled her over.

His eyes grew wide as she buried all nine inches of the stiletto blade between his ribs. She twisted the blade, making him scream in agony. He sat back with a thump. His hands grasped the blood-slick horse at his side. By the look in his eyes, he couldn't comprehend what was happening to him. He never moved a muscle to stop her when she reached for the gun he had dropped when she stabbed him. He sat stunned, with his hands on the handle of the knife.

She pointed the gun at him. "You're gonna pay for what you've done to us!" she screamed at him. "For what you did to Eddie."

He held his bloody hands out to her. A pitiful sadness showed in his eyes. "Why'd you hurt me, Lucy?"

"Why?" she repeated. "How can you sit there and ask me why?"

She placed the barrel of the gun in the corner of his eye, against the bridge of his nose.

He did not try to fight her.

She pulled the hammer back.

He didn't flinch.

"I love you, Lucy."

"I don't care!"

She pulled the trigger.

Epilogue

T he following March, Lucy and I stood next to Carl and Joanne in the hospital corridor. I leaned heavily on the cane in my left hand. As with Lucy's father, the cane had become as much a part of me as the limp with which I walked. I shifted my weight to my good leg, and loosened my grip on the brass horse handle. I held Lucy's hand in my right.

Carl leaned close to the window and looked at the baby in the bassinet on the other side. Sarah Grace Johnson was the talk of the town, and she was barely six hours old. She was the first interracial child born in the Wixton hospital.

"She's beautiful, ain't she?" the new grandfather asked, breaking into a huge grin.

"Beautiful," I confirmed.

"Hard to hate somethin' with the face of an angel." Carl was furious when Jenny came to him and confessed her love for T, but he held her while she cried and revealed her pregnancy to him and Joanne. Standing with his face pressed against the glass, he beamed with pride. "Babies change everything, you know?" Carl said as he placed his hand on my shoulder.

"I know." I rubbed my hand across Lucy's baby-swelled belly. "I know."

Printed in the United States
38832LVS00004B/13-62